\# 1

Morning Glory

Bernadette Carson

Copyright © 2005 by Bernadette Carson

ISBN 0-7414-2848-2

Cover photo of Finestkind Scenic Cruises tour boat by Patrick McNamara Photography, Cape Neddick, Maine; © 2003 Patrick McNamara

Published by:

PUBLISHING.COM

1094 New DeHaven Street, Suite 100
West Conshohocken, PA 19428-2713
Info@buybooksontheweb.com
www.buybooksontheweb.com
Toll-free (877) BUY BOOK
Local Phone (610) 941-9999
Fax (610) 941-9959

Printed in the United States of America

Printed on Recycled Paper

Published December 2005

This book is dedicated to my parents, Sadie and Carmine Crisa, my sister, Corrine Carbo, and my brother, Frank Crisa. Though our family lived modestly during those Brooklyn years, our lives were enriched by love. You may be gone, Mom and Dad, but the beautiful memories you left will sustain and comfort us for the rest of our lives. Keep smiling down.

Acknowledgments

When thinking of which people to thank first, my mind makes a beeline to Ogunquit, Maine, where my story is set.

Leanne Cusimano, the real owner of Amore Breakfast, whose enthusiasm and willingness to help inspired me to turn a one-sentence idea into a full-length novel.

Sergeant Matt Stewart of the Maine State Police, Criminal Investigation Division, deserves extra special thanks for all the time he spent reading through several chapters for authenticity. His feedback was extremely helpful and informative and his patience unsurpassed.

Sharma Damren of the Ogunquit Police Department was another crutch for me, always eager to help and perpetually pleasant. When I met her in July 2005, I was happy to discover that the real Sharma is very similar to the lovely young woman I had created in my mind.

During my July 2005 vacation in Ogunquit, I met and spoke with Eleanor Hubbard, the owner of Finestkind Scenic Tours. I left Eleanor a copy of my manuscript that day, hoping she would read it in the next week or two. That same night she returned it, having read the entire manuscript! Summertime is Ogunquit's busy season, yet this gracious lady took the time to read my novel in one day.

Jerry Maine (yes, *Maine* is his real name!), one of Finestkind's tour guides, was excited about this novel from its inception. I was pleasantly surprised to meet him my first day in Ogunquit when he and his wife, Mary Ellen, walked into Amore Breakfast.

Thanks also to Newell Perkins of Perkins Real Estate in Ogunquit, who also took the time to read excerpts related to the real estate business.

During my 2003 summer visit to Ogunquit, my husband and I enjoyed performances given by Sally Struthers and Christa Jackson in *Always, Patsy Cline* at the Ogunquit Playhouse. The idea for *Morning Glory* was already swimming in my head and I was so excited about this outstanding production that I wanted to mention it somewhere in my story. When the production was brought to the Helen Hayes Performing Arts Center in Nyack, New York, I wrote a brief letter asking if they could look over the scene where I had written them in. I received a warm and friendly hand-written response which truly touched me.

I was hesitant to ask Columnist Bob Baird for help since I was a total stranger to this busy man and my name not exactly a household word, but again I was pleasantly surprised. He responded promptly and encouraged me to contact him again if and when I needed additional help.

My niece, Dianne Carbo, a nurse and mother of three, always finds time in her busy life to help me with medical questions, as she's done with all my novels.

I would be remiss if I failed to mention my "editing partner," Bill Carson, whose sharp mind and watchful eyes are invaluable to my writing.

To all of you I give heartfelt thanks. If any errors are found in the information you've provided, I humbly apologize and take full responsibility.

Lastly, I want to thank my family for all their support and pride in my work. Every one of them deserves to be mentioned individually here:

My son, Michael Martorelli and his wife Ellen; my son Frank Martorelli; my son, Paul Martorelli and his wife Lauren; my daughter, Bernadette Kilduff and her husband Danny; and all my grandchildren, Andrea, Lauren, Michael, Vincent, Brian, Jaclyn and Matthew.

To claim you all as my family, I'm the one who beams with pride.

Chapter 1

Glory English brushed a gentle hand over her mother's collection of literary classics. As if touching them was tantamount to the precious hands that once held them. The past eight months had been emotional hell for Glory and she ached for the loving comfort her parents could have provided if only they had lived.

Her fingers paused at the spine of one of her mother's favorites; John Steinbeck's *Grapes of Wrath*. She pulled it off the shelf, poured herself a glass of merlot and curled up on the sofa. Her mother's presence enveloped her as she fanned the book's pages.

That's when she found the letter.

My darling daughter,

I don't know if I'll ever finish this letter or if I'll have the courage to leave it for you. There's so much I have to say, I don't know where to begin. All your life I've been afraid of how you would react. Why hurt you with this shocking revelation? What purpose would it serve?

Yet, I feel compelled to tell you. You have a right to know the truth about your birth.

Glory's hand trembled. Her fingers turned icy cold. A numbing weightlessness gripped her entire body. Her imagination was far ahead of her mother's words. As though it were on fire, she flung the letter across her living room floor. She didn't want to read any more, afraid of what it would reveal. But since the Pandora's Box had already been opened, there was no turning back. She retrieved the folded letter off the floor and continued reading while her heart pounded away.

I was young and relatively happy. My college years were behind me and I was enjoying a fun-filled, carefree summer before settling down in an exciting new job with NBC News, scheduled to begin right after Labor Day.

Remember my friend, Paula Howard? We were so close, but lost track of each other as the years passed. Anyway, Paula's parents owned a summer cottage in Ogunquit, Maine, and Paula had invited me to spend the entire month of August with them.

I thought I couldn't have been more thrilled until the day finally came and we arrived at the "cottage," which could more aptly be described as a mansion. It faced the ocean and had three levels of balconies so that the fabulous view and sounds of Maine's rocky shore could be enjoyed by all its guests. After spending most of my life in the city, it was like another world to me. What a beautiful wind-down of this transitional period in my life.

I was not the only guest that summer. There were fifteen spacious rooms in that "cottage," they called Ratherbee, and all were put to good use. The Howards treated me like family and introduced me to all their friends. By my second week, I had become very close to one particular friend, and that, my darling Glory, is the beginning of my bittersweet story. Bitter because of what I loved and lost (a woman never forgets her first love), but sweet because nine months later, that bright morning in early May, you were born. When I saw your tiny round face for the first time, I cried and called you my little flower, my morning glory, and, as you know, that's how you got your name.

"Oh, my God! Oh, my God! What are you telling me, Mom? *Why* are you telling me this?" Glory cried aloud. All the love she ever felt for Steven English seemed to surface and wrap around her heart. But now it invaded like an icy storm, not with the warmth and comfort she had known for thirty-two years.

"Daddy, daddy, daddy!" she screamed, her cries half-love, half-anger. How could they have deceived her like this?

But she couldn't even vent her anger. Both her parents were gone. Her mother's life was cut short six years ago by a massive heart attack and her dad had succumbed to prostate cancer two years later. The cancer was discovered only three months before her mom died. At first he had accepted his fate with calm resolve and optimism. He studied and dwelled on all the success stories. After his wife's death, though, his will to live drained out of him like sand in an hourglass.

He never knew, my special friend. We parted that Labor Day weekend making all kinds of promises. He lived in Arizona and with twenty-four hundred miles between us, our summer romance was ill-fated. Love has to be nurtured to stay alive, they say. How true. We saw each other every day that August, lived under the same roof. Although he had intended to stay for only a week, he was between jobs and didn't have to start his new one until mid-September. When the Howards invited him to stay longer, he eagerly accepted.

That September we spoke on the phone several times. We made sketchy plans about spending our next vacation together, but with the distance between us, our new jobs and busy lives, we both knew that would never happen. Soon after, the phone calls stopped. I was disappointed, but not devastated, not yet.

By October, I knew for sure that I was pregnant. Yes, then I was devastated. The thought of telling my parents was killing me. My job with NBC News was even better than I had anticipated, but I went through the motions halfheartedly because I knew it would be short-lived. All I could think of was the life growing inside me and how long I could keep that life a secret.

I did a lot of soul-searching those days. Naturally, for me, abortion was never an option. Aside from the moral and religious issues, I loved you from the moment I knew you existed and couldn't wait to hold you in my arms.

A sob caught in Glory's throat. Despite her mother's shocking revelations, she ached to feel her arms around her one more time. Especially now.

She hadn't noticed until she reached the third and last page that it ended abruptly. There was no "Love, Mom," or any other closing words. The tears that had welled in her eyes now stained her cheeks at the discovery. Thirsting for more, she read on.

A decision had to be made soon and finally I made it, without looking back. Your father was a constant in my life. (Yes, I mean Daddy, the only father you knew and loved.) I loved him in a special way, for the special person he was, but I can't honestly say I was in love with him then. My friend, the father who gave you life, was a strong presence in my heart and mind those days, but I think I told myself I loved him to ease the guilt of giving myself so completely to someone I had known for only a few short weeks. It was all like a passing dream.

Daddy loved me unconditionally. At first he was heartbroken to hear that I was pregnant. He was the first person I confided in. I hadn't even told my parents yet. I guess you know, Glory, where this is going. Daddy knew I had no intention of telling my friend about the pregnancy. A loveless marriage for the sake of a child who was born from a brief summer romance could never survive. And so, when Daddy offered to marry me and claim you as his own, I accepted. Grandma and Grandpa already adored him and after the initial shock wore off, I had no doubt they would welcome him – and most certainly you – into our family.

It ended there, unfinished. What else did her mother intend to tell her? Why did she always refer to him as "my friend"? Would she have told me his name if she had finished the letter? she wondered. Her mother had to know it would be easy enough to learn his name. He was a house guest at the Howards' home that summer. And *why* hadn't she finished it? Her stomach tumbled over when she realized that the answer stared her in the face. The date on the first page said, "March 10, 1997." Two days later, her mother was dead.

Chapter 2

A stream of sunlight warmed Glory's face. Her eyes squinted at the unwelcome brightness that awakened her. Startled to find herself on the sofa, she shot up erect and remembered last night. She had read her mother's letter over and over again until she obviously dozed off, mentally exhausted. Repeatedly she had cried out in angry frustration to both her parents because neither one could ever answer the myriad questions that kept spinning in her head. Now, this morning, they had materialized into a huge, throbbing headache.

There it was again, the letter. It had fallen off the sofa. She picked it up, stared at it, and without warning, a new flood of tears filled her eyes. Glory brushed them away, drew a deep breath and sucked back the sobs. No. No more. She couldn't subject herself to any more anguish. She had to function. Her editor had already rescheduled their meeting once to suit her convenience; she wasn't about to ask him to do so again.

Six years ago Glory had been given the chance to write a weekly column for The Reporter, the newspaper that employed her fresh out of college. *Glorious Cooking,* which started out with quick and easy recipes for the working mother, had a slow start. They were about to pull it, but gave in to Glory's pleas for a chance to kick up its format. That decision had turned out to be a good move. Glory added humorous anecdotes about cooking, children, husbands, jobs and life in general. She welcomed questions from her readers and selected for publication those queries that allowed her to write amusing, witty, yet informative responses. Her new style took off like a rocket, right into syndication.

In the bathroom, she went through the usual routine of brushing her teeth and giving a quick brush to her thick, chestnut-brown hair. When she caught sight of her image in the mirror, she winced. Her eyes were bloodshot, her lids puffy, her cheeks swollen. Her Elizabeth Arden makeup kit would have a hell of a challenge this morning.

She stood back and took another good look at herself. *Stupid, stupid woman. Not the slightest suggestion anywhere on that face that you are your father's daughter.* Why hadn't she ever noticed that before? Only her mother's features were evidenced; the high cheekbones, the same crescent-shaped eyebrows, deep-set, smoky-blue eyes, generous lips and strong, perfect teeth. Her mother used to say Glory had inherited from her father only his passive personality; not an angry bone in his body, she'd say. *Did you hear me last night, Mom? You would have changed your tune.*

***

Her meeting with Marty Clark, her editor, could have been handled by telephone or e-mail, but Marty liked to see his key people look back at him from the other side of his desk. The open exchange of ideas with a view towards wider circulation was, of course, always the focal point and most often yielded positive results.

When the meeting broke and the other three men and two women gathered their paraphernalia to leave, Marty crooked a finger at Glory, the gesture meaning he'd like her to stay. With narrowed eyes, he gave her a quick study.

Oh, no, he wants to talk to me alone. Not today of all days.

"Are you okay?" he asked after the others left.

There they are. Those three words whispered from the lips of a concerned friend. That's all a person needs to open up those proverbial floodgates.

She dabbed at her eyes, managed a half-smile. "I'm sorry. I'm having a bad heart day. Am I that transparent?"

"What's that supposed to mean?"

She waved away his thoughts. "No, no, it's nothing medically-related."

Marty blew a sigh of relief. "Okay, then. Nothing else can be that bad. Want to talk to poppa?"

"Maybe eventually, Marty, but not today."

With genuine concern, he watched her troubled face. He couldn't decide whether to pull it out of her and try to help or to mind his own business. "Okay," he said. "I'll back off. I don't mean to pry, but we're friends. If ever you want to talk, call me, here or at home, okay?"

Glory bit her lips and struggled to keep from crying. With her gaze fixed on her clasped hands, she whispered, "Okay."

"Promise?"

"Promise," she said and left the room.

When she left the building, she drew a deep breath, relieved that she had managed to get through the meeting without falling apart. Mechanically, she walked over to the garage for her car and drove off. By the time she had weaved her way out of the city streets and onto the highway, she was blinded with tears again. She kept seeing her father's face; that gentle, loving face. "Damn you, damn you, Daddy," she yelled out and slapped the steering wheel. "Why didn't you tell me? *Why?*"

She couldn't help but feel that her whole life had been one big lie. Both her parents had never intended to tell her until her mother had this change of heart and had begun to write the letter. And Glory would never know if her mother would have ever given it to her.

Feelings of anger, love and frustration melded together and put a knot in her stomach that rivaled her throbbing head. When she finally pulled into her parking space at her condo complex, she was dry-eyed and determined. A plan had shaped in her mind and she was about to put it in motion.

Chapter 3

Stacy Nappi, Glory's closest friend, stood before her, hands on hips. "What do you mean you're going to Maine *indefinitely*? What's going on?"

"I couldn't get into it on the phone," Glory said. "That's why I asked you to come for coffee." Her lips had already begun to quiver at the thought of confiding in Stacy, but she had to talk to someone or she'd burst. "Sit down, Stacy," she said, pointing to her rocker. She hadn't intended to share the letter with her or anyone else, but when those sobs shot up in her throat, she took the easy way out. She handed Stacy the letter. "Read it," she said.

At the sight of Glory's tears, Stacy was almost afraid to read it. "My God! What's wrong?"

Stacy was rendered speechless when she finally looked up. Now she understood the pain in Glory's face. For a few silent moments, she wrapped her arms around her and they cried together. When she let go, Stacy lifted Glory's chin with a finger and handed her a bunch of fresh tissues. "C'mon, Glory, talk to me. This is such a shock, even to me, that I can well imagine what you're feeling."

Glory forced a smile. "That should explain why I said I'm going to Maine indefinitely."

"Not really. The man lived in Arizona. If you're set on finding him, why Maine?"

"Because I'm not sure I want to find him, but I feel some unexplainable pull to be where it all happened. Where I was *conceived.* And I want to look up the Howards and see what I can find out. In a very subtle way, of course."

Stacy gave her an incredulous look. "Glory, this is crazy. You're making these plans based on an emotional shock. Think it out first. How do you know the Howards are alive and still own that house? It's been thirty-five years!"

"That I've already checked. Easy research. The deed is still in that name and the house and property is still called *Ratherbee.*"

"Did you know your mother's friend, Paula Howard?"

"I only remember hearing *of* her, when my mother reminisced about her college days. The memories would light up her face whenever she talked about that time in her life, but you could always see a hint of sadness. I assumed it was simply nostalgia that had put it there."

"So you have no idea what ever happened to her?"

"No, not a clue. She was part of my mother's life, not mine. Chances are, she's married, has another name. I'll find out."

"Guess I can't blame you. In your shoes, I'd probably do the same. But you can do it from here, can't you?"

Glory shrugged. "Maybe. But I'd rather be there. Consider it a vacation. Maine is supposed to be beautiful in the summertime, and I'm leaving around the Fourth of July."

"Want company? I can probably switch my weeks."

"No way. You already made your vacation plans. I wouldn't dream of asking you to change them. Besides, Stacy, I'd be miserable company for you. Since I found that letter, I haven't been able to concentrate on anything else. I think I need this time alone."

"I think you need a friend. You've been having enough trouble battling your emotions since your marriage broke up. What are you going to do there all by yourself?"

"I'm not sure but it's not as if this is a pleasure trip. And if you were with me, I'd feel worse to see you bored."

"So? Did I say I wanted to go out partying every night? What's wrong with a little relaxation? We can swim, take long walks and eat leisurely lobster dinners at oceanfront restaurants."

Glory felt a slight impatient frown form on her face before she could stop it. She replaced it quickly with an apologetic look. "Please, Stacy, not this time. I appreciate what you're trying to do, but this has to be a solo trip."

Stacy threw her hands up and blew a sigh. "Okay, I give up. I guess I can understand how you feel, but if you change your mind –"

With a sincere appreciative smile, Glory cut her off. "I won't change my mind. Go enjoy the Jersey Shore vacation you planned and forget about me. I'll be fine."

"Yeah, I guess so. I just hate to see you go through this alone."

"I'm a big girl now. I can handle it. I just went through a divorce, remember?"

Stacy shot her a look. "My point exactly."

Glory forced a laugh and continued. "Once I can control these annoying tears I'll be in much better shape. It's been like one huge waterfall. You know how it is; tears can exacerbate a problem. If you succumb to them, you get no place fast. If your head is on straight, you can focus on the root of your problem, meet it head on and deal with it."

Stacy paused to search Glory's face for hidden emotions. "Is that how you categorize finding your father, Glory? A problem to be dealt with and discarded? You can't start out hating him – "

"I never said I hate him."

"Okay, then change that. You can't begin your search with this angry, hostile attitude. Remember that your father – your biological father – never knew about you. It's not as if he abandoned you."

Glory digested that fact again and tossed it around in her mind. "Maybe the anger and hostility you see in me is against my parents for going to their graves and never telling me."

"Glory, they obviously loved you too much to hurt you. You had a happy, stable life. Why would they want to upset that? Would you have loved them the same way if they had told you?"

Glory sucked in a breath and exhaled slowly. "No, probably not," she admitted.

***

Later, after Stacy left, Glory felt relieved to be alone, but she smiled thinking about how hard her friend had tried to drag her out socializing again. Get out, make new friends, have fun, find someone else, she would say. The usual clichéd words of wisdom. As if any old guy would suffice to erase twelve years of being married to and crazy about a man you thought loved you back but didn't. Like buying a new battery to charge you back to life.

Not a single day had passed since that fateful night that the scene hadn't flash through her mind. Glory had been pleasantly surprised when he came home unexpectedly early. Like the loving wife she was, she had hugged him, smacked a noisy kiss on his lips and said, "Are you hungry? I wasn't expecting you home so soon. What can I give you? Want pizza?"

"No, Glory. I want a divorce," he'd said.

She went numb; thought he was making some sort of sick joke. He had actually tried to hold her then. Whether his intent was to brace her for what he was about to say or whether he couldn't bear to look her in the eyes, she didn't know, but in less than an hour he was gone. If the roof had caved in on her, Glory couldn't have felt more crushed.

That night, her husband, Dr. Jason Vance, the successful orthopedic surgeon, had left her to move in with Marilyn Stillwell, the medical supplies salesperson he had been having an affair with for the last fifteen months.

Chapter 4

It took weeks for the sharp edge of shock to subside, but finally the anger, the denial, had dissipated. She had planned and packed for her trip with a calm resolve. Maine, with its inviting tranquility, seemed like the perfect place to sort through or put aside your problems.

She had searched the Internet and contacted the Chamber of Commerce to inquire about accommodations in the Ogunquit area. There were dozens of motels, inns and bed-and-breakfasts to choose from and it was difficult to make a choice. Finally, she chose one called Ocean Cliff Lodge for several reasons; first, it rated among the highest; second, it faced the sea with a magnificent view; and third, it was set on a hilltop along Shore Road, away from Route 1, with its steady stream of traffic.

That location was another plus for Ocean Cliff Lodge. Her inquiries had disclosed that everything she could want or need was either within walking distance or a short trolley ride away. She could walk to the beach, to Perkins Cove, and to the many quaint shops, galleries, outdoor cafes and countless restaurants. For anywhere else she wanted to go, like Ratherbee, she'd have her car. Everything sounded perfect.

She tightened her lips and nodded her head to underscore the thought, then threw her suitcase in the trunk of her Lexus and slammed it shut.

***

It took Glory almost five hours from Rockland County, New York to reach Ogunquit, Maine, but she hadn't minded.

Particularly at this time of year, the last week in June, when the exodus begins for vacationers, traffic tie-ups were anticipated.

A breath caught in her throat when she finally slipped in her key card and opened the door. Her second-floor suite at Ocean Cliff was spacious and beautifully furnished. The oversized plushy sofa was done in a soft, cool blue with two side chairs in blue and beige checkered fabric. A fully-equipped white kitchen was separated from the living room/dining area by a light blue countertop and four stools.

The suite's floor-to-ceiling windows provided a panoramic view of the ocean. Even from the king-sized bed she could stare out at the ocean and let it lull her to sleep at night. She stepped out on the balcony and stood pensively for a while listening to the slapping sound of the surf against the black rocks. The salty scent filled her nostrils as she stood mesmerized by the golden rays of the sun dancing on the water. Her body and her senses yielded to it all. It was as though she were breathing freely for the first time since Jason left her and all her emotional pain triggered by the shock of her mother's letter had finally drained.

Acceptance of her parents' deception was settling in. What could she do, stand at their gravesite and scream at them? What was their worst sin, loving their daughter too much to see her hurt? She couldn't agree with their choices, but could understand their motivations.

And so, these past weeks, she learned to let go. But there was an excellent chance HE was still alive. How old could he be? Late fifties; sixty maybe? Still young by today's standards. She had to find him. He probably has a full, loving family that he would want to protect, she suspected, but she couldn't let him pass through life never knowing she existed. Nor could she pass through hers without seeing his face and putting her arms around him. If he let her.

Glory took a shower, slipped into shorts and a tank top and went out to explore the area. She had psyched herself to be slightly disappointed. From past experiences she had learned that Internet photos and brochures don't always tell the true story. Not so here from what she had seen thus far.

The sidewalk of the narrow tree-lined street was crowded with tourists headed towards the beach or just out for a leisurely stroll. She lingered at a charming little restaurant called *Amore Breakfast* that looked more like a private home. Freshly painted white with red shutters and red window boxes filled with geraniums, its wholesome Americana look was accented by red, white and blue buntings draped over each of its support columns. Charm with a capital C.

She noticed that the customers waiting to get in were comfortably accommodated. Self-service urns of coffee were set up for people to enjoy at the little tables on the restaurant's open porch. It was twenty minutes past noon and they were still serving breakfast, and unless they intended to turn people away, they would be serving for several hours more. She had eaten a light breakfast four hours ago, but found *Amore Breakfast* too inviting to ignore. Her feet found their way to the porch where she helped herself to coffee and browsed at the framed pictures on display. One of them boasted a photo of the young female owner, Frances Oliveri, wearing a proud, ear-to-ear smile. The article below told the story of Amore Breakfast's humble beginnings and ultimate success. It had never been a private home, as she had guessed, but a farm stand.

Her name was last on the list but she was first to be called since she didn't need a table. See, there are some advantages to being unattached, she mused. Inside, nostalgic plaques and photos of old Hollywood in its heyday enhanced the irresistible mood that drew tourists to its door even before tasting its food.

Glory took a seat at the counter and spotted the life-size cardboard cutout of Elvis, with his signature sequined outfit and guitar, his handsome face captured in song. It brought a smile to Glory's face. She was among the multitude of fans that were too young to appreciate Elvis when he reigned as king, but learned to love him through his music, his movies and his immortality among entertainment giants.

She studied the menu, intending to choose something light, but as she glanced around at some of the tantalizing dishes being served, her appetite piqued. She had eyed a French toast creation made with lemon bread and stuffed with cream cheese and blueberries. When it passed her by, she couldn't resist; it smelled like it had sailed down from heaven. When the waitress served it, she dug in and promised herself dinner would be strictly salad.

Her dish was half empty when a friendly female voice came over her shoulder. "Hi, how are you doing? Everything okay?"

Glory turned and recognized that pleasant face of the owner, Frances Oliveri, who preferred to be called "Frannie," according to the article she had read on the porch. She blotted the syrup off her lips and smiled back at her. "Excellent. Your food is outrageous. I wanted to eat only half, but after tasting it, I don't think there's a chance of that."

"Good. I'm always happy to hear from satisfied customers. Enjoy," she said, and left her to finish eating undisturbed.

When Glory paid the check, Frannie was still at the door greeting the incoming customers and thanking the outgoing ones. She wore a perpetual smile, Glory noticed; not the plastic, artificial kind people are often forced to wear for business, but the sincere smile of a person who truly loved what she was doing.

Glory shook her hand as she was leaving. "I'm glad I found this place," she said. "I'll be here in Ogunquit for a while, so I'll definitely be back."

"That's great. Glad to have you. What's your name?"

"Glory English."

"Yes, come again, Glory. New friends are always welcome."

Glory had been there less than two hours and she was madly in love with Maine.

Chapter 5

The little seaside town of Ogunquit was packed to capacity for the Fourth of July weekend. According to the Ocean Cliff staff, there wasn't a vacancy to be had for miles around.

She realized what a stroke of luck it had been to catch a cancellation when she had called. Glory suspected there might have been a waiting list, but when the reservations clerk heard her name, she realized she had found a fan. The woman's personality had bubbled right through the phone. "Glory English? Do you happen to be the same Glory English who writes the *Glorious Cooking* column?"

"Guilty as charged," she'd answered.

"What do you mean 'guilty'? I *love* your column, Miss English," the clerk had said before putting her on hold with an apology. When she came back, the girl happily informed her that the suite was hers for four weeks if she wanted it.

She sat now on a bench at the dock in Perkins Cove soaking in the salty breezes and watching the couples and families bouncing in and out of the shops and restaurants. Everyone wore a smile despite whatever troubles they had left at home. The spirit was contagious and Glory found herself smiling more these past few days than she had in months. Her thoughts were absorbed with how she could stretch it out to the whole summer. The thought of leaving Ocean Cliff put a frown on her face. Even if she could find availability elsewhere, she imagined it would pale by comparison.

The weather had cooperated this holiday weekend. Parades and celebrations were everywhere. Patriotism surged through the hearts of all Americans more than ever on this special day in American history. That eleventh day of September, 2001 left an indelible mark in our minds and hearts, Glory thought. It would burn forever and we'll never again take for granted the precious gift of freedom. Tears filled her eyes as she licked her strawberry ice cream cone remembering that horrific day. An incongruous combination, she mused; ice cream and tears.

Patriotic music filled the air and Glory sucked in a deep breath. She blinked back the tears and let pride take their place while she chatted amiably with other vacationers who shared her bench. They watched the small cruise ship take off for a shoreline tour. Glory's gaze lingered as it sailed away leaving a trail of snow-white foam in its wake. She made a mental note to prioritize that tour on her itinerary.

On Tuesday Glory decided to drive up to Ratherbee with no preplanned speech, no prior contact. She'd just hope for the best. Sounded simple enough in her mind, but her heart raced and her stomach did flip-flops every time she imagined herself ringing the doorbell.

First she needed some comfort food. The food at Ocean Cliff was better than good and the ambiance couldn't be beat. Still, Glory missed that down-home feeling of Amore Breakfast and she was ready to sample another specialty dish off that menu.

It was 7:45 when she got there and, to her surprise, was seated immediately.

Frannie greeted her again with her sunshine smile. "Hi! Nice to see you again. Glory, isn't it?"

Glory put her menu aside and returned the friendly greeting. "Yes, and I'm impressed that you remember my name considering all the people who walk through these doors. I haven't been here for days."

"Just as well, maybe," Frannie said, darting a sideways glance. "It was pure bedlam here; too many customers, not enough help. I had to grab an apron and help serve. That doesn't allow much time for friendly chit-chat with my customers. But I'm not complaining. I thrive on this. When I look at that line of people outside waiting to get in, I say 'God bless 'em for waiting. Keep 'em coming!"

When Frannie walked away to seat other customers, Glory ordered her breakfast. She chose an Eggs Benedict creation this time loaded with vegetables and sipped her coffee while she waited.

"Now I remember!"

Glory turned to face Frannie who had shouted the three words. She laughed when she turned to her. "You sound as though you just won the car on *Wheel of Fortune.*"

Frannie's hand went to her mouth, her look of surprise fading into an apology. "I'm so sorry. How stupid of me! Me, of all people, should have recognized you."

Glory smiled. It still pleased her to be recognized by her readers. The thrill of success hadn't worn off yet. "Not necessarily," she answered. "That photo is a few years old. My hair is different and I've added a few wrinkles, I guess."

Frannie waved it away. "Wrinkles? Where?" she said. "I always read your column. When you said your name, I thought it sounded familiar, but nothing clicked and it slipped right out of my mind." She shook her head. "I must be getting early senility. Even 'Glory' should have put my antennas up. It's not a common name."

"Forget it. It's no big deal," Glory said. "Listen, if you have time, I wanted to ask you something."

"Sure. Shoot."

"I love Ocean Cliff, but I can only have it for four weeks, and I think I'd like to stretch my stay here to the entire summer. Do you know of any place decent – something with an ocean view – that could possibly have availability?"

Frannie's lips twisted with her frown and she shook her head sympathetically, but she stopped short and smiled.

Glory searched her face. "What are you thinking? I can see your wheels are turning."

Frannie hesitated, then gave a why-not shrug of her shoulders. "I was about to say probably not, especially oceanfront, but then I had this crazy idea you might go for if you're desperate."

"I'm listening."

"My house faces the ocean and I have a whole separate apartment downstairs with a private patio. I made it for my parents to use when they visit, but they've got their summer all mapped out, starting with an island cruise, so I won't see them until late September. And even that's a maybe."

Incredulous, Glory remained with her mouth open. "Are you saying you'd offer that to me?"

"Don't look so surprised," Frannie said with a laugh. "It's not as if you're some bum off the street. You're a successful columnist and a nice person. I can tell. In this business, you sharpen your people skills. So? What do you say?"

"I say when can I see it?"

They both laughed while Frannie wrote her home phone number on a daily specials menu and handed it to Glory. "Call me tonight," she said.

Chapter 6

After heading out for Ratherbee twice and losing her courage both times, Glory was once again on Route 1, determined not to turn back.

According to her map, she was only minutes away. Words began to take shape in her mind, but none of the opening lines she came up with sounded credible. She shook them all out of her head and felt a funny, tingling sensation when Ratherbee, the stately mini-mansion, came into view. She drove slowly up its narrow dirt driveway. A canopy of tall pine trees provided an umbrella of shade. A thick layer of pine needles blanketed the drive filling the air with its heady scent. Glory steeled herself not to let her emotions interfere with her plan. Her intent was to pass this off as an impulsive decision prompted by nostalgia.

It was easy to see how a setting like Ratherbee could wrap around a girl's heart. It's mood alone suggested romance, and if the right guy stepped into the picture…well, it would be merely a matter of time.

A late model Ford Escort stood alone parked in a shady spot at the end of the driveway. Two long, weathered stone walls covered in moss ran parallel to the trees.

To the left, the gated pool area appeared abandoned. Apparently, there were no guests this week or, if there were, they were probably all down at the beach or out enjoying other pleasures.

The end of the driveway opened to a large bright clearing revealing a massive shingled home, its windows sparkling in the sun. Its wraparound porch was outfitted with assorted pieces of wicker furniture with plump, colorful cushions.

Facing the sea, on the sweeping grassy lawn several Adirondack chairs were positioned under a shade tree, but none were occupied. Two women, however, were on the porch. One of them stood up now and observed Glory as she approached.

Glory looked up at the gray-haired woman. "Excuse me. I'm sorry to bother you," she said, "but I'm looking for Paula Howard, or Mrs. Howard, her mother." A touch of humility coated her words which came out in the form of a question. She anticipated the possibility that the elder Mrs. Howard might be dead.

The woman gave her a guarded look before answering, then said, "May I ask who you are?"

"My name is Glory English," she said, hoping the woman might be familiar with her column and invite her up onto the porch. No such luck. "My mother and Paula Howard were roommates in college back in the '60s; Wheaton College. I'm staying in Maine for the summer, I hope, and…well, my mother passed away, and I had hoped to meet and talk with her friend."

Glory's explanation didn't earn her a welcoming smile, but the woman's gaze shifted to the steps and she nodded. "Come up if you like."

She climbed the few steps and nodded a polite hello to the other woman, who still remained seated, unmoved by curiosity. Then, with a sudden jolt of her head, she peered at Glory with one long, unnerving stare.

"It's about time you got here," she said. "Some daughter you are!" Her arms crossed her chest and her lips tightened. "Chester will be here at six and I have a lot of shopping to do before then. You expect me to go to his cocktail party in this?"

The woman was rail thin, her hair dark brown with gray roots that made a strong showing in the sunlight. Her skin was brown and leathery; her eyes soft amber brown, her features delicate remnants of a once-beautiful woman.

The gray-haired woman threw her arm out, pointing an open hand to the seated woman. "This is Paula Howard, but her married name is Grant."

An involuntary "Oh, no," passed through Glory's lips. She shifted slightly to exchange a private word with the gray-haired woman. "Alzheimer's?" she asked. "She's so young!"

"Yes, that's everyone's reaction. But it happens." She shrugged and paused. "I'm Nancy Sheridan. I'm sorry if I seemed ungracious, but you can't be too careful these days. Mrs. Grant's family hired me and two other nurses to care for her round the clock."

Glory glanced over at Paula Grant, who was now engaged in conversation with some imaginary person. Disbelief, sympathy and disappointment swept over her simultaneously. "How long has she been like this, Ms. Sheridan?"

"It was gradual at first; barely noticeable. Once it accelerated…" She didn't bother to complete her sentence, let her face brighten instead with an unconvincing smile. "She still has her moments of lucidity. It's wonderful to see when it happens. Like a dead person coming back to life." Her gaze shifted from her charge back to Glory. "Maybe if you care to stop by again, you might be lucky enough to catch one."

"No, I don't think so. It would seem so intrusive and insensitive now. Excuse me for prying, but where is her family? Does she have any? She's young enough to even have parents alive."

Nancy Sheridan made a negative face. Her bottom lip protruded as she spoke. "No, her parents are gone. They were both in their late thirties when they had her. In those days that was a rarity. Her husband, poor soul, died from liver cancer when he was still in his forties."

"And her children?"

"No, she could never conceive, I'm told. Her brother makes sure she's well taken care of, but he rarely visits her. For some family members, this is very tough to take. The more the disease progresses, the less you see them."

"And her sister?"

The nurse dismissed the subject with a hand wave. "Oh, you don't want to hear that story and I don't want to tell it."

Glory drove away from Ratherbee feeling as though she had lost her mother for the second time. After all these weeks of anticipation, her hopes of piecing together that vital part of her mother's life had died in a few brief moments.

Chapter 7

When Glory arrived at eight o'clock that night to see the apartment, Frannie gave her a quick tour of her home. It was modest compared to Ratherbee, but "adorable," "charming" or "cozy little cottage" were the descriptive words and phrases that came to mind when she saw it. She was becoming so enraptured with all of Maine's tranquility and laid-back lifestyle that her real life back in New York held no bonds of affection, she realized. Especially since Jason left her. She'd like nothing better than to leave it all behind like a bad dream. In her line of work, she had the advantage of being able to live anywhere she chose; all she needed to earn her living was her laptop.

Frannie was standing outside on the patio waiting to greet her. "Did you have any trouble with my directions?"

"No, not at all," Glory said. She had feared that the ocean view might be somewhat obstructed from the lower level patio, but as she had hoped, the house was built on a hilltop overlooking a rugged landscape and that spellbinding ocean that took her breath away.

"I love it already. As long as you put that ocean in front of me, I'm hooked."

Frannie laughed at Glory's enthusiasm. "Well, come and see inside anyway. I made a fresh pot of coffee and I have a few muffins from the restaurant on a warmer tray in the oven."

Glory threw her a look of mock defeat. "Oh, no," she said. "I'll never be able to resist. One drawback of hanging around you and your restaurant is that I'll probably be two sizes larger by summer's end."

Frannie cocked a brow as her gaze dropped to Glory's size six body. "And you'd *still* be thin," she said.

Glory regretted having made the comment. She had a bad habit of opening her mouth to speak before thinking about the impact of her words. Frannie was a fairly tall, well-proportioned woman and was probably a size twelve. She'd never describe her as overweight, but she clearly packed on a good twenty pounds more than her own one hundred twelve.

"Oh, wow! Where did you find this stuff?" Glory asked when they stepped inside. Two full-size sofas, both in a green colonial print, were surrounded by an eclectic collection of Early American furniture that faced a stone fireplace and sliding glass doors that invited the ocean view indoors.

The bedroom was a modest size, but Glory let out a sigh when she saw the four-poster canopied bed with its thick patchwork quilt comforter and matching accessories. She couldn't wait to sleep in it.

The kitchen, like Amore Breakfast, was done in red, white and black with copper and cast iron pots hanging from the ceiling. A wooden table with six red ladder-back chairs was cornered in the room, leaving the cooking area, which included an island counter and two stools, free and unobstructed.

Although her suite at Ocean Cliff was more spacious and more luxurious, she fell in love with the apartment's Americana charm. "When did you say your parents would be back?" she asked.

Frannie laughed, pleased at Glory's reaction. She too was proud of the way the apartment had turned out. Shopping for everything had given her months of pleasure. "I guess that means you like it?"

"Are you kidding? What's not to like?"

"Fine. It's yours till the end of September, if you'd like, and possibly more, depending on my parents' plans. How does three hundred dollars a week sound?"

Glory gave her an wide-eyed look. She was paying two-hundred-sixty a day at Ocean Cliff. "It sounds like a bargain," she admitted.

"Great. Then it's a done deal. Come, let's sit in the kitchen and talk. The coffee's ready."

After two cups of hazelnut coffee and every last crumb of a warm blueberry muffin, Glory found herself telling her newfound friend details of her life and deep-seated feelings she hadn't even confided in Stacy. There was a genuine sincerity about Frannie that made her open up.

They exchanged confidences with ease. Glory had wondered if there was presently, or had ever been, a man in Frannie's life, and Frannie had volunteered the information without being asked. She was now thirty-eight, but when she was twenty-five, she had been in love with and married to a man she thought was the greatest gift God had sent her. His job, however, required that he travel a great deal. Three years later, Frannie learned that his out-of-town business included another wife and two children.

After that, she had locked up her heart and hadn't allowed any relationship to grow beyond a certain point. Yes, there had been a few men over the years, she said, but she dated only occasionally, and always on a swinging-door basis.

When Frannie finished her story and tried to discreetly hold back her emotions, Glory patted her hand empathetically. "I have a similar story," she said. She spent the next hour telling Frannie all about herself; starting from when Jason left her to her mother's letter and the real reason for her trip to Maine. She hadn't intended to, but once it was all out and she had shed fresh tears, she felt better.

"My God, Glory, you've had a double blow to deal with. I'm glad we found each other. Sometimes it's easier to talk to a stranger than to someone you've known all your life. Not that we're exactly strangers to each other and certainly will be friends now that you'll be living here. Who knows, maybe if we put our heads together, we can find your father."

"My father, if he's still alive, may not want to be found. He probably has a family and wouldn't want to hurt them. That part scares me – having him reject me."

"Don't be such a pessimist. How do you know he has a wife and children? Maybe when you find each other, it'll be a glorious event and your presence will make him happier than he's ever been."

Glory peered at her under hooded brows. "Boy! Are you a dreamer!"

"Well, it *is* possible, isn't it?"

"Yes, it's possible," Glory conceded.

"Fine. Then let me chase you out of here. I have to get up at the crack of dawn. We'll get together later this week and maybe figure out a way to find your mystery man."

"You make it sound like a romantic love story."

"Hey, it may not be *romantic*, but it sure is a *love* story."

Chapter 8

Glory sat on her balcony at Ocean Cliff the following night, eating her dinner – a bowl of popcorn and a Diet Coke. She stared down at her cell phone on the table and heaved a sigh. If she didn't make those two calls she had promised, one to Marty and the other to Stacy, they'd both be calling until they tracked her down.

Marty's answering machine picked up and Glory was relieved by the temporary reprieve. He probably wouldn't be too happy with her plan to be away all summer, and she wasn't in the mood to listen to his objections.

She called Stacy next and caught her just as she was about to leave for dinner with friends. After giving her a quick summation of her visit to Ratherbee and a promise to call again next week, she hung up and went back to her popcorn. Minutes later she realized that she hadn't mentioned her summer-long plans. Just as well, Glory thought. Stacy would surely begin mothering her again with all kinds of warnings and advice. And right now she could do without another mother figure. She was still battling with a whirlpool of mixed feelings about her real mother. And her real father.

How is this possible? she asked herself. I never saw his face, heard his voice, never knew of him, never saw his picture, and yet, I love him. Why is that? Then she remembered her mother's line in the letter about how love filled her the moment she knew her baby was growing inside her. Blood ties. Yes, that's what it's all about.

In the middle of the night, Glory shot up in bed. "Oh, my God! Why didn't I think of it?"

She looked at the red numbers on the digital clock. Three-forty. If I get an early start, I can be home and back by tonight. The idea was crazy and could fall apart like her trip to Ratherbee, but this one had possibilities. Strong possibilities.

Glory jumped out of bed and into the shower, her adrenaline pumping.

***

The long drive back to Rockland County seemed to take forever with no one to talk to, but if she found what she was looking for, the nine or ten hours for the round trip drive would be worth it. Her mother's life was captured in photographs, most neatly arranged in albums, and stored in Glory's attic at the condo.

The first thing she did when she walked in was to put on a pot of coffee and defrost two slices of multigrain bread for toast. While her coffee perked, she pulled down the attic steps and climbed up. Three cartons of her mother's photos were stacked in one corner, all labeled to cover a span of years. Unquestionably, the one she wanted was the bottom one, labeled "1960-1979."

She pulled it out, brought it down and put it on the kitchen table. Her stomach had been growling like a cement truck while she drove, but now anxiety diminished her appetite somewhat. The hot coffee soothed her angry stomach and once she bit into the jellied toast, she ate every last crumb.

Glory took a long pensive moment as she peered down at the box. In the next few seconds she could possibly find a photograph of her biological father. The same mixed feelings that she had felt with the letter swept over her now. She wanted to see his face, but the part of her that wanted to deny his existence kept her hands clasped.

As she knew it would, her heart took the lead and her fingers followed. When she took the lid off the box, Glory felt a smile form on her face while an ache tugged at her heart. The contents were meticulously organized; so typical of her mother. Sometimes her compulsion for neatness would exasperate Glory and her dad, but now that she was gone, those memories were erased and her mind conjured up only feelings of affection.

She immediately rejected all the albums after glancing at their labels. Most were special family occasions or vacations, none of which would include the face Glory was looking for. There were at least two dozen envelopes stuffed with photos, but thanks to her neat-freak mother, who had them all arranged chronologically, she flipped through to 1967 and there it was, labeled, "August 1967, Ogunquit, Maine."

Glory's mouth went dry.

She found a group photo and spotted her mother's young face. She felt as though she were seeing it for the first time. Her sand-colored hair was teased high and wide, and its ends were turned up in a pronounced flip. Her mom had always been thin and petite, and always looked younger than her years, but looking at her in this photo, youthful and trim in shorts and tee shirt, she looked more like an adolescent than a college graduate ready to face the world. Staring down now at her radiant, carefree smile, Glory found it hard to swallow that this innocent-looking young woman would soon conceive a child, if she hadn't already. The writing on the back identified everyone in the photo. They were Howard family members, young and old. Glory put the photo aside and slowly scanned the others.

She stopped dead when she found a photo of two couples with their arms locked together, all beaming like one continuous smile. Her gaze locked in at the couple on the right. A chill shivered in her chest and trembled its way straight down to her toes. There was her mother with her head tipped and leaning on the shoulder of a tall young man. She flipped the photo over quickly, but this one had no names. It merely said "At Mrs. Howard's Birthday Barbecue."

Glory couldn't stop staring at that face. His smile was inviting, his teeth a little too large for his face, but the flash of white against his coppery skin was magnetic. His hair appeared dark, but Glory attributed that to the fact that it was soaking wet and slicked back behind his ears. One rebellious curl fell onto his forehead. She couldn't determine the color of his eyes because it was a full-body shot, but if this was *him,* Glory could see why her mother had become attracted to him. He towered over her. Even with her teased-high hair, she just about reached his neck, and his long, lean build was muscular, boasting broad shoulders and strong thighs.

I shouldn't make that assumption, Glory reconsidered. It might not have been a physical attraction. Judging by his smile, their relationship might have been triggered by an amiable, gregarious personality. She fumbled through her desk drawer to fish out her small magnifying glass that was buried among all the other miscellaneous items. Its bright red plastic case facilitated her search.

She positioned the glass over the face she suspected was her father's and examined it carefully, hoping to discover some unique characteristics that would identify it as the masculine version of her own face. As much as she wanted to, it was impossible to make that determination. His eyes were squinting from the sun, his lips widened with his smile. Unlike the nose of her adoptive father – *God, I hate that term,* Glory thought – which took command of his face, the nose in the photograph was straight, strong and well-defined.

She found him in two more group shots, but both were taken at a distance, and neither one had captured him full-face. Disappointed but by no means defeated, Glory threw the entire packet of Maine photos into her tote bag. I'll scan and enlarge them on my computer when I get back to Maine, she told herself.

After replacing the box in the attic, she curled up on the sofa and closed her eyes, hoping to catch a short nap before she started the long trip back, but her mind refused to shut down. A whirlpool of memories circled her head. Scenes from the past took shape again with remarkable clarity, but were somewhat jaded now, as though it were the same scene with different characters.

Glory let a full hour pass, then gave up. If she felt drowsy on the way, she'd pull into a motel and sack out till morning. She grabbed her tote bag, locked the door and headed back for Maine.

Chapter 9

A balmy breeze floated past her the moment Glory stepped out of her car. She walked through the shaded parking lot of Ocean Cliff and rubbed her bare arms to chase away the sudden chill.

She had made good time; it was only 6:10 p.m. when she arrived. The sun was still blazing in the sky to warm the sun worshippers at the beaches and pools, although it did nothing to remove the ocean's icy sting for the few who were brave enough to venture in.

A fresh shower, a change of clothes and a walk into town was the best plan she could come up with for the evening. If she had someone to share it with, it would be high on the entertainment scale.

The light on her phone was flashing when she opened the door to her suite. She dropped her tote bag on the sofa then sat on the edge of the bed to retrieve the message. Frannie Oliveri's recorded voice came on and asked that she return the call when convenient. Hearing that it was Frannie who had called, not Stacy, her lips curled up in a smile, giving her mixed feelings of relief and guilt. Yes, Stacy had proved herself to be a true and faithful friend, having carried Glory through the agonizing months since Jason dumped her like an old, worn-out shoe, but she was a glaring reminder of those dark days.

Sweeping the memories out of her mind, she picked up the phone and returned the call. "Hi, Frannie. What's up?"

"Oh, Glory. Hi. Where you been? Out playing tourist?"

Glory laughed. "No. I made an unexpected trip back home." A thought came to her that wiped the smile off her face. "Why did you call? Don't tell me your parents had a change of plans and I won't be able to rent the apartment."

Now it was Frannie's turn to laugh. "No, you're way off base. I called because I have two tickets for tomorrow night's performance at the Ogunquit Playhouse. The friend I was supposed to go with had to cancel. I'm going anyway, but I hate to see the other ticket go to waste."

Glory's eyes brightened. "Oh, wow! That would be great. I noticed when I drove by the Playhouse that they have a show about Patsy Cline, with Sally Struthers. I had intended to call for a ticket."

"Well, now you won't have to. It's called *Always, Patsy Cline.* Everyone who's seen it says Sally Struthers is terrific as Patsy's friend, and the girl who plays Patsy has a voice that's not to be believed."

"Say no more. I can't wait to see it. And tell your friend I'm sorry she had to cancel, but I'll of course pay for the ticket."

"It's a he, not a she. And forget the money. I wouldn't even think of offering him money. He'd be highly insulted."

Glory slipped off her sandals, unzipped her jeans and peeled them off while she spoke with the phone crooked between her neck and shoulder. "Okay, then," she said, "but how about an early dinner before the show. You say where and I'll treat."

Frannie hesitated. "Let me think about where. There are a million great restaurants around. I'm on my way out now. I'll call you tomorrow."

"Great. Thanks, Frannie."

When she hung up, Glory realized she never mentioned a word about why she unexpectedly went home. Fannie was probably curious, but too polite to ask. The thought widened her smile. After the long, soul-baring conversation they'd had in Fannie's kitchen, she had no more secrets left buried.

Rather than call her back, she decided to wait. When they were comfortably seated at a dinner table tomorrow night, she'd yank out the photographs.

Chapter 10

Instead of waiting for Frannie's afternoon call, Glory walked to see her at Amore Breakfast. After a restless night of getting in and out of bed to look at the photographs, she had finally fallen into a deep sleep sometime after sunrise.

The restaurant was mobbed. Cars that came in were circling their way out when their occupants saw the crowd waiting on and around the porch. She needs to expand this place, Glory thought. She has a turn-away business here.

When she walked inside to put her name on the waiting list, she changed her mind. The wait staff was moving about so fast, it looked like a silent movie. Frannie spotted her from afar and threw her a sorry-can't-talk-to-you-now look.

"Can I help?" Glory called out to her.

Frannie's eyes widened, pleased by the offer, but her expression changed to a you-asked-for-it warning. Her hand went up, gesturing that Glory stay put till she could talk to her. A minute later, Frannie approached her, nearly breathless. "It's insane, and we're down two people today. As long as you offered, do you think you can fill the guests' coffee mugs so I can stay at the door?"

Glory gave a quick shrug. "Sure. I can bus tables too if that helps. We need to maintain your reputation for running a well-oiled machine, right?"

"You got it! You're a lifesaver, Glory. I owe you."

It took more than two hours for the pace to slow down, but Glory loved every minute. She was so busy trying to play the part of congenial waitress that she never had time to think about what brought her to Maine. By 1:30 the last few customers had finished eating, but lingered over their conversations. Glory brought a tall glass of iced tea out on the porch, plopped in a chair and put her feet up on another one.

Frannie joined her shortly after. "You were a godsend today. Thanks a million. I didn't intend for you to get stuck that long. I'm sorry."

Glory waved it away. "Don't give it a second thought. It was fun to get caught up in all that hustle-bustle activity among all those happy faces." She stopped for a second to give it more thought. "Actually, I enjoyed myself," she added with a satisfied grin. "I'd be glad to walk over in the mornings and help out while I'm here."

Frannie swept away her offer with a hand gesture. "Are you kidding? No way! Even if I paid you the going salary, I would never consider it. You're on vacation, for goodness sake. There's plenty to see and do in Maine. Your days should be free to take it all in."

Glory gave her a sidelong glance. "If you recall our long conversation, you'll remember that the purpose of my visit was not to admire the scenery. That's secondary."

"Yes, I know this is all about your biological father. All the more reason why your time should be free."

Glory put her tea glass on the table alongside her and turned to look squarely at Frannie. "Look, I'll be here all summer. Time is not a problem. I'm serious about my offer. And you *certainly* don't have to pay me. It'll be my pleasure and, thank God, I don't need the money."

Frannie said nothing, but scrunched her face in dubious consideration. "You're a crazy lady. A glutton for punishment."

"I totally agree. So is my offer accepted?"

"If I said no, then I'd be crazy too. You're on! But if something else comes up or you just change your mind – "

Glory didn't let her finish. "I know, I know," she said and rippled her fingers to wave away further discussion. "So, where are we eating tonight and what time?"

Frannie looked at her with a face about to erupt with laughter, and it did. "You could have saved yourself a lot of hard work and grief if you had waited for my phone call."

"Grief had nothing to do with my time spent here."

Frannie gulped down the rest of her iced tea and stood up, ready to get back inside to close up for the day. "I'll pick you up at 5:45. The show is at eight, so that'll give us plenty of time. We're going to Marcello's. It's close to the theater and I've never heard a bad word about their food or their service."

Chapter 11

Glory had eaten in countless fine restaurants in her lifetime and Marcello's could shine among the favorites. Both women agreed that their appetizers and entrees scored high in presentation and taste. The magnificent paintings and murals that lined the walls brought the Amalfi coast to life in the modest-sized Italian restaurant. The romantic ambiance triggered memories with Jason that stabbed at her heart, but she quickly blinked them away.

They chatted amiably through their meals, about their work, their families and politics. When they fell into discussion about the war in Iraq, their mood darkened. Fortunately, they forced themselves to break away from the frightening subject of war and terrorism when the waiter arrived with their coffee and dessert. Glory sliced the one cheesecake they had decided to share into two even portions. Then, without preamble, she reached into her purse and put the computer-enlarged photographs on the table.

Nonplussed, Frannie glanced down at them and met Glory's eyes, waiting for an explanation. Glory stared back at her, waiting for Frannie to make the connection. She eyed the photographs again and made a hand motion for Frannie to take a second look.

"Oh, my God! Don't tell me," she said, then reached in her bag for her glasses and held the photo closer to the candlelight. "It's him, isn't it? Which one?"

Glory shook her head as if to clear it. "Oh, how stupid of me. I assumed you'd pick him right out, without realizing you don't even know which girl is my mother. Here..." she said, pointing, "that's my mother and I'm assuming that's *him*, my real father. He showed up with my mother in four photographs. He looks like a kid, doesn't he?"

"Well, they were both in their early twenties. From where we are now, everyone that age looks like a kid."

"That's for sure," Glory acknowledged with a smile.

"How did you find these pictures?"

"That's why I went home yesterday. You know how things click in your head in the middle of the night sometimes? Well, I remembered the boxes of my mother's family photos and thought, just maybe..." She went on to explain with a sprinkle of pride her mother's meticulously organized boxes and how easily she had found them.

"So now what?"

"I'm not sure."

Frannie gave the photos and Glory's face a closer scrutiny, her eyes darting back and forth for a comparison study.

Glory laughed. "I did the same thing. I even brought the picture with me to the mirror to look for a resemblance. I didn't see one, and I can see by your face that you don't either."

"No, not really. But that doesn't necessarily mean anything," she said handing the photos back to Glory.

To lighten the mood, which fell somber again, Glory asked Frannie questions about how Amore Breakfast got started and how much knowledge she had needed to handle the business end along with learning all about food preparation.

Frannie's enthusiasm and pride in telling the backstory kept their conversation alive for the next half-hour. Glory listened with rapt attention, surprised by the inexplicable, sincere interest she was developing in the restaurant business. She was well aware that many people would give their right arm for her successful career, but Frannie had a way of making food service sound more exciting and rewarding. Was it all those pleased customers that paraded in and out of Amore Breakfast every day? Maybe, but something compelling about the business piqued Glory's interest.

***

After the performance, groups of people clustered in the theater lobby talking about the show while they waited for their cars. Praise for the Patsy Cline production was on everyone's lips. Christa Jackson, who played Patsy, did indeed have a singing voice that brought the audience to their feet. Sally Struthers' narration, with her innate flair for comedy, added her talents to capture the hearts of the audience as well.

Frannie was approached several times by different people. She seemed to know everyone. Proudly, she introduced Glory as "Glory English, the columnist." As usual, Glory's name drew blanks on some faces while others were clearly impressed and full of questions. A tap on her shoulder interrupted her conversation.

"Excuse me, Miss English. Can I speak privately with you a moment?" the woman asked.

For a brief moment, Glory didn't know who she was, then realized she was looking at the dressed-up-out-for-the-evening version of Nancy Sheridan, Paula Grant's aide. Noting the serious look on her face, Glory stepped out of the circle.

"I was planning to call you tomorrow at Ocean Cliff, but I might as well tell you now," Ms. Sheridan continued. "Alex Howard called to check on his sister. I hope you don't mind, but I told him about your visit. He said if you should stop by or call again, I should tell you to feel free to call him." She shrugged as if to say she didn't know why, but it's none of her business. "Guess he's curious about you."

Glory's heart quickened. Her mind raced trying to think of how old this brother might be. *Maybe he knows something about my father.* "Really? That's nice of him," she answered. "Tell me, Ms. Sheridan, how old a man is he...about?"

The woman's eyes shot up thoughtfully. She pursed her lips and placed her index finger over them. "Mid to late forties would be my guess."

He would have been ten to fifteen that summer. *Old enough to remember,* Glory thought, trying to veil her anxiety. "I don't suppose you have his name and number with you now?"

"As a matter of fact, I do," she said, reaching into her bag. "I keep it in my wallet just in case I have a problem."

Chapter 12

Glory made it her business to get to Amore Breakfast the next morning at 7:30, before the mad rush. She helped herself to coffee and a warm zucchini-nut muffin and sat at the counter. Again, she considered eating only half, but wolfed it all down before her conscience denied her the pleasure.

"It's no use. I'm doomed to gain twenty pounds this summer," she said to Vicki, the waitress working the counter.

Vicki scooped away the empty dish and refilled Glory's coffee cup. "Nah. Don't you know you should never count calories when you're on vacation?"

Glory gave her a smirk. "Yeah, a week maybe, but a whole summer?"

"I've been here three years and look at me," she said, proud of her trim figure. If you start working around this place every day, it won't tempt you as much. You see so much food you develop an immunity."

With her hands supporting a huge tray of food, Frannie paused at the counter to throw a question to Glory. "Did you decide yet about calling him?"

Glory wrinkled her face indecisively and Frannie took off, not waiting for an answer.

For the next three hours, Glory had no time for idle chatter with Frannie or any of the other wait staff, but as she manned the door, she did extend her congeniality to the hungry customers.

By 11:30 Frannie literally threw her out. "C'mon, you've been here too many hours," she said. Frannie had a hand on each of Glory's shoulders and gave her a polite shove out the screened door. "We can handle it from here. Go do something relaxing. You're giving me a guilt complex watching you work for nothing."

Glory blew an exasperated sigh. "I told you I don't need the money – "

"Yes, I know, and you enjoy it, but force yourself to do something leisurely. For my sake, okay? It's a gorgeous day out there."

Glory gave up the protest and left the restaurant, but she didn't head directly back to Ocean Cliff. She walked along Shore Road until she reached the entrance to Marginal Way, Ogunquit's oceanside walking path.

Once she began her walk, she was sorry she hadn't done it sooner. The view from high up was breathtaking. A relentless ocean breeze fanned her face, providing relief from the inescapable blazing sun. Along the way, other walkers were friendly; they'd smile and say hello, and others even struck up a pleasant conversation as they paused to share a bench and soak in the view. What a life! she thought. I think I could take a steady diet of this Maine lifestyle.

As she walked her way back and off Marginal Way, Glory decided to make this pleasurable trip part of her daily routine. It had totally relaxed her body and her mind. In one short hour, she had already cleared her head enough to organize thoughts for her next column and come to a decision on her latest pressing problem. She headed back to Ocean Cliff for a much-needed shower, a refreshing and invigorating swim in its luxurious pool, followed by an important phone call.

Yes, she had decided, she *would* call Alex Howard. *I hope he has a sharp memory.*

***

Glory sat on her balcony for over an hour that Saturday afternoon, staring at the phone. It was already past four o'clock and if she didn't call soon, he might go out for the evening. That would give her another sleepless night agonizing over whether or not she should call.

She felt like a jerk. If she didn't tell this total stranger the real reason behind her call, she'd be embarrassed to bother him. He'd probably classify her inquiries as pure feminine sentimentality.

Oh, the heck with it, she thought. Why should I care what impression he gets? I'll probably have one phone conversation with him and that'll be the end of it.

When his voice mail picked up, she was half-relieved and half-disappointed, but she stumbled through her message. "My name is Gloria English. Ms. Sheridan gave me your number. I appreciate your willingness to talk to me. Thanks anyway. Maybe I'll call again."

She felt foolish when she hung up, but decided to get out and browse in the shops. The distraction would do her good. She slipped into her thick rubber-soled slides and was almost out the door when the phone stopped her. She ran back to answer it and breathed a friendly "hi" into the mouthpiece, expecting to hear either Stacy's or Frannie's voice.

Alex Howard realized by her tone that she'd expected someone else. A slight laugh accompanied his words. "Well, hi yourself. This is Alex Howard."

Glory echoed his little laugh with one of her own. "Oh, I'm sorry. You didn't have to call me back. I said I'd call again."

"You said maybe you'd call again. I knew from Nancy Sheridan that you were staying at Ocean Cliff, so I thought I'd better call you. I got the feeling that you were uncomfortable about talking to me."

"Wow! You're a very perceptive man, Mr. Howard. You were able to glean that much from that brief message?"

"I'm not always right. First tell me, Miss English, are you the same Glory…"

"Yes, I am."

"The columnist? Really? I read your column often; even tried some of your recipes, but don't ask how they turned out."

That eased her and she laughed.

"I understand that your mother and my sister were friends?"

"Yes, in college."

"Well, I guess we might have some thoughts to share."

"I'd like that, Mr. Howard, if you can spare the time. At your convenience, of course."

"First of all, 'Alex' is fine. Your mother and my sister made us fast friends. But actually we might enjoy reminiscing about them over lunch or dinner. I'll be in Ogunquit for four days next week to see Paula and arrange for some necessary house repairs. Could I interest you in dinner?"

"That might be nice," she heard herself say. His voice had such a throaty, sexy tone that she wondered whether he was married or involved with someone. She quickly swept the thought away but not before she felt her cheeks flush.

"Good. I'll call you. I should be there, say, late morning Friday. So we'll do dinner that night, okay?"

Glory hesitated for several reasons. Only one reached her lips. "What about your sister?" As soon as she said it, she realized instantly it was the wrong thing to say. An awkward pause fell between them for a moment until he spoke the words Glory anticipated.

"I don't think she'll miss me. She doesn't even recognize me anymore."

"I'm sorry…"

"Don't be," Alex said. The smile was back in his voice. "I'm looking forward to meeting you, Miss Glory English."

Glory was so excited at the prospect of meeting Alex Howard and learning more about that "summer of '67 that she put off her shopping trip to call Stacy and Frannie with the news. She didn't reach Stacy, but Frannie picked up after the first ring and Glory told her, almost verbatim, about her conversation with Alex Howard.

"Wow, this *is* a giant step. And by the way, I picked up a little news for you too. This fine gentleman you have a dinner date with is forty-eight years old, so he was thirteen that summer. And my sources tell me he's Gregory Peck, reborn."

"Oh, stop. He could be short, fat and bald for all I care as long as he can fill in some necessary blanks for me. Besides, don't you start playing cupid too. I already have Stacy in New York who drives me crazy with that stuff. He's probably married and might show up with his wife on his arm."

"No chance. He's not married because his wife died eight years ago. And the jury's still out on the circumstances of that mysterious accidental death."

"Are you kidding? Where did you get this information?"

"When you have a business like mine, you get more information than *The New York Times.*"

Chapter 13

Glory chose her black pants suit for her dinner date with Alex Howard. She had plenty of clothes, but favored this old standby. It seemed the correct choice for almost any occasion. A dusty pink shell underneath broke it up nicely. She played with stubborn strands of hair until she finally accepted defeat. The last touch was her creamy pink lipstick which matched her shell perfectly. She took one long look in the full-length mirror and decided the image before her had long passed from girl to woman, but was still attractive. People generally assessed her more favorably, but Glory had always dismissed the compliments as exaggerated attempts at congeniality.

Glory tried to convince herself that the anxiety she'd been feeling since his late-morning call was attributable to what this gentleman could or could not divulge about that fateful summer. Not entirely true, she admitted to herself. Although her business had often necessitated luncheon dates with men, those were different; all strictly business. At the time, she had been the proverbial happily married woman who looked forward to her evenings at home with her perfect husband.

Her face went sour at the thought.

***

Despite his tall, lean build, his lips grabbed her attention first. She stood there on Ocean Cliffs's front lawn, shook his hand, met his gaze two or three seconds too long, but the lips held her captive. She hoped her reaction wasn't transparent, but long-dormant feelings stirred inside her.

"Your photograph doesn't do you justice, Glory."

She paused for a second, then realized he meant the photo that appears with her column. "Actually, it's six years old. I like the photograph better than the real me."

"Well now, we've just met and already we disagree."

Deep velvet. Yes, those were the words that best described his voice; deep velvet framed by full, smooth lips. She chased away her sensual thoughts and looked up at him with an amused smile. "Where did you make the reservation?" she asked.

"Well, after you left it to me to decide, I chose a wonderful oceanfront seafood place, The Chowder House. Have you been there?"

She shook her head as they walked to his car, a late-model Jaguar. "You have to remember I'm a newcomer to Maine, Alex. I haven't been here long enough to explore it all."

"Well, maybe you'll consider taking me on as a tour guide. I still have three days, and with the situation at Ratherbee, I could use some good company. We can take in a lot of sights if we plan it well. If you're free, that is."

Her mind wasn't ready to send an answer to her lips yet, so she simply gave him a breath of a smile and a "we'll see" shrug of the shoulders.

***

Glory selected Chilean sea bass with a Caesar salad and Alex ordered a broiled lobster without bothering to look at the menu. She let him select the wine, a Sauvignon Blanc, which helped ease her into the subject that brought them together.

Their conversation began with his sister Paula's medical misfortune. She had been an intelligent, active and vibrant woman. As a child, he resented her self-imposed authority, but once he matured into a young adult, that resentment had reshaped itself into profound admiration and love. His face revealed that fact as he spoke and reminisced about his sister.

"It's like she's dead already," he confided. "I wish I were a stronger person, but I just can't handle seeing her like that. There's no chance of communication and when I look at her face..." He paused and swallowed. "Yes, her features are all there, but her eyes tell you her mind is far off in some distant, unreachable place."

Glory remembered Nancy Sheridan's words about the declining frequency of his visits. Her heart went out to him as he spoke about how the disease had progressed, with the infrequent, insignificant signs at first to her present stage. In some ways, his pain was worse than the shock he would have felt if she had died suddenly.

He squared his shoulders finally, sat back in his chair and flashed a smile big enough to erase all the depressing details of his sister's illness. "Hey, I'm sorry. I didn't mean to dump on you. Let's talk about something pleasant."

She had intended to respond with what she went through when her mother left for a quick shopping trip to the mall and never returned. His wide smile prompted her to save it for another time. If there was another time.

"Alex, as Nancy told you, I have this quest to put back pieces of my mother's life. She had mentioned your sister often when she reminisced about her college days. Do you have any memories of my mother?"

His eyes narrowed as he searched his mind. "I do remember that my sister brought her home a couple of times. What did you say her name was? Mandy, was it?"

"Yes, short for Amanda."

His lower lip protruded just a fraction more as he concentrated, exposing the pink plumpness. He shook his head. "Nancy told me you said your mom spent a whole month with us the summer after they graduated. My parents, bless their souls, had guests constantly. Our house was like a hotel; some people checking out and others checking in. Paula always had friends around; some from college and some locals. Remember, I was thirteen that summer. My sister certainly didn't want me tailing along with her friends, nor did I want to."

The Gregory Peck resemblance was coming to light. The shape of his mouth, the strong, well-defined features, and the arched left brow were all mirrored in the face and mannerisms of Alex Howard, whose wife had died mysteriously. She couldn't stop thinking about that.

"Your mother stands out in my mind for one reason, though."

Glory nodded to the waiter who came to clear the table. After eating all the succulent fish and half her salad, she waved away her untouched baked potato wordlessly so as not to interrupt Alex. She folded her arms on the table and leaned forward to listen.

"Your mother was a great swimmer...entertainingly so. We all used to watch and admire her in the pool."

Glory smiled with pride. "Yes, she was. She mentioned several times how she loved Esther Williams, the Hollywood swimming star of the 50s. She used to see her movies over and over to study and imitate her style."

"And she looked just as good in the water. Your mom was a beautiful woman. At thirteen I was already starting to notice. Anyway, I used to have a fear of the water, so I never learned to swim. Your mother changed that. By the end of that summer, I was as good as she was."

"Ah! That's nice to hear. Maybe you inspired her to teach swimming. She did that for years, privately and at the Y."

Glory veered away slightly to probe elsewhere. Nancy Sheridan's few words had sunk with a thud. Her curiosity got the best of her and, who knows...maybe what Alex doesn't know his other sister does.

"I understand you have another sister. Is she younger or older?"

"Younger. That's Allison. There's six years between us, so she's forty-two now."

She would have been seven, Glory thought. No help there. The one word "now" tagged on told Glory that brother and sister hadn't seen each other for a long time. That and the absence of his smile when Glory broached the subject.

"I'm sorry," she said. "I get the impression I touched on a sensitive area. It's none of my business."

He shook it away as if it was an insignificant detail. "It's no big deal. Happens in families all the time. My sister and I both have strong personalities. She's always been opinionated and stubborn, and we clash, so we avoid each other. Simple as that."

She had wanted to ask him about his wife's "mysterious" accidental death, but that would be pushing it.

"Is there anything else you remember about my mother? You've already made me feel good knowing she helped you conquer your fear of water."

His eyes squinted closed as he focused again on rolling back more than three decades. He opened them seconds later and gave her a rueful look. "I'm sorry, Glory. I wish I could remember more for you, and maybe I will at another time, but right now my memory is blank, or dim, I should say. I do remember that she was tiny and trim and everyone loved her. She had a way about her that put everyone at ease."

"Yes, my mom was always a warm, loving person," she eagerly agreed. "What about other friends? Is it possible that she became close to any of your sister Paula's other friends?"

"You mean friends here in Maine?"

"Yes, or anyone who might have any recollection of my mother."

A long, silent moment fell between them. Glory felt his penetrating eyes searching hers. She rubbed at the goose bumps crawling up her arms.

Finally he spoke. "Glory, I know we've only just met, but I think your interest in my memories runs deeper than you care to discuss. If I'm right, and you want to talk about it..."

She cast her gaze downward. Before she had a chance to respond, he reached over and patted her hand. "I'm sorry. I didn't mean to make you uncomfortable. I'd just like to offer my friendship, okay?"

Glory looked up at him and nodded. Her expression held a hint of concession. Without words, her eyes said yes, there is more, but nothing I'm ready to speak about now, if ever.

"Okay, so we'll forget about it for now. Let's think forward instead of backwards. How would you feel about a long car ride out to Boothbay Harbor tomorrow?"

Glory couldn't think of a reason fast enough to refuse him, nor did she want to. "I did hear that that area is supposed to be beautiful," she said. "Sure. Why not?"

Chapter 14

Alex Howard returned to Ratherbee that night and found it draped in a blanket of darkness. Yes, there were subdued lights in the driveway and at the back door; enough to help find your way, but the lights of life were long gone. Memories tugged at his heart. He remembered when the Howards were a well-to-do happy family whose biggest problem was which caterer to use for their next celebration. Life back then was one long party, strung together with days and nights filled with love and laughter among family and friends.

Elena had slowly destroyed Alex's blue skies and sunshine lifestyle. All the carefree gaiety had faded into dark storms. As much as he tried to shield his troubles from his parents, they too had suffered seeing their son's misery.

As if that weren't enough, his sister Allison had suddenly turned from a sweet, precocious child to a wild, rebellious young adult, obsessed with material possessions and men. In that order. Almost a mirror image of Elena.

Another heartache for his parents. But at least they had been able to draw strength from Paula, their firstborn. Alex was grateful they hadn't lived to see her under the grips of Alzheimer's disease. Hadn't had to watch her mind die a little more each day.

Don't go back, he admonished himself. *Let it go. Let it all go.*

Alex found Josephine Britton, the night nurse, seated outside Paula's bedroom door. She put a finger to her lips when he approached. Her plea for silence together with her widened eyes told him instantly that Paula had been difficult.

He walked closer to her and whispered," She gave you a hard time again, Josie?"

Josie blew out a sigh, but her eyes were forgiving. "It's the illness, Mr. Howard. She can't help it."

Alex looked in on his sister in the darkened room, illuminated slightly by a night light plugged into a floor socket. He tiptoed through that funnel of light and stared down at the sister who used to be. She slept peacefully now, free of the demons that possessed her most of the time; those demons that sucked away her ability to be cognizant of anyone or anything around her.

He brushed a limp lock of hair away from her face and stared for a moment, letting himself imagine that her eyes might open wide with recognition and sensible, intelligible words would flow from her lips. But that wasn't going to happen. Alex knew that well. His sister was lost to him forever; her mind locked in some ominous sea of darkness from which she'd never escape. Only death would free her.

He kissed the tips of his fingers and brushed them across her lips. The lump in his throat went down with a hard swallow. Feeling the moisture building in his eyes, Alex turned abruptly and left the room. He mumbled a soft good-night to Josie, who remained seated outside the bedroom door settled in a club chair with a cup of tea and a paperback novel.

***

The roaring sea and cawing gulls were not the sounds that awakened Alex the next morning. The peal of his sister's screams electrified the house. Nancy Sheridan, the day nurse, was with Paula now, trying to calm her enough to sedate her.

Instead of helping, Alex watched from a distance, immobilized by the sickening display of his sister's diseased mind. When Nancy finally gained control of Paula's flailing limbs, he breathed a sigh of relief, as though he himself had been through the physical struggle. He went back into his bedroom quietly thinking about the nurses. When he had first hired them, he felt their fees were exorbitant. Now, he decided, he'd leave each of them a generous tip before he left.

In the shower, a complete mood reversal took over Alex. The warm spray of water and the clean, musky fragrance of the soap washed away his earlier depression. He had a full day to look forward to with the very pleasant and very beautiful Miss English. Alex's energy quickly returned. He found himself shaving the crevices of a smiling face instead of the grim image that usually greeted him in the morning.

Chapter 15

Glory's eyes opened at 5:10 that morning. For the next twenty minutes, she forced them closed by holding her fingers over the lids, but sleep evaded her. Racing thoughts kept her wide awake. At 5:30 she settled for the five and a half hours of sleep she'd already had and threw the comforter aside.

She had plenty of time to enjoy a brisk early morning walk along Marginal Way, but she opted to skip it today and walk down to Amore Breakfast. Frannie opened for business at 7:00, but was there every day by 6:00.

The screen door was locked but Glory knocked when she spotted Frannie pouring coffee grinds into one of the urns. One of the waitresses swung the door open.

"I thought you were going to call me last night?" Frannie said.

"It was late; close to 9:30. I know you go to bed early."

"True, but I was anxious to hear how your date went."

Glory went palms up. "Let's stop right there. It was *not* a date. My only interest in Alex Howard is his long-term memory."

Frannie shot her a look. "That may be so, but according to what I heard about him, his looks are a fringe benefit. Is it true?"

Glory grabbed a handful of paper placemats and a basket of silverware and napkins. She busied herself setting up the twenty tables. "Yes, I guess so. I can see what they mean about the Gregory Peck resemblance. He's not quite *that* good-looking, but there's something about him…"

Frannie pointed a finger. "Ah ha! See? Regardless of the true nature of your plight, I smell an attraction. Am I right?"

"Don't be ridiculous," Glory was quick to answer, but felt that tell-tale blush in her cheeks again.

"I just met the man, for goodness sake!" She kept her attention focused on her table settings to avoid her friend's gaze.

"It only takes one look for a person to feel attracted to someone. So are you going to see him again?"

Glory blew a defeated sigh. "Yes, but only because I barely scratched the surface with him. It was difficult to probe too much without telling him why. I'd rather avoid that if I can."

She followed Frannie into the immaculate, well-organized kitchen where the cooks were busy preparing batter and cracking dozens of eggs into blenders. Glory pitched in by washing the assortment of vegetables that would be chopped up for the specialty omelets. There was something exciting about Amore Breakfast's morning rush. Something pleasantly challenging. From what she had observed so far in her time spent there, Frannie and her employees enjoyed a harmonious working relationship. She treated them fairly and without condescension and their reciprocation was reflected in their job performance. She loved the teamwork, the camaraderie; two essentials lacking in her career. Yes, Glory was fully aware that independence was not to be frowned upon, but mornings at Amore Breakfast revealed that an independent career choice did not necessarily mean a *lonely* career choice.

Her conversation with Frannie had to be put on hold once they had moved to the kitchen. Questions were thrown at her from left and right and Frannie handled them all without missing a beat. Glory worked along with them, but flashed her eyes up to the wall clock several times. That repeated action did not go unnoticed by Frannie.

"Glory, we can handle this. If you want to make a break, just go. If you have plans I don't want to hold you up."

"Well, I have a little time yet. It's only 8:10. I'm being picked up at 10."

Frannie's brows shot up in anticipation. "Picked up?" she asked, but didn't want to push for more than Glory was willing to yield.

"He offered to take me sightseeing for the day. The guy looks for something to get away from Ratherbee when he comes. Seeing his sister like that..." She let her voice trail off.

Frannie's hand went up like a stop sign. "Hey, you don't owe me any explanations."

The two friends exchanged a knowing look.

"If you get home before ten tonight, call me. If you feel like talking, that is."

"Oh, I'll be home long before ten. What the heck would we do in all that time?"

Frannie threw her a suggestive grin. "You put your foot in it that time."

Glory laughed, yanked off her apron and threw it at her. "You're hopeless!"

Chapter 16

She looked pretty enough to paint when Alex drove into Ocean Cliff Lodge. Seated on a wooden bench that wrapped around a huge oak tree, she looked stunning, though casually dressed in crisp, white cropped pants and a navy scoop-necked stretch polo with a gold nautical design. When she stood and stepped into the sunlight, Alex felt a stirring in his loins. The sun's rays danced in her silky chestnut hair and when she smiled her hello, her perfect white teeth illuminated her creamy tanned face. The polo hugged her tiny waist accentuating the fullness of her breasts and the slight swell of hips that tapered into legs he'd love to touch. Sunglasses covered her almond-shaped, smoky-blue eyes, but Alex remembered them well.

He realized he'd been staring and quickly jumped out of the car to greet her. It was a struggle to pull his eyes away from her perfectly proportioned body, but he managed to settle his gaze on her face, which also held him spellbound. Even her voice captivated him; a deep, seductive tone, albeit devoid of flirtatiousness.

"Have you been waiting long? I'm sorry."

"No, don't be. You're not late. I enjoy sitting under that tree and listening to the sounds of summer. I purposely came down earlier to enjoy it awhile."

Alex touched her waist slightly to lead her into the car. He felt a sensation that took him by surprise. He hadn't reacted to a woman like this in ages, if ever, and his vulnerability made him uneasy.

They drove in silence until the traffic ahead of him cleared and Alex turned off the narrow road onto the highway. Out of the corner of his eye, he caught her gaze fixed on his bare thigh. The cool flow of air coming through the vent could not stop the rush of heat seeping through him. For a split second he considered that her thoughts could have been far away; that she had been oblivious. But no, there was no disputing her embarrassment when their eyes met. He fought back his smile while she fumbled through the moment.

"I was noticing your white shorts and navy golf shirt. It's so similar to what I'm wearing, you'd think we planned it."

Alex released that smile that wanted out. "Yeah, I see what you mean. Even the emblem on my shirt is gold like the anchor on yours."

Eager to let the moment pass, Glory switched to safer ground. "So, how long a ride is it to Boothbay Harbor?"

"About three hours, but we can stop along the way. Are you hungry? Have you had breakfast?"

"No, but I'd rather pass if we're going to have lunch when we get there. I won't have an appetite."

"Yeah, me too. I thought we'd do an early lunch and a late dinner. I'd like to slip in something extra that I think you'll enjoy." He waited for her reply, but all she returned was a curious look. "I thought we'd take a cocktail cruise in the early evening, then have dinner at one of the restaurants at the Perkins Cove dock when we get back. How does that sound?"

"Sounds great!" she said, her enthusiasm genuine. "Actually, I'm glad you thought of it because that cruise has been high on my 'to do' list. It'll be even more pleasant with someone to enjoy it with."

On the long ride to Boothbay Harbor, they fell into comfortable conversation. Alex filled her in with interesting facts about Maine's history and geographical highlights. Glory listened with fascination, awed by his keen knowledge and ability to retain the most trivial facts.

The subject of the friendship between Mandy Stewart and Paula Howard never came up until they settled at a table in one of Boothbay Harbor's many scenic restaurants. They both sat sipping iced tea at an outdoor table shaded by a green umbrella. The temperature had reached eighty-six degrees, but the sun's rays were cooled by the steady breeze.

"I find myself wondering how much of this beautiful state my mother got to enjoy that summer. It's mesmerized me since I got here."

"She never came back since that one summer after college?"

"No, not to my knowledge." Her silent gaze drifted out to the bay.

Alex released one of those empty coughs intended to fill in time. "Excuse me if I'm pushing where I don't belong, but you seem so sad when you talk about your mother. When we first spoke, it seemed important that you learn whatever you could about that one August she spent with us. You miss her terribly, I'm sure, but is it more than that?"

When she opened her mouth to speak, he quickly added, "If it's something you can't or won't speak about, just tell me and I'll keep my big mouth shut."

Glory pondered whether she should jump right in with the truth. In the short time she had known him, she felt an inexplicable ease; a bond maybe, perhaps due to that old '60s friendship. Conversely, her body tried in vain to ignore the sensations his nearness created. All kinds of excuses flashed in her head, but her body was winning the battle with her mind.

"I'm sorry," he said when she offered no immediate response. "Forget everything I said."

Glory broke through her ruminations. "Alex, think hard. Can you remember who my mother might have dated that summer?" She blinked her eyes closed, embarrassed by the words she hadn't planned to say, but the subject was introduced and she decided to take the plunge. "Was there one special guy who hung around her?"

Alex saw her lower lip quiver before she stopped it with her teeth. An obvious prelude to tears. The curtain was lifting now on whatever was troubling her. He had an uncomfortable feeling that was a loaded question. "Gee, it's hard for me to remember," he said. "As I said before, I was a teenage kid at the time. I didn't pay much attention to what my sister and her friends did. And it *is* thirty-five years ago..." His words stopped dead in their track. The "thirty-five years" triggered bells in his head. She had mentioned her age the night before. He was beginning to see light behind the dark cloud. His voice softened to a whisper when he spoke. "You were conceived that summer, weren't you?"

"Yes, but as you might have guessed, the young man who fathered me was not the man my mother married. I recently found a letter she had started to write to me, but she never finished it. She died two days later. I can't believe that all my life I loved a man who conveniently stepped into my real father's shoes. Now both my parents are dead and I'm looking for answers."

Although he had suspected something like that, Alex was stunned by her revelation. "More than ever now, I wish I could help you, but I barely remember Mandy. I can only visualize her general appearance; her petite frame and her full head of hair that flipped up at the sides. But her face...it's a blur. I couldn't possibly recall who she might have been dating that summer. I'm so sorry."

"Just one last thing." She reached in her bag for the photo and handed it to him. "Do you know who this young man is?"

"I know what you're thinking, but no. His face is not at all familiar. I'm sorry."

"No, don't be sorry," Glory said. "It's crazy for me to expect you to remember faces from thirty-five years ago."

"Still. I wish I could be more helpful."

While they waited for their lobster rolls, Glory attempted to break the somber mood. "So, tell me about your job. You said last night you're a pharmacist and live in New Jersey. Where do you work?"

"Generally, I'm at my Hazlet location, but I keep tabs on my other two stores as well."

"*Your* locations? You own three drug stores?"

"And negotiating a fourth."

"Really? Good for you. That sounds like a huge responsibility."

"So does writing a column that the whole country can read."

"Well, not the *whole* country. Do you enjoy it or do you find the responsibility confining?"

Alex wrinkled his nose and gave it a moment's thought. "In the early years I was sort of glued to it, I suppose, but now that I have enough pharmacists and reliable employees, I have more freedom of movement. Those twelve- and fourteen-hour days are long gone."

"I can imagine how a routine like that can run you ragged," she said. "It was probably tough on your wife." She silently cringed hearing her own words which were a definite plant for information. The waiter unknowingly offered her a chance to cover her flash of guilt by serving their lunch with a polite smile and a few courteous words.

When he left, Alex answered her question with a shrug of his shoulders and a quick twist of his lips. "She did her own thing."

Those five words and the way they were delivered told Glory all she needed to know about Alex Howard's marriage. The reporter in her nudged her to probe further. Before she could befriend or become involved with this gorgeous hunk of a man in any way, she needed to know what exactly caused his wife's death.

"Do you want to talk about how she died? People usually avoid talking to a grieving person about their loss, not realizing that the grievant wants and needs that release."

His face grew taut, his smile forced. "Yes, that's true for some people, but not all." He leaned forward and patted her hand. "Our plan for today was to enjoy the scenery, the weather, a couple of meals and each other's company. If you don't mind, I'd like to put death and sickness out of our minds for today. Okay?"

His smile was ear-to-ear, but something about his facial expression told her to cut it right there.

The softness returned to his face by the time they started back to Ogunquit. Their conversation went from Maine lifestyle versus New York lifestyle, to politics, to the situation in Iraq, to the pros and cons of running a business. She told him all about Frannie and how she would be moving into her parents' apartment the next weekend.

The sun was preparing for its glorious descent when they boarded the boat for their cocktail cruise of Ogunquit's picturesque shoreline. They sipped their Vodka tonics and listened to the captain. While the first mate manned the pilot house, he explained the purpose of the varying colors of the buoys attached to the lobster pots. All of the buoys were color-coded, he said, to identify the owner. The passengers listened to the distinguished gray-haired gentleman tell his stories with an engaging style. Glory and Alex were particularly fascinated and amused with the tale about the long-ago Maine prisoners who were regularly fed lobster and eventually revolted to protest the diet they considered inferior.

Whether it was the cocktails, the ambiance, the Gregory Peck charm, or the long-time absence of a man in her life, Glory couldn't quite define, but Alex Howard had awakened feelings she thought were long dead.

They ended their long day with a quiet dinner on the outdoor deck of a Perkins Cove restaurant, watching the lights shimmer on the calm waters. The fluttering in her stomach left her meal barely touched, but they were never at a loss for words. Laughter found its place in their conversation. Although Alex's aversion to discussing his wife's death had unnerved her, she couldn't believe he was in any way responsible for her death. No way. He was too nice a guy. Yet Glory was convinced that there was more than grief behind that closed door. If any grief at all.

It was ten o'clock when he dropped her off at Ocean Cliff Lodge, too late to call Frannie. Besides, she wasn't in the mood for conversation. She had a lot of thinking to do. When Alex invited her to spend the next afternoon at the beach, she said yes without hesitation, knowing full well that she was headed for trouble. If you could call it that.

Chapter 17

Alex recalled with regret how he had stiffened when Glory asked about Elena. His response, both verbally and emotionally, had been sharp and transparent. He knew it, had felt himself tighten at the time, but his reaction had been spontaneous. If he had seen it coming he could have steeled himself and smoothly steered her away from the subject.

On the other hand, it might have been better to deal with it head on. If a meaningful relationship was possible for him and this beautiful, intelligent woman whose very presence excited him, he didn't want to jeopardize that chance. Glory English made him remember what it was to feel alive again. He hadn't laughed or even smiled as much in the last eight years as he had in the short time since they met.

Besides, if she stays in Maine long enough and makes their relationship known, sooner or later someone will say something about Elena's death. Gossiping tongues offered much speculation at the time and the press was delighted to sensationalize it for their readers. All Glory needed to do if her curiosity got the best of her was pay a visit to the library and read all the old articles.

His thoughts were interrupted by the arrival of the contractor who had come to give an estimate on repairs to the roof, the porch and several other areas in and around Ratherbee that could no longer be neglected. Alex hurried out to speak to him. The faster their business was concluded, the faster he could call Glory and pinpoint a time for their day at the beach.

He couldn't wait to see her in a bathing suit.

Alex slipped past his sister whose body appeared calm, positioned in her usual Adirondack chair. Her once luminous eyes were vacant now; two pools of nothingness. He didn't allow himself more than a fleeting glance before he nodded and murmured a polite good morning to Nancy Sheridan.

If it weren't for Glory English, he would have concluded his business with the contractor and made his escape back to the near normalcy of his New Jersey life.

Chapter 18

Glory's mind was somewhat troubled Sunday morning, filled with positive and negative thoughts of Alex Howard. Those same thoughts trailed with her as she walked along Marginal Way. She was glad in a way that he was leaving Ogunquit the next day. Maybe there was some truth in the old adage, "Out of sight, out of mind." She hoped so, but on the plus side, she realized that Alex's temporary presence in her life had almost totally obliterated thoughts of her parents. All three of them. And barely a thought about Jason. Is that a sign of healing? she wondered. Or was she just trading in one set of heartaches for another?

Frannie's last words haunted her. "The jury's still out on his wife's mysterious death." The line pulsated in her head.

***

People were already waiting on Amore Breakfast's porch when Glory arrived at 7:45. She took her place in line for her day's first cup of coffee and sat at one of the tables to sip it leisurely before going inside.

Frannie mocked a devilish look when she saw Glory. "How did it go?" she asked.

Glory answered with a smile, a shrug and a simple "okay" response. She had plenty more to say, but Frannie had no time to listen.

"I can stay and help till about ten this morning. Is that okay with you?"

"Of course it's okay," Frannie answered. "You work your tail off for free, and you have to ask my permission when to leave?" She tilted her head, shot her brows upward. "Alex again?"

"Yes, but don't build it into something it's not. He's going home to New Jersey tomorrow. End of story."

"New Jersey is not the other side of the world. Especially for someone who lives in New York."

"For now I live in Maine," Glory said. "I did want to talk to you though, Frannie. Can I call you tonight?"

"Sure. And don't worry about the time if you need to talk."

She did need to talk. Even if her relationship with Alex died when he left tomorrow, she needed to know the facts surrounding Frannie's casual comment about his wife's death.

***

Glory's bathing suit had a matching wraparound skirt which would come in handy today. At the beach, her bare legs would blend in among all the others. But for now, in the more intimate confines of his car, if she felt his eyes on them, she'd need more than the ocean to cool her off.

Alex rented two beach chairs and an umbrella. The young beach attendant positioned them close to the water, but far back enough to avoid the racing foamy bubbles that rolled onto the shore.

Glory filled her lungs with a deep breath of the clean ocean air. Its salty breeze stroked her face and rippled through her hair like massive yet gentle fingers.

"Are you ready to go in or do you want to relax awhile?"

She pretended not to notice how gorgeous he looked stripped down to a bathing suit. His body was lean and muscular; not that unnatural look produced by weight lifting, but tightened by diet and exercise. She admonished herself for her thoughts. Since she first met Jason, she had never been conscious of another man's body. It scared her. Especially since this was the man whose wife died mysteriously.

"I think I'll sit here awhile. I love to look out at the ocean. It's mesmerizing. But you go in if you like. It takes me time to work up the courage to plunge into that icy water."

"No, I'm in no hurry either. That ocean's not going anywhere."

Behind her sunglasses, Glory watched him stretch out in the beach chair inches away from hers, glad that he would slip out of her life as swiftly as he had slipped in. Effective tomorrow. And he has no memories that could help her identity and find her biological father. What did she need him for?

Alex lifted the back of his chair to match Glory's sit-up position. "If I had known how much fun I'd have this weekend, I could have enjoyed looking forward to it," he said. "Instead, I dreaded this trip."

Glory flashed him a quick smile. "I guess we're all lazy in a way. Even to move for the things we enjoy, we procrastinate. It's always tomorrow, next week, or some day."

He leaned forward and twisted his torso to meet her gaze. "I wasn't referring to the ocean, Glory."

"I know," she acknowledged. "I've been enjoying your company too. Here in Maine, we're two lost souls. Starting tomorrow, my afternoons will be spent reading, writing and relaxing again. Also pleasant, but it can get lonely at times. Although these days, I need that time to myself."

"What are your plans, if you don't mind my asking."

Glory knew by his tone what plans he meant. "I'm still not sure. If I pursue it, chances are great that I'll find him, but whether I want to screw up his life – or mine – " Her lips formed a thin line and she shrugged, rather than complete her sentence.

"It's a tough decision, I can imagine. But if you want my two cents worth, I think you've got to go with it. You'll never find peace if you don't."

She faked a laugh. "And I may find war if I do."

They both stared ahead at the hazy sky a few moments until Alex broke through their separate, private thoughts. "We're losing the sun. If we plan to take a swim, now's the time."

Glory nodded in agreement, stood up and tossed her wraparound skirt on the back of her chair. The mention of her biological father triggered another mind battle. Alex was right; she had to find him and deal with the consequences; one being that he could be long dead and buried. That possibility she didn't want to face.

Glory was so lost in her thoughts that she neither saw nor sensed Alex's eyes on her. She ran into the water with him and matched his skilled strokes with ease. They swam parallel to the shore in perfect unison. He gave her a look that reflected his admiration. She smiled complacently and said, "Did you think you were my mother's only swim student?"

When they left the water a long time later, invigorated and refreshed, Alex took her hand as though unaware of the liberty he had taken. Yes, a minor, harmless liberty, Glory thought, but a definite step along a path she wasn't ready to travel, but wished she were.

Gregory Peck indeed.

***

"These past few days with you have been wonderful," Alex said as he drove into Ocean Cliff. "I hate to go home to Jersey. He gave her a sad smile then rested his warm hand gently on her cheek. An unwelcome feeling shot through her like an erupting volcano. Part desire, part fear. Glory wasn't sure which part was the dominating force, but her mind took control before he could go any further.

"Thanks for another lovely day," she said with polite formality, then popped the lock on the door and had her feet on the gravel driveway in one swift second.

Chapter 19

With some trepidation, Glory had accepted Alex's invitation to one last dinner late that evening. She was losing control of her emotions and it made her uneasy. She could have used the time more productively anyway. There were a few New York calls to return, information she needed to research for her next column and a late afternoon nap sounded good. If she could turn off her mind and relax. Most important was the call to Frannie.

At 5:30, she decided to try her at home and lucked out.

"Why are you calling now? I thought you were going to call tonight? Is anything wrong?"

"Not really. Just that something's been bugging me. Is this a good time? Did I interrupt you from anything?"

"Just some mall shopping. It can wait. What's on your mind?"

"Alex Howard. He seems so nice, the perfect gentleman type, but so do a lot a serial killers."

That drew a hearty laugh out of Frannie at first, but her tone sobered quickly. "What put that thought in your head?"

"His wife's mysterious death. That's your quote, not mine. What do you know about how she died?"

On the other end of the line, Frannie blew a sigh, pausing to shape her words as objectively as possible. "No one knows anything for sure, Glory. She supposedly died from a fall down the stairs; hit her head, but neighbors often overheard or witnessed some heavy-duty arguments. That triggered a lot of rumors that he might have done it intentionally. Pushed her maybe."

Glory couldn't contain her shock. "Pushed her? You mean some people thought he was actually capable of murder?"

"Well, I wouldn't go that far. For a while there, it looked like they were going after him, but the DA never charged him."

"Gee, Frannie, this has me spooked. Why didn't you tell me before I agreed to have dinner with him?"

Frannie took a pensive moment before answering. "You were so hopeful that he might be able to help you identify your father. I didn't want to burst your bubble. Besides, although I never met the guy, from what I heard and pieced together, I couldn't condemn him. Too much reasonable doubt. No one will ever know the real story. His wife was no angel, I heard. And his sister – the younger one – was even worse."

"And what do you know about them?"

Frannie's hesitancy was veiled with guilt. "Actually, I don't *know* anything for sure. A lot of stuff passes through my restaurant. You hear so much, it's hard to determine what's fact and what's fiction. But anyway, shake it off. Your business with Alex Howard is done with. As you said, tomorrow he goes home to New Jersey. End of story, right?"

"Right," Glory answered. She didn't bother to add that Amore Breakfast would have to manage without her Monday morning. After the beach, when Alex dropped her off, he asked her to keep breakfast open for him too. She had started to refuse since they were having dinner together that night. They could say their goodbyes then. But when he put that pleading look on his face, there was no way she could look into those deep-set cocoa-brown eyes and say no.

Chapter 20

The two glasses of wine she had consumed through dinner should have relaxed her into long hours of uninterrupted, dream-free sleep. They should have, but didn't.

After her talk with Frannie, Glory had resolved to clear her mind of all dark thoughts concerning Alex. She had planned to get through dinner and breakfast with him as if he were any other friend, casual acquaintance or business associate. Then he'd be gone. Past tense.

Her determination had worked through the entire evening—almost. Their conversation never waned, but Glory kept it focused on impersonal, mundane topics. She had decided to close the book on his wife's death, declare him innocent of all speculative charges and simply enjoy his company.

But she couldn't ignore her body's reaction when she recalled their goodnight scene. It brought to mind a similar scene from an old classic black and white movie where Joan Fontaine is high on a cliff somewhere with Cary Grant, the husband she half loves, half fears. Yes, she remembered the title now. *Suspicion.*

After several restless hours, Glory finally fell asleep only to be haunted by a nightmare. In her dream, she was Joan Fontaine and Alex was the handsome, albeit feared, Cary Grant. But unlike Joan, Glory got shoved off the cliff.

She shot up in bed, her body cold and clammy. There you go again, stupid, stupid girl, dramatizing everything way out of proportion.

By seven o'clock, when a clear, blue sky and a blazing sun smiled down and shimmered on the ocean, daylight erased all last night's dark and ominous thoughts. She laughed to herself while in the shower recalling her crazy dream.

While she still had the towel wrapped around her, she picked up the phone to call Frannie. First to warn her that she wouldn't be able to help this morning, and second, to alert her that she'd be coming in with the infamous Alex Howard. "I'm curious to see what impression he makes on you," she told her friend.

"In other words, you want to know if I think he's the killer some people think he is?"

"Exactly."

"Great, bring him on." She paused to let a short giggle escape, then said, "I was about to say I'm dying to meet him, but under the circumstances, that's probably a bad choice of words."

Glory rolled her eyes. She suppressed the urge to laugh with her, cleared her throat and said, "Frannie, this is *not* funny."

"Who's laughing?" Frannie answered in her most serious tone, but the laughter spilled out anyway.

Chapter 21

Alex had arrived early for their goodbye breakfast. He was there when she came down, leaning against his car. His arms were crossed against his chest, accentuating broad shoulders, centered by a spray of sun-tinged hair at the open collar of his golf shirt. The flash of his white teeth when he saw her brought to Glory's mind that glorious sight of the Christmas tree lighting at Rockefeller Center. A one-second gesture that made the breath catch in your throat and swelled your heart. A strange comparison, perhaps, but similar feelings. One was electrically charged and the other only felt that way.

"Good morning," she called out as she approached him.

"Good morning to you too," Alex answered. He thought she looked delicious in white shorts and a pale pink tank top. His eyes remained glued to her and he made no attempt to admire her with any degree of discretion.

"I forgot to suggest it last night, but how about Amore Breakfast after our walk? I can't believe you've never been there."

"It hasn't been there too many years. And in the old days, I used to enjoy hanging around Ratherbee. Whenever we dined out, it was usually dinner."

Glory wondered who the "we" was, but didn't dare ask. She assumed he meant his wife. There had to be a period in their lives when they were in love and enjoyed being together. The thought brought bittersweet memories of Jason that pained her still and probably always would.

***

Their walk along Marginal Way bore no resemblance to her dream of the night before. There were too many walkers this early in the morning. Not a good time for murder, even if he was a killer, which he wasn't, and even if he did have strong motivation, which he didn't.

On the way back, they stopped to sit on a bench to relax and talk awhile. He reached for her hand again when they were ready to continue their walk back. That now-familiar electrical shock feeling made her pull it away the moment they began to walk. Fortunately for Glory, the morning people traffic necessitated walking single file anyway. Now she only had to deal with the discomfort of knowing his eyes were exploring her body from behind.

***

Frannie made it her business to escort them to a table that morning. Having already told Alex all about Frannie, her restaurant and the charming apartment that would soon be hers, conversation among the three fell easily. But after a few congenial minutes, Frannie retained her image of pleasant proprietor/hostess and attended to other customers. From a distance, she managed to throw Glory a wide-eyed look and circled her fingers to illustrate her approval.

Frannie obviously liked what she saw, but Glory smirked back. She didn't need her approval on his looks. No one would dispute that. What she needed was her vibes on what lies beneath that gorgeous exterior. Next chance she got, Frannie wrinkled her nose and waved. Glory understood that to mean "We'll talk later."

With Alex sitting across from her, even Frannie's fabulous cheese omelet had lost its appeal. Maybe it was the fact that they'd be parting ways soon, but his eyes never seemed to leave her face. It was as if he were searching for something.

***

"Do you mind if I hang around a few minutes more?" he asked when they arrived at Ocean Cliff Lodge. "I've always admired this place from a distance. I'd like to see it; walk around the grounds." His eyebrows arched questioningly as he waited for a response.

Glory visualized herself in the intimacy of her suite being kissed by another man for the first time in fourteen years. A rush of desire burned through her but like a gust of wind it made its power be known, then whipped away.

Recalling her resolve, Glory answered with a benign expression that she'd be glad to give him a quick tour of Ocean Cliff. *But not her suite.*

She led him on a brief walk-through of the Lodge, then along the winding path that circled the property. The sun was intense, so they settled at a table poolside, shaded by its green and white striped umbrella. Guests had already placed towels on the backs of almost all the lounges to ensure availability after breakfast. Glory and Alex shared a laugh at the sight of a middle-aged, heavyset woman who decided to fight for her rights. With her mouth thinned into a determined grin, she removed two towels from the lounges she chose, threw them into the used towel bin, and replaced them with her two Disney World towels. She gave her husband a complacent nod, and pointed a finger at one of the lounges, practically ordering him to occupy it. He sneered his disapproval and shook his head, but meekly followed her direction. The wife, with her black and neon green print bathing suit, plopped herself down on her lounge as if she had won it in battle.

The scene struck Alex so funny that he had to turn away from the couple's line of vision. Watching him enjoy the humor of what had transpired softened Glory momentarily. Even if he and his wife were in the middle of a heated argument, she still couldn't imagine that he would have intentionally pushed her down the steps. His personality seemed too passive for that behavior. Unless he was a hell of an actor. Like her parents. Or unless that part of him remained dormant until provoked.

Alex grew serious as he turned his attention back to Glory. "What would you say if I told you I'd like to come back next weekend?"

"Why?" she said without thinking, then realized her one-word answer was replete with innuendoes.

He laughed at her feigned naiveté. "Do I really have to answer that?"

Her gaze fell and rested on her nails. She looked up again when she realized she had the perfect excuse. "Next weekend I'll be busy, Alex. Remember I told you I'd be moving into Frannie's apartment?"

"Of course I remember. But that can't monopolize all your time. It's not like moving from one permanent residence to another, right?"

"Right," she conceded. "But I might want to shop for some little incidentals. You know...the comforts of home."

"And I'd be invading your privacy if I tagged along?"

She scrunched her nose. "I sort of made tentative plans with Frannie."

His hands went up in defeat. "Okay. I'll give up on next weekend. How about the one after that?" He shook a teasing finger at her and added, "If you refuse me again, I'll take the hint."

Glory blew a sigh. "It's not you, Alex," she said. *A partial truth.* "I haven't been – this is embarrassing – I haven't dated anyone since my divorce. As a friend, I enjoy your company, but..." She let him figure the rest out for himself while she tried to hide the blush that surely stained her cheeks apple-red.

"And I enjoy yours. That's what we'll be; two friends who like to spend time together." His gaze drifted off and, with one hand turned outward, he nodded. The gesture clearly spoke the unsaid words, "for now."

An awkward pause followed while her mind searched for the right words to refuse gracefully. Not that she wanted to, but for the past few days, her mind had lost total control. That gave her an unsettling feeling.

With his head tilted, Alex watched her and waited with an anticipatory smile.

Finally, she was about to tell him next week would probably be all right, but her two conflicting emotions reached a compromise. "I guess the weekend after next will be okay, as long as we have that understanding."

Alex drew a deep breath and beamed, showing off his milk-white teeth. "That's a relief. You had me bracing myself for a gracious brush-off. How about a phone call or two in between? Can you handle that?"

She gave him an easy smile, noting his cautious approach. "Sure. Maybe towards the end of the week, before I check out here."

He leaned closer, bringing his gorgeous face inches from hers. That tremulous shock bolted through her again. "I'll look forward to talking to you," he said. His tone was friendly, but his eyes betrayed him.

Before she had to fake another amiable response, she covered her mouth to suppress laughter. "Don't look now, but I see a war brewing."

Instinctively, Alex turned around anyway. A younger couple had approached the lounges they thought they had reserved earlier. An exchange of controlled words began between the two women, but escalated into an argument that had heads turning. The older woman refused to give up her territory, arguing her case against the practice of reserving lounges. When the younger couple walked away in a defeated huff, Alex and Glory got up to leave too. They laughed their way back to his car poking fun at the petty poolside argument.

Their mood sobered when finally it was time to say goodbye. He squeezed her hand before slipping behind the wheel of his car. "Two weeks," he said as though it were half a lifetime.

"Yes, see you then," she said and waved him off. She walked her way back to the Lodge and up to her suite where she spent the next hour on her balcony. That ocean always helped her sort out her thoughts. Her attraction to Alex Howard couldn't be denied, but why did she feel like she was walking into fire?

Images of her biological father drifted back again. She tossed that ball around in her head for the next few hours. By evening, as she walked to Perkins Cove, she promised herself that right after she moved into Frannie's apartment, she'd seriously pursue the search for her father. She would no longer cloud her desire to find him with fears of rejection. *Get ready to open your arms wide, Daddy dear, 'cause you're about to get the shock of your lifetime.*

A bittersweet smile tugged the corners of her mouth when, for the first time, she considered the possibility that she'd reject him. Who's to say he isn't some beer-guzzling, foul-mouth loser?

Either way, she was going to find out. *Just be alive, Daddy dear. You can't desert me too.*

Chapter 22

Stacy had been thrilled to hear Glory's edited version of her weekend with Alex. She romanticized it all the way to the altar.

Frannie was less demonstrative, more guarded. She sat quietly on her counter stool, waiting for the last of her employees to leave, while Glory fed her a bland, passion-free version of her days with Alex. Certainly, Stacy had known Glory years longer, but Frannie had the advantage of watching her. She listened with her arms crossed over her chest and a grin on her face that required no verbal interpretation.

"Why are you looking at me like that?" Glory asked. She tried to brush it away with a laugh, but her friend wasn't easily fooled.

Frannie shook her head and smiled. "I wish you could watch yourself in a mirror. Your body language gives you away."

Glory gave up, relaxed with a long, deep sigh. "Okay, so I'm human. So a guy pays a little attention to a woman whose wounds are still raw and she eats it up. A classic reaction. Anyone would feel flattered. Especially someone who's been dumped."

"Tell me about it!" Frannie shot back with twisted lips. "So when and where are you going to see him again? Is he coming back or are you going home?"

"No, of course I'm not going home. I can't wait to move into that adorable apartment of yours. And who said I was going to see him again?"

"You didn't have to say it."

Exasperated, Glory threw her head back and gazed upward. "Why do I get this feeling that your eyes snake their way through the deepest, darkest tunnels of my mind? I feel exposed."

Frannie went instantly contrite. "I'm sorry. I was just having fun teasing you. Just feel free to tell me to shut up whenever the urge strikes you."

"No, don't apologize. It's not you, it's me. Since our first night together, I've had this ongoing battle with my own emotions. I couldn't wait for Alex to go back to New Jersey so I could sweep him out of my mind. But then when he offered to come back again, stupid me said yes." She paused and shifted her gaze to meet Frannie's. "He's coming back the weekend after next."

"Ah hah! So the romance continues..." Frannie teased.

But Glory sensed a hint of cautious displeasure in the way she said it before slipping off the stool to lock up for the day.

Chapter 23

On Thursday night, Glory was restless with indecision. She had wanted to take a long walk in and around Ogunquit or maybe sail out on another cruise from Perkins Cove. The memory of that delightful boat ride with Alex ignited her sensuality again. She paced the floor of her suite, shooting glances at the phone. Of course, if she chose to go out and he called, she'd find his message later. She never gave him her cell number because she didn't want to be out in public when he called.

In the end, she opted to go out for ice cream. There's nothing as soothing as comfort food and she needed the distraction of being among people, even if they were all strangers.

To her disappointment, she found no messages when she returned. A part of her had hoped he'd call tonight, rather than Friday night, which is technically the end of the week, but if he were really anxious to talk to her...

She made herself a cup of tea and went out on the balcony to throw her thoughts out again to her magnificent ocean. But tonight the ocean returned them with an ominous roar. The cascades of crashing white foam became faces; Alex, Jason, her mother, her father and her FATHER, who now had an image created in her dreams that could come crashing down the instant she found him.

And then there was the distorted face of Frannie. That last expression haunted Glory. Something troubled Frannie; something she was reluctant to discuss. If Alex was the core of it, surely she would have cautioned her. Twice Glory had passed the library and resisted the urge to go in and read what she could find about that tragic night, but too often people recognized her. She couldn't chance a local librarian passing word around that Glory English, the columnist, was probing into the cause of Elena Howard's death.

The Internet, of course, would eliminate that problem.

In the seclusion of her suite, Glory sat at the oak desk and began her Internet search. Her fingers scrolled and clicked until she found the articles. Her mouth went dry as she read. She tried telling herself the newspapers had sensationalized the story to generate sales, but a chill crawled up her back anyway.

Alex's explanation sounded credible, she told herself, wanting desperately to lift that cloud of suspicion that hovered over him. Even Frannie thinks he's innocent, she rationalized. Her face brightened at that thought, then fell into a troubled frown when she recalled Frannie's piercing look of unspoken words.

Saturday was only one full day away. Most of her belongings were already packed. As much as Glory had enjoyed the serenity and spacious luxury of her suite, the move to Frannie's apartment reveled her. She loved its quiet intimacy, its New England charm that Frannie's efforts had so tastefully captured. Between the restaurant, the apartment, and Ogunquit itself with all its natural scenic treasures that the locals might take for granted, Glory's sense of home was strangely taking root here. No, not strangely, she reconsidered. Perhaps its natural beauty and laid-back lifestyle were only contributing factors. Perhaps it was the promise of a fresh, new start away from the memories that rocked her emotions this past year. That promise had planted new seeds to help her through the dark moods that often enveloped her. And those seeds had blossomed in a new and exciting challenge that could possibly chase away all those black clouds.

And then, of course, there was that compelling force that held her steadfast. That little matter of her conception. This is where her life began. Maybe now, after thirty-five years, Glory was home to stay.

For a while, sleep evaded her again. Myriad thoughts, new and old, melded together. She opened the sliding glass doors of her bedroom. As she had hoped, the salty, sea breeze across her face and the crashing sounds of the surf lulled her into a deep, dreamless sleep.

The phone startled her at 7:15. "Good morning," said that voice she had waited to hear last night. She mumbled back a scratchy response.

"I woke you. I'm sorry, but I wanted to catch you before your walk on Marginal Way."

"I would have been there already if I had fallen asleep at a reasonable hour."

"Oh, I'm sorry again. I know what it's like to be haunted by dark thoughts and bad memories."

I'm sure you do. "My thoughts weren't all that dark, actually." She propped herself up to a sitting position and stuffed the two thick bed pillows behind her back. "Many were happy, stimulating. The kind that keeps your adrenaline flowing and your mind racing."

His voice deepened suggestively. "In that case, I hope I slipped in there somewhere."

"Once or twice," she admitted, but kept her voice even, its tone amiable.

"That's nice to hear. But I'd like to get those numbers up. I've missed you. By next week, I'll have withdrawal!" He gave a short laugh and Glory saw in her mind's eye perfect white teeth lighting up a perfect tanned face. "So are you packed and ready to go?"

"Just about."

"Will you call me once you get settled in? If you don't reach me, leave a message and I'll get back to you."

"Sounds good," she said and threw her legs over the edge of the bed.

"So what else have you been up to?" he asked.

Doing research on you came to mind but, of course, never escaped her lips. "Alex, can we continue our conversation sometime this weekend? I want to get out for my walk and over to Amore Breakfast." What she really needed was to use the bathroom but she wasn't about to tell him that.

His hesitancy reflected his disappointment. "Sure, I guess so. Want to give me a rough idea of when?"

"Sunday would probably be best. The move on Saturday will keep me busy and I'd like to treat Frannie to dinner that night."

"Fine. I'll be waiting for your call. And say hello to Frannie for me. She's good people. I can see why you two became friends."

Her friendship with Frannie was pulling her in another direction. To take her mind off Alex's nebulous side and the fallout if and when she found her father, she allowed her ideas to take shape and develop. Once she moved in at Frannie's, she'd take the next step, which could drastically alter her life.

Chapter 24

In the apartment that Glory would now call home, Frannie helped put the last of the groceries away, grabbed two bottles of Evian out of the refrigerator and threw one to Glory. They both collapsed onto the soft cushions of separate living room chairs. Their feet shared the same ottoman.

"So what's this crazy idea you want to discuss?" Frannie asked. "My curiosity piqued when you said it had nothing to do with your father or Alex."

"Well, maybe in an indirect way, I can tie it to my father," Glory answered. "But that's a stretch. What I wanted to say – you're going to think I'm nuts." She gave an embarrassed laugh.

With a curious smile, Frannie took her feet off the ottoman and leaned forward. "C'mon. Don't make me pull it out of you," she said.

Glory drew a deep breath. "Okay. Here goes. Do you ever think about an Amore Breakfast II? You already built an excellent business and reputation. Of course, you'd know better than I, but I'm sure you'd have no trouble filling the place with customers."

Frannie's hand went to her mouth, covering her easy smile. She nodded thoughtfully a few seconds before responding. "It's funny that you should ask that question because I've been bouncing around a business-related opportunity for weeks now. But not for an Amore Breakfast II." She waved off her own thoughts and returned full attention to Glory. "Why do you ask, anyway?"

To stall again, Glory sipped from her water bottle. "What would you think if I said I'm giving serious thought to making radical changes in my life? Like, for instance, moving to Maine permanently and investing in a restaurant. Preferably as a partner with you. I could never handle it on my own."

Frannie gave her an incredulous look, then exploded with laughter. "I don't believe this! Yes, it sounds a little crazy, but I love the idea. What about your column? You have a whole career going. You can't just throw it away."

"I don't intend to. That's the beauty of being a columnist. You can write it from anywhere. Owning or managing a restaurant can only help, not hinder. Food is the crux of my column." Her expression made a quick change. "You said 'not an Amore Breakfast II' though. Why not? Are you free to discuss the other opportunity you mentioned?"

"Actually, you just gave me that freedom." Frannie stood up, paced. Glory watched as her friend wrestled with accelerating thoughts, all positive judging by the sparkle in her eyes. "Glory, we're talking big bucks here, but if you've got enough money to invest in a partnership arrangement – a working partnership, that is – we might have something going here. Only this one will not be an exact spinoff of Amore Breakfast. This will be strictly dinner. A classy place with a classy menu and a romantic setting. How does 'Amore Evenings' sound?"

The image brought Glory to her feet. "I love it! But where? Are you buying someone out? Building new? Tell me!"

"The place is Heaven-sent. It's right on the water down in Perkins Cove. It's old, weather-beaten and needs plenty of work, but if we can get enough money together, we can jazz it up in no time. Right now it's a private house, but practically abandoned. It's been through three generations of family, but the present-day heirs apparently have no sentimental attachments. They know the property is worth a fortune and they're just holding out for the highest price."

Breathless, Glory tried to contain her excitement. "How much do they want?"

"How much you got?"

They began with a burst of laughter that soon diminished when they got down to the monetary problems. Three hours later, they sealed their business arrangement with the formality of a handshake followed by a bear hug. A simple phone call to the realtor assured them that the property was still available. The woman had evaded the question of price while she rambled on with her sales pitch, promising to discuss all the details the next morning at the site. But Frannie wouldn't be put off.

She hung up the phone and beamed. Her lips were forced closed, but a huge smile was bursting through.

"Well? Don't keep me in suspense. How much?" Glory eyebrows rose to new heights.

Frannie shrugged. "A steal, she said."

"Give it to me fast. Don't torture me."

"Two million," Frannie said, then with a giggle, "What's two mil' between friends?"

"Two million dollars?" Glory drew in a deep breath and exhaled slowly while she let the numbers sink in. Her hands went up in defeat, but the smile never left her face. "Small potatoes," she mimicked with a hand wave.

"Now I *know* you're nuts. But I'm sure glad you are!"

Chapter 25

The old Crawford house that sat on prime property in Perkins Cove needed a hell of a lot more than "jazzing up." They might have done a broom-clean job on it before listing it with the realtor, but the place was still an eyesore. Glory couldn't fathom how a family could allow a valuable piece of real estate to deteriorate like this.

At first glimpse, Frannie reacted with a jolt that Pamela Eggars, the realtor, had noticed. The woman had also caught the look Frannie threw to her friend. "I had no idea it was *this* bad," it conveyed.

Pamela jumped into action. "Now ladies, don't let first impressions cloud your judgment. If you're looking to use it for commercial purposes, a restaurant, you'll have to gut the entire first floor anyway. Keep your eye on the prize. Turn around and look at the breathtaking view your customers would enjoy. Many people would come here for the atmosphere alone. They won't place too much emphasis on the food. If it's halfway decent, they'll come in droves just to sit here."

"Our menu won't be 'halfway decent,'" Frannie said, her indignation unshielded.

"I didn't mean to imply –"

"I know what you meant and I apologize if I came on too strong, but I take pride in my business. I have an excellent reputation and I intend to maintain it."

Pamela Eggars raised a hand. "You won't get an argument from me. I've been in your restaurant enough times to know. You've certainly earned that reputation."

The compliment restored the smile to Frannie's face.
"Thank you. I never get tired of hearing good things about
Amore Breakfast. I think I'm more surprised than anyone at
its huge success. Let's hope we can do it again. If we can
negotiate a fairer price, that is." She gave the realtor a
sidelong glance, her brows raised in disbelief. "Oceanfront
property aside," she continued, "we both know this place is
in sad shape. Worse than I imagined."

Glory left the finances to Frannie while she walked
around and put her imagination to work. Frannie caught up
with her moments later and, with pursed lips, mumbled her
complaints. With her effervescent realtor's personality,
Pamela tagged along making her best effort to quash all
Frannie's negatives with positives. She pointed out all the
features conducive to a restaurant; the wraparound windows,
for one. The upper level already had a deck which could be
utilized for additional oceanfront seating. Right now it
looked like a party of four would cave it in. The five upstairs
bedrooms could be converted into three large rooms for
private parties.

"The layout is great," Glory whispered. In response,
Frannie put a gleam in her eyes and raised her brows twice, a
la Groucho Marx. Glory stifled a laugh.

They spent thirty or forty minutes checking it out, the
complaints mounting in dollar signs. Finally, Frannie threw
her hands up in defeat. "Sure it has great possibilities. You
know how it is; money buys everything but health. And we
need big bucks for renovation costs. I hate to pass it up, but it
looks financially unreachable."

The realtor took her cue. She furrowed her brows and
fingered her chin for a display of concerned concentration.
This theatrical gesture had become routine over her years in
the business. After exhaling a long breath, she threw Frannie
a pessimistic look. "The owners are pretty firm with their
price. What would you consider reachable?"

"I think that would depend on estimated renovation costs. To bring it up to code, outfit and furnish it, my guess would be around a million or more."

"I assume you'd use your cousins' company, Duca Brothers?"

"Naturally." She knew exactly where the realtor's mind was going and helped her out. "I'm sure they'll give me a fair price, but after all, they're in business to make a profit."

"Oh, of course," Pamela said and moved on. "Why don't you have Carl and Mike take a look and give you an estimate. Then we'll talk again."

Frannie nixed the suggestion with a frown. "That would be putting the cart before the horse." Her gaze shifted to Glory, but she continued to speak to the realtor. "Give us a few minutes to discuss this further. We'll come up with an offer. If the sellers go for it, that's when I'll call my cousins."

Pamela extended an arm towards the living room where her two potential buyers walked off to deliberate. In less than five minutes they returned.

"One million-five," Frannie said. "If they agree, and if I'm in the ballpark with my guesstimate of renovation costs, we'll be ready to go to contract."

Pamela cocked a dubious brow. "Half a million is a stretch. I doubt if they'll go down that far. There *has* been some interest, although I haven't accepted any binders yet."

Glory interjected with a pleasant smile. "Look, why don't you present them with our offer and we'll take it from there?"

"Okay," Pamela said. She blew a sigh, dramatizing her pessimism. "I'll contact them when I get back to the office."

The three women exchanged handshakes and left the premises they all hoped would soon become "Amore Evenings."

As Frannie pulled her car away from the property, she beamed with anticipation. "They'll probably refuse our offer and push for one and three-quarters."

"Which we'll accept, right?"

"Sure. But not without a fight."

Glory laughed but her admiration came through. "You're one tough cookie, lady."

"I'll take that as a compliment. If there's one thing I learned early on in this business, it's if you want to succeed and keep your head above water, you have to toughen up."

Glory fell silent a bit, but a faint smile lingered on her lips. "I can't believe I'm doing this," she said.

Frannie shot her a look fraught with warnings. "It *is* a big decision for you; more so than me. Are you sure you've given it enough thought? Your move from New York to Maine is change enough without taking on a business partnership with a person you barely know. Do you want more time to think about it?"

"Maybe I do..." Glory said, letting her voice trail off. Seconds later, she squared her shoulders and said, "There. I gave it more thought and I've never been more excited about anything in my life!"

Frannie echoed her pleasure with a slap on the steering wheel and a howl that would have turned heads if her car windows had been opened.

Chapter 26

Her Sunday morning hours at Amore Breakfast took on new meaning for Glory. It was more than the congeniality that energized her today. She observed everyone and everything around her in the restaurant with a new attitude. A thirst for knowledge. Her excitement had completely obliterated her usual insatiable appetite. Juice and coffee was all she took time for before springing into action. She had plenty to learn and she'd need a crash course if this Amore Evenings dream materialized.

The phone call couldn't have come at a more inopportune time. At 11:30 the late sleepers were still pouring in for breakfast. Frannie literally yanked Glory back into the kitchen as she was about to go out on the floor to take orders from new arrivals.

One look at Frannie's dancing eyes and Glory knew the news was good. "They took it?" she asked.

"No. It went just like we said. They went down to one and three-quarters. I took a chance and tried for a million, six. The sellers were there in her office. She put me on hold while she spoke with them. The suspense was killing me. I was ready to say forget it; we'll give them the one and three-quarters, but then she came back on the line and said they went for it. I'm so excited I can't think straight."

"Me too. Just for once I wish it weren't so darn busy in here so we could spare a minute to congratulate each other and come down off the clouds," Glory said. "Tonight when we're relaxed at home, we'll break open a bottle of champagne and celebrate."

"Can't wait," Frannie answered, then both went their separate ways to handle their customers.

***

Alex had barely entered her mind all day. She had been on her feet for too many consecutive hours at the restaurant and her body ached in protest. But there was something satisfying about the pain that Glory couldn't quite define. Like a physical reminder of a job well done.

She freshened up with a cool shower, slipped into shorts and a T-shirt, popped open a Diet Coke and went out on the patio to give her legs a well-deserved rest on the chaise lounge. She picked up the novel she was into but couldn't absorb a single line. She visualized her mind like a fully saturated sponge, rejecting all new thoughts until the old ones had been squeezed dry.

Anxiety about her new life here in Maine made her restless; impatient to see dreams shape into reality. Eventually she succeeded in pushing them aside and hoped to doze off for a while before Frannie got home, but those two faces shrouded in mystery flashed for attention. They came on strong, pulling her with powerful force. Like hurricane winds, if you didn't find safe shelter, it would suck you up. Perhaps Amore Evenings would provide that shelter.

Still, she reached for the phone and made that call she had been putting off.

"Glory, how *are* you? I had hoped to hear from you sooner. Are you all settled in now? What's happening?"

The sound of Alex's voice made her body react with unparalleled sensations. She laughed anticipating his surprise when she answered his casual question. "So much is happening, I wouldn't know where to begin."

"Try," he said, his voice piqued with curiosity. "Is it good news or bad?"

"Good, very good, I hope. First of all, I've decided to become a permanent Maine resident, and secondly, I'm embarking on a whole new business venture that I'm so excited about, I can't think of anything else," she said, thinking he should only know the images she has of him.

"Wow! That *is* exciting news. In one week you made such monumental decisions? C'mon, give me the details." Before she had a chance to answer, he added, "Wait, let me guess. I bet it has something to do with Frannie and her restaurant. Am I right?"

"Almost. Frannie and her *new* restaurant."

He let out another surprised laugh, then said, "I hope that doesn't mean you'll be too busy to see me next weekend?"

There was her opening. She could have bowed out gracefully, but that inexplicable force spoke for her. "No, of course not, but why don't I save the details for then? I'll enjoy chewing your ears off about all our plans."

"Can't wait for Friday. Late dinner okay? Eight o'clock?"

"Perfect," she said. She still hadn't asked Frannie what, if anything, bugged her about Alex but for now she decided she'd rather not know. Sunshine had finally blanketed her life again and she wasn't about to invite any rain clouds.

Chapter 27

Duca Brothers Construction lifted the last element of doubt that hovered over Frannie and Glory. Sometimes the eye of a professional sees problems the prospective buyer is oblivious to. Problems that could skyrocket renovation costs.

But that didn't happen. Carl and Mike Duca's design plan, which covered more remodeling than the women had hoped to accomplish, still came in just under $500,000. The lawyers for both sides set a contract date for two weeks later.

Glory needed a huge chunk of that time. She had to sell her condo and most of its furnishings, discuss with Marty how her relocation could impact her responsibilities to the newspaper. She couldn't imagine that it would have much adverse effect other than her inability to show up in Manhattan as often as she used to. Hopefully, Marty would have no quarrel with that. It wasn't the long drive that would present a problem; it would be her responsibilities at the restaurant.

Stacy, she anticipated, would go *nuts.* Glory laughed to herself imagining that scene. Her friend would play amateur psychologist and go into her spiel about all the emotional reasons that triggered this insane decision. Stacy thrived on analytical discussions.

A sobering thought struck her. Who else but Stacy and Marty would really miss her? Not a soul. Not a damn soul. And that was reason enough to make this move to the beautiful, tranquil state of Maine. Although with the creation of Amore Evenings in the works, Glory doubted there would be much time for tranquility. Butterfly sensations tingled through her. She couldn't recall ever being this excited about anything before; not even when Jason proposed.

***

They were sitting in Stacy's apartment, sitting at her dinette table, halfway through a dinner of grilled chicken and stir fry veggies when Glory broke the news as though it were an everyday occurrence. "I'm selling my condo and moving to Maine permanently."

On cue, Stacy dropped her fork. "No wonder you couldn't tell me your news on the phone! You wanted to watch me freak out."

Glory's amused smile slanted. "I knew you would, but I waited to tell you because it was too much for a phone conversation."

"What the hell prompted this? Don't tell me this is all about your mother's letter?"

"Some, not all," Glory answered, then fixed her gaze on her plate. She continued cutting her chicken breast into bite-size pieces.

"Not that your mother's letter justifies such drastic, radical action anyway, but what may I ask is the other contributing factor?" She pushed her dish aside and crossed her arms. "Tell me you fell madly in love. Maybe I'll feel better. And not with Maine," she added with a finger in Glory's face.

Glory's broad smile broke into laughter, then sobered slightly. "If you thought I was crazy before, what would you say if I told you I'm entering into a partnership arrangement with the woman who is at present also my landlady for the purchase of a two million dollar oceanfront property that will soon be a fine dining establishment known as *Amore Evenings?*" She stopped to inhale deeply after rambling it all out in one breath. The grin never left her face because even to her own ears the whole idea sounded ludicrous.

"Do you hear yourself? Are you flipping out? What the hell happened to that mature, sensible businesswoman who left here only a few weeks ago?"

"She's still a businesswoman, about to become a restaurateur, and hopes her dear friend will wish her luck and promise to visit often." She got up from the table, cleared off the dishes and cleaned the tabletop. "Where's that cheesecake I brought?"

Stacy stared in silent disbelief as Glory put the tea kettle on and went about playing hostess. In the end, Glory's flashing eyes and spirit when she detailed the story convinced Stacy that Glory was truly happy and excited again. It was a pleasure to watch her; she positively radiated. Whatever turned her around like this had to be right.

Chapter 28

Her talk at the office with Marty was similar to her conversation with Stacy. They agreed that Glory's appearances at the office would be less frequent, but on a regular basis.

Both scenes ended with hugs and sincere good luck wishes and, both times when she left, Glory exhaled long sighs of relief. Looking towards a brand new life where painful reminders of Jason could no longer haunt her. And maybe, once she worked up the courage again, she could snuff out all the tiny flames of fear and resume her search for her father.

For now, de-establishing her New York residency was first on her list. Alone in her condo again, she looked it over once more, as though to say good-bye. This time, although memories of Jason in every room were still vivid, they no longer stabbed at her heart. She picked up the phone and called a reputable realtor who assured her that an agent would be at her door promptly at ten the next morning.

Satisfied that all New York ties were being severed, Glory stretched her arms out triumphantly and did another walk-through of the condo with a pen and yellow pad to jot down all the furniture and household items she wanted shipped to Maine. They'd have to be stored, of course.

Her list was very small. Whatever she couldn't sell, the Salvation Army would be happy to take. "Good-bye, good riddance," she mumbled, but her voice was devoid of bitterness. She was consumed with a sense of freedom she had never realized was lacking. But now that it filled her, she embraced it and vowed to remain totally independent. She would answer to no man ever again.

***

The realtor, Andrea Shaw, arrived ten minutes before ten. A pleasant older woman, somewhere in her late fifties, she went about her business amiably and efficiently. Glory had a good feeling about the woman. She felt that once she signed the agreement, the woman would make a diligent search for a buyer. She recommended a listing price of $600,000, which was more than Glory had hoped to ask, and promised to start showing it as soon as possible. An hour later, Glory had no qualms about giving the realtor her key and leaving the rest to her. More exciting things awaited her in Maine and she planned to start back in the morning.

Andrea Shaw was more adept than Glory had imagined. At five o'clock that night she returned with a young engaged couple who appeared to love every room, although they both tried to contain their enthusiasm. They were full of questions and from the nature of their concerns, Glory suspected they were eager, prospective buyers.

It was almost seven when they left and Glory went straight to the bathroom to fill the tub. A warm bath followed by soup and a tuna sandwich was the best she could offer herself for tonight. When the phone rang at 8:15, her eyes were fixed on the television, but she had no idea what she was seeing. She sprang to life when Andrea Shaw told her the engaged couple had offered $550,000 and there would be no mortgage problem, she added, but they had no use for any of the furnishings.

"Fine," she answered. "Take it." The moment she hung up, she called Stacy, then Frannie.

Her eyes were dry and her voice strong when she made her next call. "Is Mr. Templeton in?" she asked the receptionist.

"He's on the phone at the moment. May I ask who's calling and what it's in reference to?"

Glory shook her head and smiled to herself. *There's such a thing as too polite,* she thought. "Yes, this is Glory

English. Ask him to call me when he's free. I'm relocating to Maine and I'd like him to represent me for the sale of my condo."

It had been a long day, but definitely productive. She drew a breath and looked around the place she once loved to come home to. Now she couldn't wait to permanently slam the door behind her.

Chapter 29

Frannie had news for Glory that piled up the pressure. Her parents would be back the last week of September for a two-week stay.

Glory knew the apartment was a temporary arrangement but she had hoped to stretch it out awhile in light of all these life-altering events. Now she'd have to go back to Ocean Cliff or one of the other hotels until she found a place she liked enough to buy. But Frannie had another suggestion.

"For the first time in my life I was wishing my parents *wouldn't* come. My mother has a big heart, but she's very opinionated, and God forbid my father disagrees with her, I get caught in the crossfire."

They were sitting across from each other in the living room that was temporarily Glory's. Frannie went to the refrigerator for a cold drink but stopped short just before opening it. "Sorry," she said, "I forget this is yours for now. I'll get used to it. Mind if I get an Evian?"

Glory made a face and tossed a throw pillow at her. "Are you crazy? Don't ever ask me such a stupid question again! Now come back here and tell me what you were about to say. What's up?"

Frannie popped an Arizona tea and poured it into two glasses. "Thoughts started spinning in my head after my mother called." She paused, handed Glory the glass and a coaster. "I felt bad that you'd have to be pushed out when they come and I happened to mention it to Carl."

Glory cocked a curious brow. "And?"

"And that started a whole new discussion. He got me all keyed up." Another pause. "What do you think about a place above our restaurant? There's plenty of room for a spacious, luxury apartment for you, looking right out at the ocean you love, with enough left over for three dining rooms; two indoors and one outdoors. The way he sketched it out, you'd have complete privacy; no interference at all from the business."

Glory was momentarily silenced. Nonplussed, she tried to sort out the pros and cons. Her first reactions were you couldn't overlook the convenience, and once most of her money was sunk in Amore Evenings, her chances of buying an oceanfront house were slim to none.

"How much space are we talking about? How many rooms could I have?"

"He said you'd have five good-sized rooms; about 1,500 square feet, all told."

It sounded too good to be true and could be fraught with problems. Glory tried to suppress her excitement in case some unforeseen detail cancelled it out. One in particular came to mind.

"Well?" Frannie asked, disappointed at her hesitancy. "I couldn't wait to tell you. I thought you'd be thrilled. Instead you look like I threw a monkey wrench in our plans."

"No, no," Glory said. She fanned her fingers upward to nix Frannie's erroneous impression. "I *am* thrilled. The troubled face you see is concerned about the financial impact; the partnership. If we're splitting this straight down the middle, and I get 1,500 square feet for personal use as my permanent residence – "

Frannie cut her off. "Carl and I talked about that too. I'm sure it's all workable. We'll talk to our lawyers and tip the scale a bit monetarily to cover that. Don't worry, you'll pay your fair share."

Glory shrugged and widened her smile. "Then I'm all for it. Can I talk to Carl myself to discuss my options pertaining to the floor plan?"

"He said just give him a call if we decide to do it. He'll come here to discuss your needs and sketch it out for your approval."

"Then what are we waiting for? Get on the phone and call him."

Frannie tapped out the numbers on her cordless. "Hi, Carl, it's me," she said when he answered. "Yes, Glory's back from New York and I told her. She's all for it. When can you come over and discuss it with her?" She paused while he checked his schedule, then turned to Glory when she had his answer. "Friday night okay?"

Alex's gorgeous face flashed in her mind. She hesitated, not wanting to break her dinner date with him if she didn't absolutely have to.

Frannie handed her the phone. "Here, you talk to him."

"Hi, Carl. How are you? Yes, I'm excited about your proposal, but is Friday night my only choice?" She was staring at Frannie as she spoke and knew the imaginary light bulb had flashed over her head. She had slapped her forehead, obviously remembering Glory's date, but said nothing.

Glory hung up after agreeing to meet with him Saturday morning to walk Marginal Way. She refused his invitation to breakfast in order to help Frannie. She needed all the help she could get on weekends. Now that she was committed, she wouldn't consider not showing up. But Alex probably intended to walk Marginal Way with her too. She'd have to cancel that part out.

Oh, well, Glory thought, guess I can't complain. Although one was business and one was pleasure, both men were certainly easy on a woman's eyes. And both made her feel like a woman again.

Chapter 30

Dinner this time was casual; jeans and sandals. At Viola's recommendation, they had decided on Rick's by the Sea, a drinking hole with a great steak and seafood menu, live music, a dining room with dark, knotty pine booths and candles flickering in red glass. Peanut shells were strewn all over the wood floor, adding just the right touch to add to the mood of the place. The sound of crunching footsteps could be heard despite the loud music.

When the hostess called their name, Glory and Alex carried their icy mugs of beer from the bar to their booth. Conversation was never at a loss; there were so many future plans and dreams to discuss now that Amore Evenings would become a reality.

Realizing she had been monopolizing most of their conversation, Glory drew a deep breath and sipped her beer. "I'm sorry I barely let you get a word in edgewise, so why don't you tell me what's new with you, and I'll do the listening for a while."

He gave her an affectionate laugh, patted her hand. "No, I don't mind at all. It's a pleasure to watch you. It's a pleasure to watch anyone who's as animated and excited about something as you are. It's contagious. I'm very happy for you. And for me."

Glory went serious for a pensive moment; decided not to respond to his last comment. "Tell me about your wife, Alex. Does it still hurt to talk about her?" The words in her mind had already escaped her lips. Too late to suck them back in. Besides, sooner or later she needed to know. She needed to watch his eyes as he talked about her, to listen while he told his version of the night she died. Only then could she judge for herself whether this man's gentle, amiable personality was only a façade. Was the real person within prone to explosive violence? The thought chilled her bones.

In answer to her question, his long, deep breath and tightened lips clearly indicated to Glory that he'd rather not. Still, rather than apologize for asking, she waited.

"What's there to tell, really? Elena and I were married for six years when we were both not ready to settle down." Grim-lipped, he sipped his beer, then added, "Especially her. Certainly not because we were too young. I was thirty-four, she was thirty. Maybe we were both too used to our independence. Who knows?"

"I'm sorry. I don't mean to intrude. It's just that every time I think of how she died, that accident – " Her hand went up. "Forget it. If it upsets me, I can imagine how rough it is for you."

But Alex went on. "When someone dies like that, the survivor torments himself with guilt. You start going through all the 'if onlys'…if only I hadn't said this or that. But life is full of regrets. You can't blame yourself for everything or you'll go crazy. I've learned to turn that guilt around a bit. Elena, rest in peace, was a very high-strung young woman who was pampered and spoiled all her life. She could be fun and even loving if you agreed with her one hundred percent on any issue and let her take complete charge of your social life."

He paused just long enough for the waiter to serve their salads, but when he opened his mouth to continue, Glory stopped him. "Please, I'm sorry I brought it up. It's none of my business. We can talk about something else. It's just that…" She shrugged, indeed sorry she had brought it up.

"You heard the local gossip, didn't you? Even after eight years, people still enjoy sensationalizing. I'm sure every time it's mentioned someone embellishes the story to add a little sizzle to their conversation. At my expense. Who told you? Frannie, I suppose."

"No," she lied and shivered to think of how he'd react if he knew she had researched Elena's death on the Internet. "Actually it was a customer who heard me talking to Frannie. I guess your name grabbed her attention and she listened. Before she left, she tapped me on the shoulder...."

"And warned you against me, I'm sure."

Their salads remained untouched while Glory tried to ease her way out. As much as she wanted to hear his side of the story, something about his reaction made her squeamish. Her instinct hadn't determined whether his sour smile was caused by repeated unwarranted attacks against his reputation and credibility or the memory of his intentional criminal act.

She drew a breath and tried to laugh it off as insignificant. "The woman impressed me as your typical gossip, Alex. Believe me, if I had given any credence to what she said, I wouldn't be sitting here tonight. Can we please change the subject now? It's making us both uncomfortable."

His face softened and he reached for her hand again. For a few fleeting moments before, she thought she saw shades of Anthony Perkins as Norman Bates in *Psycho,* but the gentleness of Gregory Peck was back. One broad smile with those captivating eyes locked with hers, and her insides went weak. The fluttering sensations made her feel weightless. She wondered if she'd be steady if she had to suddenly stand. There was such an innocence about him as he gazed at her silently that she couldn't imagine him capable of any violence – not even a hot temper.

Rather than let her eyes reveal what she was feeling inside, she speared a tomato from her salad and waved her other hand at his. They ate in silence, but what had passed between them through eye contact needed no words to convey.

Oh, the power of gossiping tongues! she thought as she chewed away.

If any of those people knew him, had looked into those gentle eyes, they could never suspect him of foul play. With all due respect to the dead, Elena must have been quite the bitch.

Chapter 31

She had come dangerously close to kissing him last night. Heaven knows she wanted to, but something made her pull away and mumble a string of polite amenities before dashing off to her apartment. It was almost rude, now that she thought about it. What would have been so terrible about letting him see the place after she had described it so enthusiastically?

Temptation, that's what. They had only spent a few days together and she didn't like this out-of-control feeling. She had to concentrate on Amore Evenings and all the changes that'll come with it.

A knock on her kitchen door interrupted her thoughts. That would be Carl, she thought with a smile. He had left a message that he'd swing by and pick her up.

"Hey, how are you?" she called out.

He put his palms out in a can't complain gesture and returned her friendly smile. He watched as she snapped on her fanny pack and locked her door.

"Did I drag you out of bed too early for this? I would imagine weekends are your only chance to sleep late."

He didn't answer till they were inside his pickup truck and he had turned the ignition key. "I don't get much chance to sleep late on weekends either. I should but it never works out. We're always backed up fighting to meet completion dates. And sometimes we're out on estimates." He shrugged. "I was never a late sleeper anyway."

Glory thought she detected a slight hint of discontent in his tone.

"So, Frannie said you liked the apartment idea but were concerned about the finances."

"More for Frannie than myself. I want to be sure everything is split down the middle. Without her, this dream would never be possible so I want to be fair."

His eyes darted to meet hers and he grinned. "My cousin has a good head for business. One look at Amore Breakfast any day of the week can tell you that."

Her eyebrows rose and she nodded in agreement. "No one can argue that."

She drew a deep breath and kept her gaze on the scenery, all aglow with the early morning sun. The open windows of the pick-up allowed her to soak up the summer fragrances and soft ocean breeze. Two minutes later they arrived at Perkins Cove and the entrance to Marginal Way.

Again, as she experienced when she walked with Alex, the narrow path was not conducive to any in-depth conversation. But they managed to exchange some small talk and Glory enjoyed Carl's easy-going way. His personality worked well with his rugged good looks. He wasn't strikingly handsome like Alex, but his face had a look of strength; a weathered roughness suggestive of many hours outdoors. The Mel Gibson type, she decided. A frivolous thought came to mind that brought a smile to her lips. What woman wouldn't welcome attention from Gregory Peck and Mel Gibson? To be fair, though, Carl hadn't uttered a single flirtatious word today or the day she had first met him and Mike. All four of them had met that day to discuss renovation choices and estimated costs. Whatever conversation had passed between them was strictly business. Yet there was something about the way Carl looked at her...or was it her imagination seeing what her bruised heart hungered for? Male attention. Not necessarily with sexual connotations; she just needed to know that men could still find her attractive. Jason's wounds had sliced deeper than she realized.

Her serious face put a frown on his. "You look jittery; worried about something. Are you getting cold feet about the new restaurant?"

"No way," she was quick to respond. "Frannie and I are both excited about it."

"Good. You should be. You're doing business with the right person. Frannie is damn good at what she does and people love her. That's a can't miss combination."

Glory crossed her arms loosely and smiled. "If I didn't agree with that totally, I'd never be jumping into this. I'm not one bit worried."

He winked and squeezed her arm. "Good for you. It's gonna be great, you'll see. I wish both of you the best of luck."

She mumbled a thank you and her gaze fell to the spot on her arm where his fingers had been.

Carl pretended not to notice and Glory pretended not to have seen him notice.

Moments later they arrived at the site of Glory's future home and workplace. Carl put her imagination on a grand tour of the luxury apartment he envisioned for her. They exchanged ideas and easy conversation. When they left an hour later, Glory felt good. Really good. In that short time, she and Carl had become friends. First Frannie, then Alex, now Carl. In all those years she had spent almost exclusively with Jason, she never realized what she had been missing.

Too many good things had been happening. Too much, too soon. It gave her a sense of foreboding.

Chapter 32

"Yes, I am seeing Alex tonight," Glory said when his name came up in their conversation. "He's picking me up at seven."

Frannie cocked her head. Her expression shifted from eternal optimist to cautious pessimist. "Be careful, Glory," she said and punctuated it with a pointed finger as she climbed the first step to her own apartment upstairs.

Glory yanked at Frannie's sleeve to pull her back. "Wait, don't leave on those parting words. Tell me what's bothering you about Alex. First you tell me you could never condemn him and lately you're giving me the creeps with that long worried face. C'mon, Frannie, if there's something I need to know, I think you should tell me."

Frannie stepped down and swung back into the kitchen. She leaned against the counter, drew a deep breath and took her time exhaling. For a few seconds her gaze was everywhere but on Glory. Discomfort and indecision about what was on her mind was mirrored in her face.

Glory prodded. "Frannie, that serious face is scaring me..."

Frannie blinked away her thoughts and looked directly into Glory's eyes. "Okay. This is a little embarrassing for me...I have no right...but my concern is twofold. A part of me is troubled by the mystery of who he really is; what kind of guy he is."

Glory said nothing while Frannie paused. Neither one sat down; both stood up against the L-shaped counter, facing each other.

"I told you," she continued, "rumor has it that they used to argue a lot. Maybe she provoked it. Who knows? But the fact is there was some form of violent behavior in that house and maybe, just maybe, she pushed him over the edge."

"So now you're thinking he *did* intend to kill her?"

Frannie's hand went up. "No, I never said that, but his anger could have caused her death. Whether or not that was his intent, no one knows, but the point is, do you really want to get involved with that history?"

"Not if it *is* history."

"And if it isn't?"

Glory's gaze fell to the tiled floor. She searched for an honest answer for herself as well as for her friend. A shrug was all she offered.

"I'm sorry, Glory. Ordinarily, I would never invade anyone's privacy like this. But you are my friend. We tied our lives together with this Amore Evenings idea. Your husband did a number on you – "

"So did yours."

"Yes, probably more so, but Alex Howard is turning the charm on you, not me."

"Why are you suddenly against him, Frannie? It was your supportive attitude that made me put my guard down in the first place."

Frannie pulled out a kitchen chair and sat down. She crooked a finger for Glory to do the same. "I said there were two reasons. One, even if I don't believe he had murder in his heart or on his mind that night, I can't rule out the possibility. But the fact remains he probably does have a hot temper, considering what people have said about their arguments. And believe me, I know how destructive that can be. In my family, we were all victimized by my father's rage. The slightest thing would provoke it. It was hell to live with; we were always in fear. But my mother suffered the most. I wouldn't want my worst enemy to go through that."

Glory watched in silence as Frannie's lips began to quiver. She pulled tissues from the box on the counter and handed them to her. Frannie blotted the tears that had welled up in the corners of her eyes and sucked in a deep breath. "I'm sorry," she said to Glory with a forced smile.

"No, *I'm* sorry. The two men who should have loved and protected you treated you like shit. It's not fair."

"It may sound weird, but my father did love us when he was normal. When he lost his temper, it was like some kind of fit that made him temporarily insane; turned him into a monster. And we were supposed to accept that as an illness. Even my mother made excuses for him." She waved the memories away. "But we were talking about you, not me. The threat of you getting tangled with a potentially explosive personality is only part of my concern. The second part zeroes in on our business venture. If something develops between you two, I have to worry about how that will impact Amore Evenings. If he starts influencing your decisions, that could be bad news."

This time Glory thought hard before she spoke, then finally whispered the words she didn't want to say. "Do you want to forget the whole idea?"

"No! I want you to assure me that I'm doing business with Glory English, not Alex Howard."

Glory gripped Frannie's right hand and shook it vigorously. "There. Consider yourself assured. If there's one thing I can thank Jason for it's being forced to think for myself, make my own decisions. I never realized how much he controlled me and how I unknowingly allowed it until he left and I was suddenly on my own. There's no way I'm about to make that same mistake twice. Forget it!"

Frannie studied Glory's face a few moments, then relaxed her own into a soft smile. "I guess if you keep that attitude, I have nothing to worry about."

***

She was swimming in Frannie's pool when the phone rang. Rushing out to catch it could have bought her a few broken bones, but she was able to grab the back of a beach chair to break her fall. A sinking feeling went through her at the sound of Alex's voice. There was a problem with his sister or some other crisis at Ratherbee and he had to cancel, her mind quickly imagined.

"Would I be rushing you if we moved up from 7:00 to 5:00?"

Glory heaved a sigh of relief. Her conversation with Frannie, replete with warnings, flew out of her mind.

Chapter 33

Anxiety set her heart racing while she waited for Alex. She had been ready forty minutes early and didn't know what to do with herself. She was too restless to sit still.

If she were in Frannie's shoes, she probably would have had the same concerns. But Frannie wasn't in a position to make a fair evaluation. She had met Alex only briefly at Amore Breakfast and hadn't exchanged more than ten words with him. Maybe if she got to know him better…

She put it out of her mind for now. Alex was due any minute and she intended to invite him in to see the place. She grinned at the memory of how she had chewed his ears off about it. But when his car came down the driveway, Alex had a plan of his own. He jumped out of the car to open the door for her.

"I was thinking," he said, glancing at his Movado wristwatch, "it's such a beautiful clear night; almost a shame to stick ourselves indoors. If we hurry we can catch that cocktail cruise again if you're in the mood."

Glory looked down at her eggshell-white silk dress and her high-heeled sling-backed shoes. Not what she would have chosen for a boat ride, but there was no time to change. "Sounds good," she said with a bright smile. "Let me run in for a sweater and lock up."

When she came back she said, "I was going to invite you in before we left. I thought you'd want to see the apartment, but if we're going to catch that boat…"

"I do want to see it, but later, when I take you home, okay?" He said it ever so politely but his slanted look suggested he was interested in more than the furniture.

***

The cruise boat captain gave a warm greeting to all his passengers as they stepped off the gangplank onto his boat. When he extended a hand to Glory, and then to Alex, his squinted eyes gave them a quick study. *You look familiar,* they said.

"We enjoyed this ride a few weeks ago," Glory offered. "We wanted to repeat it."

The captain's smile widened. "My pleasure. Welcome."

Capt. Daniel Madison, his nameplate said, but he introduced himself as "Captain Dan." A strong, masculine name to match a strong, masculine face, Glory thought as he disappeared up into the pilot house.

The scents of summer and the cool ocean breeze relaxed her body and mind as they headed off for Bald Head Cliff. The passengers were served their drinks and a pleasant young woman named Tracy, the narrator, told the stories she and Alex had heard before, but enjoyed hearing again.

"I always wonder how people who narrate for a living can stand saying the same lines over and over again, ad nauseam. It may be interesting stuff for their audiences, but the repetition must be so boring for them."

Alex pursed his lips and pondered that a moment. "Not necessarily. If you love what you're doing, telling the same stories to new faces might be more satisfying than we think."

"Yes, I guess that's true. Most actors prefer the stage to movies. I think I'd rather have the diversity of different roles, but to them appearing on a stage, particularly the Broadway stage, is the ultimate prize."

Captain Dan had come down from the pilot house when his first mate took over. His congenial smile suddenly flashed down on them. "Excuse me," he said, "but I couldn't help overhearing." He shifted his gaze to Alex. "You're right, sir. It's never boring to us because we love meeting all the different people who come from different parts of the

U.S. and other countries as well. They're full of questions and often tell us interesting stories of their own."

Glory took an immediate liking to the captain. He had an engaging personality and was strikingly handsome for an older man. His hair was gray-white and thick; he wore a pencil-thin mustache and his build showed no signs of age. His legs were bronzed by the sun and looked strong as tree trunks. Anyone can see he loves what he does, she mused; his spirit for life radiates on his face.

"How long have you been doing this?" Glory asked.

The captain waved his hand over his shoulder as though he were throwing the years behind him. "Oh, it's almost twenty-two years now." Pride broke through his smile.

Glory's curious mind wondered what he had done before. She opted not to ask. The guy didn't have to tell his life story to everyone.

Apparently Alex didn't see it that way because he asked that same question. "Were you drawn to the sea all your life in some way? What did you do before this?"

Captain Dan waved a finger. "Now *that's* what you can call boring. I was stuck in a stuffy office all day and half the night working with a bunch of ruthless cutthroats. There were a few halfway decent people, but I could count them on one hand. After a while, the long hours and tensions of the job got to me. I chucked it all, moved to Maine, and never looked back."

"Wow! Good for you." Glory considered telling him that they had something in common, but if she started talking about her move from New York to Maine, she'd monopolize too much of his time. Instead, she asked, "Where had you lived before, New York?"

"Oh, no. Phoenix. I was born and raised in Arizona, but when I was a young man, I spent a summer vacation in Ogunquit and I was hooked. Phoenix is a beautiful city, but there's no ocean. I always wanted to come back and here I am."

The steady roar of the boat's engine and the splashing sounds of the ocean could not drown out the sound of Glory's thumping heart. She pressed on for one final question. "How long ago was that? What year did you vacation here?"

Alex squeezed her hand as if to brace her for what she might hear.

"Oh, that was way back, before your time. It was '67, right after college," he said, then winked. "I shouldn't have said that. Now you can figure out how old I am."

He had spoken in jest, but Glory couldn't fake even a smile, much less a laugh. A lump shot up in her throat like a rocket and a rush of tears filled her eyes. She was thankful for the sunglasses that shielded her emotions. "Excuse me, please," was all she managed to murmur before she raced to the tiny bathroom where she succumbed to an explosion of tears.

When she finally composed herself enough to come out, she found Alex leaning against the side of the boat.

"Are you all right?" he asked, leading her toward the rear of the boat, away from the crowd of people, clustered in the benches up front.

She put her hand up and nodded to hold him off while she sucked in a few deep breaths. "Can you believe this?" she said, her lips quivering.

Alex didn't hesitate to wrap his arms around her. The temperature was still somewhere in the 80s, but she was trembling from shock.

"It's him. It has to be him!"

His arms tightened around her, his lips were in her hair. "Probably," he acknowledged, "but we don't know for certain."

"Alex, how can you say that? He said '67 and he's from Arizona. How coincidental is that?"

"I know, I know. But you have to talk to him and you can't do it here. No way."

Another tourist had captured the captain's attention when Glory and Alex finally went back to their bench seats at the bow of the boat. He managed to look away from the portly gentleman to throw Glory a concerned look. "Are you okay?" he mouthed.

She flashed him a weak smile of assurance to let him assume she had a bathroom emergency.

The hour passed with no other opportunity for conversation with Captain Dan, nor did she and Alex exchange a single word about him. They were sandwiched in on their bench, with people on all sides. Her sunglasses, however, allowed Glory to steal long looks to study his face. With the image of the youthful face in the '67 photo burned in her memory, she searched for a match. But time and sea had weathered Captain Dan's face and thickened his body. Waves of recognition sent her head spinning. The height appeared about right, but she concentrated on the nose and mouth for a stronger resemblance. In the '67 photo, the young man's eyes were squinted under a summer sun and his smile widened for the photo.

It was the teeth that sent a chill through her again. Not exactly a match, but a similarity. The shape could have been altered by cosmetic dental work but as she recalled the photo, the smoke began to clear. Something about the curve and the width of his smile had her heart racing again. She drew short, quick breaths to calm her anxiety, but the eyebrows grabbed her attention. She swallowed hard as the realization struck her like lightning. In the photo, one eyebrow arched higher than the other. She had attributed that to the glare of the sun; his natural struggle to keep his eyes open for the photo. But it wasn't sunlight that caused it, she discovered, because Captain Dan's eyebrows had that same unique distinction.

Her mouth went dry. She sipped the remains of her drink, now watered down by the melted ice cubes. On her right side, she felt Alex's eyes peering at her, but he remained silent.

It's him. There he is, only ten feet away and I can't say a word. Can't hug him, can't claim him as the father I was denied for thirty-five years.

The minutes passed by too quickly. She hadn't paid any attention to what the narrator was saying since the moment the word *Arizona* left his lips. Now they were approaching the Perkins Cove dock and soon Captain Dan, her *father*, would be ushering her and all his passengers out with a broad smile, a thank you and a good-bye.

Glory managed to maintain her composure as she shook his hand and thanked him like everyone else.

A young attractive woman, somewhere in her 20s, was waiting at the dock for someone. She wore a straw hat over long, silky blond hair that was tucked behind her ears.

"Hi, Sweetheart," she heard from behind. The voice of her father. She turned to steal a glance, but what she caught only upset her further. Captain Dan blew a kiss to the woman who had to be half his age. Not the daddy image she had allowed herself to dream up since she learned of his existence. It gave her a sickening feeling to think of her father involved with so young a woman. But that reaction was soon replaced by another when the woman called back to him.

"Hi, Daddy!"

Glory had no choice but to watch in silence as he hugged and kissed his daughter who had obviously paid him a surprise visit.

That makes two surprise visits, Daddy.

Chapter 34

"Want to skip the restaurant?" Alex asked as they walked away from the dock. "You're upset, understandably."

"Do you mind?"

"Not at all, but I *am* hungry and you said you were too before you spoke to the captain."

"*My father,*" she said, trying to accept that fact, but a saddened, rejected image of the father she had loved kept popping in her mind. "I thought nothing could match the shock of my mother's letter but this, tonight..." She couldn't finish, just threw up her hands.

He left her to her thoughts all the way home and when they arrived, Alex didn't bother to wait for an invitation. He simply escorted her inside.

They walked in through the kitchen and settled on the living room sofa. Glory reached for the box of tissues, dabbed at her eyes and blew her nose. She gave him an embarrassed smile. "Sorry. I'm okay now."

"Hey, you don't have to apologize. You had quite a shock. If I were in your shoes, I'd probably have tears to shed too."

"Thanks," she said and patted his hand lightly, then averted his gaze. "My head's in a fog. I'm not sure what to do next. I'm still shaking."

"Can I get you anything? Do anything?"

"There's an open bottle of wine that Frannie and I started. You can pour us each a glass. The wine glasses are in the cabinet to the right of the refrigerator."

"Okay," he said and walked into the kitchen. "If you're feeling woozy, though, I think you'd better eat something with it."

"Gee, again I apologize. You must be starving." She gave him a hopeless look. "I wasn't prepared –"

He handed her the wine glass, sat opposite her in a club chair and rested his own glass on the end table. "Forget it," he said. "Like pizza?"

She sipped her wine and broadened her smile. "I *love* pizza. The phone book's right under the phone in the kitchen."

Glory had no appetite whatsoever when Alex had ordered the pizza and thought she would force down a slice just to be sociable. But by the time it was delivered, she was feeling a bit lightheaded from the wine and once that fresh-baked aroma wafted through the air, her usual ravenous appetite returned.

They sat at the kitchen table with their wine glasses and pizza slices. Glory folded hers in half and brought it to her lips, but abruptly put it down in her plate. "It's too hot," she said. "I'll let it cool awhile, but you go ahead and eat. I know you're hungry and I'm sorry I spoiled your dinner."

"You *did not* spoil my dinner, Glory. I rarely get to eat pizza, so this is a treat for me." He took a huge bite and chewed silently while Glory seemed to be lost in her thoughts again. "I don't know whether to be happy or sad for you. You look so troubled."

She managed a little laugh. "Troubled sums it up, I guess. I was thinking 'confused.' How the heck do I approach him? And privately, no less. And do I *want* to?" She made a question-mark face. "I'm scared to death." Her lips quivered at the admission.

Alex put his pizza slice in his dish and reached for her hand. "It's your decision, Glory, but I'm sure you know you have to talk to him. And soon, or you won't be able to function. And you have to consider the possibility that it isn't him. Maybe several guys from Arizona vacationed here that summer. Prepare yourself for that possibility. I'd hate to see you so terribly disappointed."

"I'm not sure if I'd be disappointed or relieved."

He cocked a brow. "No, I'm sure you'd be disappointed. I think you should arrange a meeting."

She nodded. "Yes, I've been tossing around a sketchy plan in my head. I think it can work. I only need one missing element."

"What?"

"Courage." This time, her laughter came naturally. "C'mon, stop worrying about me," she went on and waved her hand over his dish. "Eat before it gets cold."

Glory ate two slices herself and moved the conversation to Amore Evenings and her new apartment.

Alex wasn't quite sure whether her incessant chatter was prompted by her resolve to get Captain Dan out of her head or because she sensed what he was feeling.

Either way, it didn't matter because when she stood up to put their dishes in the sink, he came behind her, turned her face to his and kissed her. It happened so fast, without warning, that Glory had no chance to resist. Nor did she want to.

When their lips parted and her eyes opened, Glory broke away from his embrace. She leaned against the sink, arms crossed, and her gaze shifted to the floor.

"Your timing is all wrong, Alex."

He stood next to her, their bodies touching, but their eyes never met. "You're absolutely right, Glory, and I'm truly sorry. But please understand that the shock you sustained tonight is probably what I reacted to. You looked so confused and frightened. My first instinct was to comfort you, but this attraction, or whatever it is I feel for you, took control of me. If you're offended, I apologize. But am I sorry

I kissed you? No. Absolutely not. I've been wanting to do that since we first met."

She lifted her gaze and looked at him. "No, Alex, I'm not offended. It's just that so much has been happening lately – I shouldn't complain because much of it is good – but it's put me on an emotional roller coaster ride. I need time to sort it all out."

He gave her a long, penetrating look. "Do I hear a message in there somewhere? I hope not."

She returned an easy smile. "No, not the message you suspect. I just want to keep our relationship friendly, but cool. The situation with my father is first and foremost in my thoughts. I don't think I can handle anything more for now. If you can't handle that..." She finished off with a shrug.

He put his hands on her shoulders. "Depending on how long, it won't be easy, but as long as you added the words 'for now,' I'll hold on to that."

For the next half-hour they ate, sipped wine and made small talk to mask their feelings until they reached an uncomfortable lull. The urge to kiss him again grew stronger in the silence. That's when Glory stood up and led him to the door.

"Alex, I hate to pull the plug on what started out to be another pleasant evening, but – "

He placed a gentle finger on her lips. "Forget it. I understand. Just think it all out carefully, and whatever you decide to do, I'm sure it'll be the right decision."

"Thanks, Alex. That's exactly what I intend to do; just crawl in bed, think it all out, as you said, and wake up with a plan. Right or wrong, I'll just go with it."

"That's the best attitude you can take. Have faith in yourself. I'm sure it'll all smooth itself out once everyone gets past the initial shock stage."

Glory nodded, both hands clutched to the kitchen door. "I hope so," she said. "You're probably right, except for one minor detail." Her lips twisted with her negative frown. "My father is not the only one I'm worried about. I doubt that my brand-new kid sister is going to welcome me with open arms. I'd like to dream it'll be something beautiful, but I'm afraid it could turn into an ugly scene."

"Don't start again worrying about bad things that may never materialize. Stay focused on the good stuff. If and when the crap starts flying – excuse the expression – you can deal with it one at a time."

Glory laughed. "Now *that* sounds like a plan. In the talking stages, it always sounds easy."

She gave him a quick sisterly kiss on the cheek, opened the screen door and waved him off. The guy is like one huge tranquillizer, she thought. Her eyes stayed glued on his car as it pulled out of the driveway. She stood there until the crunching sound of pebbles under tires faded away and the glow of his headlights was lost in the darkness.

I'll bet his wife didn't see him as one huge tranquillizer, she thought. And what about *his* kid sister? I don't think she's too crazy about him either. But by the time Glory's head hit her bed pillow, Alex and his family were tucked in the back of her mind. Captain Dan, a/k/a *Daddy*, and his beautiful daughter were right up front.

Chapter 35

After another restless night, and despite her heavy eyelids, Glory felt better when she got out of bed in the morning. She had decided to follow Alex's advice and contact Captain Dan immediately. Today. Now that she was near certain she'd found him, there was no turning back. No more what ifs. Whatever happens, she'd deal with it and accept.

It was only 5:45 a.m. She could linger in bed for another hour or so if only to rest her eyes, but she decided against it, opting for an earlier start on Marginal Way.

Frannie's voice from upstairs changed that plan.

"Glory? You up?"

Glory came out of her bedroom, where she had begun to shed her pajamas in exchange for shorts and a T-shirt for her morning walk. She furrowed her brows, wondering what brought Frannie down at this unearthly hour.

"Actually I knew you were up. I heard the toilet flush." She paused as though she might change her mind about what she had wanted to say, but the words blurted out. "Glory, you know I have to go open up the restaurant...I wish I could stay – "

"What's wrong?" Glory asked, a sense of foreboding filling her.

"I just heard something on the radio. I'm sure it'll upset you just as it did me."

Glory's eyes widened with frightened anticipation. "Oh, my God. What?"

"Paula Grant was found dead last night. Drowned. Apparently her nurse had fallen asleep and Paula had somehow slipped out of the house and wandered off, as Alzheimer's patients often do, unfortunately."

Horrified, Glory stood silently shaking her head a few seconds while she tried to absorb this shocking news. "Drowned? In the pool?"

"Not the pool, the ocean. The dock attendant found her early this morning."

"I'm speechless. I can't believe this."

For lack of a better idea, Frannie poured her a glass of water from the Brita.

"Alex must be out of his mind. He was probably sleeping while his sister ran out to her death. If I know him, he'll be crazy with guilt."

Frannie just looked at her, but her silence and expression exposed her inner thoughts.

Glory studied her face. "Oh, forget it. I know you don't agree with me."

"It's not that I disagree. It's just that I'm not sure about him. It's very possible he's everything you say he is, but it's also possible…" She shrugged and let it go.

Glory's tone became defensive. "Frannie, think about this. If it weren't for all that gossip about his wife's death, would you have anything to substantiate that feeling?"

Frannie tilted her head and smirked. "No, I guess not."

"And I still don't understand this reversal. You didn't react this way the first time I told you about him. Why the change? And don't tell me you're afraid he'd influence my business decisions."

"When you first met him, he was just a man who might help you learn about your father. A man who happened to be gorgeous."

Glory waved it over her shoulder. "Don't read into my relationship with Alex something that doesn't exist."

Frannie responded with only a lifted brow and twisted lips.

"Anyway, let's forget it for now. I have to go to him, Frannie. Do you mind? I'll come down to the restaurant as soon as I can. Okay?"

"Of course it's okay," Frannie said and gave her an impulsive hug. "I'm sorry I'm a little standoffish about Alex. I'm just afraid for you in case those gossiping tongues were right. I'm thinking maybe you'd be better off not getting involved with him."

"Well, don't be afraid for me. I've spent enough time with him to be in a better position to judge. I can't believe Alex would hurt anyone. No way."

Frannie threw her hands up in defeat. "Hey, you may be one hundred percent right. I certainly hope so."

"I *know* so. Let me go. I want to go to him. I'm sure he'll need help with funeral arrangements and stuff. I'll see you later."

"Sure. And don't worry about the restaurant, Glory. Stay as long as you need to. I won't have a problem." She wanted to say she'd been handling it on her own for years, but thought Glory might misinterpret her meaning.

"Thanks, Frannie," she said, leading her out. "Thanks for understanding."

Chapter 36

He cried when she walked into Ratherbee's spacious living room. It was beautifully furnished, but death seemed to shadow everything. Without a word, Glory opened her arms to embrace him. They hugged for one long, silent moment, then broke apart.

"I never heard her. I was in a dead sleep. She might have been roaming around in the house before she found her way out. I should have heard her – " His voice broke.

"Stop, Alex. Don't do that to yourself." She held his hand between hers. "This is not your fault. All you did was sleep, like the rest of the world does at night. Besides, where was his nurse?"

His eyes rolled upward, still disbelieving. "Out like a light. Sound asleep in her chair."

Glory tried to imagine that scene. "How is that possible? I can't imagine how someone like Paula, with such limited brain function, could slip out without making a sound and with the nurse right outside her door."

"I'm sure my sister didn't plan it. To my knowledge, Alzheimer's victims don't have that capability. They act on whatever impulse strikes them."

Glory nodded in agreement. "Yes, you're probably right. But I still can't believe she got past that nurse."

Alex's mouth twisted into a bitter snarl. "Paula had a little help there. When the police arrived, it didn't take them long to figure that out. Apparently, Miss Britton spikes her tea."

"You're kidding! Are you saying she was drunk?"

"I don't know about 'drunk,' but definitely well-sedated."

They sat silently for a few moments, each with their separate thoughts. "And what exactly did the police say? Do they think she just unlocked the door somehow, ran out to the water, threw herself in and drowned? And the tide sent her back in?"

"Something like that. It may not sound sensible to us, but to Paula – who knows what was in her mind. Maybe she wanted to swim. Her mind might have put her back to a time when she loved to swim in the ocean." He threw his hands outward and shrugged.

Glory stared down at the floor while she searched for comforting words, but nothing came to her. She was still shocked herself, having felt an attachment with Paula simply because she had been her mother's friend. And maybe because locked somewhere in Paula's mind were memories of confidences she and her mother shared; all the unanswered questions about her father. All vanished forever now.

That ocean she loved to watch certainly had its dark side. God only knows how many lives it swallowed up. And only last night, Paula Howard Grant became another victim of its timeless wrath.

"What can I do for you, Alex? Let me help."

"There's not much to do," he said. "The funeral director was already here. They take care of mostly everything."

"How about phone calls? Are there any relatives or friends you'd like me to contact?" Her first thought was his sister Allison, but of course Glory wasn't about to mention her.

"Allison's already been contacted. She wasn't home, so they had to leave a message for her to call here."

Glory's voice became a gentle whisper. "And did she? Have you spoken to her?"

He shook his head. "Couldn't handle it. Not *yet*," he added, knowing it would be inevitable now. "Nancy spoke to her when she called. She told Nancy she'd be here tonight." He made a face that translated to *who cares? Who needs her?* But the bitterness was gone for the moment.

"Anyone else I can contact?"

Alex raked his fingers through his hair. His face was sweaty, his skin darkened by his unshaven face. His eyes were slightly bloodshot, his lids heavy.

"What time was it when you found out?"

"Oh, who knows? It was sort of pre-dawn when the police came. Josephine went crazy when she realized what she slept through. Hysterical with guilt. They had to take her away. I wish I could say I feel sorry for her, but I don't."

Their conversation was interrupted by the arrival of a group of neighbors, all of whom carried a tray or a casserole dish of food. Glory began to feel awkward under their curious gazes, but Alex quickly came to her rescue with introductions. He included a brief explanation of what he and Glory had in common.

One of the women, Hannah something-or-other, had come in red-eyed and sniffing back her tears, but her face brightened when she learned Glory's identity. First because she was well-familiar with her column and also because she remembered Mandy. A little bit of a person, a ball of energy, and she swam like a fish, Hannah said.

Glory smiled back at her, wishing she could pick her brain, but again remembered where she was and why. In a way, the urgency had waned. She was almost certain Captain Dan was her father, but anyone who had been at Ratherbee often enough that summer to watch her mother's romance develop might be able to help. It was strangely important to Glory to know that her mom had loved her father; that he wasn't just a summer fling.

Later, when everyone had left, she sat beside him again on the sofa. "Are you okay?" she asked.

"Sure. But I need to shower and shave."

She stood up to excuse herself and leave, but he held both her hands. "Do you need to go, Glory?" he asked. His eyes held a pleading look, but he said nothing more.

Glory saw the sadness that cloaked his face and didn't have the heart to refuse him although the desire to run to her father burned inside her. She never dreamed she would stumble upon him so easily, yet now that she had, he was still unreachable.

"No, Alex," she answered. "I don't *need* to go, but if I can't help, I feel sort of in the way. After all, I'm not family."

"But there is a favor I'd like to ask, Glory, if you can handle it."

"Name it."

"Come with me to Hodge's Funeral Home? I have to finalize the arrangements, but more importantly, I have to pick out a casket." He had been dry-eyed through all the company, but now a rush of tears surfaced. "I can't go through that again," he said through sobs.

She hugged him till he calmed, then thought with anger about all the faceless people who suspected this gentle soul of murdering his wife.

Chapter 37

In all fairness to Alex, he had no idea she had intended to approach her father that day. And it never occurred to him that selecting a casket would bring back painful memories. His thoughts were focused on his sister Paula's death. And how she died.

It did finally dawn on him when they were already on their way to the funeral home. His face was replete with apologies when he stopped for a red light. "Oh, God, Glory. I was so wrapped up with my own grief that I never stopped to consider your feelings. You've already been through that twice and I don't want you to relive those dark days. I'm going to drop you off and go myself."

"No, Alex, don't," she started to protest, although he had already changed lanes to head towards Frannie's house. "I'll be okay. I feel terrible about your sister, but this time the loss is yours, not mine."

He acquiesced with a silent nod, but stayed on course to take her home anyway.

She gave up with a sigh, and when he stopped at the house, she said, "Call me when the arrangements are made."

"Of course. And thanks so much. It meant a lot to have you with me today."

***

She sat on the patio with a glass of iced tea to relax and think clearly. The ocean, though still beautiful and hypnotic, frightened her today. Its powerful roar, its depth and magnitude were ominous reminders of its superiority over mankind. It could be loved, but always respected. Despite the sunshine that warmed her face, she shivered as she imagined Paula drowning; how completely helpless she was to save herself against the sea's infinite force.

A tug of conscience told her she should sit around and wait for Alex's call, but visions of her father at the mercy of that ocean every day flashed in and out of her mind steady as a heartbeat. How quickly pleasure could turn to tragedy, she thought. What if something happened to him before she had a chance to tell him who she was?

With that in mind, she freshened up with another shower and a change of clothes. She selected a comfortable sundress with a matching hat and wedged sandals. A touch of makeup helped complete the picture and, for a change, she decided to let her hair fall loose on her shoulders rather than pin it all up.

Her heart was beating wildly as she slipped on her sunglasses and studied her image in the mirror. What would he think of her? *This is as good as it gets, Daddy.* No match for the beautiful, youthful daughter she had seen at the dock, but not bad either. Deciding her looks wouldn't and shouldn't matter once she introduced herself, she picked up her car keys and left to meet her father.

***

The girl at Finestkind Scenic Cruises told Glory that the boat was due back in about twenty minutes. "Do you want to reserve for the next tour?" she asked.

"No, not today," she said pleasantly. "I just wanted to speak with Captain Dan."

The girl gave her a curious gaze. "Anything I can help you with?"

She laughed a little, thinking how innocently ridiculous the girl's question was.

"No, it's a personal business matter. I can wait," Glory said.

She left the young girl to her curious thoughts and walked leisurely around Perkins Cove, the very site that would become her home and place of business. A smile crossed her face as she visualized sitting at an oceanfront table at Amore Evenings, having dinner with the new and special man in her life, her *daddy*.

Her smile faded when her thoughts shifted to Alex and all her confusing feelings about him. How would a relationship with him affect her friendship and business relationship with Frannie? And if her father welcomed her into his life and took an immediate protective role, how would he feel about Alex?

She was making small talk with an elderly couple that shared her bench when her stomach suddenly flipped and that weightless feeling washed over her again.

Out on the horizon, Captain Dan's tour boat came into view.

Chapter 38

With a rapid heartbeat and a dry mouth, Glory watched from a distance as Captain Dan gave thanks and good-byes to all his disembarking passengers. When the last one stepped off the gangplank, Glory left the bench. He remained on the boat, but not alone. She could see that at least two crew members remained with him, both busy with their respective tasks.

Again, she approached the girl at the ticket booth, whose name she had learned was Brittany. "Do you think I could have a few minutes to speak to the captain, alone, if possible?"

Brittany gazed at her with suspicious indecision. Clearly, she didn't want to annoy her boss, but sensed that the woman had something important to say. She walked over to Captain Dan and gave him the message, Glory assumed, because he stopped untangling the rope in his hands and looked up.

She was only steps away from him now and a numbness ran through her as their eyes met. She felt as though she were sinking in sand with cement legs.

God, how do I say this? All the opening lines she had imagined she'd say seemed trite now.

The interruption put an annoyed look on his face, Glory noticed, but he approached her with a polite smile.

"I understand you wanted to see me about something personal?" he said, then added, "I can't imagine what."

Glory's thumping heart echoed in her ears. She licked her dry lips and glanced around her. "I'm not sure this is the right place. I'm sorry," she said as she considered the fleeting impulse to run away.

Dan Madison gazed at her with cautious eyes, perplexed by her transparent anxiety. She either had a profound tale to tell or she was mentally unstable, he concluded. "Well, I'm afraid I can't invite you on my boat. My crew is still aboard and busy, as I am. But I must admit you've piqued my curiosity. Brittany seemed to sense an urgency in your message."

At that moment, Glory spotted a couple vacating a nearby bench. It looked like the most privacy she was going to get. "Could we sit there?" she asked, pointing.

His forced smile switched to a scowl as he hesitated. He didn't want to be trapped into a long conversation with this total stranger who obviously had a problem. Still, there was something compelling about this beautiful and troubled young woman that prompted his silent response. He shrugged, threw his gaze to the bench and nodded.

Glory pulled herself together and jumped right in. It was clear to see he was uncomfortable and impatient to hear her out so that he could get back to his work.

"When we spoke briefly on your boat last night, you mentioned that you had spent the summer of 1967 here in Ogunquit. Did you happen to meet a girl named Amanda Stewart? She was a house guest at Ratherbee, the Howard family's estate. Her friend was Paula, their oldest child."

His expression of tolerant impatience quickly transformed into one of shocked surprise, albeit a pleasant surprise, judging by his smile.

"You mean Mandy? Do you *know* her? This is incredible!"

Glory was relieved to see his joyous response at the mention of her mother's name, but knew it would disappear with her next breath. "I wish I could say I know her, but I'm afraid I have to use the past tense. She died six years ago. A heart attack."

He reacted to the news at though he too had been stabbed in the heart. He clenched his teeth and squeezed his eyes closed. Glory let a silent moment pass before she spoke again. "She was your friend, wasn't she?"

"Yes, a very dear friend actually, but we lived in different parts of the country and somehow we lost touch." His eyes were clear reflections of regret. His gaze went out to the ocean while old memories surfaced. He turned to her and asked, "But how did you know we were friends? This is an amazing coincidence. Who are you?"

"My name is Glory English, Mandy's daughter." She shifted her gaze from the ocean to his eyes. Tears welled in hers, but she managed to spill out the words that had to be spoken.

"I'm not here only to tell you that she passed away. There's something else." She paused for a deep breath and searched for fresh and natural words to break the news. "I was born in May of 1968." Again she paused, but her gaze never shifted from his eyes.

"What are you saying?" he asked, his voice a breathless whisper. His eyes revealed that his mind was making the right connections. Confusion, denial and instantaneous love all seemed to break through at once.

"I'm saying what I imagine you might be thinking now. Yes, I'm your daughter." She let the tears fall undisturbed onto her cheeks while she stared up at the face of her father. Now that the last traces of doubt were obliterated, a powerful surge of love swept through her like a tidal wave. She couldn't deny it if she wanted to.

Nor could he. Stunned out of his mind, he reached for her hands at first and just stared at her. "Oh, my God, oh, my God," were the only words that reached his lips. Then, when he too could no longer hold back the tears, he wrapped his arms around her, oblivious to the crowds of people. Together they cried, but their tears were soon replaced by joyous laughter.

Chapter 39

When their emotions had calmed somewhat, Captain Dan broke from their embrace, put his hands on her shoulders and pushed her away slightly. He wanted to enjoy and savor a long look at the daughter he had never known. The daughter of Amanda Stewart, the girl he had fallen for hard and fast. But their love hadn't survived the difficulties imposed by time and separation.

He shook his head, creased his forehead, and stared down at her with incredulity. "I never knew. Please believe me, I never knew. I have so many questions, I don't know where to begin. My body still feels numb from the shock. I've never experienced a feeling like this in my life."

"Me neither," Glory said. Her hand still trembled as she dabbed at her eyes with a tissue.

An I-need-you wave from one of the crew members on board brought Dan back to earth. He stood up. "Glory, please don't move. Can you sit here for just a few minutes until I settle things with my crew? Once they're done, we'll have time to talk privately on the boat before the next cruise."

With the same smile that hadn't left her face since he embraced her, Glory merely nodded.

She waited only ten minutes, but it had seemed like forever. Finally, she saw two men and the young female leave the boat and head for the parking lot. Her father waved for her to come aboard and, with wobbly legs, she went to join him.

He handed her a Diet Coke and they sat starboard side, where they were hidden from the throngs of tourists on shore.

"What did your mother tell you?"

His question brought a trace of bitterness to her lips. "She didn't *tell* me anything. I found a letter...accidentally. I'll never know if she ever intended to talk to me about it." She reached in her bag for the letter and handed it to him.

Captain Dan creased his brows and, with parted lips, he slipped the paper from the envelope. Before he unfolded it, he hesitated and gave her a long look.

She nodded. "It's okay. Read it."

Glory watched his eyes grow watery as he read. His face seemed weighted down with the shock of its contents and his mouth remained open while he drew deep breaths.

He gave her a pained, questioning look when he discovered that Mandy had never completed the letter.

"She died two days later," Glory said and filled up with tears again. "I like to think that she was writing the letter to get all her thoughts out in some kind of order. Maybe she felt her emotions wouldn't allow her to convey to me what was in her heart for almost thirty years. Maybe she planned to hand it to me, watch me read it, and then fill in the rest."

"That's probably exactly what happened. Why would you think any differently?"

She shrugged, thinned her lips. "I don't know, but I don't like thinking that she had either planned to leave it for me to find after her death, or she had abandoned the letter, deciding that I'd be better off never knowing the truth."

Dan made a face that disagreed, but she cut him off before he could respond.

"That's what she did to you, isn't it?"

"Maybe so, Glory, and I must admit that I think my initial reaction would have been fury, but once you told me she died...." He paused, swallowed. "Your mom *chose* to exclude me from your life. God knows what made her reach that decision. Maybe in her mind she felt it was an unselfish and noble act. I probably would have changed career plans to marry her and assume my responsibilities as a husband and father."

"In her defense, I don't think Mom wanted to force that on you. She sort of alluded to the fact that your romance had cooled once you went back to Arizona."

He nodded with unseeing eyes, his thoughts rolling back to that special summer. He tried hard to recall what words had been exchanged in those few phone calls. What had been said to make Mandy arrive at that decision? What had he told her or not told her? But too many years had passed; his memory of those conversations clouded by time.

"I wish she would have told me, Glory. I never would have denied you. You believe me, don't you?"

She held his hand, this man who was a stranger to her yesterday, and today the father who swelled her heart with love.

"I do believe you – " She was about to call him *dad*, but a pang of guilt stopped her. The gentle, loving image of her father, Steven English, surfaced and held fast. She lowered her eyelids and suppressed a nervous laugh. "I'm sorry. This is awkward. I don't know what to call you."

"Call me whatever you feel comfortable with. *Dad* would sound really great to me, but if you can't handle it, Dan is fine."

"If you don't mind, I'd like to try *dad*, especially since the father I've known is gone, but bear with me if I stumble. Now that we found each other, I'm in shock too. Not only you."

They shared a laugh then Dan went on. "Tell me about yourself, Glory. Are you married? Do I have grandchildren?"

"Wait. First let me show you something." She pulled out the old photograph. "Is this you?"

He laughed with surprise. "Oh, wow, does this take me back! Yes, that's me. I was a handsome devil then, wasn't I?"

"You still are. A little older, maybe…"

He threw her a look that said *a lot older.* "So go on, talk to me."

"I was married for twelve years, but we're divorced now. His name is Jason Vance, but I never used his name. And no, I did want children but now I guess it was better that it hadn't happened."

The moment he had asked, he noticed the hurt in her eyes and wanted to move away from the subject of her marriage. "So talk to me, Glory. Go back as far as you can remember, to your childhood. I want to hear every memory of your life."

"Wow! That's a tall order. How many years can we sit here?"

"For now we have two hours before the next cruise. I'm sure we can cover the first chapters at least."

Her face grew serious. "I have a few important questions of my own first. What about your family? Will you tell them?"

He paused, but only briefly. "I'll have to. I can't keep you a secret as though I was ashamed of your existence. No way. Your mother and I fell in love long before they came into my life." He sliced the air with his hand as though cutting off any possible objections. "Oh, I nearly forgot," he said, lifting a brow. His smile boasted an excellent set of teeth considering his age. "I have a wife, Louise, two daughters and a son. Vanessa, Amy and Todd." A sobering thought made his smile disappear for the moment. "It'll be a shock to them – no question – but they have to be told. And they'll have to meet you eventually. Soon, actually. Are you okay with that?"

She shrugged. "I may lose a lot of sleep over it, but I've been doing a lot of that lately anyway. So yes, I'd like to meet them." The corners of her mouth went up as she entertained dreamy thoughts of a welcoming family, siblings she'd never had. "They may already know me a little when you tell them my name." She said it with a modest grin, aware that he hadn't a clue about Glory English, the food columnist.

He gave her a quizzical look and an easy smile. "I don't follow you. What do you mean?"

"Have you ever read or noticed the *Glorious Cooking* column in your newspapers?"

He tried to think but came up blank. "Sorry," he said, "maybe I did, but I don't recall it. I'm not big on cooking, unless manning our outdoor barbecue counts. Why? Don't tell me it's your column?" His face brightened with the revelation.

"Yup! I'm syndicated in thirty-six states," she said, unable to mask her pride. "I still pinch myself every now and then to make sure I'm not dreaming it. It got off to a slow start, but it eventually kicked off."

"That's fantastic!" Dan said. "We just met and already you made me a proud papa."

Ninety minutes passed while they tried to fill in decades of their lives. But the crew members had returned and a line had already formed for the next cruise.

"Glory, why don't you ride with us? We won't be able to talk much, but I'd love to have you nearby after missing thirty-five years."

Disappointment cloaked her face. "Me too, but tonight of all nights, I can't. A friend of mine here had a death in the family and I thought I'd keep him company. He's really down. His sister had Alzheimer's. Last night she wandered off and drowned."

"Paula Grant, yes. I heard about it. That means you're a friend of Alex Howard?" He said it as though she had befriended a snake.

"You know him?"

"Not personally, but I know of him. I'm not so sure about him, Glory. I certainly can't tell you how to choose your friends, but I wish you'd reconsider that friendship."

"Dad," she said with a mix of discomfort and pleasure. The title would take some getting used to. "I've spent a lot a time with Alex and I've heard and even *read* all the stories about his marriage, his wife and her death. Believe me, he's not capable of any kind of violence. He's a pussycat who's just a victim of gossip."

"Well, gossip is already spreading that his sister's death was no accident."

Chapter 40

Glory had considered giving Alex her cell phone number when they last parted, but was glad she hadn't. She would have turned it off anyway while she shared those very special moments with her father.

When she arrived home she was disappointed to find that Frannie's SUV was not in the driveway. She had been excited about sharing the details of her glorious day with her father. As expected, though, Alex left a message on her answering machine. She tapped out his number.

"Where were you? I was concerned," he said when he heard her voice.

He did sound sincerely concerned, Glory noted, but she felt a tinge of annoyance. After years of being married to a man who micro-managed her life, she didn't want to answer to anyone else about where she was, what she did and with whom. Her three-second silence had apparently sent that message to Alex because he quickly apologized.

"I'm sorry. I had no right to say that. I'm still in such a state of shock. I'm not thinking straight."

"Forget it, Alex. There's no need to apologize. How did you make out? Was it difficult for you?"

"No, not really. When you have no other choice, you do what you have to do. In my case, the worst part is that both times – with Elena and now with Paula – the grief is compounded with guilt. If Elena and I hadn't been arguing that night, she'd still be alive, and if I hadn't slept last night like a baby without a care in the world, Paula would still be alive too."

"Alex, you can't beat yourself up with all this guilt. Both deaths were horrible, tragic accidents and neither one was your fault. I can't believe you're punishing yourself for sleeping! After all, you did provide your sister with full-time nursing care. Now put that stuff out of your head and tell me about the arrangements."

Glory pressed the off button without saying a word about her day with her father. She had been so anxious to tell him but the moment wasn't right. Mixing her joy with his grief seemed disrespectful. Besides, his sister Allison was due to arrive within the hour, he'd told her. Glory didn't want to intrude on that unpleasant family scene nor did Alex ask her. Tomorrow Paula would be waked and she'd see him then, during the evening viewing hours, they'd agreed.

She was relaxing on the patio and still euphoric about her father when she heard Frannie's car pull up. Glory jumped right off the lounge and went out to meet her. But Frannie wasn't alone. Her cousin Carl pulled up right behind her.

"How was he?" Frannie asked.

Glory shrugged, took one of the two large bags from her friend's overburdened arms. "As well as can be expected, I guess. It was a shocking, unexpected death, so it's tough to accept." She eliminated the guilt part, knowing Frannie had swung the other way in her assessment of Alex's credibility.

Carl slammed the door of his pick-up and joined them. He greeted Glory as though they were old friends who hadn't seen each other for years. "Hey, Glory, how are you doing, pretty lady?"

She returned a friendly albeit less enthusiastic greeting and approached him. Now the paper bag filled with food and supplies from Amore Breakfast went to Carl's hands and they both followed Frannie up the few stairs and into her kitchen.

"I understand you were pretty shaken up about Paula Grant's death last night, Glory," Carl said.

She looked at him curiously.

"Frannie told me," he continued and glanced over at his cousin, who nodded her okay. "I had already heard that you've been seeing Alex Howard, so I asked her." He made a face that mirrored concern. "That's good for him, but bad for you, maybe."

An angry flame shot up through her. "What's that supposed to mean, Carl? What the heck is going on in this town? Did someone initiate a class action lawsuit against Alex Howard? Is there anyone at all in this whole town who at least gives him the benefit of the doubt?"

Carl's hands went up in surrender. "I'm sorry, Glory, really sorry. It didn't dawn on me that you could be that attached to the guy in so short a time."

"And what did you hear? That he and I are having a wild passionate affair? Well, not that I owe anyone an explanation, but you can pass the word around that I had an entirely different reason – a perfectly innocent reason – for befriending Alex Howard."

Carl remained silent and open-mouthed while she vented, then said, "Again, I apologize. It's your life, your business. It's just that we like you and care about you, Glory. No one wants to see you get hurt. Be careful. And that's it. I spoke my piece." He made a two-finger gesture to show that his lips were sealed.

Glory heaved a sigh. "I'm sorry too. I got excited over nothing. It's just a culmination of a lot of built-up stress. I know you and Frannie mean well."

Carl put on a bright smile. "Okay, then, speaking of Frannie, she invited me to dinner, and do you know how I answered her?"

Glory's arms were folded and an easy grin broke through her face. "No, I don't know, but I'm sure you'll tell me."

"I said if Glory can join us, I accept. If not, can I have a raincheck?"

She made a well-creased frown, touched with humor. "Oh, Carl, that was an awful thing to do! If I were Frannie, I'd be insulted and not invite you at all."

He waved it off. "Not Frannie. We're family. In her eyes I can do no wrong," he said, again throwing a look at his cousin. "Right, Frannie?"

Frannie was silently busy at her refrigerator, fighting for space to accommodate the food she had brought home. But Glory sensed that she never missed a word of their conversation. She strongly suspected that Frannie had invited Carl to dinner hoping he'd get a chance to work his down-to-earth charm. She hadn't been successful in discouraging Glory, but maybe Carl could get through to her.

If that were the case, it could sure put a damper on their friendship. Alex Howard, like the proverbial forbidden fruit, was beginning to look better and better. And Glory had always been a sucker for the underdog.

But not another word about Alex was mentioned the entire evening. The sudden flash of anger she had felt earlier when Carl offered his friendly words of warning had totally dissipated.

They had begun talking about Paula Grant's shocking death, followed by a discussion about Alzheimer's disease, and how the number of its victims had escalated to frightening proportions. The subject depressed them and when Carl asked a question about the status of their business venture, both women welcomed the new conversation. Carl answered several of their questions concerning renovation of the house and property which took them through dinner and long past dessert.

The moment Carl left, Frannie turned a serious face to Glory. "I guess I owe you a huge apology, Glory. It's true. I asked Carl to talk to you. I'm sorry. I'm going to try real hard to put all those scary thoughts out of my mind and see him through your eyes. I trust your judgment. If you trust

Alex, I'll trust Alex. I don't want anything to stand in the way of our friendship."

Glory broke into a wide grin. Neither her decision to move to Maine nor the dream of Amore Evenings had excited her more than having Captain Dan, *her father,* practically fall into her lap. She wasn't about to let anything put a damper on her mood. "Oh, forget it. It's not important at all compared to what I have to tell you. I had the best afternoon of my life!"

Chapter 41

It was as though a dam had burst. Glory couldn't contain her excitement. She laughed and cried at the same time. "I found him, Frannie. I *found him!* I didn't know if I ever would and suddenly there he was, right here in Ogunquit." She lifted a hand. "Look, I'm trembling again."

Frannie couldn't make a sound at first. Stunned, she stared at Glory wide-eyed and open-mouthed. "No, it can't be...she finally managed, afraid to be happy for her in case her facts were screwed up. "You'd better sit down again and start from the beginning. Who told you what?"

"Don't give me that scared look. *He* told me. I talked with him for a long time today. *My father.*"

Frannie threw her a guarded look that grew into a pessimistic frown. She pulled out a chair and sat down with Glory. "Okay. From the beginning, I said."

Glory pulled in a deep breath to prepare for a long talk. "It really started last night when Alex and I were out. You and I never got to talk when he left, and this morning, when you came down with that bad news..." The joy left her face for a brief moment, but returned brighter than before. "Anyway, thank God for Alex's suggestion to change plans. He asked if I wanted to repeat the boat ride we enjoyed the first night we met. On the boat, we somehow got into a conversation with him, and Arizona got thrown in. When he said he had fallen in love with Maine on a vacation when he was young, my heart went wild. I asked him what year that was and – "

"Frannie cut her off. "Glory, who's *him*?"

"The captain. My father."

"Are you telling me that Dan Madison is your father?"

"Why? Do you know him?"

"Not personally, no. Only by name. He's been running that tour like forever. But he's here only in season. He's a snowbird; lives in Florida during the winter months." She shook her head to let the news settle. "This is surreal, amazing. You thought – and I agreed – that God knows where he settled. Without a name the search would be tough. After so many years, he could be anywhere. Even in another country. And now you tell me it's Dan Madison, and he's right here in the very same town where he and your mother – " She pursed her lips and shook her head again rather than complete her sentence.

Glory laughed. "It's all right. I can handle it. Where he and my mother had a love affair and I was conceived. Actually, how can I not be glad they did? Their love gave me life."

Frannie wiped away some involuntary tears. "This is such a tear-jerking soap opera story. It's unbelievable! Tell me the whole story. I want to hear every detail."

"Okay, but first promise me you won't say a word to anyone. Not until he tells his family."

She raised a hand. "Absolutely," she said, then remembered where Glory spent half her day. "Did you tell Alex?"

"No, not yet."

"But you're going to?"

Glory made a face suggestive of an apology. "Well, he was with me when it all happened. There was no way I could hide my reaction when I realized Captain Dan Madison could be my father."

Frannie gave a dismissive nod. "Tell me about your father. It isn't often that I can listen to a heart-warming, happy story."

The two friends dumped their cooled coffee and switched to wine. The next hour was spent talking about Captain Dan's presence in Glory's life and how beautifully it could fill the void caused by her parents' deaths and Jason's betrayal.

When finally they had squeezed the subject dry, the talked about plans for Glory's new apartment above their restaurant, their present and future plans for Amore Evenings and all the magical places they'd like to travel to during the winter months when the restaurant would be closed.

Dreams. All beautiful dreams. And all of them possible with dedication and sweat. They talked about all of them. Whatever thin layers of frost had formed because of Alex had temporarily melted away.

Chapter 42

The following morning father and daughter went about their separate lives. Before Glory left the Finestkind the day before, they had agreed not to see each other until he had the chance to tell his family. He didn't want to start lying to his wife, making excuses for his absence. Nor did he want to be seen in the company of a young and beautiful woman before he could make her identity known.

But he would do it very soon, Dan promised. Within the next few days. In the meantime, he would try to call her late at night, after Louise fell asleep, or whenever he found the right moment.

***

After spending six hours at Amore Breakfast for what she considered her crash course in food service, Glory would have liked to rest her aching legs on her patio lounge, but tonight her legs would have to settle for a chair in Hodge's Funeral Home.

Paula Grant looked beautiful in death, as is often said when a person dies suddenly. Her face seemed relaxed, peaceful. When Glory had first seen her, her wrinkled brows and piercing eyes reflected a frightened and confused mind. Now, ironically, she looked normal. They put her in a peach-colored chiffon dress, her makeup a bit heavy, but tastefully done. She wore pearl button earrings and her brown hair was framed softly around her small face, the white roots no longer visible. From a distance she looked as though she was taking a short nap before going to a wedding.

Although the chapel hours didn't start till 7:00, at 6:45 there were only two people in the room. Alex and Allison. They were both seated in the navy blue crushed velvet chairs in the front row, one empty seat between them.

Both stared at their dead sister. Neither one wore a mournful face. Their only common emotion, Glory noticed, was hostility. Paula's death had thrown them together, but they both despised being forced to breathe the same air.

Glory gave Alex the customary hang-in-there hug and hand squeeze, then moved on to his sister. "You must be Allison," she whispered.

"I'm sorry. Do I know you? Your face is vaguely familiar but I can't place it."

Glory took the seat between them. It was obvious there had been no social conversation between the two siblings since their sister's death brought them together. "My name is Glory English. I just moved to Ogunquit from Rockland County, New York. My mother was your sister Paula's good friend during their college years."

"Oh? And did you know Paula? When she was well, I mean?"

"No, I'm sorry to say. I only met her recently. I had hoped to reminisce with her about my mom. She died six years ago."

"Well, I'm sorry you never got the chance to talk to her. Excuse me," she said, and turned her attention to the arched entranceway, where people were starting to walk in. Alex and Allison played their parts graciously, accepting condolences and listening to stories that sung the praises of Paula's life.

As the room filled up, the mood changed. Gone were the somber faces; conversations grew louder, spurts of laughter erupted occasionally, although quickly subdued. And everyone seemed to forget where they were and why.

Alex tried his best to keep Glory at his side and introduced her to a whole bunch of people she'd probably never see again. But his attention was often diverted and she found herself sitting alone with her hands clasped in her lap.

It was during one of those awkward moments that Allison approached her again. She was all smiles and slipped into the next chair. A friendly hand touched Glory's arm. "Now I know why you looked familiar. I hear you're Glory English, who writes the *Glorious Cooking* column."

"That's me," Glory answered modestly, as she had done a thousand times before when people recognized her. But she couldn't help wondering why Allison was pouring on the congeniality knowing full well that she was a "friend" of Alex's. She hadn't seen a single word exchanged between them in the hour she'd been there. Conversely, she hadn't seen any eye daggers exchanged either. Whatever wall of fire hung between them, they kept it under control for the sake of appearances.

"Well, it's nice to have a celebrity among us," she said, her smile too cheerful for the occasion. It disappeared just as rapidly, replaced by the standard more suitable one which toned it down to polite amiability touched by grief.

"It was so nice of you to come," Allison continued, "considering you never knew my sister."

The line was loaded with innuendos. Allison was cutting her way through for information on her relationship with Alex. Just as Glory's lips parted to respond, she caught the look Alex threw her under hooded brows. Across the room, although surrounded by people, he managed to convey his warning to get away from his sister. She met his gaze and merely blinked back an acknowledgment. Message received, her response conveyed, but I can handle it myself, thank you.

"I felt compelled to be here for my mother. They were close at one time," Glory answered, then added, "And for Alex. We're friends too."

Their conversation was interrupted when someone tapped Allison on the shoulder. Allison was apparently surprised and pleased to see the older woman because they exchanged a warm embrace. Sincerity softened her demeanor, Glory observed, making her think of the old adage, *There are two sides to every story.*

The room was crowded now since Paula would be waked this one day only. There was a long line of mourners backed up into the vestibule waiting to view the body and give condolences to the family, which consisted of Alex, Allison and two female cousins, both elderly and widowed.

Alex grabbed his first opportunity to rescue Glory from his sister. "You okay?" was all he said or could say with a crowd of people within earshot. "I didn't mean to leave you alone, but – "

"No, don't bother to apologize. You have to be up there to receive the callers. Don't worry about me. I'll be fine. And if I don't get the chance to see you when I leave, I'll just slip out and see you at the Mass tomorrow."

He looked disappointed. "Oh, but the neighbors brought over a ton of food. I thought you'd come back to the house."

She gave him an *I-don't-think-so* frown, her eyes darting over to Allison who was now engaged in animated conversation.

"There'll be loads of people, I'm sure," he said, noting her hesitancy.

But Alex had misinterpreted her reaction. It had nothing to do with the strained relationship between Alex and his sister. It was all about her father and the remote chance that he might call her at home. And she certainly couldn't explain that now. Even if the opportunity for a private conversation had presented itself, she never would have mentioned meeting her father. A funeral home was the last place she'd want to share such a joyous, memorable occasion. Instead, she gave him a partial truth.

"Alex, I have to answer a few e-mails and send a few of my own. If I don't get the information I need for my column, I'll run into a serious deadline problem. I'll see you at church, okay?"

"Sure. And you'll come back to Ratherbee when it's over, won't you? Half the town will be there. Who knows? Maybe you'll connect with the right person." He didn't elaborate, of course, but gave her a shared secret smile.

Glory wished she could yank him out of there for an hour or two so she could tell him every glorious detail, but she just returned his smile and accepted his thanks-for-coming kiss on the cheek. On her way out, she suppressed a giggle as she admonished herself for the sensual charge his polite kiss had ignited.

At the front steps of the funeral home, she literally bumped into Allison, who was smoking a cigarette and laughing with friends. They looked about her age, so she assumed they were friends. But something about them made Glory think they'd be ready to party as soon as they drove out of the parking lot.

"Glory English!" Allison called out and reached for Glory's arm. "Come. I want to introduce you to my friends. Hey, guys, this is Glory English. Do you know who she is?" Then she cupped a hand over her mouth and jokingly said, "Half of them barely read a newspaper, much less cook!"

Glory forced a smile and a nod at the group and searched for an opening to escape to her car.

Allison's hand was still gripped on her arm. "She's not only a syndicated columnist, but she's also my brother's *friend!* Can you imagine Alex having a *friend?*" She pursed her lips and waved a hand as though it was an inconceivable, absurd thought. Her friends followed her lead and laughed too, albeit with less enthusiasm.

For a brief moment when she'd met Allison inside the viewing room, Glory had allowed herself to search for something to like about her. To think maybe somehow, in time, she could be instrumental in bringing them together again. She imagined that maybe she could play arbitrator, listen to both sides, let them get it all out, and the scene would end with happy tears and hugs.

Another fairy tale. There *are* two sides to every story, she thought, and without a doubt, she was already on Alex's side without hearing a word of either story.

She pulled her arms away, waved a silent goodnight and rushed to her car.

Chapter 43

There were no phone messages when she got home. Frannie was out with friends and even the ocean couldn't calm Glory's restlessness. She sat at her computer, making a diligent effort to put together an amusing and informative column.

But she wanted that phone to ring.

She wanted to hear that he had told his family, and that they were all shocked, but ready and anxious to meet her. Not with hostility, but with instant love for the half-sister they never knew.

Yeah, right.

It was possible, but definitely not probable. Still, she wanted to face it and brace herself for the fallout.

At 11:10 p.m. the shrill sound of the phone jolted her like a tongue of lightning. Glory was in her pajamas with a mouthful of toothpaste. She spit it out in the bathroom sink without the benefit of rinse water, grabbed the hand towel to blot her face and raced to the living room. In her haste, she collided with the leg of a living room end table and picked up the phone with a grimace of pain.

She managed a breathless hello. The butterflies in her stomach were a positive distraction to the pain in her big toe.

"Glory, did I wake you?"

It was another voice that usually fired up her emotions, but this time it deflated her. "Not at all. I'm wide awake, working on my computer. How did it go tonight?"

"Pretty much the same. I'll be relieved when it's all over. Josephine came and fell apart. They had to help her out. She feels responsible for Paula's death, not to mention the shame of having her drinking habit exposed to the whole town."

"Poor thing. What she did was certainly irresponsible, but I'm sure she never dreamed her drinking would cause someone's death. I feel sorry for her."

A short silence fell between them.

"I missed you, Glory. I need to spend some private time with you after the funeral. Are you okay with that?"

"You mean *right* after?"

"I mean right after the last of the guests, or mourners, or whatever you call the mob that congregates after the cemetery. When the last one leaves the house."

She hesitated, reluctant to fan a fire, then asked, "What about Allison? How did you manage spending two nights alone with her?"

"I *didn't* spend the last two nights with her. She was out and I wasn't about to ask her where and with whom. We're long past that. For the short time we were in the house and alone together, we simply ignored each other."

She blew a sigh into the phone. "I don't mean now, Alex, but maybe someday you should tell me what happened between you. It's all bottled up inside. You might feel a hell of a lot better if you talk about it."

"Maybe. We'll see. Let's put Allison out of our minds for now," he said dismissively. "So, will you stay tomorrow after the funeral?"

Glory's single word response, "Sure," was barely audible.

Alex's tone suggested that he wanted much more than the company of a good friend. How she wished she could chuck all her fears and the weight of all those fingers of suspicion.

"I'd like to stay awhile, Alex, for my own reasons. We haven't had time to talk and I have a lot to say."

"Oh, you sound serious. Will I like what you have to say?"

She let a laugh escape. "Definitely." Her grin grew wider when she hung up, realizing that their minds were on different wave lengths. His was moving to the beginning of a love affair, hers bursting with love for Dan Madison and the need to share her joy with Alex.

Not that a love affair with Alex had never entered her mind.

First she needed to trust him; to erase all doubts. Then she needed to convince Frannie and her father to trust him.

And Carl.

Chapter 44

In the front pew of All Saints Church, Alex and Allison left a noticeable gap between them. Neither seemed to care what people thought or said about their turbulent relationship. If anyone knew why, everyone knew why. But no one was ready to share that information with Glory. And chances were great that the facts had been distorted as they channeled ear-to-ear, mouth-to-mouth throughout Ogunquit.

But not to be compared with what sensational stories their imaginative minds had come up with on the subject of Elena's death. A whole bunch of hypothetical, thrilling scenes of the events preceding that fall down the steps.

With her elbows rested on the pew, Glory shielded her eyes by framing her face with her hands, as though absorbed in prayer. But Glory wasn't praying. Her gaze was fixed on Alex, and her hands were being used to block other curious eyes that might be studying her as she studied Alex.

There was nothing she could glean from his body language or his facial expressions to suggest anything other than her first impression. He was a decent and fine gentleman – *a gentle man* – whose reputation and credibility had been tainted by a few suspicious minds who thirsted for sensationalism.

Yet, when she allowed that shadow of doubt to snake its way in, she too couldn't shake it out. With all her heart she wanted to bury it in some dark corner of her mind and never think about it again. Better yet, she'd like to completely obliterate that doubt, not only from her mind but from the minds of his accusers. Only then could she release the emotional barriers she created and let the surge of love spill in. God knows she wanted to.

The sound of Allison's sobs broke through the somber silence.

Glory's gaze shifted. If she had left the funeral home last night with only the memory of her first impression, she would have filled with tears herself at this heartrending scene. But her second and lasting impression, the one of the laughing, ready-to-party Allison on the steps with her friends, held fast and left Glory dry-eyed.

Alex never moved a muscle. He neither reached out to her with a comforting gesture nor acknowledged her display of sorrow. His gaze remained fixed on the altar. That, in itself, revealed something more about Alex. A certain coldhearted resolve, she observed. And a deep-seated hatred for his own flesh and blood.

She had to know why.

***

As anticipated, Ratherbee's living and dining rooms were filled to capacity with people drinking, eating and laughing, all relieved to be free from the sorrowful and frightening moods of the church and cemetery. In the face of their own mortality, all were celebrating the fact that they were still alive and well.

The excess spilled outdoors. The sun was strong but a steady summer breeze wafted across the porch and lawn.

"I can't wait till they're all out of here," Alex whispered.

Her body's sensual reaction to his suggestive words left her uneasy. She felt too vulnerable; too weak to stick to her resolve.

She gave him a benign response. "I don't blame you. It's been a rough three days."

He cocked a brow. The silent gesture made it clear that wasn't what he meant and she knew it.

A little giggle slipped out. "Okay, okay. Don't look at me like that. I know what you meant. I could use some quiet time too."

"With me, I hope?"

"Sure," she said, the laughter still tugging at the corners of her mouth.

***

The caterer's crew was wrapping the last of the leftover food and tidying up the downstairs rooms along with the outdoor areas where the guests had gathered. Glory's cursory glance revealed no evidence that a crowd of people had been there for the last few hours.

Allison, who made herself very visible and social all day, disappeared without a word. She had apparently floated out with her friends.

Glory and Alex were seated on lounge chairs on the back lawn, facing the ocean. The huge branches of the birch tree under which they relaxed carried the glorious scent of salty water and summer flowers.

"It amazes me how you and your sister Allison could have put the whole wake and funeral together without speaking to each other. I would imagine you'd have a lot to discuss now with Paula's death."

"I'm sure she was only too glad to leave that all to me so she could turn it into a social event."

Glory raked her fingers through her hair to let the breeze flow in. Then, without meeting his gaze, said, "Is it possible you're being a little too hard on her, Alex? I thought I saw some reflections of grief at times." *Not always,* she thought, but kept that to herself.

He lifted his brows and shot her a look.

Her hands went up. "Okay. Guess I'm wrong. Forget it."

She glanced around towards the house and driveway to double-check that there were no lingering workers.

Alex followed her gaze and smiled softly, all traces of bitterness now gone. "Yes, they're all gone. All three of them came and left in the same van."

She blew a sigh. "What a mob you had here! It always bothers me a little to see how funerals turn into parties."

He waved it off. "That doesn't bother me. I don't think anyone means to be disrespectful. It's just a release from sorrow. They need to feel happy and alive. When I go to other funerals, I'm guilty of the same behavior."

"Me too, I guess. It is a release, but when you're the grieving party, still stinging from the pain of leaving someone you loved in a cemetery waiting to be buried, a party atmosphere is the last thing you're in the mood for. It hurt me with both my parents, but it's one of life's normalcies, unfortunately."

She waved the subject away, swung her legs off the lounge and sat up to face him. "Alex, I've been bursting to tell you something, but I had to wait till this was over."

He assumed the same position in the adjoining lounge chair and reached for her hand. Her enthusiasm was contagious and his face also lit up with an anticipatory smile. "Yes, I was going to ask you about that anyway. You left me hanging yesterday. So tell me, your eyes are full of excitement. I could use some good news."

"I told him, Alex. After you dropped me off the other day and went to make the funeral arrangements, I made an impulse decision right then and there. I couldn't put it off any longer."

He squeezed her hands. "Oh, my God," he said, looking as excited as she was. "Tell me what happened."

"Let's walk," she said. "I can't sit still. I want to tell you every detail so I can relive it all again."

They were walking towards the water and Alex stopped her abruptly. "Wait. Before you start, I need to say something; to make a wish, a promise." He put his hands on her shoulders and held her gaze. "I wish someday I can give you the same joy I see in your eyes now. I'm sure gonna try. And that's a promise."

There in the sunlight, with the sound of the sea for music, he hugged her first, their cheeks touching. When their eyes met again, their lips followed. For the moment, Glory forgot all she was about to say and yielded, body and mind, to the overpowering feeling of newborn love.

When their lips parted, he cupped her cheeks with his hands. "Glory, I want to hear about your father as much as you want to tell me, but can it wait just a little while?"

His pleading eyes completely destroyed what little resistance was left. It wasn't supposed to happen this way. She was supposed to be strong, to keep their relationship platonic until she could break through the mystery surrounding him. But once he held her in his arms and she felt the depth of his kiss and all that it conveyed, her strength had dissipated like the ebbing tide.

Involuntarily her voice found the words Alex was waiting to hear. "Yes, I guess I can."

Together they walked hand-in-hand and silently into the house. Glory didn't know if it was the sudden change from the warmth of the sun to the coolness of an air-conditioned house, but her whole body trembled. An inexplicable mixture of desire and fear took complete control. She wasn't quite sure how to define the fear. Was it fear of falling in love or fear of the man she was falling in love with?

Chapter 45

Glory would never know if she would have succumbed to the temptation or if the fear would have drained her desire for Alex. The decision was made for her. She and Alex never got past the kitchen when the front doorbell rang. She remained frozen with the discomfort of nearly being "caught in the act," particularly right after Paula Howard's burial.

She wished she could escape unnoticed, but it was too late for that. Whoever it was probably thought Alex was alone because only his car was in the driveway. Her car was still parked far from the house because of the multitude of people that had come after the funeral services.

Glory made no attempt to hide her presence, though, knowing it would be a futile effort. Wouldn't it be plausible that she was a casual friend who happened to linger longer than the other guests? Sure. Why not?

Alex opened the door to a young couple that Glory assumed were late callers who had come to pay their respects.

Her assumption was far off.

"Mr. Howard, I'm Detective Sergeant Tony Gerard and this is my partner, Detective Patricia Carney. I'm sorry, we thought you were alone, but we need to ask you a few questions." The sergeant's gaze went to Glory. He gave her a polite and apologetic nod for interrupting whatever it was they had interrupted.

Glory was relieved that he had given her an opening to leave. "No, it's okay," she said, grabbing her bag off the entrance hall table. "I was just leaving anyway."

Alex threw a hand up to stop her from leaving, then turned to Sgt. Gerard. "Can I ask what this is about? Will it take long?"

Glory didn't wait for the answer. "Take care, Alex," she said with polite formality. She nodded a quick good-bye to the two detectives and left, dying to know why they needed to question Alex.

"What can I do for you, Sergeant?" he asked, leading them into the kitchen. With a hand wave, he offered them each a chair, but he remained standing. "You do realize I just buried my sister this morning, don't you?" Alex heard the annoyance in his own voice, but didn't care.

"Yes, and I'm sorry, but we didn't know when you planned to return to New Jersey."

"I'm not sure myself," he said. "When I came here this weekend, who ever dreamed it would end like this?" His lips twisted to a sour scowl, as though he still refused to believe it had all happened. He shook his head dismissively, then turned to the sergeant. "So?"

"Okay, Mr. Howard," the sergeant began, "Let me tell you why we're here. We spoke again to your sister's night nurse, Josephine Britton. She's extremely distraught over this, but still insists that she remembers locking the bedroom door to prevent your sister from wandering out. And I'm inclined to believe her."

"Why?"

"Because she claims she had done it routinely, every night, once Paula was asleep."

"All the more reason to believe she might have neglected to lock it," Alex retaliated. "When you do something routinely, it's easy to think you already did it when in fact the picture is in your mind from doing it repeatedly in the past."

Sergeant Gerard's hand went to his mouth to wipe off the condescending grin he felt coming. "That's very intuitive, Mr. Howard, but although there's some merit to that theory, I still tend to believe Mrs. Britton. She's a good nurse with an excellent record and her mind is quick and sharp."

"And she's also a drunk!" Alex made no effort to shield his bitterness.

"That too is a troublesome issue. With much remorse and humiliation, Mrs. Britton admitted to us that she does 'spike up' her tea at night – her words, not mine – but swears with not more than a tablespoon or two. Says she's been doing it for years to help her relax at night. I'd hardly classify that as a drunk."

"That's arguable, I think, but what's your point? Where is this leading?"

"It's leading to a huge gray area. Assuming Mrs. Britton did lock the door. And she's pretty adamant about that." His shrug carried the implication that he had no reason not to believe her.

Alex leaned against the kitchen counter, his arms crossed defiantly. He didn't like the smell of this. He threw his gaze over to Detective Carney, but her blank expression was unreadable and she hadn't yet uttered a single word. Alex was several inches taller than Sergeant Gerard and peered down at him, waiting for him to continue.

"I understand, Mr. Howard, that you are an heir to your sister's fortune, which is substantial. Eleven or twelve million, correct?"

Alex had been controlling a slow simmer inside him, but it had begun to boil over. "What the hell is that supposed to mean?" His hands went up, palms out. "No, don't answer that. I don't want to hear it and I'll be damned if I'm going to stand here in my own house and listen to this crap."

"Your family's house, you mean."

Alex's face mirrored his anger. The veins in his forehead and neck were visible and pulsated with every word. "Yes, Sergeant, that's correct, but I've been solely responsible for the care of my sister and Ratherbee since her

Alzheimer's disease was diagnosed. And if you want to turn that into something more, so be it." His hands went out in a gesture of defeat.

"Hold it right there, Mr. Howard," Sergeant Gerard said. "Why don't you sit down and try to calm yourself. We're only here to clear up a few things. I'm sorry our presence upsets you."

"Well, can you blame me? I loved my sister, damn it, and I don't like your suggestions that her death was not accidental."

Detective Carney's cell phone rang and she seemed annoyed by the interruption, but stepped away into the entrance hall to take the call.

"Mr. Howard, let's back up here," the sergeant said. He made a sweeping wipe-the-slate clean motion on the table. "Why don't we start over? Again, I apologize for coming here today. We realize it's been hard on you coping with the shock of your sister's death and her funeral today. If we could have waited, we would have, believe me. And no one is pointing a finger at you, sir, understand that. But until we're completely satisfied that your sister's death was an accident, we're going to ask questions and hope we can depend on your cooperation."

Alex closed his eyes, steepled his fingers over his nose for a brief moment to calm himself. He had let too much anger escape and it would behoove him, he knew, to eat a little humble pie. He drew in a long and deep breath, allowing the anger to drain from his face, then threw his arms up in surrender. "Okay, sergeant. I apologize too. I know you're just doing your job, but as you said, I'm still trying to get past the shock of my sister's death and the guilt of sleeping through her escape from the house..." He paused to clear his throat and continued, "...then to be questioned and accused – "

Sergeant Gerard's hand went up this time. "No one is accusing you, Mr. Howard. Our questions are just part of the investigative process."

Detective Carney rejoined the scene. Alex gave her a quick study, tried to read her thoughts, but she remained silent, her face impassive.

"Okay," Alex said. He pulled out a kitchen chair and sat opposite them. "Ask your questions, Sergeant. I really didn't mean to be sharp with you, but I'm a little worn out and I need some time alone."

Tony Gerard threw his gaze to the door where Glory had left only minutes before, but made no comment.

Alex caught the sergeant's gesture but ignored it. His love life was none of the sergeant's damn business.

"Tell me about your sister, Allison. How long have the two of you been on no speaking terms and why?"

Alex's eyes darted sideways and locked with the sergeant's, who undoubtedly thought he already knew the answer, but wanted to hear Alex's interpretation.

Keep a lid on it, Alex, he told himself. *Stay calm and tell your story. It's time.*

Chapter 46

Frannie was doing laps in her pool when Glory drove up. Her arms sliced the water at a speed that made Glory do a double take. As soon as she opened her car door and felt the heat again, the water looked too good to resist. She ran inside, stripped out of her clothes, and pulled her bikini out of her dresser drawer.

The cold water was just what she needed to shock her body and relax her tense muscles. She had run away from that embarrassing situation as fast as her feet could carry her. At thirty-five years old and in this age of sexual freedom, she couldn't fathom why she should have been embarrassed, but was. After so many years of being married, it was tough adjusting to new attitudes.

Frannie was at the ladder climbing out when Glory dove in. She hadn't been in the pool for days and the sun was fierce today, with the temperature pushing ninety. She swam with her face in the water and came up feeling totally refreshed. Not only her body, but her conscience as well. As much as she had wanted intimacy with Alex, she still felt married to Jason. Not that he deserved a faithful wife.

When the detectives had arrived their presence had thrown that black cloud over Alex again. Without hearing what they had to say, she sensed that Sgt. Gerard already had a strong and unfavorable opinion about Alex. She had only caught that first look in his eyes, but that was enough.

Even if she had stayed and waited for them to leave, nothing would have happened between her and Alex. The detectives' appearance, with questions no doubt about his sister's death, had immediately smothered her sexual appetite.

She inhaled a deep and slow breath of the chlorine-scented water and shook the excess water from her hair, tucking the dripping strands behind her ears. She grabbed her sunglasses off the lounge where she'd left them and joined Frannie, who sat on the ledge of the pool with her feet in the water.

"So, how'd it go?" Frannie asked. "Stupid question, I know. What could be good about a funeral?"

"It wasn't bad, actually. Paula had no husband, no children, so there were no heartrending scenes."

"What about Alex and his other sister?"

Glory waved it off and made a hopeless-situation face. "They act like total strangers and never even sneaked a glance at each other. At least not that I noticed." She turned and looked at Frannie with concerned curiosity. "Did you ever hear what the story is between them?"

Frannie took a moment to consider the question and looked a little unsure herself. She stared at her feet kicking in the water while she tried to shape an honest answer. "We hear so much, sometimes you have to sort through it. That's why some people believe gossip is sinful. It can destroy people, especially those wrongfully accused."

Glory crossed her arms and peered at her with a smirk of satisfaction. "Excuse me? Isn't that what I've been preaching about you-know-who?"

Frannie smiled and gave Glory a conceding pat on the arm. "Yes, true, but gossip is often based on facts. Exaggerated maybe, but there are usually underlying seeds of truth."

Glory sliced the air with a swift hand wave. "No, I disagree. Not *usually*. Sometimes."

Out of Glory's line of vision, Frannie's eyes rolled upward. It looked like Alex was going to get thrown into all their conversations. If this pattern continued, Amore Evenings may never come to pass. Better to air it all out now, she thought, before we sign the contract. "Okay, she said, "Let's try to get this settled or sorted out. First of all, as far as the brother/sister relationship is concerned, it sounds to me like an advanced case of sibling rivalry. There's a big age difference and supposedly – "

Glory pointed a finger, but with a touch of humor. "Ah-ha! *Supposedly* being the key word here."

"Okay, smartass, but let me go on. *Supposedly* once she reached her teenage years – her father was already dead – Alex came down hard on her. He was stricter with her than her father had ever been and she fought him tooth and nail, defying him every chance she got. She told everyone who'd listen what a monster her brother was. She hated him and still does, probably."

Glory scrunched her face, a clear rejection of Frannie's explanation. "I can't buy that completely. Allison's been an independent adult for too many years. Alex had to let go a long time ago, I'm sure. I can't imagine that they'd still be so bitter now. All families go through those rough teenage years. I put plenty of gray hairs in my parents' heads too, but once you get past that, all that bad stuff is behind you. We grow up; mature. And maturity, thank God, is the great equalizer."

Frannie rubbed her fair skin with another coating of sunblock and took her time digesting her friend's argument. "You may be right. My sister and I used to fight like cats and dogs. We couldn't stand the sight of each other. But she's three years older. When she left for college, although I never admitted it, I missed her." A nostalgic smile took shape on Frannie's face. "Right after she finished college, she got married and moved to Vermont. That's when our relationship healed and strengthened. Now I talk to her on the phone often, but we only see each other two or three times a year. It's sad to think how many good years we wasted."

Glory felt a fleeting tinge of sympathy for Frannie, but at least she *had* a sister.

"So, see? That's my point exactly, Frannie. Doesn't it seem to be the norm that once siblings separate – get out from under the same roof – everything calms down? All the anger and jealousy dies and out comes the love."

Frannie couldn't hold back her laugh. "That sounds like song lyrics. 'Out comes the love.' So dramatic."

Glory saw the humor and laughed with her. "Yeah, listen to me. Like I'm an authority on the subject. Me, an only child. But seriously, I've seen enough through friends, haven't you? Especially during high school."

"Okay. So back to Allison Howard. That's all I can recall hearing. Nothing earth-shattering that would stay in my mind. And now that you put the bug in my head, I have to admit I'm inclined to agree with you. I doubt that sibling rivalry would leave such deep battle scars."

"So you agree with my instincts…that it had to be something pretty awful, right?"

Frannie pursed her lips and gave it more thought. "More or less," she said, "My money's on a connection between Allison and your friend Alex's dead wife."

Glory threw her head back, looked up and heaved a sigh. She wished she could solve the mystery behind Alex with facts rather than all this speculation.

Frannie paused to study Glory's face. "I'm sorry, Glory. I really am. I know how much you want me in your corner. And that's where I should be. We're friends. But I can see more objectively. I'm not – " She stopped herself; made a *forget-it* hand wave.

Glory persisted. "You're not what?"

"I'm not in love with the guy."

Exasperated, Glory made an impulsive dive back in the pool, but came up still hot on the topic. She mopped the hair off her face and went on. "Frannie, I am *not* in love with Alex. At least not that I'm aware of. He's just a friend who's fun to be with. You don't *know* him. How can you be so judgmental? Alex is a Class A gentleman. And yes, I will admit we do have a strong attraction to each other, but so what? Heaven knows his attention has done wonders for my morale."

"Oh, Glory, I wish I had a movie camera to catch your face on film. I never saw so much fire in anyone's eyes to defend a *friend.*" She crooked her two fingers to form imaginary quotation marks.

"Somebody has to defend him. It seems everybody's against him."

"Why? Did someone else warn you against him?"

"No. But two detectives paid him a visit today after everyone left. I was still there, but then I left too."

Frannie's interest piqued. "Why? What did they want?"

"I have no idea."

Frannie gave her a defeatist look. "Ah, damn, Glory. See what I mean?"

"No, see what *I* mean?"

Frannie picked up a white paper napkin from the basket on the table and waved it. "Truce? Can we talk about something else?"

Glory broke into a hearty laugh, then hugged her friend. "I know I give you a hard time. Please be patient with me. I'll work so hard to make Amore Evenings a success, I won't have time for Alex. Especially if my father lets me into his life."

"Nothing yet, huh?"

"Not even a message."

"Give him time, Glory. It's a rough spot to be in. He's stuck in the middle."

Glory's eyelids lowered. "I know. I can wait. As long as I know he's alive and he loves me, I'll be fine. It's just a little nerve-racking waiting to hear how his family reacts to the news."

"Well, looking on the bright side, we go to contract in three weeks."

That thought did lift Glory's spirits. Her smile widened. "I can't believe we're actually doing this. We have so much to look forward to, it makes me feel like something's sure to burst our bubble."

Glory shook her head to dismiss the ominous feeling. "Let's talk about Amore Evenings. That keeps us both smiling. We still haven't decided on the colors, the furniture, the mood of the place. I know all oceanfront restaurants go nautical, and although I like the feeling it creates, I'd like to add something new and different. Let's think..."

Frannie went inside the house and came back with the pile of food service trade books to pore over again. Here they had common ground. Their tastes were similar and whenever Glory was unsure, she left the decision to Frannie's expertise.

After fifteen minutes, she was so immersed in the business of Amore Evenings, that she totally forgot this morning's funeral and the conversation she'd just had with Frannie. Still, her eyes darted occasionally to the silent phone. No news from her father and no news from Alex. She'd been home an hour already. Why hadn't he called to tell her what those detectives questioned him about?

Her racing imagination threw out a vision of Alex being led out of Ratherbee in handcuffs. The thought chilled her but she chased it away and stayed focused on Amore Evenings.

Then, finally, the phone rang.

Chapter 47

The smile slipped off Glory's face at the sound of Alex's voice. Before she had found her father that voice was sure to ignite a small flame inside her, but now it was Dan Madison's voice she longed to hear. The fact that she couldn't contact him or try to steal a few moments with him at Perkins Cove made her desperation more agonizing.

"I thought you'd be glad to hear from me," Alex said, having heard her less-than-enthusiastic hello. "Considering where we left off."

That familiar flame snaked its way through her now. She gave him a nervous laugh. "Yes, actually we were lucky they came when they did. It could have been very embarrassing for both of us. But who knows, Alex? Everything happens for a reason. Maybe we were rushing into something too soon. We let our emotions get in the way of our thinking. I did say I wanted to keep it cool for a while, didn't I?"

Alex blew a defeated sigh into the phone. "You did," he said ruefully.

"Let's not get into that now, Alex. What's more important is why those detectives showed up on your doorstep today. Is it something you can talk about?"

"Basically, we pretty much went through some of the same Q's and A's we covered the night Paula died."

Glory paused, waiting for him to continue, but when he offered nothing more, she pressed on. "What do you think they're looking for?"

"Who knows? If Sergeant Gerard is to be believed, they're just rehashing routine questions they say must be addressed before a final report is issued declaring it an accidental death."

"Accidental instead of what?"

"Well, I'm sure you know the answer to that. Murder, of course."

Glory did know the answer when she had asked the question, but hearing it spoken aloud sent her stomach plummeting. "That's crazy, Alex. Who in the world would want to murder someone like Paula? She was as helpless as an innocent baby. What possible motive would a person have?"

"Money, what else? Isn't that supposed to be the root of all evil? People have been killing each other for money for centuries."

The next question got stuck in Glory's throat. The question and answer was so obvious, she didn't want to bring it up. An uncomfortable few seconds of silence elapsed, but that question hung between them like a collapsing bridge.

Alex made a weak attempt at levity. "Now, c'mon, Glory. Don't tell me you're thinking of me as the Big Bad Wolf too? I thought you could rise above all that gossip."

"That's not true at all, Alex. I'm just concerned about you, that's all. I'm assuming that you stand to inherit Paula's assets, not that I want to discuss it. That's strictly your business," she said. "And Allison's," she added.

"I think maybe we *should* discuss it, Glory. I'd much rather put my cards on the table and let you decide for yourself. You've been in my head day and night since we met. I'd hate to let it go any further then find out that you don't trust me. I've been through enough, Glory. I don't think I can handle it."

Glory just listened. She wished she could have cut in and yelled at him for even *thinking* she didn't trust him implicitly. But she couldn't. Because she didn't. Not implicitly. Yet she couldn't deny the feelings he stirred in her. She felt as though she were being pulled in a tug-of-war battle with her emotions, not knowing which way she'd fall.

"Glory, are you there?"

"I'm here, Alex. I was just thinking. Are you trying to tell me something?"

"Yes, I *am* trying to tell you something. I want you with me, any way you want it. But I don't want to lose you, Glory, especially now. Since we met, I feel like a new person. I have something to look forward to, to care about. Life became such a routine for me these past years, I didn't even realize what was missing. What do you say? Don't let me babble like this. And that's another thing – I never knew I could be such a talker till I met you!"

Glory laughed at that. "Guess I bring out the best in you," she said, then went serious again. "I am with you, Alex. But that road runs both ways. If you want me to trust you, you have to trust me. Maybe it's time for you to open up. Not now. Tomorrow. Before you leave for New Jersey because if we're moving in the direction I think we are, I need to hear it all. I need you to start with Elena, how she lived and how she died. And finish with Allison. I need to know why there's been so much poison in your family. And why it's all centered around you."

Chapter 48

Sara Baisley and Timothy Waite had a lot in common.

They had recently turned eighteen and had graduated from Wells High School this past June, where both had excelled scholastically and athletically. They also loved beer, adventure and each other. They both lived in a neighborhood where real estate begins at three million. Both sets of parents were civic-minded citizens, well-known and active in the community. The two couples, like their children, also had something in common. After feuding on personal and public issues for years, they finally settled down to a nice, comfortable hatred, with no need for further confrontations. Such a relationship between their parents became the catalyst for "hooking up" their children.

Their parents would be furious to know that Sara and Timothy had even befriended each other, much less become physically involved. This knowledge amused the two teens; it had become an exciting game to them to sneak into any dark corner, dangerously close to their homes, to satisfy their insatiable appetites for excitement.

But on Saturday night, the second of August, at approximately 11:30 at night, the fun had stopped dead.

Now, two days later, on a hot and sticky afternoon when they could have been at the beach having fun with their friends, they chose instead to ride their bikes and meet at the Jansen property, a favorite spot of theirs this summer. Bike riding had become a resurrected sport since they began seeing each other. Bikes were much easier to hide than their parents' cars. When they met at the Taggerts' property, they didn't even need bikes; it was a short walk for both.

Today was not a pleasure meeting, however. They had to decide what to do with their haunting piece of information.

Too jittery to sit, Sara stood up to pace. She burst into tears the moment she allowed eye contact. "I'm scared to death, Tim. We're on top of a cliff on this. However we fall, we're dead in the water."

Tim pulled her back down on the grass, where they were shielded by thick shrubs. He made a disagreeable face and stared ahead towards the ocean, deep in troubled thought. "It's not that bad, Sara. Don't go dramatic on me. Here's our choices. We can tell what we saw and face the consequences – which would be hell for both of us – or we can keep our mouths shut and hope the police will eventually get him."

"We don't know that it's a *him.*"

Tim rolled his eyes. "Or her. Whatever. My vote's on shutting up. I like my life just the way it is, and if you open your mouth everything will change. You can bet on that."

"You think I'm looking forward to their fury? I could be twenty-five, but according to them, as long as I'm under their roof, I have to live by their rules. I can just hear them!" She threw her head back and shook the image away. "We don't have to tell them what we were actually *doing,* but once they hear I climbed out my bedroom window to meet you while they were sleeping, that'll make them crazy enough." She stroked his face to make him meet her gaze. "Maybe we can sell them on the idea that this is just a budding romance. We're good friends who never did more than kiss."

Tim threw her an incredulous grin that broke into a laugh. "You've got to be kidding! They may be a little in the dark ages, but they're not that stupid."

"It's better than admitting the truth," she pleaded. "As long as we leave them a little room for doubt, they'll grab it and accept what we tell them because they'll *want* to accept it."

Tim didn't agree with her, but conceded that she had a point. He didn't answer, just plucked a blade of grass and chewed on it pensively. Then he looked her straight in the eye and lowered his voice just above a whisper. "I hate to say this, Sara, but let's be realistic. The old lady had Alzheimer's. She was half-dead anyway. Once your brain gets screwed up – "

Sara was horrified by his callous remark. She reacted with a punch to his arm. "My God. I can't believe you said that. Just because she had Alzheimer's doesn't mean she deserved to die."

"I never said she *deserved* to die. Don't put words in my mouth. All I said was her brain was already dead, unfortunately."

"Oh, so that means in this case murder is justified, huh? So we can go around killing all the mentally ill or diseased people because they're already partly dead? Is that what you're trying to say?"

Tim drew a breath through clenched teeth and neither answered nor looked at her.

Sara couldn't keep the sarcasm out of her voice. "No, come to think of it, I take that back. I think what you're trying to say is we should just let this one murderer get away with his crime because it would upset our lives for a while. Isn't that right?"

Tim had had enough. He stood up, grabbed his bike and raced off.

It wasn't till Sara watched him speed off that she realized she had gone too far. They were both extremely upset over what they saw and the ramifications that would surely follow their confession. She jumped on her bike and followed him, only seconds behind, but his legs were stronger and fueled by anger. She gave up, slowed down to a comfortable speed and pedaled her way home. Maybe if she gave him a few hours to cool off, she could call him on his cell phone and apologize.

She resolved to try to convince him calmly one more time. If he wouldn't budge, she'd just have to pray the police will eventually get the bastard without their help.

Chapter 49

The phone rang so soon after she'd hung up on Alex that Glory assumed it was him again. "Alex? Forget something?" she asked.

"No, sweetheart, it's not Alex. It's me."

Glory's heart soared. Finally, the call she had been waiting for. Breathless, she was afraid to ask her father the big question, but did. "Did you tell them?"

Dan's voice took on a deflated tone first, then rose to an optimistic level. "No, I never found the right moment. This won't be easy, Glory. But it'll happen. Count on it."

She couldn't cloak her disappointment and felt a little foolish when all she could say was "I know."

"I do have a plan, though. I'm just not sure it would be fair to Louise."

"Dad," she began. It still felt awkward to hear herself say that and it filled her with a sense of betrayal to the father she had loved. She blinked away the image of her deceased father's gentle face and went on. "Dad," she repeated, "the timing will never be right for what you have to tell them. It'll be a terrible shock, we both know that." She didn't add *but it has to be done,* but the words were implied and silently heeded by Dan.

"Here's what I was thinking. It might be the best way to handle it or it might blow up in my face."

She heard his sigh and understood his agony. Her love for him was already so strong she wished she could spare him the pain, but knew she didn't have the strength of character to be that unselfish.

"Sunday is my wife's birthday. All my children will be at the house. It's not easy for me to find an opportunity to gather them all together. They all have busy lives. So I thought – "

Without knowing her father's wife, Glory cringed. "You're going to tell your wife on her birthday? And at the same time you tell your children?"

"I know. I've been agonizing over that decision myself, but I want to do it in the privacy of our own home when the whole family is together. If I tell her first, there'll be no birthday celebration. I figured I'd wait till after the cake. It's the best I could come up with. No matter when and how I do it, it'll be tough."

Glory tried, but couldn't think of any way to soften the blow and make it easier for him, except to give him up totally. And that was a price she was not willing to pay. "I guess it is better that you just do it and get it over with as soon as possible. Let's face it, there'll never be a time when it'll be less shocking. And I'm sure this must be killing you, keeping it all in, knowing they have to be told eventually." She paused, hoping he'd say something that might ease her conscience, then said, "Dad, I'm *so* sorry I'm causing you this tremendous problem – "

"Glory, stop. Don't even think about apologizing. You are not a problem. You're an innocent victim in this. You just found out that I exist and that you have siblings. And now that I found you, I love you just as I love them. The feeling amazes me too, but it's probably a natural parental surge of love that hits you the moment your child is born. And Glory, as far as I'm concerned, you've just been born."

The lump in her throat sent tears to her eyes. Her voice broke up. Scratchy words flowed out. "You can't imagine what a relief it is for me to hear you say that, although it's bittersweet. I've been so afraid you might deny me, get angry for upsetting your life, and even though you've opened your heart to me, I'm still upsetting your life."

"Glory, please stop apologizing and please stop crying. It hurts me to hear you cry. I told you none of this is your fault. Somehow it'll all work out. Let's hang tough."

She sniffed away her sobs and felt a smile on her lips. *God, how she loved this man!* "Okay, Dad, I'm with you, whatever you decide."

"Good girl. And don't be concerned if you don't hear from me. I may not get a chance. It's funny, you don't realize how little privacy you have until you need it. But soon we won't have to sneak phone calls. I have a good feeling this will all work out. It would be a different story if you were conceived during my marriage, but you weren't, so I'm going to think positively and I want you to do the same, okay?"

Her heart swelled. "Okay, Dad. I promise I'll try."

When she hung up, she did try to look at it with her father's reasoning. Maybe after the initial shock and all the tears, it *will* be okay and they'd all welcome her into their family.

Sure. And maybe Santa Claus will slip down her chimney this Christmas.

Chapter 50

Alex wasn't sure he had made the right decision in spilling all that garbage he fed the detectives. Their faces were both devoid of expression as he told his story. He had no idea whatsoever if they believed him or not. He hoped so, but if not, the hell with them. Let them prove otherwise.

These were the hardened words he told himself as he left for his breakfast with Glory. He hadn't even left for New Jersey yet, and already he was trying to figure out how soon he could come back.

***

She looked so radiant when he pulled up in the driveway that he had to fight an urge to push her back into her apartment and carry her, Rhett Butler style, to her bedroom. Instead, he reached for her hands, kissed them ever-so-gently, then caressed her face with gentle fingers and brushed a kiss on her mouth.

"You look gorgeous," he said, stepping back to admire her. Glory wore an apple green sleeveless knit shirt that clung like skin and allowed that peak of navel just above her low-waist crop jeans. Sunlight behind her created a crown of gold through her silky chestnut-brown hair.

She took a quick glance down at herself and laughed. "Are you seeing something I missed? I'm wearing jeans and you say 'gorgeous'? I can't wait to get really dressed for you," she joked.

"Ah, hah! But it's what's inside them – *who's* inside them, that's gorgeous, not the jeans."

She waved away his flattery but inwardly she glowed and the warmth that ran through could not be blamed on the weather. For the moment, she had completely forgotten the shock and sadness of the past few days. But she had never known Paula Grant. Alex was a little too congenial for a man whose sister died so tragically only a few days ago.

She tucked the troublesome thought away and held her smile. "I have breakfast all ready, Alex. Come in and grab one of the trays for me, will you?"

He followed her in and together they carried out a tray of croissants and muffins, bran and corn, another filled with bite-sized pieces of watermelon and cantaloupe framed with strawberries and blueberries. A carafe of coffee and a pitcher of orange juice completed the picture on the patio table to whet their appetites for this summer morning breakfast.

"Are we expecting company?" he teased.

She laughed looking at the spread and realizing how much she'd overshot her target. "This is actually a light breakfast. No hot food. I guess I did get carried away on quantity."

"Well, I'm hungry. Let's give it our best shot," he said, pulling out two chairs.

"You can only stuff yourself for one hour, Alex. I want to get down to the restaurant by 8:30. The crowds really start pouring in at that time."

"You're pretty dedicated to Amore Breakfast already. Frannie is lucky to have you."

"No way. It's just the opposite. Without her, Amore Evenings would never be possible. At this stage, I'm not there every morning to help her. I'm there to *learn,* just as I didn't invite you for breakfast to watch you eat, but to *listen.* So start talking, Alex."

She bit into a plump strawberry and waited for him to speak.

He chose a croissant first and smeared it with cream cheese. "I don't know where to start."

"Start with whatever turned sour first and why."

"That would be my marriage. But if I get started on the why, an hour won't be enough," he said bitterly, then smiled. "Can I finish this first?"

"Sure. See how much you can wolf down in five minutes, then talk." She said it jokingly, but was dead serious and determined. To soften the impact of her words, she leaned her elbows on the table, bringing her face closer to his. "Seriously, Alex, I realize this makes me sound very forward, and ordinarily I'm not at all like that, but we do have a..." She paused to search for the right phrase. "*A growing relationship* might best describe where we are. You want me to trust you and I want the same thing, believe me. But first I have to know what you're all about." Her eyes searched for his understanding and she touched his hand with hers in another gesture of her support.

Alex poured them each some coffee and kept his eyes on his task. He drew a deep breath and threw his chest out as though he'd need a lot of air to fuel this story. "We had a good marriage for a while. At least the first year, I'd say. We had fun together, were sexually compatible – "

"You can stay out of the bedroom, Alex. I don't need to know that."

He acknowledged her comment with an understanding smile. "Gotcha," he said and continued. "We developed a relationship with a few couples at the country club here, played tennis, had dinner parties with them regularly, went out on each other's yachts...you know, all the fun stuff. It was great. I loved it too in the beginning."

"So what went wrong?" she asked, nibbling at the blueberries while she listened.

He shrugged. "I'm not sure. Boredom, I guess. After a while, when even the fun falls into a pattern, it becomes monotonous. At least it did for her. She started breaking away, looking for friends of her own. Girl stuff, she told me. I didn't mind at first until I realized she was spending more time with them than with me. Still, I closed my eyes, rationalized. After all, I had a business to run. My first drug store was right here in Ogunquit."

Glory raised her brows in surprise. "Really? You never mentioned that."

"I tried to skip over the 'Elena years' when we talked before. Anyway, it was doing very well, thankfully, not that I can credit myself entirely. My family had money and I was able to give it a good jump start and still had a nice cushion to fall back on. I was putting in a lot of hours, so being the nice guy I am..." He stopped for an effective pause, his tone implying not everyone would agree, including Glory. "I figured why shouldn't she enjoy herself with friends while I was busy?"

"She never helped out at the store?"

He made a face that told Glory her question was ludicrous, then laughed. "If you had known Elena, you'd see the humor in that too. She was definitely not the type to humble herself to stand behind a counter and handle a cash register. No way."

Glory had switched from blueberries to chunks of watermelon but her appetite craved substance. She cut a corn muffin in half, buttered both, and handed one to Alex. She took a healthy bite of her half and washed it down with coffee. "Okay, so she was a party person, a social animal." She shrugged. "That's not so terrible."

Alex waited to swallow his mouthful of corn muffin before he spoke. "It is if you're partying with drugs, alcohol and both sexes."

She stopped chewing and sat erect to look at him with questioning eyes. "I had a feeling Elena had someone else, but this is worse. Once drugs and alcohol are involved, it's got to be the pits."

"No doubt about it," he said.

Glory thought the bitter edge in his voice bordered on hatred.

"And let me correct your assumption. It wasn't 'someone else'; it was some *others,* male *and* female."

"Oh, Alex," she said ruefully, regretting that she had forced this out of him. But once he started pouring out the details, she didn't stop him or interrupt. He had a hell of a lot of poison to expunge.

Chapter 51

Alex called her from New Jersey that same night and again on Thursday night. He had hoped to make it back for the weekend but he had a mess of problems to iron out and couldn't manage to break away that soon. But he'd definitely make it back by the following Friday, he said. She missed him mostly when she spoke to him. One whispered "hello" was all it took to stir her up. Her imagination ran wild as they spoke but she kept their conversations light and chatty. At their breakfast Wednesday morning, he had given her a vivid picture of his life with Elena. They had never gotten around to Allison before they had to say their good-byes, and she hoped to bring the subject up again on his next visit.

Her life had become so busy, though, that she couldn't dwell on it. Their contract date was set for Wednesday, only days away, and Amore Breakfast was going hot and heavy with the summer season in full bloom.

On top of that, and most prevalent in Glory's mind, was what would happen in the Madison household when her father drops that bomb. *If* he drops that bomb, she thought. He could easily chicken out despite his best intentions. She smiled remembering her last two conversations with Alex. Before he left for New Jersey, after their serious talk about Elena, she was glad she had saved her good news for last. Just before he left, she told him about her father's phone call. He was thrilled for her. Now, in both nightly calls, he tried to gently prepare her for disappointment. "He may not get the courage or the opportunity to tell them," he said. "Or worse, they may want no part of you."

How sweet of him to be so sensitive to my feelings, she mused. "Don't worry about me, Alex," she'd told him.

"When it comes to worrying, I'm the champion. I'll never need any help worrying."

On that line, they both enjoyed a good laugh and hung up smiling and feeling good.

***

Frannie had a standing dinner-and-whatever appointment with three friends every Friday night. It was understood, though, that if some knight in shining armor happened to show up and capture the heart or attention of any one of them, she was free to cancel at the last minute. With her usual witty humor, Frannie told Glory that all four of them were still waiting for the chance to exercise that option.

Although Frannie invited Glory to join them, she reluctantly refused, knowing she'd probably miss a good time, judging by Frannie's stories. But somehow word got to Carl that Alex was back in New Jersey and Glory didn't need more than three seconds to figure out how. When he called her that afternoon, she didn't have the heart to refuse him. She *had* promised to have dinner with him sometime soon, and this would fulfill that obligation.

***

Carl Duca had missed his calling, according to Glory. Luckily, they were seated in a back corner of a dimly lit restaurant in Wells, a neighboring town. He had a flair for telling jokes and amusing true stories with a style that had her sides splitting. She was laughing so hard she could hardly talk.

"I don't believe you!" she said, wiping the laugh tears off her eyes. "Why the heck you chose construction instead of stand-up comedy is beyond me. Is construction your natural family calling?"

Carl sipped his wine and threw his gaze upward to think. "Construction *is* a family thing, yes, but natural, no."

She gave him a perplexed look.

"I mean it's not natural for me. I was a foster child."

"Foster! Really?" She giggled, embarrassed. When he and Mike were first introduced to her, she had remarked that they didn't look at all alike. "How long did you live with the Duca family?"

He slapped his pot belly. "Do I look like I ever left?"

"That's fabulous that you've had such a strong lifetime relationship, enough to put you in business with a foster brother. I guess you and Mike were always close."

Carl let a little laugh escape and his only response was a nod.

Glory gleaned an awful lot from his simple responses. She had no idea what had happened between them, but was sure that he and Mike were not as close as she had thought.

If at all.

Chapter 52

Four days had passed since Sara and Tim's argument. She was fuming over his stubbornness and stressed out holding that explosive secret all by herself. But he wouldn't talk to her, not since she laced into him last Tuesday. What he had said about Paula Grant being half-dead already when she died was technically true, but she cringed remembering his indifferent attitude about Paula's death. No matter what, the woman was still a live, human being, and no one had the right to kill her.

Tim had done plenty of soul-searching these past few days and eventually came to the same conclusions. At ten o'clock on Saturday morning, he called Sara on her cell phone, knowing she'd still be sleeping.

"It's me," he said when he heard her groggy voice. "We need to talk. I didn't mean what I said exactly the way it sounded. And the bottom line is you're right. No one has the right to kill someone else, except in war or self-defense."

Sara sat up in bed, wide awake now. "So does this mean you'll go along with my plan? We'll tell them but just edit our story a little."

"Pretty much. But we have to fine-tune the details and get them absolutely straight. In case they question us separately, we have to be sure we're on the same track."

"I can't disagree with that. So now what?"

"So now we get together and figure it out. Did you make any plans for today?"

"I told the girls I'd go to the beach with them, depending on how the weather looked. The TV said chance of afternoon showers. Actually I was hoping we wouldn't get rained out because I figured you might go with the guys later. I missed you, Tim."

"Me too. Bad," he said, his voice just as contrite as hers. "But right now the sky's just hazy. Let's plan to meet there. It's easier and safer to be out with our friends. You won't have to invent cover stories for your parents."

"And what if it rains between now and then? We're planning to go about one o'clock."

Tim thought about that. He didn't have a Plan B ready. "It won't rain," he said confidently. "Why are we worried about a chance of rain anyway when we're trying to catch a killer?"

Sara laughed at his logic. "I hope it helps in some way. It's not as if we can make a positive identification of the killer."

"But at least they'll be thinking *murder,* not accidental drowning."

"True."

***

By noon, the sun broke through the hazy sky and stayed put all afternoon. They played volleyball on the sand with their friends, cooled off in the salty surf, ate hot dogs and fries from one of the concession stands and eventually broke away from the others to walk along the shoreline, which they did under normal circumstances. Today their walk on the beach had a much stronger purpose. Today they weren't simply two teens giddy and glowing with the incomparable feelings of first love. Not, not at all. As soon as they had walked a safe distance away from their crowd, they chose a spot that looked fairly private and sat on the sand. Their eyes locked for just a moment and a second later they were lying down, wrapped in each other's arms. Their kisses had a special urgency today. The sweetness of young love reunited, but burdened by the weight of their consciences and the knowledge of what troubles awaited them.

"This better be worth it," Tim said when they finally broke apart and sat up.

"What?" she asked, making a futile attempt to shake the sand out of her hair. Still wet from the ocean, their bodies were caked with sand.

Tim laughed. "What? How can you say *what?* I'm talking about this noble act we're about to perform. The one that may not be of any help to the police, but will certainly make a hell of a lot of trouble for us." He threw his hands out and smirked. The gesture and facial expression conveyed his reluctant acceptance to do it anyway and hope for the best. "Okay. I've been working on this all day. I think I've come up with a simple, believable story. Tell me what you think.

"First, let's not tell them we've been meeting secretly for almost two months. It'll be tough for them to swallow that we've been behaving like two little angels in all that time. Let's say we saw each other a couple of times a week, with our friends, but just started to meet alone, say, once a week for the last three weeks."

Sara considered that a moment and nodded. "Sounds good. Actually we had met alone more than three times before we got involved so it is believable."

"As far as our meeting place is concerned," Tim went on, "let's say we always meet on your neighbors' property, the Taggerts, because it's easier for you to get to. No sense revealing our other spots. We need to keep them secret so our parents won't be patrolling them every time we're out of their sight."

Sara made a face that nixed that possibility, almost disappointed. "I doubt my parents would take the time out of their busy social lives to hunt me down."

Tim disagreed. "They would if they knew you were meeting the son of their arch-enemies."

Sara laughed, jabbed a finger in the air. "Point taken." She furrowed her brows in thought, then asked, "Did you think of a way to eliminate the window, Tim? How about if we say that night was the first time we met at night, in the dark? Like you said, I don't want to blow our chances for the future if we come out of this alive."

"Well, you're the one who said it would be impossible for you to get past them using the front or side door. And certainly not the sliding doors out back, you said, remember? That's how we decided on the window."

Her finger was on her lips now while her mind searched for something workable. "Look, how's this: We'll say you were going to wait one hour, between eleven and twelve. If I didn't show, you'd know I couldn't sneak out. But since they both usually went to bed early and watched TV in their rooms, I decided to chance it that one night, hoping they wouldn't hear me with the TV on or, better yet, that they were in a sound sleep."

Tim digested her idea. "Sounds okay to me for a one-time only try. Too chancy for a regular basis, so they might believe we only met that one night. Let's go with it."

"Fine. I wouldn't want them nailing down my window."

They both laughed, but both were aware that neither of them found this amusing. They were just trying their hardest to get through it.

"Okay, so we covered when, where and how we'd been meeting for three weeks only in the daytime and how we met the night Paula Grant drowned. Next we work on what we saw and how."

"Well, at that point we can just tell the truth, right? Eliminating what we were actually doing, of course."

Tim's eyes squinted with a troublesome thought. "Not exactly. I have one kink to work out and in order to do that, I'll have to sneak back there to check it out."

"What kink?"

"Position," Tim answered. "We were lying down on the grass. What we witnessed we saw through the bottom of the hedges. If we were sitting up, we might not have seen anything. The hedges from that position would have been too thick for us to see through, I think. But I'll check it out again."

Sara took a deep breath to think that one over. "So we were lying down. We were scared someone from somewhere might see us, so we lay down on the grass, just as an extra precaution."

Tim had to laugh. It sounded ridiculous in a way. "And we were just talking, I suppose?"

"No. We were kissing. What eighteen-year-old has never been kissed? In *any* generation? I'm not going to sweat the small stuff. I have no problem admitting to kissing, even with the son of Rachel and Gregory Waite!"

"So, we were down on the grass kissing. And?"

"And the reason we didn't come forward at first—"

"Is because of our parents. Which is the truth, right?"

"Right. Okay. Let's wait till I check out those hedges. If we can, I'd feel better saying we were sitting up talking, which we might have been doing if we had just met there. Then Monday we'll go talk to the police."

Sara clenched her teeth. "Oh, God, Tim. Talking is easy, but the doing is going to scare me to death."

Tim hugged her although he was scared himself. He was afraid of his father's wrath. And *her* father's wrath. But he had to put on a courageous front for Sara. "Don't be scared. What we're doing is the right thing. You're the one who convinced me. It'll all work out."

Neither one felt confident about that, but they both fell back down on the sand again and let their love for each other push aside their fears.

Chapter 53

Glory stayed glued to the house all Sunday afternoon and evening waiting for that most important call. She was a bundle of nerves and had already warned Stacy and Alex not to call her that day or night. Although she had call-waiting, she didn't want her hopes to soar at the sound of the phone only to be deflated not to hear her father's voice.

By 10:30 that night, she was sitting up in bed, crying her eyes out and feeling very sorry for herself. Her sky had fallen. It probably all blew up in his face. Most likely, the whole scene had been so bad that calling her had been impossible.

Glory threw the blanket off and got out of bed. Why even try? There was no way she was going to get any sleep tonight, so she poured herself a glass of wine and took it outside on her patio where she could talk to God and His ocean. The setting did relax her body somewhat, but her mind continued to race. Involuntary tears still stained her face.

Maybe some unforeseen incident occurred that destroyed his chance to speak to them, she mused hopefully. Something as simple as unexpected company, friends or neighbors Louise might have invited to stop by for some birthday cake. She sniffed away her sobs and considered that possibility. If that were the case, it would be disappointing, but not to be compared with her first instincts.

She had no idea how long she had been there, lying on the lounge, hoping the mesmerizing sounds of the surf would lull her to sleep. The creaky, banging sound of an aluminum door closing broke the silence. Glory bolted upright and turned her head to see Frannie coming down her back steps.

Finding herself on the lounge in daylight confused her for the moment. "Don't tell me I slept out here all night!" she said. "What time is it anyway?"

"Almost 6:30."

Frannie got close enough for Glory to get a good look at her face. That brought her to her feet. "Are you all right? What's wrong?"

Frannie's watery eyes glistened in the sunlight. The corners of her mouth quivered.

Glory felt a sickening surge of panic. "Oh, my God, Frannie. What *is* it? What's wrong?"

Frannie hugged her friend first to brace her for the news she dreaded telling. "I had just come out of the shower when something on the TV caught my attention. The local newscaster was saying something about an accident last night on Route 1. Three vehicles involved; a truck, an SUV and a motorcycle."

Glory's eyes widened with fear.

Frannie could no longer hold back her sobs. Her words spilled out in tears. "They identified the driver of the motorcycle. Dan Madison."

Glory collapsed in her arms.

Chapter 54

Glory was breathless when she got to the hospital reception desk and had to wait her turn. The drive had seemed to take forever, not knowing the severity of his injuries – if he was even still alive.

The elderly volunteer worker, whose name tag said simply "Elsa," gave her a broad smile boasting perfect dentures that brightened her face. But Elsa's furrowed brows grabbed Glory's attention next when she gave her the name, Dan Madison. *He's dead,* was her immediate reaction. *He's not listed because he never made it here alive.*

The woman's face relaxed into a satisfied smile. "Oh, here it is," she said, finding his name on the computer. "I'm afraid Mr. Madison is in recovery." Her smile disappeared, replaced by sympathetic concern. "Are you immediate family? You can wait with the others in the family waiting room."

The frustration of not being able to say yes to that question brought a fresh flow of tears. Elsa thought she understood Glory's pain and came around the desk to comfort her. She grabbed the box of tissues and led her to a dark corner of the reception waiting room, leaving the front desk to a co-worker.

Embarrassed but touched by the older woman's compassion, Glory blew her nose and apologized for her outburst. Before she realized what she was doing, she had blurted out a quick explanation of her relationship to Dan Madison and his family.

"I'm sorry," Glory said, forcing a smile. "You must think I'm a lunatic dumping all that on you. But as you can imagine, I need a friend in the hospital. How else can I find out how he is?"

Elsa patted her shoulder. "Don't worry. After listening to that sad story, how can I refuse you? Give me a little time and I'll see what I can do," she whispered. "You stay here and wait. Can I get you coffee or water, maybe?"

Glory looked at this woman as though she had found her guardian angel. "You're so kind, Elsa. I don't want to trouble you."

"One cup of coffee is no big deal," she said. "How do you take it?"

***

She sat in the quiet corner by herself sick with worry. She tried to distract her thoughts by looking through a Time magazine, but she couldn't concentrate. After forty minutes, she stopped at the reception desk again to tell Elsa she'd be in the chapel, just in case she had any news.

Ten minutes later, Elsa came in with a young doctor. She introduced him as Dr. Mark Seidel, a third-year resident. He sat in the pew with her after Elsa left to man the reception desk again.

"Elsa confided in me, Miss English. I hope you don't mind. She probably felt, and rightfully so, that if she didn't tell me that story, I wouldn't be here."

"Do you know how my father is, Dr. Seidel?"

"Yes, I examined him in the Emergency Room. His injuries were serious. A CAT scan revealed a subdural hematoma in his head. A blood clot. And don't ask me why his helmet didn't prevent that from happening, but it obviously wasn't secured properly because it went flying off his head.

"Anyway, we had to perform surgery to relieve pressure on the brain. And, of course, we'll keep a close eye on him for the next few days."

"Wasn't the surgery successful, Doctor? I sense a warning in your tone."

"Yes, as far as we can tell at this point, his chances for a full recovery are good."

Relief washed over Glory's face. "Oh, thank God."

"But we have to watch for certain neurological changes that could occur when he wakes up."

"Like what?"

"Like confusion, slurred speech…a number of changes, perhaps, but let's not concern ourselves with that now. He may come out of this perfectly fine, so why anticipate trouble? If and when it shows up, we'll deal with it, okay?"

"Could I possibly see him, Doctor? Of course, I'd wait until his family leaves."

The doctor made a doubtful face that answered her question before he spoke. "There are four of them here now. I don't think any of them plan to leave anytime soon. Even if they slip out for a break, or go to the cafeteria, I'm sure one will stay on the floor to be near him."

Glory nodded. She understood her chances of seeing her father were slim to none. "Well, just in case there's an opportunity, I'll be here."

"Sure," he said kindly and excused himself.

Glory sat alone in the tranquil silence of the chapel. She couldn't remember when she had last prayed. Oh, she'd call out to God occasionally, please this, please that, but always as she went about her business. But now she found herself really praying. All the memorized prayers she learned as a child came back to her…Our Father, who art in heaven…

The sound of the chapel door opening startled her. Her head automatically turned towards that sound. Three women walked in; one she recognized immediately as Dan's daughter, the one she had seen on the dock at Perkins Cove. Glory's heart raced.

Just as they were slipping quietly into a pew, the older woman took a double take at Glory's face. "You're Glory English, the food columnist, aren't you?"

"Yes." *What a time to be recognized,* Glory thought. How could she have a casual conversation with this family?

Louise Madison studied Glory's face a few silent seconds. "Then you're my husband's daughter. These are our daughters," she said, putting the emphasis on *our.*

Glory felt as though she had been punched in the chest. "He told you," she said.

"He told us," Louise acknowledged with an icy voice while her two daughters stared at Glory with contempt, the older far more than the younger.

All three looked at her as though she were the "other woman" rather than the "other daughter."

"And if he *hadn't* told us, he wouldn't be in this hospital fighting for his life!"

These angry words came from Vanessa, the older daughter, not that Louise had offered their names.

"What do you mean 'fighting for his life'? Dr. Seidel said – "

Louise interrupted. "We know what Dr. Seidel said. What Vanessa means is that anything can happen."

Louise's voice was calm but effective. Glory recognized the suppressed anger and interpreted the unsaid words. *And it's all your fault.* Her mind visualized what had probably happened. It was undoubtedly awful, all of them angered by the shock. Her father probably couldn't handle it and stormed out to cool off alone. By motorcycle.

They were all still standing, including Glory. She looked at them in one agonizing glance, her eyes pleading for understanding and acceptance. But their eyes were cold, their lips tightened. Only in Amy, whose adoration for their father she had witnessed at Perkins Cove, appeared to have a touch of a guarded something. In that fleeting moment she couldn't identify what it was, but maybe she too felt this involuntary surge of love for the half-sister she had never known. Glory knew in that instant that if she hoped for the slightest chance of reserved acceptance, Amy would be the first to open her arms.

And she hadn't even met Todd yet.

"I'm sorry. I'm *so* sorry," she mumbled and rushed out to the parking lot where she could pull herself together in the privacy of her car.

Twenty minutes later, Amy came out, lit a cigarette, and spotted her.

Chapter 55

Sara and Tim had opted to put off telling their parents the edited version of that night. They concluded there was a remote chance the police would reject their statements as vague and inconclusive, thereby eliminating the need to confess to their parents. They both anticipated that once they heard they had been meeting each other secretly, the news that Paula Grant had been murdered would take second place.

Yes, they were both eighteen and not legally bound to involve them, but eventually they'd find out. With an investigation going on about the death of a lifetime Ogunquit resident, there would be no chance of keeping a lid on it, particularly since it involved another member of the Howard family. Surely it would resurrect the questionable death of Elena Howard, Alex's wife.

And so, on Monday morning, eight days after Paula Grant's drowning, Sara and Tim approached the Ogunquit Police Station on Cottage Street with much trepidation. Both had shaky stomachs and tongues thick and dry as cotton.

Something else in common.

"We called the State Police barracks and spoke to Sergeant Gerard," Tim told the dispatcher. He cleared his throat to help his voice sound stronger, less frightened. "He told us to meet him here."

Before the dispatcher had a chance to respond, Sergeant Gerard came up from behind them. He introduced himself with a handshake to both, and led them inside a conference room. Now that they had reached this point of no return, Tim's attempt to mask his fear was futile.

Sara kept rubbing her fingers and hands as though they were arthritic.

Detective Carney dragged a folding chair and sat alongside the teens rather than give them another face of authority to squirm under. She introduced herself with the warmest, friendliest smile she could manage. "Relax, kids," she said. "Sergeant Gerard may look tough, but he's a softie and loves kids. As long as they stay on the right side of the law."

Seated in a swivel chair behind a small and worn metal desk, Tony Gerard stretched back, laced his fingers together behind his head, and matched his partner's wide smile. "Yeah, she's right about me, but what she didn't say is *she's* the one to watch out for. Don't let her size fool you."

Tim and Sara understood that the banter was intentional, designed to ease them into telling their story as completely and truthfully as possible, but it worked anyway. One easy smile and Sergeant Gerard transformed from the stereotyped hard-boiled detective who could read your mind into an ordinary "my favorite uncle" type person.

"Want something to drink?" he offered. "Coke? Sprite? Bottled water?"

They both nodded, eager to quench the thirst their fears had triggered. Detective Carney stepped out and returned seconds later with two Cokes.

After his brief phone conversation with Tim, Tony Gerard had decided to waive an SOP rule. Standard operating procedure would require that the youngsters be interviewed separately so as to avoid the possibility of contamination or influencing each other's statements. But sometimes rules backfire. Seeing the two frightened faces and the way Sara had clung to Tim for dear life sent Tony different vibes. Something told him separation might freeze them silent or at least cause them to hold back information. Together he could relax them and study their reactions to each other's comments.

"Okay," the sergeant said. "So before you begin, I want you both to keep in mind that you're not here to confess a crime. Your message said you have information that might be helpful about Paula Grant's drowning. That puts you on our side, so there's nothing to be afraid of. Just tell us what you know."

Sara and Tim exchanged a look that questioned who would speak first. Sara nodded and gestured with a hand wave that she'd gladly allow him the lead.

Tim began talking with a downward gaze, avoiding eye contact. "Well, first of all, Sergeant, it's not that simple. Yes, we are on the same side of the law. We had nothing to do with Mrs. Grant's death, but we should have spoken to you sooner. We know that."

Detective Carney cut in. "But you're here now, so forget it. We understand how frightening this can be to anyone at any age." She nodded for Tim to continue, but Sara interrupted.

"It wasn't the fear of talking to you," she said, swinging her finger to cover both detectives. "We were mostly afraid of our parents finding out we were together in the first place."

Tony Gerard lifted a curious brow. "Why?"

Again Tim shot a look over at Sara that asked *Why don't you tell them? I don't want to get into that.*

"Well, to make a long story short, Sergeant, our parents can't stand each other – this has been going on for years. They'd never allow us to be friends."

"How do you know that?" Patricia Carney asked.

"Trust me. I know," Sara quickly answered while Tim underscored her comment with a sour smirk.

"Okay, but you both came here in spite of that. That took guts. Your parents should be proud of you. I get the impression you're both decent, responsible kids. Tell us what you know and Detective Carney and I will do our best to make it easy for you."

Tim took a deep breath and blew it out fast. "Paula Grant didn't fall into the ocean and drown on her own. We think someone pushed her in."

Both detectives were silent, not wanting to interrupt Tim, but both reacted physically as though someone had plugged them in. Their bodies and faces were suddenly less relaxed and more attentive. Foul play had not been ruled out of their investigation and when Tim and Sara had called the State Police this morning, this is what they had hoped to hear.

"It was about 11:30 that night. Sara had sneaked out to be with me. We meet sometimes at the Taggerts' property, so I guess you can get us for that too...trespassing," he said ruefully. "But they're away all summer anyway and we didn't go there to vandalize, just to meet. It's close enough not to get caught."

Tony Gerard struggled to keep the smile off his face. Memories of his own youth surfaced. "How did you get in?"

"There's a break in the fence," Tim mumbled.

"Okay. So tell us where you were exactly, what you were doing and what you saw. Nice and easy now. Don't leave anything out even if you think it's insignificant. Very often it's those tiny details witnesses omit that hold the key to solving the crime."

Tim had a vivid memory of what they were doing at the time and couldn't imagine how that knowledge could help them solve this crime, so he swallowed hard and hoped his guilt didn't show up on his face.

"We were on the northwest side of the property, lying down on the grass, kissing. Just kissing." Tim realized he shouldn't have repeated it. It was probably a dead giveaway; an admission of guilt.

Sergeant Gerard's face remained impassive but from the corner of his eye he caught the suggestion of a knowing smile on his partner's face. Apparently she too had surfacing memories.

"Anyway," Tim continued, "at the bottom of the hedges the leaves are sparse. You know what I mean, they thicken as they grow up." He unconsciously illustrated their shape with his hands.

"If we had been sitting up, we might never have seen it," Sara threw in, wishing that were the case.

"It was dark where they were, but I caught a flash of white, something flapping in the wind. It was probably Paula Grant's nightgown."

"What makes you think that? Would you know her by sight?"

"Yeah, pretty much. My parents used to invite her to their house parties before she got sick. And she was pretty active in the community, so her face got around."

"But you couldn't say for sure it was her you had seen that night?"

"Well, no, but I saw somebody, and the next day, once we heard – "

Sergeant Gerard stopped him with a hand wave. "No, forget the next day for now. Let's stick to that night and what you saw."

"Okay. Like I said, the first thing we saw was that white something flapping in the wind. We took a closer look. It was definitely a person, but it was pitch black there, so we couldn't say who. Then we spotted this other person, all in black – at least it looked black. All we could make out was the movement of another body. My first instinct was to laugh. I figured maybe Paula Grant's nurse had a boyfriend coming to visit once the old lady fell asleep. But Sara got panicky. She was afraid they might see or hear us. Or see *us* see *them* and give us more trouble. So while they were walking towards the ocean with their backs turned, we took off."

"And you never saw the faces of either one?" Sergeant Gerard asked, looking at both of them.

"Not really," Tim said, wishing they had something more conclusive to offer.

Tony Gerard took a pensive moment, just looked at Tim who never lifted his gaze. "Tim, you just said 'not really'; you're not sounding completely sure. Is there something else you can tell me or do you remember anything more?"

Tim shrugged, then made eye contact. "What I mean is I can't say I got a good enough look to identify anyone."

"How about hair?" Detective Carney asked. "Did you notice any particular shades? Black, white, blond?"

"The woman in the nightgown had light hair, yes," Tim said. "Could have been blond or white. I'm not sure."

Both detectives' eyes moved hopefully to Sara, who shrugged. "I can't remember either. Except that it was definitely light and short."

"Let's get back to the other person; the one in black. Describe that person to us to the best of your recollection. First you, Tim, then you, Sara."

Tim looked upward, then narrowed his eyes in concentration. "This is so hard. Trying to figure out what you saw as opposed to what you *think* you saw."

"Don't try to figure it out. Just go with your first instinct. That's usually where the truth lies anyway."

Tim went palms up as if to hold off all interfering visuals and stick with his first recollection, as the sergeant instructed.

"Okay. As far as I can recall, this guy was all in black. He definitely wore pants because I could make out legs in motion. It could have been a woman in slacks, I suppose, but if I had to guess by body language, I'd say man. From the waist up all I can still see in my mind is black, except for his hands. I did see him take her hand first, then her upper arm as they walked toward the ocean."

"Did the woman appear to resist?"

"Not at all. She seemed perfectly relaxed, like she was just going for a stroll."

Tony Gerard wheeled back his chair to pour two cups of freshly brewed coffee. He handed one to Pat Carney, but never took his eyes off Tim. "Did the man appear to be pulling her along?"

Tim paused, closed his eyes to search his memory. "Maybe 'led her' would better describe it."

"And you never saw his face?" Detective Carney asked.

Tim shrugged and lifted his brows. "Seems funny, I know, but I guess my eyes were focused on her. That white nightgown flowing in the wind grabbed my attention first."

"How about you, Sara?" the sergeant asked, putting his coffee aside to cool.

She waved off his question. "You can't go by me, Sergeant. My memory is a little different, but I have a weird imagination."

Sara could see at a glance that neither detective was going to settle for that. They both waited for an answer. She gave them a you-asked-for-it look first, then said, "I do remember eyes. Not that I could actually see eyes, we were too far away, but let's say two circles of light against a black head. So I'm thinking ski mask."

The two detectives locked eyes. Sergeant Gerard continued. "So, Sara, other than that, is there anything else you remember that hasn't yet been mentioned here?"

"I could have sworn I heard a mournful cry seconds later, but I took off for home like a mouse in flight and left Tim to do the same. Tim said what I heard was probably an animal and maybe he's right. My heart was beating so fast it sounded like war drums. I could never say for sure what else I heard."

Sergeant Gerard let a long moment of silence pass while he sipped his coffee thoughtfully.

Chapter 56

Glory felt a little awkward sitting alone in her car and being watched. She didn't actually see Amy look at her, but this young beauty was certainly stealing glances while she puffed away on her cigarette. With her head leaning on the headrest, Glory closed her eyes, pretended to be catnapping, but she too was watching, observing, through slitted eyes.

She sat right up when Amy crushed out her cigarette and walked over. "Mind if I join you?" she asked.

Her face was naturally beautiful; her skin peachy and smooth, framed by long, straight hair, pure silk. Her eyes were a shade of brown she couldn't quite define, but somewhere between milk chocolate and brown sugar. The good Lord, with a little help from an orthodontist probably, had blessed her with perfect teeth resulting in a radiant smile. All told, a striking combination.

But her breath smelled of tobacco. Still, that long dormant craving came back strong to Glory. If there ever was a time she needed a smoke, it was now. She popped the door lock and Amy slid in. Glory was too stunned to speak and waited for Amy to break the ice.

"I feel for you too, Glory – okay if I call you by your first name?"

Glory gave her an are-you-kidding look which waived the formalities.

A slight smile came and went on Amy's lips. "Okay, then, what I started to say is I feel for you. I wouldn't want to be in your shoes." She laughed a little. "Four against one is tough."

Glory wanted to say she hadn't realized they were engaged in battle or even in competition. She also wanted to say their father was also on her side, but didn't dare. Besides, he wasn't really; he was more like stuck in neutral.

She waited for three or four thumping heartbeats more, then turned to Amy with strange sensations stirring through her. Involuntarily, her expression humbled and her voice came out soft and contrite. "Look, Amy – your dad told me your names – " *Not your dad, our dad,* she thought. "We've all been through a tremendous shock. Until a few years ago, I had a father I adored. It wasn't easy for me to learn that he and my mother had harbored this secret all my life, leaving me to find out after they both were gone. I think anyone in my position would have done as I did, look for my real father. Don't you think if the situation were reversed, you would have done the same?"

Amy just looked at her in the darkness. The lights in the parking lot cast a glow over Glory's face. "I guess so," she answered finally, but not convincingly.

"Amy, it's not as if he had an affair while he was married to your mother."

"That's what my dad said," Amy threw in. "But your mother should have told him she was pregnant. I'm glad she didn't, though. I wouldn't be here."

"By the time she knew, it was over, or at least the handwriting was on the wall. She didn't want to force him into marriage."

"She could have told him and let him make that choice."

Glory shrugged as if to say *Maybe so, but she didn't, and we can't change that.*

"I'm just saying that objectively. But as I said, I'm glad it worked out the way it did. My whole family would be nonexistent if it hadn't." She released another nervous laugh.

"I know everyone's wounds are raw right now, Amy, but do you think there's a chance for me?" An unexpected sob lodged in her throat, causing her voice to crackle. "I was never aware I missed having siblings until I knew I had them." She switched her gaze from her half-sister to the driver's side window in a futile attempt to hide her teary eyes. Amy tapped her lightly on the shoulder. When Glory turned to face her, Amy's glazed eyes mirrored her own. In an impulsive hug, they both let loose their tears.

"I can't speak for the others, Glory, but I'm sure willing to try."

"Do you think they'll come around eventually?"

Amy played with the ring on her finger, giving serious thought to the question. "It's too early to tell. I think inwardly they all understand your need to find your father and our father's reaction to a daughter he never knew he had. Can't blame him. After all, you *are* his flesh and blood too." She pursed her lips and paused, searching for descriptive words. "It's sort of like we were all having a great time at a summer picnic; a fun family thing complete with blue skies and sunshine. Then suddenly, out of nowhere, black clouds open up and it rains like hell. There goes our happy family picnic."

Glory's "Oh, God," was barely audible.

Amy opened the car door. "I'm going back in to see if my father's out of recovery yet," she said, then added, "I'm sorry, *our* father."

That brought a smile back to Glory's face. "Wait for me," she answered.

Chapter 57

It killed Glory to stay back knowing Dan Madison was her father too, but she understood their pain and hadn't wanted to make matters worse by defiantly presenting herself as a true-blue family member. Elsa was nowhere in sight, so Glory went back to the chapel where she would welcome the solitude. She'd been talking to God a lot these past months, but more often in anger than prayer. When the anger had finally ebbed and she'd accepted that Jason was never coming back, she made her peace with God as well.

Elsa came in twenty minutes later with a long, sad face.

"Nothing, huh?" Glory asked. Her voice was weak. She couldn't keep her eyes open, but she had hoped they'd all go home and she could get to see him, if only for a minute or two.

"The children want to take their mother home but she won't budge. She wants to wait at least till he comes out of recovery and they settle him in a room." Elsa held Glory's hand. "Look, I'm leaving now. I'll be here again at ten in the morning. Why don't you come back then? Your father's condition is serious, but not critical. I have an idea that might help you get in to see him," she said with a confident smile.

Glory perked up, then wrinkled her brows with concern. "I don't want you to get in trouble, Elsa."

Elsa threw her hands up and laughed. "I'm a volunteer. What can they do, fire me?"

Glory laughed with her. The woman's lovable personality was like finding a pot belly stove in a snowstorm. "Okay. I'll be here."

***

She had gone home without seeing him, but as long as he was pretty much out of danger, she felt better, although totally drained, mentally and physically. Without even brushing her teeth or washing her face, she had fallen into bed and slept through a dreamless night until 7:00 a.m. when the phone rang.

Oh, dear God! Something happened. Don't let him be dead.

She exhaled a long sigh when she heard Frannie's voice with the familiar background sounds of Amore Breakfast's busy kitchen.

"I'm sorry to wake you, Glory. I don't know what time you got home last night, but I was worried. Tell me, how is he?" Frannie asked, afraid to hear the answer.

"They say he'll be okay. They have to watch him a few days." She went on to explain about the blood clot and emergency surgery followed by a condensed version of her brief exchange with his family.

"Give them time, Glory. They'll come around. At least Amy is trying to accept you."

"If they let her," she said, then heard Frannie's name being called. "Go. You're too busy. We'll talk later. I'm going back at ten. I found this little angel of a volunteer worker who thinks she can get me in to see him when the others are not there. I don't know what she has up her sleeve, but I hope it works." She paused, then asked, "Do you want me to come in? I can probably help for an hour, at best." The moment she asked the question she cringed, anticipating Frannie's reaction.

"Are you crazy? What the hell do you think I'm made of, ice? Get your ass over to the hospital and make sure you call me later to let me know what's going on."

Glory deepened her voice playfully. "Yes, boss."

"Yes, *partner,*" Frannie corrected.

After a long, stressful day waiting for the call from her father that never came and later, the shocking news of his accident, Glory was surprised to feel herself smiling. She had to look at the bright side. Maybe God was listening last night. He'd sent his angels in the forms of Elsa and Amy. Now, waking up to hear Frannie's supportive and caring voice was another way of making His presence known.

But she needed to hear one more caring voice. And since she had told Alex not to call all day Sunday, he'd be anxious to hear from her.

Chapter 58

"Oh God, Glory, I'm so terribly sorry. I don't know what to say," Alex said when she told him. His voice sounded so sincere and caring that it choked her up. "No, there's not much you can say," she answered. "Let's just hope he comes through this okay. They say he should."

"I want to be there for you – "

"No, Alex. Don't change your plans. I know you have a busy week there. Friday is fine and I have Frannie for support. I'm a big girl. I can get through this. It's just that I'm such a crybaby lately," she said with a laugh that feigned surprise. "I hate that about myself."

"You've had a couple of jolting shocks to deal with," Alex offered in her defense. "You have every right to shed some tears. It's good to let them out. Besides, I wouldn't label you a crybaby, just a sensitive, caring person who's suffering some bad times."

"I'm sure half the world would exchange their troubles for mine. In spite of what I didn't know about my parents and Jason, I still had a good life. And I *did* find my real father who didn't reject me. Let's not forget about that. So I count my blessings."

"See what I mean about you? You really are special. What you say is true, but another woman in your shoes might drown herself in self-pity."

"Oh, I have my moments," she answered with a laugh that came easy this time.

Her eyes darted to the kitchen wall clock. Elsa said she'd be in at ten. Glory wanted to be there waiting when she came in. With a smile tugging at her lips, she listened to

Alex go on with a string of praises about her, not all well-deserved, but wonderful to hear.

But her mind was on her father and the hospital. She was banking on Elsa getting her in to see him. "Alex, I can't say I don't love hearing all your compliments. They're great for my morale. But I've got a major challenge this morning. I want to get to the hospital early. Maybe if I beat his family in getting there, I can get in to see him."

"You'll call me to let me know what's happening, right?"

"First chance I get."

***

At 9:45, Glory passed through the automatic doors to see Elsa already at the reception desk. She beamed when she saw Glory, a little because they shared Glory's secret, and a little because of Glory's celebrity status.

Elsa stood up immediately, left the desk and waved Glory over to follow her. At the elevator bank, she told her that his family hadn't arrived yet, and she could probably grab some time alone with her dad. "I can't guarantee that they won't be in soon. You might run into them," she warned.

Glory waved it off with hopeless resignation. "Doesn't matter. We already ran into each other in the chapel, then I later met his youngest daughter, Amy, alone in the parking lot."

"Oh?" Elsa said, her voice curious. But the elevator came down and opened its doors, so all Glory could say with a shrug was, "It'll be okay. And thanks, Elsa."

Elsa handed her the pass to Room 422 and with bright eyes and a broad smile mouthed "good luck" just as the doors closed.

Her father appeared to be in a deep sleep, but when Glory approached his bedside, he had probably sensed someone's presence because his eyes opened wide for a second. He glanced around and squinted as though he wasn't quite sure where he was or why. A scary thought swept through her. *Oh, God, not his memory,* she prayed silently.

But Dan's face quickly relaxed when recognition came and memory focused. He winced at the frightening flashback, that moment when he stared death in the face.

His smile, though brief, brought Glory instant relief. She brushed his forehead with a kiss and stroked his hand. "I'm so-so-sorry, Dad. I feel this is all my fault." Her mouth quivered and her eyes blinked back unshed tears when she saw the huge discoloration on the left side of his face. He had obviously hit more than the back of his head when he was thrown from his motorcycle.

In response, he winced again. A mix of frustration and pain marked his expression and Glory immediately understood his thoughts. With a finger to her lips, she cut him off before he had a chance to speak. "Okay, okay. I take that back. So it's not my fault. Don't get upset. Tell me how you're feeling, but not if it's difficult for you to speak. If it is, I can ask a few questions and you can just blink or nod your answers. And if that's too much, I'll just sit here and hold your hand for as long as they let me."

His eyes seemed to capture new light and a suggestion of a smile tugged at his lips. "Your mother was a chatterbox too," he said. His voice was audible, but scratchy and weak.

Glory's relief released with a good, hearty laugh. The fact that he had a head for humor told her that he'd be fine. "You remember that after all these years?" she asked, incredulous but pleased. "She did love to ramble on and my dad used to – " She paused for just a second, still stunned into disbelief about her two fathers.

With a smile of assurance, Dan nodded for her to go on. "It's okay. He was your dad too. Certainly more than I was."

"Through no fault of your own."

"True."

Her head turned to the voices behind her. Her eyebrows lifted and her expression changed to a deer-in-headlights look. But the voices belonged to two staff workers and she breathed another sigh of relief.

Dan Madison's mind was working just fine. He made a hand gesture towards the chairs at the foot of his bed and pointed a finger to the right side of his bed. "Relax. Sit and let me look at you. And don't worry. They won't be here till noon."

A smile crossed Glory's face at his ability to read her thoughts. She lifted a chair and positioned herself at his bedside. She stroked his hair and studied his face for a moment, so grateful to God for sparing his life. Gently, she broached the sensitive subject. "Do you think you can handle telling me what happened?" she asked, then quickly added, "But not if you're not up to it."

Dan gave her a sidelong glance and a mocking smirk.

Glory laughed and laced her fingers with his. "Okay. There I go again. I'll shut up. Promise," she said, raising one hand to make it official.

Dan felt he owed her the truth. She'd been lied to all her life. Sure, maybe it was in her own best interests, or maybe not. It certainly wasn't in his. Mandy had no right to deny him his daughter for thirty-five years. But he'd never reveal that bitterness to Glory now that her mother is dead. He had no intention of denying his daughter the comfort of knowing her parents were at least in love when she was conceived, and that he had nothing but precious memories of that first love.

He shook away thoughts of Mandy and focused on Louise, the woman he'd loved for thirty-three years. In all that time, he'd rarely, if ever, seen Louise lash out in anger. It wasn't her nature to display any temperament beyond "upset." Unless you count disciplining the children. They had taxed their patience too many times to count.

But Sunday night Louise was way beyond upset. She was livid; her temper tantrum was so out of character; so unlike her passive personality. Even their children were shocked, though no one tried to calm her until she was spent.

Glory's questioning eyes met his and broke his ruminations. "It could have been better," he said, forcing a smile.

"That's what I thought."

"You have to understand what a shock it was to them. Louise carried on as though I had been unfaithful to her, the girls behaved like they'd never be able to face the world again – but you can't go by them – they can be very emotional at times." The corners of Dan's mouth lifted into an uncertain smile; half pride, half disappointment.

Glory nodded, heeding what he'd said and imagining how they probably dramatized the shocking news into a scene that might have resembled what fires Chelsea had stormed through when her world-famous dad confessed his White House indiscretions.

"And Todd?"

The smile fell from Dan's face at the mention of his son's name, but the disappointment remained. His head tilted a bit when he raised his brows thoughtfully. He seemed to be searching his mind for a catch-all phrase to best describe Todd's reaction.

"I'm not sure," he said with a sigh. "I think I would have liked it better if he'd lashed out too. All I remember is that long, cold steely look. Then he softened to comfort his mother and sisters, but not before he gave me one of those 'I hate you for this' dagger looks and never said another word or asked another question."

Dan shrugged it off, but Glory saw him swallow the lump that shot up in his throat. She felt her stomach roll over. As she had feared from the start, a lot of people would feel a lot of pain, primarily her dad. "You need to talk to him alone," she said.

His amber eyes rolled upward as he nodded in agreement. The fleeting gesture sent a clear message that he dreaded doing it, but such a confrontation could not be avoided. Glory hoped, for his sake, that it would be a conversation, not a confrontation, but she pessimistically suspected the latter would prevail.

Their conversation went silent a few moments while they each pondered this problem they shared. Their thoughts differed sharply, though. Dan did not want to lose the loving relationship he had with his family, nor did he want to deny himself the same relationship with Glory. He intended to fight until he could knock some sense into their heads, but he feared what price he'd pay before and after that happened.

Glory's thoughts were troubled in different ways. Even if they did relent eventually, could she accept being with them if they merely tolerated her as a means of compromise? But she had no right to expect more. She would always be seen by them as the product of the sins of their father. Unfair, but inevitable.

"What's going on in that pretty head of yours?" Dan asked finally. "Maybe I shouldn't have answered your questions so honestly, but it's better in a way. I want you to be prepared. This is going to be an uphill battle, but we'll win in the end, right?" He pinched her chin softly to get her full attention. Glory raised her downcast eyes and gave him a thin-lipped smile. "Right," she answered, but wished she believed it.

A nurse came in for blood samples and Glory turned to the door, but the nurse stopped Glory from leaving. "That's not necessary. I'll only be a few minutes," she said, nodding to the other chair at the foot of the bed. Glory took that seat and began to read the newspaper that someone had left.

The nurse had completed her task and was marking Dan's chart when another person entered the room. His son Todd came in smiling, obviously pleased to see his dad awake and alert. That smile vanished when he noticed who occupied the chair.

Chapter 59

Putting an end to Paula Grant's useless life was not the least bit challenging, nor did it evoke even the slightest trace of remorse. Who knows, in her state of mind, maybe I did her a favor, he reasoned. But how can you know her state of mind? That flash of conscience raced through his head faster than a whipping wind. No, I did what had to be done, he mused. It was time I did something all on my own, with no one to help me. They think I'm not capable of handling my own problems or making my own decisions. A man's got to do what he has to do to attain self-respect.

True, sending Paula Grant off for her final swim was literally like throwing the baby out with the bath water. That's what she was, really; a full-grown baby. The pathetic old broad never had a clue, he thought with a smirk. It was comical, in a way, to watch that childish innocence on a shriveled face.

But the down side of this easy job troubled him. There was a good chance he had been seen leading her to the dock. He had heard voices somewhere behind him. Nothing he could decipher with the roar of the ocean and a pounding heart to contend with, but definitely voices. He had assumed it was two people; either two people involved in a clandestine affair, or two people preparing to burglarize a targeted home. Question is what did they see, if anything? Maybe nothing at all, but he couldn't take that chance.

Even if they had seen him thrust her frail body into the ocean, they could never identify him. Dark clothing and a ski mask had obliterated that possibility, but still, he had made the wrong decision and run off. He realized later that he should have chased them down; eliminated even the chance of launching a murder investigation. An Alzheimer's patient who wandered off in the middle of the night and drowned – well, hey, that's tailor-made for a guy like me, he thought complacently.

Conversely, if he had chased them down, he would have put himself in an extremely high risk situation. He might have been seen by some insomniac who happened to be looking out a window. A call to 911 would have sent patrol cars to the area and trapped him like a rat. Even if he had caught the witnesses and silenced them permanently, he couldn't begin to fathom the intense investigation a triple homicide would launch.

But all that reasoning was behind him now. Now he had no doubt. He had driven through the area a few times at about the same time. Finally, his patience had paid off. He spotted the two stupid kids taking off; first the girl in one direction, then the guy, in the opposite direction.

A sardonic smirk framed his mouth as he thought about the idiotic things kids do, never giving thought to possible consequences. By meeting again in that same spot, they had given him an open invitation to come and get them.

Chapter 60

Todd Madison's amber eyes might have been the same color as his father's, but that's where the resemblance stopped. They peered down at Glory hooded by thick black eyebrows. He never said a word or acknowledged her presence. But he didn't have to. This young man that her father loved – her half-brother – held fire in his amber eyes.

Glory sprang from the chair, blew her father an air kiss and ran from the room and out to the elevators. She clenched her jaws then pulled in a long, deep breath to fight off the tears that wanted out. No more, she resolved, I've shed enough tears these past months to last me a lifetime. A woman has to be strong to fight for the man she loves. Only this time, the man she had to fight for was her father and her antagonist is not another woman, but her own siblings. And their mother.

When the elevator opened its doors on the main floor, Glory stared into another pair of striking eyes. But these eyes held no anger, only surprise. Rather than take the elevator up, Amy stepped aside to speak with Glory.

"You look upset. Is my dad all right?"

Glory's fingers fanned off her concern. "He's fine. Better than I expected, thank God."

Amy's eyes lowered. "He told you, I guess." Her lips made a sour twist. "It was not a Brady Bunch scene."

"No, it wasn't that. I had already psyched myself for that reaction. He said all of you wouldn't be here till after lunch, so I wasn't prepared when your brother walked in."

"He's up there? *Our* brother?" she asked.

This time, her emphasis on *our* was indiscernible. Glory wasn't quite sure whether it was meant sarcastically or whether Amy had said it aloud to help herself get used to the idea. She responded to the question with only a grim-faced nod.

Amy punched the elevator's up button and took hold of Glory's arm. "Come back with me," she said, although her tone made it clearly an order, not a suggestion.

With an appreciative smile, Glory resisted. She politely peeled Amy's hand off her arm. "Look, it's okay. I can come back later when no one is here. I have tons of work to do anyway. Besides, I don't want to upset him or cause any embarrassment. There's bound to be a scene."

Determination tightened Amy's face, adding unflattering creases. Glory recalled that day at Perkins Cove when Dan had proudly referred to his youngest child as "feisty and strong-willed."

"There won't be a scene. Trust me." Amy gave her a not-too-gentle shove when the elevator door opened. It was packed shoulder-to-shoulder with visitors now, so Glory couldn't say another word. She did, however, send Amy a strong, sidelong glance that said, "I hope you know what you're doing."

Amy pursed her lips, returned a quick but confident smile and winked.

Glory shook her head as though she disagreed but was willing to give it a try. She silently admitted to herself that she felt a new rush of confidence now that she had Amy to help. The odds had narrowed to 3-2. Success not imminent, but possible.

***

Amy had intended to drag her in like a wounded puppy, but this time Glory was adamant. She'd wait in the visitors' lounge until Amy gave her an all-clear signal.

Glory sat there with her arms folded, wondering if Amy had mentioned her yet. Probably not, she thought, since there were no voices to be heard that rose above the ordinary sounds of morning on a busy hospital floor. The lounge was unoccupied but the TV was on, tuned in to a talk show, but today was one of those days when you stare at the screen but don't absorb. The words seemed to go in one ear and out the other.

A long ten minutes passed before Amy appeared at the doorway. One look and Glory could read what Amy wanted to say but didn't know how to take out the sting. Glory helped her out.

"I appreciate your help, Amy, but I didn't expect any miracles."

"It wasn't a total loss. He didn't flare up. Just flatly said no. I could see he was in no mood to discuss it so I didn't push."

"It's just as well. I didn't want to upset your father. *Our* father," she added. The more they rejected that fact, the more she'd remind them.

"Too late. He *was* upset. He told Todd he was acting like an immature child. When he insisted I come and get you, Todd walked out."

"Oh, God. I don't believe this. It's so unfair." She picked up her bag and headed back to her father's room. Anger filled her now after hearing how stubborn and yes, immature, Todd had behaved. How could they do this to her? Maybe she could allow some resistance on Louise's part – not that she could condone her behavior either, but Glory allowed her some slack. My father's wife and I are not blood relatives, she reasoned, and I *am* the offspring of another love. But that love between Dan Madison and her mother was born and died long before Louise and Dan had ever met. She just couldn't excuse their attitudes and told her father so when she reentered the room.

"Maybe I'm being selfish, Dad, but if the situation were reversed, I don't think I could turn my back on any of them. Gee, I was all excited to learn I had a brother and two sisters. I never dreamed it would turn out like this. It's like they made a concerted decision to hate me. Except for Amy. She's sticking her neck out for me and I already love her for that."

Dan reached for his daughter's hand and kissed her fingertips. "Hang in there, Glory. They'll all cool off. To tell you the truth," he confessed with a half-smile, "when I opened my eyes in this hospital and that ugly scene in the kitchen came back to me, I was almost glad the accident had happened. I thought they'd be so worried about my health, it would erase all those hostile feelings."

Despite his forced laugh, Glory knew it hurt him to think they had taken his injuries so lightly.

"In all fairness to them," she said, " – not that they're being fair to me – by the time you opened your eyes, they already knew you were not in grave danger."

Dan nodded, conceded that possibility and asked, "Where's Amy? Did she leave with Todd?"

Glory turned to look and saw Amy standing outside the lounge. Their eyes met and Glory waved her in. "I think she wanted to give me some alone time."

Amy came in, took her place at her father's bedside next to Glory. The facial expressions of all three revealed that they shared the same awkward feeling. So now that we're gathered together, what do we talk about, the weather?

Amy broke through with an attempt at levity. "Well, Dad, at least our surprise sister is someone we can be proud of. She's a celebrity, after all!"

Glory lifted a brow and a modest smile touched her lips. "Now that would depend on how you'd define 'celebrity.' My name is not exactly a household word."

"I'm sure it is in some households," Amy said.

"Doesn't matter," Dan said to Glory. "You don't have to be a celebrity to be special to me. You're a fine young woman and I'm proud of you." The moment the words rolled off his lips, Dan quickly grabbed Amy's hand and kissed it. "You too, of course," he said.

Glory cringed. "You too" sounded almost like an afterthought. She hoped Amy realized that his demonstrative affection for his newfound daughter was merely temporary, an outpouring prompted by shock.

Chapter 61

Glory stayed away from the hospital after her short Tuesday morning visit. Her dad had tried to convince her to stay, hoping he'd have a better chance of dissolving their icy defiance. A hospital setting for such a delicate discussion might work to allay any argumentative eruptions.

But Glory needed space. She wasn't in the mood to deal with their selfish and insensitive attitudes. For now she took comfort in the fact that she had the love and support of her dad, a guarded acceptance from Amy and, of course, Alex and Frannie. And today they'd sign the contract for the beachfront property that would soon become Amore Evenings where she'll also have the convenience of a luxury apartment with a magnificent ocean view. The realization had her beaming. Yes, count your blessings, girl, she told herself.

Both attorneys agreed to hold a late afternoon contract signing so that Frannie could conclude the day's business for Amore Breakfast. To their relief, there were no surprises that would adversely affect the sale and purchase. They were out in less than an hour and the closing date had been set. In three weeks the Duca Brothers could commence the renovations that would transform the property into what Glory and Frannie hoped would be a huge success.

Glory drew a long breath when they left the lawyer's office and couldn't contain her excitement. She remembered how thrilled she had been when she was given the *Glorious Cooking* column. At the time, she had thought nothing could top that, then came syndication, now this.

She laughed to her friend and new partner. "I can't believe this is happening, Frannie. When I left New York for

Maine, if some psychic had predicted I'd be in the restaurant business, big time, I would have laughed in her face! But here we go. The wheels are in motion. I'd be scared to death if it weren't for you. Your sharp business acumen and success with Amore Breakfast is what gave me the courage to do this, but I'm still a little frightened. Actually, it was me who talked you into this – "

Frannie made a hand wave to erase her words. "Forget it. Don't go there. You *suggested* it, yes. But I loved the idea. It would never have entered my mind, true, but that's only because of the big bucks. For me alone, it would have been too risky. And let's not forget how your column and your name connected to any restaurant will help. It's great publicity."

Glory tipped her head and smiled. "Okay. I won't try for modesty. That's probably true. So we're a winning combination. Let's celebrate and go out to eat. Someplace fancy, maybe."

Frannie threw her a sidelong glance. "Glory, in a few weeks we'll have a lifetime commitment to a 'someplace fancy.' So I say we celebrate with pizza and beer or Mexican and margheritas."

"I could go for Mexican. My mouth is watering already."

Cocktails and dinner lasted almost two hours. Glory and Frannie talked nonstop about their immediate and long-term plans for Amore Evenings. The subject of Glory's problem with her father's family came up twice, but only briefly. Glory's spirits were so high after signing the contract that she didn't want the "afterglow" to dissipate.

Alex was not mentioned at all, but his face and the sound of his voice popped into Glory's head often, despite her attempts to chase them away. With all that was going on in her life, she should have been too preoccupied to dwell on Alex, but there he was, ever-present like a heartbeat.

When they got back to the house, they said goodnight and parted, each to her own private living quarters. Before undressing, Glory went to the phone to check for messages. The first warmed her. "It's me. Give me a call whenever you get in. I want to hear how everything went with the contract signing." Then his voice lowered. "I also want to hear your voice. I miss you."

Glory felt a flutter inside her and a catch in her throat. It's no use, she thought, I'm sinking fast.

She listened to the next message before returning Alex's call.

"Glory, it's Amy. Please call me when you get this message. And don't worry about the time. Just call."

Glory tapped out that number first. She didn't like the tone of Amy's message.

Chapter 62

Tonight Tim and Sara enjoyed the comfort of his father's Infiniti. Air conditioning and soft upholstery seemed like the ultimate luxury for this young couple who were used to stretching out on damp and buggy grass. But sometimes the hassle his parents put him through in order to get the car just wasn't worth it. The whole exchange was always all lies and promises. And beer was totally out of the question. A caffeine high on soda was as good as he would feel whenever he had the car. One of his parents was always up when he got in. They'd never admit it, but Tim was sure it was to check for alcohol on his breath.

Since he got his driver's license, Tim had made it a practice to look for obscure spots to take girls where they wouldn't be seen by residents or cruising police cars. One of those spots was exclusively for his Sara now, whenever the rare opportunity presented itself. Once Sara was in his arms, he never missed beer or thought about anyone or anything else. She could be a pain in the rear sometimes, but he was crazy about her. Enough to let himself get involved in a murder. But maybe that's what he loved about her; her conscience wouldn't allow her to hold back such pertinent information. Not when their silence would cause Paula Grant's death to be declared accidental, rather than a homicide, and letting her killer run free.

After an hour together in the seclusion of this perfect private hideaway, passion, love and reason fought a raging battle. Finally, when they had gone too far, Sara broke away, inhaled a long, deep breath and exhaled slowly. Tim crossed his arms and locked his hands under his armpits to keep them under control.

They stared ahead into the darkness. The moon and stars peeking through a cluster of trees provided a romantic setting, but little light. The whites of their eyes were luminous, like snow on black coal.

Sara broke the silence. "Maybe it's not such a good thing that you found this place. For whatever it's worth, Tim, I have as much trouble holding back as you do," she said, then added with a sly smile, "It's just that your problem is more visual, of course."

"And tangible," Tim threw in.

"Yes, and tangible," she agreed.

They both loosened up enough to laugh then Tim grew serious. "Why are we torturing ourselves, Sara? We both know it's just a matter of time before we both give in or explode."

She sighed and nodded. "You're probably right, Tim, but I need more time. I made a mistake before and the guy dumped me soon after. I've been dragging a lot of guilt around since then. I was only sixteen at the time."

Tim sat forward and turned to look her in the eyes. His were fiery. "Oh, so you think because one jerk hurt you, I'm gonna do the same? Is that how much trust you have in me? After all the times I said I love you?"

In one swift move, he yanked the seatbelt, locked it and turned on the ignition.

Sara gave a frustrated eye roll. "So now you're mad at me, right? What did I do?"

"It's not what you did. It's what you *didn't* do. And I'm not talking sex here; I'm talking trust."

"Be patient with me, Tim. He said he loved me too. Ignorant jerk that I was, I believed him. I felt so dirty after he dumped me, so used."

"Well, I don't want to be compared to that creep."

Sara wiped away the tears that had fallen onto her cheeks. "Okay, I'm sorry. I *do* believe that you love me and I do love you. Just give me a little more time, please?"

Her pleading tone melted his anger. The car was already in motion so he simply reached over and pinched her cheek affectionately. "I'm sorry too. I guess it's jealousy that sets me off. But when my head is clear, I can understand what you're thinking. We'll wait till you're ready."

***

They pulled into the parking lot at Perkins Cove where Sara had prearranged to meet her friend, Andrea. Andrea had picked Sara up and dropped her off there where she had connected with Tim. Now she would take her home and Sara's parents would remain clueless.

It was a perfect summer night, warm enough to enjoy the cool ocean breeze, but dry enough not to feel the discomfort of humidity. As usual, the area was packed with tourists. Today they were a half hour early for Sara's designated pickup time. All the benches were occupied but she and Tim stood up against the railing and looked out at the ocean. Moonlight painted magical stripes on the rippling water.

A very attractive woman deep in thought stood only inches away. Sara took a moment to admire her. She was strikingly beautiful and awfully familiar. Sara struggled to remember where she had seen that face before but nothing came to her.

When the woman caught her staring, Sara had no choice but to speak. "I'm sorry. I didn't mean to stare. It's just that you look so familiar and I can't place where I've seen you before."

Glory laughed. *Here we go again.* "Well, I'm sure you don't know me. I've only lived in Maine since the beginning of summer. I moved here from New York. My face is probably familiar to you from newspapers. I'm Glory

English. Maybe you've seen my column, *Glorious Cooking?*"

Sara let out a shriek and even Tim seemed impressed. They introduced themselves and immediately started throwing questions at Glory. "Wow! This is exciting. Didn't I read awhile back that you and Frannie Oliveri bought that Crawford property and you're opening a new restaurant there?"

Glory beamed at her youthful enthusiasm. "Yes, you did." She looked out in the direction of the house that would soon become Amore Evenings. "In a few weeks we'll begin renovations."

"People are excited about it. It's a great spot. I bet it'll be the classiest place in Maine."

Glory laughed. "Well, I don't know, but hopefully it'll be considered *one* of the classiest. That's our goal."

"Excuse me," Tim cut in politely. "What are our chances of getting weekend work? We're both going to local colleges soon and it would be great for us to have jobs here. Some of our friends make big bucks as servers in these restaurants."

Glory raised her brows and gave an approving nod. "I'd say they're pretty good. We're going to need a good-size competent staff who are patient, polite, congenial, ambitious and reliable." She glanced from Tim to Sara with an easy smile. "How do you two think you score in those areas?"

"High. Very high," Sara quickly responded. The thought of working in Frannie Oliveri's new restaurant together with Glory English, the food columnist, absolutely thrilled her.

Glory's questioning eyes went to Tim. "And you, Tim? What do you think?"

"I think we'll both pass the test with flying colors. When do we start?"

Glory smiled at the obvious. She waved a hand towards the private home that would remain untouched until after the closing. "Well, inasmuch as a hammer hasn't even touched the place yet, I'd say it'll be awhile yet. A few months. But we intend to put our employees through some serious training – paid training, of course – to shape them into providing the excellent service we intend to offer our customers." She handed each of them a business card. "Here. Why don't you call us in about a month? Frannie and I plan to start interviewing almost immediately after closing."

***

As soon as Glory excused herself and left them standing alone, Tim smacked the railing and let out a howl. "Wow! I don't believe our luck. Talk about being in the right place at the right time! Not only do we get to work in a classy place, but we're sure to make great tips. Anything Frannie Oliveri owns is sure to turn to gold." He turned and gave her a quick but hard kiss on the lips. "But the best part is we get to work together too."

"I'm excited about it too, Tim. Sounds too good to be true. Did you ever get the feeling when something good happens that there's got to be a down side?"

Tim wrinkled his nose and frowned. "Where did that morbid thought come from? Hey, we lucked out. Why can't you just enjoy it?"

Sara smiled and waved it off. "I am. But it just gave me the creeps for a second when something dawned on me. Glory English, I hear, is seeing Alex Howard. We saw Alex Howard's sister get murdered. And you know what they always said about Alex Howard."

"That he might have killed his wife. So? What's that got to do with us? The guy might be perfectly innocent anyway."

"I know, I know – "

Tim tried to laugh off her concern. "Let me tell you something, Sara. You were right on when you told Sergeant Gerard you have a weird imagination. I know what's spinning around in your crazy head, but how the hell is Alex Howard supposed to find out we saw him – assuming it was him?"

"You're right, but even if it wasn't him, the thought of being connected to the Howard family even remotely gives me the creeps."

Tim shook his head, gave her a you're-useless smirk, but inwardly he pondered Sara's concerns. He then dismissed them as ludicrous, but the thought lingered.

Chapter 63

"A heart attack! How could he have a heart attack right there in the hospital?"

The shock was too much for Glory. Denial overshadowed her ability to accept the truth. She could barely hear, much less understand. Amy's sobs rendered her nearly incoherent.

Glory felt her own hysteria rising but fought to stay in control. "Amy, *please,* try to calm down a little. I can't understand what you're saying. How bad was it? How is he?" She wanted to ask if he was still alive, but those words couldn't pass her lips.

"We think he's okay. I mean we don't really know how serious it was – how much damage – "

"Well, what did the doctors say?" The palpitations in Glory's heart felt like a minor earthquake.

"Oh, you know how they are. They only give you that 'we'll see' attitude."

Amy's heart-wrenching sobs had diminished to frustrated whining, but Glory felt the urge to hug this young sister of hers. Even in the height of panic and fear for her dad, Amy had chosen to include her in this critical family crisis. She wondered with pessimism whether any of the others would have eventually relented.

This can't be happening. This can't be happening. The words pounded in Glory's head, but she opened her mouth, pulled in a long breath and blew it out quickly. Again, the fear of losing her father so soon after finding him numbed her. How in God's name can they be heartless enough to shut me out now? she thought. "Does your family know you're calling me?" she asked, clinging to hope.

"Hold on," Amy said and broke away.

A few seconds of silence followed until she heard an unfamiliar voice. "Miss English, this is Vanessa Madison."

Miss English rippled through Glory's body like a rush of ice water.

"Amy's told us how concerned you are for our father, and yes, I do believe you are, but you have to understand and respect our position. He's been our father for a lifetime and now you come in at the eleventh hour expecting us to immediately accept you into our family? I'm sorry, but I don't think so. This is a very stressful time for us and your presence doesn't help."

Vanessa's cold formality and unyielding heart stunned Glory. Only one thought blew into her head. *My sister's a bitch. A cold-hearted, nasty bitch.*

Glory stiffened. "So, if that's how you all feel, why this phone call? Just to tell me to stay away?"

Vanessa heaved a sigh into the phone. "No, not really," she said. Her tone was suggestive of indifference with an air of authority. As though being born to Dan and Louse gave her more right than the child born to Dan and Miss Somebody Else. "What we want to convey is this: we don't want you in our faces now. My dad's in ICU and the hospital is strict about their five minutes per hour rule. Certainly no one in my family is willing to relinquish that time to you. If you want to see him, you'll just have to wait until we've all left the hospital."

Glory cringed at Vanessa's arrogant and superior attitude. "And how am I supposed to know when that is?" She couldn't contain the sarcasm in her voice even if she wanted to. Which she didn't.

"My sister Amy will call you."

Well, isn't that big of you? she wanted to scream. This instant family she had inherited was growing uglier by the minute. Except for Amy, she wanted no part of them either. She shook her head in disbelief that Dan Madison, her father, had also fathered these cold selfish children. No, it had to be a mean streak that ran in their mother's blood. "Who's my father's cardiologist?" Glory asked, this time taking full possession of the father title.

"My father's cardiologist is my uncle, my mother's brother," she snapped back with emphasis on *mother*. "I don't think he'd be very receptive to your questions, so don't bother to call him."

"Miss Madison," Glory retaliated, "don't *you* think about telling me what to do. How dare you talk to me this way? I can't believe we have the same blood in our veins!"

"Maybe we don't," came Vanessa's snide reply.

Impulsively, as though touching something poisonous, Glory slammed the phone back in its cradle. She wanted to scream out a string of obscenities but bit down on her lip instead. "I'll be damned if I let them win," she mumbled aloud. Rage steamed inside her. But Vanessa's last remark which attacked her mother's morality was the last straw. She equated those words to a declaration of war.

Chapter 64

The guy who first said, "It's a small world" knew what he was talking about. But the guy who came up with the line "Can you keep a secret?" did not. Paula's killer laughed to himself wondering how many secrets went from ear to ear; how many promises never to reveal a confidence broken.

Both these familiar phrases worked to his advantage. Apparently this Sara what's-her-name couldn't keep a secret. She couldn't resist telling her girlfriend what she and her boyfriend had seen that night. And the next day, sure enough, the girlfriend cupped her hand over her mouth and shared Sara's secret with someone else who shared it with him. He shook his head and laughed. So much for secrets. And isn't it a hell of a small world if the secret travels around and lands in the ears of the guy who put Paula Grant out of her misery? Sure is.

He found himself amused with it all, knowing if they did go to the police, they could never finger him. There was no way they could have seen him close enough to identify him. Even when he yanked the friggin' itchy mask off his face. The damn thing was soaked with his sweat and falling over his eyes.

But do I want to take that chance? He asked himself? Hell, no! The kids will have to be wasted. Too bad. Too young to die, that's for sure, but you know what they say, better you than me, kids. It'll be a romantic death though – like Romeo and Juliet. I'll think of something special. And it'll be fast. I'll do you that favor. You'll never know what hit you and you can shoot right on up to heaven together, wherever that is.

He nodded as he thought it out, satisfied with the plans being formulated in his mind. "Yeah, it'll be romantic," he said aloud. "I promise you that."

Chapter 65

It was after eleven when Alex got home and listened to his messages. "Hi, Alex. It's me. Sorry I didn't catch you. I sure can use your shoulder to lean on." Her voice came through broken, the kind of sound indicative of a forced smile and suppressed tears. "My dad had a heart attack," her message continued. "Can you believe that? I'm still in shock and his family is doing such a number on me…. I can't get into that. You don't have to call me back. I'll call again tomorrow as soon as I find out how he is."

He didn't call her back. The desperation in her voice made him want to jump in his car and take off for Maine. But realistically he had to make a few stops in the morning to put certain business problems in the hands of his subordinates and hope for the best.

He couldn't sleep much that night. First he kept imagining how Glory would react if her father died. She didn't say much or know much about his condition. It'll kill her to lose him now.

His thoughts shifted to his sister Paula and those detectives. All those questions. I guess it's normal in any type of investigation, but it's the questions they didn't ask that bothered him. He could see right through that silence. They think Paula's death might not have been an accident. And after the way Elena died, who would be the number one suspect? Me, of course.

But I'm not the only one who'd inherit a bundle with Paula dead. Just thinking about Allison twisted his gut. He could never forget what she did. And yet, buried somewhere deep inside him was a tiny flame of love that refused to die out. Sometimes, in a weaker moment, when he wasn't gripped by fury, he imagined that Allison would redeem herself; that remorse might wash away all her sins. Then Alex could forget the past and love again the only family he had.

Pipe dreams. It was never going to happen; he knew that. But did he think Allison, with all her faults, was capable of harming even a hair on the head of her sister? No way. The thought was inconceivable.

Alex stripped off his clothes and took a hot shower as though it would free him of all the dark thoughts surrounding his sisters. The realization came to him that once the police find no reason to suspect and accuse him of murdering Paula, their next step would surely be to take a long, hard look at Allison. And they won't like what they see.

His mind was racing ahead trying to think of how he could protect her if that should come to pass. He shivered as he towel-dried his long, lean body. The remote possibility that Allison had cracked haunted him. They hadn't spoken or seen each other in years. God only knows what influences could have destroyed her totally. Drugs, alcohol, that wild crowd of friends? Yes, anything was possible and the thought made him sick to his stomach. I sure didn't murder Paula, so who else would have a motive?

He slipped on pajama bottoms, stretched out on his bed and put the television on for distraction. This is insane, he told himself. It was an accident and the police would eventually draw the same conclusion.

Glory filled his thoughts and his body reacted. His heart ached for what she was going through, but selfishly his need to make love to her superseded his sympathy. If her father doesn't pull through…

Alex punched the pillow, thought about what could develop between them soon if all went well and fell asleep smiling.

Chapter 66

Again, Glory never budged from the apartment. Just days ago, she had hung around waiting for her father's phone call. She had clung to a dream that his family would all be shocked initially, but curious and anxious to meet her. That dream had turned to a nightmare.

Now she waited for another call. This time *about* him, not *from* him. She had tried calling the hospital, identifying herself as a close friend of the family, but got the answer she had expected. They could not release that information to anyone other than previously authorized family members. But she clung to that old adage, no news is good news. If Amy hadn't called, at least he's alive, she assumed. Then she remembered how Amy had cried uncontrollably when she called to tell Glory about his heart attack. She shivered now at the image of Amy hysterical, too grief-stricken to think of making a phone call.

No. Impossible, she told herself. Not after all these hours.

By midnight she knew there was no chance of falling asleep. She threw on jeans, a sweatshirt and sneakers and headed back for the hospital. Heavy rains fell as she drove. The steady thumping of the windshield wipers sounded like a heartbeat. A strong, steady rhythm. She hoped the hospital monitors were sending that same sound for her father.

Elsa wouldn't be there but maybe someone else might help her out. Especially if she told them who she really was. The family would go ballistic knowing I was spreading what they considered to be "dirty family laundry," she thought. But too bad. If all's fair in love and war, then that line certainly justified her actions. She loved her father and had declared war on his family.

***

Two unfamiliar faces looked up at her at the hospital's reception desk; one male, one female. Glory felt defeated before she opened her mouth to speak.

"I'm very concerned about a certain patient, Daniel Madison," she said to the gentleman who raised his brows in question. "He was in the Surgical Intensive Care Unit, but I was notified that he had a heart attack and I don't know if he's been moved to Coronary Care." *Or God forbid, the morgue.*

The man gave no verbal response. If he had a ghost of a smile somewhere, it was well hidden behind a thick moustache that dominated his face, especially since his head was bald. But he didn't ignore her entirely. He simply fed the name into his computer. "No, Mr. Madison is still in SICU but I can't let you up there. All visitors are long gone."

Glory was so relieved to know he was still alive that she accepted the visitation denial without disappointment. "I'm sorry. I thought perhaps the rules are relaxed for seriously ill patients, so I took a chance."

"Oh, no," he was quick to say. "That's true sometimes. They'll let the family stay with the patient if they can, but if they're having problems with *any* patient, the curtains are drawn and all visitors are asked to leave." He made a hand motion as though they'd all be swept out. "The staff doesn't need panicky visitors bothering them with questions or scaring the other patients."

Glory put her hand up to stop him. "Absolutely understandable. Again, I'm sorry. But is it at all possible I can find out his condition?"

He gave her a guarded look. "What are you to the patient? A relative?"

She hesitated with a sigh, then strengthened by her resolve to fight back, she lifted her head, straightened her shoulders and said, "I'm his daughter, Glory English."

For some inexplicable reason, the man's expression remained guarded. Maybe he'd been on duty when the whole family came in together and wondered why she was absent then? Who knows? she thought.

"I'm from out of town," she said in answer to his silent question.

"I'm sorry, but we have to abide by the regulations promulgated by The Privacy Act, so we can't release information to anyone other than designated parties."

That explained his look. Her name wasn't listed and if she was a daughter, why not? She asked herself that same question.

Glory was about to give up when she saw someone's reflection in the mirror behind the reception desk. "Dr. Seidel," she called out. *My guardian angel in disguise* were the words gently whispered in her mind.

Dr. Seidel was speaking with someone else, but he acknowledged Glory with a warm smile and a nod towards the chapel. Glory politely thanked the gentleman for his time and went directly into the chapel to wait for the doctor.

The serenity calmed her. On her knees, she said a few prayers for her father. When the doctor came in, she stood up abruptly and took a few steps back to meet him.

"You heard about your dad's heart attack, I assume."

"Yes, doctor. Can you tell me how he is? No one ever called me back and I've been a wreck not knowing."

He gave her a concerned-but-not-hopeless look. "It's too soon to tell how much damage he's sustained, but he's stable now and we're optimistic."

"Oh, thank God."

"Is the family still giving you a hard time about visitation?"

"You can't imagine."

He patted her hand. "Look, why don't you go home and get some rest. Call me about ten tomorrow. If I'm unavailable, just leave your number and I'll get back to you when I can. Okay?"

She beamed up at him, convinced that the young doctor was in fact her guardian angel who would help her through this crisis.

Chapter 67

At 7:15 the next morning, Glory was just getting out of bed. She felt physically better after five hours of uninterrupted, dreamless sleep. The phone rang before her eyes were fully open and she sprang to her feet. *"Please, God, nothing bad...,"* she mumbled and picked up before the second ring.

"Glory, it's me, Amy. Sorry if I woke you up, but I had no choice."

"What's wrong?" she asked, afraid to hear the answer at first, but there were no echoes of grief or fear in Amy's voice.

"He's doing okay. My uncle said it was fortunate for him that he was already in the hospital when it happened. They were all working on him the minute he had the attack. He'll need bypass surgery eventually, but not until he's over this hurdle."

Glory inhaled long and deep. That was about the best news she could have expected. "Thank God, Amy. I prayed to hear hopeful words like that. Yesterday was absolute torture. Not hearing from you and not being able to get information myself made me crazy." She opted not to mention her midnight visit when she ran into Dr. Seidel.

"I'm sorry. You were on my mind all day. I knew you were probably sick with worry, but it was a bad day for all of us, and I didn't want to throw coal on the fire by mentioning your name. The only times they weren't with me were the bathroom breaks, but my cell needed charging, so I couldn't sneak a call."

Her sister's kindness tugged at Glory's heart. "Hey, you don't have to apologize. You've been wonderful, considering what you're up against."

Amy blew out a woeful sigh. "I know it's hard for you to believe, but underneath all that stubborn crap are three warm, considerate and loving people. I don't know what happened. In this day and age, they shouldn't react this way. It's not normal. And I'm a little ashamed."

Glory managed a laugh. "Don't be. Everyone is responsible for his or her own behavior. And you're right," she added without malice, "I do find it hard to believe that they're warm, considerate and loving people. I'd sure like to see that side of them."

"Maybe someday you will. Don't give up."

Glory gave that a moment's thought, then said with a shrug, "It's not that I've given up. It's just that I'm not so sure I want to win that battle. It's your family, I know, so I hate to say this, but right now they're as unwelcome in my life as I am in theirs."

"I can't blame you. But remember, like them or not, it's your family too."

Glory's laugh went sour. "Tell that to them, Amy, not me."

"I did," she answered and paused. "Look, be patient. I reacted the same way when Dad told us. I went nuts – didn't want to look at him. But when I calmed down and thought it out, there's no one to blame. And there's nothing disgraceful about your existence."

Amy had emphasized the word *disgraceful* as though she were quoting someone. Her mother, probably, but Glory opted not to ask.

Chapter 68

Tim was too excited about working at Amore Evenings to let himself dwell on ominous thoughts about Alex Howard. By the time the restaurant opens, he could be long gone from Glory English's life. And even if not, that doesn't mean the guy is about to shoot down everyone who crosses his path. Certainly his presence around Amore Evenings would not put his and Sara's lives in danger.

No. He refused to allow Sara's crazy thoughts to make him paranoid.

Such was their enthusiasm for their new jobs, assuming they'd both be accepted, Tim and Sara had agreed to chance having breakfast together at Amore Breakfast. The place was always packed with tourists anyway. They felt reasonably safe that they wouldn't be seen by any of the locals who might run into their parents and casually mention seeing them.

"I've been giving serious thought to this problem with our parents, Tim," Sara said, punctuating her words in the air with a piece of rye toast.

Tim scooped up another mouthful of scrambled eggs but cocked an interested brow while he ate.

"I'm getting sick and tired of all this sneaking around like we're criminals. We're both eighteen and their problems shouldn't be our problems. I think I'm ready to confront them with the truth."

"Hey, I've been ready to do that for months. I just haven't pushed to save you the grief or whatever your parents dish out. Although once we start working together, we can ease into that gracefully – let them think we became friendly through the training period and the job."

Sara pondered that momentarily, then wrinkled her nose and shook her head. "That might help a little, but if the truth comes out – and it will if we're called about you-know-what." She paused while her eyes darted around to see who might be listening.

Tim quickly nodded in agreement. "Whatever you decide, Sara. I'm ready for the fallout if you are."

They had hoped to see Glory, but she was nowhere in sight. Frannie Oliveri, however, was sprinkling her congeniality among her customers with quick table stops.

Tim caught her attention. With a polite smile and a circular motion of his finger, he silently asked that she stop at their table too. "Might as well try to win over *both* our new bosses," he whispered to Sara.

As Frannie approached them, Tim slid to the corner of the booth to allow her to join them.

"Are you kidding?" she said with a laugh. "There's no way I can park my behind on this or any other seat for the next few hours."

Simultaneously, Tim and Sara laughed with her and introduced themselves. "No, we won't keep you," Tim said. "We just wanted you to know we might be working for you at your new restaurant."

"If we pass all the tests," Sara threw in.

"Really? How did that happen?" Frannie asked, but anticipated their answer. Only she and Glory could employ people.

Sara explained their chance meeting with Glory and searched Frannie's face, hoping she'd have no objection.

"Sounds good to me," Frannie said. "If Glory liked you guys, I have no problem either. I'm sure you'll both work out fine." She shook their hands. "Good luck to both of you," she said. "I hope we all make buckets of money." She left them with a wink and a bright, friendly smile.

"Gee, they both seem like nice, down-to-earth people, don't they?" Sara said. "It almost seems too good to be true. I still feel like something bad is going to happen."

Tim threw his head up, rolled his eyes. "There you go again. Don't be such a pessimist! We got a lucky break. Just accept it and be happy."

Sara gave him a toothy grin. "There. I'm happy," she teased. "I only have two problems. Once they're resolved, I won't have a care in the world."

Tim took the bait. "And they are?"

"Our problem with our parents is first, and second, the man or woman who killed Paula Grant." Her smile faded. "I guess I should reverse that order of priority. I feel so responsible for that woman's death, Tim. Don't you? If we hadn't run off, we would have seen her get pushed and could have called 911."

Tim squeezed her hand. "C'mon, don't do that to yourself. How could we have known what was happening?"

"I know," she said with a frown, trying to accept his reasoning. "But I've been beating up on myself for not paying attention to that dark face. Why didn't it dawn on me then that the guy was probably wearing a ski mask? As far as I know, ski masks are only used to ski, to shield yourself from wind or snow, or to shield your identity. And since it was August –" She shrugged and left a huge imaginary question mark dangling between them.

"And since it was August," he continued for her, "it had to be used to shield his identity and for no other reason, right?"

"Well, can you think of any other reason?"

"No. But can you be absolutely certain what you saw was a ski mask?"

"Not absolutely, no."

They both exhaled a sigh of defeat and were happy to change the subject when the waitress came with their check.

Chapter 69

So the young lovebirds would be working together at Amore Evenings when it opens. What a break that could have been for me, he thought. Too bad the timing is off. It could have worked out beautifully to throw more suspicion on Alex Howard. If Howard were hanging around Glory English and her restaurant, he'd eventually get familiar with the staff. He'd have opportunity to befriend them, gain their confidence, then do them in.

At least that's what the police would be led to believe if those kids already talked to them. And if not, once I ship them off to heaven, for sure her friend will tell them all about the "secret" Sara shared.

Yes, hot-headed Alex Howard would be number one on their list, and maybe they won't even bother to look any further. With his history, his motive and his opportunity, why look elsewhere? His sister will be able to prove she was miles away with friends at the time, so who's left? Alex, of course. Easy indictment for the DA.

But Paula's killer couldn't wait that long. Too dangerous. He still felt ninety percent certain there was no way they could identify him, but that other ten percent left him uneasy. The job had to be done soon. What the hell. They'd still go after Alex Howard.

But he had to be extremely careful. He couldn't let fear of exposure push him into hasty decisions that could blow up in his face. And it certainly had to be done when Alex Howard was back in Ogunquit. That was a must, but not a problem. He had a reliable source of information concerning Howard's scheduled visits.

He thought it all out and felt confident he could pull it off and get away with it. His only concern was the risk he was taking with his "partner in crime." She had plenty to lose if she tripped up. No, *we* have plenty to lose. Tonight would be the last time they'd see each other for months. She had pouted at that part of the plan, but understood it had to be this way. The sacrifice would pay off eventually.

These damn kids were never part of their plan, though. Of all the places they could have sneaked to, they had to pick that spot, and that exact time. Shit. "Well, they're gonna get their just punishment for their sins," he said aloud and enjoyed a laugh thinking about it.

A lustful thought sobered him. He remembered the girl and how he felt when he first saw her. Be a shame to kill her without enjoying himself first. And who knows? She might die happy. He licked his lips and visualized his fantasy.

I'll have to get rid of her shitass boyfriend first, of course.

Old memories surfaced again like flames of fire. His face went taut and beads of perspiration formed on his forehead. He knew what he had to do and how. No, I won't kill him first, he thought. Just slice him up a little. Then tape his mouth, tie his hands and keep him close. Helpless and in pain, but conscious. So he can watch. Like me. Only difference is he's eighteen, not eight. And he won't have to go on living with those Parker sons-of-bitches, like I did. No, Timmy boy, he thought, you'll be better off with me in control. At least I'll let you die.

Yes, his suffering will be quick. Just enough for someone else to know what it's like. So someone can share the pain, the terror. But this kid won't have to hold that poison in his gut for a lifetime with no chance to spit it all out. Or get revenge.

The more he thought about making Timothy Waite share his pain, the more he liked it. That might just be the cure he needed. He sucked in a long drag on his joint and let it do its magic.

Yes, he already felt better.

Chapter 70

Glory refused to give in to the family's demand. Their continual denial only fueled her defiance and determination. She stepped off the elevator with her head held high. Finally, with a little help from Amy and Elsa, she was on record as Dan Madison's daughter. Perhaps only within the confines of this hospital, but it's a start, she told herself.

Her fighting spirit died an instant death when she saw her father. He was hooked up to a cardiac monitor, IV tubing and oxygen. The steady beeping noises were his links to life. His skin looked dry and gray and his eyes were partially closed. Todd and Louise were at his bedside, just watching him breathe. They both gave her a steely look that required no words. Glory cocked her head and returned a look of her own. Not here, not now, her face warned.

They acquiesced silently, but their expressions carried distinct messages.

Glory pretended not to notice. "How's he doing?" she whispered.

Louise chose to ignore the question entirely, but Todd succumbed with a shrug followed by a "not too bad." There was no eye contact, but Glory considered his three words a major breakthrough.

Dan's eyelids gave a weak flutter like it was an effort to hold them open. He managed a fleeting look at Glory which brought a hint of a smile to his lips. His gaze shifted to his wife and they all witnessed the pleas his eyes conveyed. No one spoke, but words were superfluous. Louise heaved a sigh, nodded to Glory and stepped away. Another major breakthrough. Glory took her place, wiped away a rush of tears and kissed her father's forehead. His left hand gently covered hers and his right hand reached out for his son. Todd blinked away the glaze in his eyes and tried to smile, but his lips betrayed him with a quiver.

"You trying to scare the life out of us, Dad?" Glory said. She was laughing and crying at the same time.

"I'll be okay," he said, but his words were barely audible.

She brought his hand to her lips and kissed it. "You'd better be okay," she teased. "We have to catch up on thirty-five years."

Todd stepped away. Glory wasn't quite sure whether it was to give her a few moments alone with Dan or because he couldn't watch or listen to their loving exchange. But she wasn't about to complain. At least they didn't chase her out.

She took only a few seconds more, then nodded to Louise to sit in the chair she had dragged to his bedside. Louise mumbled a quick thank you and sat next to her husband. Glory stepped outside the room just as her two half-sisters were walking in. Amy looked surprised, but smiled warmly. Vanessa looked surprised, but furious.

Chapter 71

By the time Alex turned onto the parkway for the long ride back to Maine, it was early afternoon and Glory was still unreachable. He considered the possibility that she might be working at Amore Breakfast but didn't want to call there. Considering her father's condition, chances were greater that she was at the hospital, still fighting for her right to see him.

Sight unseen, he hated them all for what they were doing to Glory. The more he thought about it, the more it pissed him off. His fingers drummed on the steering wheel as he imagined what he would say to them if given the chance. True, he didn't have the right yet to push himself into her private affairs, but he was determined to earn that right. More importantly, to earn her trust. Until she does, he thought, that wall will always be between us. That wall she created between friendship and love.

He couldn't blame her, though, after what her bastard husband did.

He took a slow, deep breath, then exhaled the angry feelings. His temper was what got him in trouble in the first place, enough to make people suspect him of murder. His face soured as his mind wandered back to those ugly years. Sure, he said to himself, let all those righteous bastards who are so quick to judge and condemn spend some time with the likes of Elena or my sister, Allison. See if they don't crack too.

The memories gave him a heavy foot on the accelerator. He switched to the right-hand lane and slowed down. He tuned his satellite radio to country music, kept his thoughts only on Glory and his angry feelings flew away as swiftly as the miles behind him.

***

Alex completely bypassed Ratherbee when he arrived in Ogunquit. He still got her machine when he last called, but hoped he'd find Frannie at the house. If not, he was heading straight for the hospital. Not to interfere, just to see if she's there and if her father's okay.

Luck was with him as he turned into Frannie's driveway. She was already in her car, backing out, but stopped when his car pulled up beside hers. Alex gave her his warmest smile but it didn't melt her hostility. The smile she returned was forced, unnatural.

"I'm sorry to bother you, but I'm concerned about Glory. Do you know how her father is? Or where she is?"

"I haven't heard from her since this morning. Supposedly, he's holding his own. Glory is there, of course."

His expression changed as he hesitated, then nodded. He and Frannie shared Glory's problem and he silently hoped she'd recognize his sincere concern. The moment he had met her gaze, he could read her eyes. Polite with uncertainty, but nonetheless guarded. *This is the guy who might have murdered his wife,* they said.

"Do you know if she got in to see him? Did anything else happen with the family?"

"I have no idea. When I spoke to her she had only spoken to one of the resident doctors who briefed her on his condition. That's all I know. Sorry."

She threw her car back in reverse and Alex took that as his dismissal. He let her pull out first and resisted the urge to stop her and defend himself against her accusatory eyes.

Chapter 72

Glory's earlier assumption was dead wrong. Her identity as Dan Madison's daughter was not contained only within the hospital walls. A slice of information of that magnitude spreads faster than metastasized cancer. One hospital employee was all it took to get it going.

The employees at Amore Breakfast were among the first to know and the place buzzed with the news.

Tim overheard his mother's phone conversation with a friend and questioned her when she hung up. She eagerly filled him in on whatever details she'd gathered, albeit somewhat embellished along the way.

Tim called Sara, but Sara was just about to call him with the news.

Paula's killer got wind of it that first day too. He got a charge out of tossing that information around at Luke's Tavern, a popular watering hole for the locals. Hell! Everyone knew Dan Madison and enjoyed speculating on missing or clouded details. Like Glory English's mother. Some of the old timers sipped their icy mugs of beer and laughed as names were thrown back and forth just for the hell of it.

It was common knowledge now that Glory English, the columnist, and Alex Howard, the guy who probably knocked off his wife, had a thing going. Money to money, they said.

"Ain't nobody warned her yet about that guy?" Charlie Singer yelled out. "She's gotta be nuts to fool around with him. One false move and wham!" He shoved his hand into the air and laughed, mimicking what Alex might have done to his wife.

Ed Gilhooley and a few of the others laughed with him, then Ed said, "We'll be seeing more of him around, I guess. She's some looker! If I were him and getting into her, I'd dump my New Jersey drugstores like hotcakes and put my ass back in Maine permanently."

"Guess he has no qualms about revisiting the scene of the crime, huh?" This from Eugene Tulley, who owned a book store in the heart of town.

"You guys are terrible," the next guy said, but his smile was as sinister as theirs. "C'mon, now. Isn't this the country where a guy is innocent until proven guilty?"

"Yeah. And he can also be innocent because he has a sharp lawyer, not because he's *innocent.*"

Paula's killer lifted his glass and returned a mock salute. "Touché," he said.

Chapter 73

Alex had second thoughts the moment he reached the hospital reception desk that evening. This might be pushing it, he decided. Glory might be mad as hell if he showed his face here. He was still nobody special in her life and what the hell was he thinking showing up where even she was unwelcome.

He was just about to reverse his steps and leave when Elsa lifted her head and flashed a smile. "Can I help you?"

"Is Daniel Madison still in ICU?" he asked.

Elsa gave him a curious look, wondering who he was and whether his presence in the Madison family picture would help or hinder Glory's position. Her curiosity was soon settled.

Glory was among the small crowd of people coming towards them from the elevator. She smiled in surprise when she saw Alex. His tall and handsome frame stood out above the people waiting in turn for visitors' passes.

Alex was relieved to see through the warmth of her smile that his presence was welcome, not intrusive.

"What are you doing here? When did you get back?" Glory asked. She had noticed Elsa's curious gaze and she nodded to her with a silent *It's okay. He's friend, not foe.* Elsa winked back in response and gave her attention to the next person in line.

Alex suppressed the urge to take her in his arms. Instead, he pointed to the visitors' lounge where several sofas were unoccupied. "I've been so worried about you," he said once they were seated. "Especially when I couldn't reach you. How's your dad?"

She shrugged. "Stable, I guess. We don't know for sure yet."

"We?" he questioned. The one word held strong but positive implications.

She gave him a half-smile. "No, I didn't mean to imply that I've been fully accepted as 'family.' Nothing short of a miracle can make that happen. But at least they allowed me to stand at my father's bedside and breathe the same air with them."

She said it with blatant sarcasm but Alex easily recognized the pleasure reflected in her eyes. He lifted his brows and nodded, heeding her words. "I'd say that was a major accomplishment. Wouldn't you?"

Glory wouldn't allow herself to be that optimistic. She needed to stay tough for whatever they might dish out next. "Yes, I would," she acknowledged," but I think they relented only because they were too concerned about my father's heart attack to put up much resistance. And, I should add, Vanessa wasn't there at the time. When I bumped into her later, she still looked like she was breathing fire."

Alex laughed, then lowered his voice. "Aw, stop, Glory. Don't make the situation worse than it is."

Immediately, he could see he had said the wrong thing. Her eyebrows shot up and she opened her mouth to defend herself, but Alex stopped her with a finger to his lips. He then spoke with a calm and supportive tone, being particularly careful not to sound condescending. The last thing he needed was to make her feel that her interpretation of their attitudes might be a gross exaggeration.

"Forget that, Glory. I phrased it wrong," he said, doing the wipe-away gesture with his hand. "It's not that I don't believe you. Their behavior towards you is inexcusable. No question. But try to give them some slack. Your father's accident and heart attack came right after they found out about you. They're all hurting like wounded animals."

Glory took a deep breath and sighed. "And they see me as the cause of his accident and heart attack."

Alex pondered that. "Maybe," he said.

"No, that's not a maybe, that's a fact. And I can't argue with that because it's true. If I hadn't stepped into his life and thrown it into turmoil, my father wouldn't be here."

Alex stared at the face that had filled his thoughts since the night they met. He could see the pain of guilt in her eyes and the tightness around her lips. He held her hand between his and whispered, "Glory, you've got to stop torturing yourself with all these *ifs.*"

She smiled ruefully. "Good advice, but easier said than done."

With a quick laugh he shook his head and gave her that "you're hopeless" look. "Why don't we take a little walk outside?" he suggested. "There's a nice little gazebo that might be empty. We can talk privately."

Glory hesitated, then gave him an apologetic frown that wiped the smile off Alex's face. "I think I'd like to hang around for one more quick visit – they only allow five minutes every hour. But then I'll head home. Maybe you can come visit me later?"

His look of anticipation sparked a similar reaction in Glory. She tried her best to mask it. "I don't have much to eat in the apartment, but I can stop and pick up some take-out. I assume you haven't eaten yet?"

He ran a playful finger down her nose. "You assumed correctly. Call me when you leave the hospital. I'll pick up the food and meet you at your apartment."

They parted like two friends whose only intent was to share a meal.

But their hunger had nothing to do with food.

Chapter 74

Glory didn't call Alex when she left the hospital, but waited until she got home. She wanted some lead time to freshen up with a shower, shampoo and a change of clothes. A flash of guilt filled her for the images her mind entertained. As worried as she was about her father, it wasn't enough to extinguish the sensual urges Alex had ignited.

She fingered through all her clothes in the closet, trying to find something comfortable but feminine. No, not comfortable, not feminine, she decided. Something sexy. Seductive.

But not too seductive, a part of her urged.

Just enough to make her feel like the total woman and to invite that unmistakable look in Alex's eyes. The one that said *I'll never understand why your jerk of a husband gave you up.* Like Jason had the Pulitzer Prize and he had chosen a bowling trophy instead.

Memories of Jason sent her hands rummaging through for the perfect outfit. She selected a satin tropical print dress Jason had bought her during a Maui vacation. It covered every inch of her with another layer of softness, he had said, giving promise to what lies beneath. Romantic words then, but poisonous now.

She wondered with a bitter taste in her mouth whether he had spoken those words for her or whether he was already hungering for Marilyn Stillwell. He had left her only three months later.

"Yes, perfect," she said aloud, and threw it on her bed. A vengeful smile crossed her face, prompted by the satisfaction of wearing something he had bought her that would now please the eyes of another man.

***

Alex's arms were full when she opened the door. Her eyes widened in surprise. "Alex, what the heck did you do?" she said, laughing. "I thought we decided on lobster rolls?"

His smile was broad and his spirits high as he placed the three bags on her counter. "Well, yes, we did, but this place has the creamiest and thickest clam chowder. I had to let you taste it. Then, of course, it all came with salad and hot biscuits." He gave her a bright-eyed shrug. "I couldn't resist."

Glory was starving before he came, but now she could have skipped the whole meal. He looked so adorable and desirable that she would have preferred to throw her arms around his neck and taste those luscious lips instead.

"What's in this bag?" she asked, peeking into the smallest one.

"That's ice cream for dessert."

"Ice cream?" she yelled, but giggled. "What are you trying to do to me?"

"I'm sorry. It's not ice cream, it's yogurt. Frozen yogurt."

"Oh, that'll help," she teased. "A few less calories."

They worked together, laughed together, setting the table and arranging the food neatly in serving dishes. Glory put the tossed salad into bowls while he opened the wine.

"This is great, Alex," she said, breaking a biscuit that was still warm. "I didn't realize how hungry I was until these aromas wafted through my kitchen." She tilted her head and chewed away. "But then, I have a ravenous appetite."

His head lowered but his eyes lifted. "So do I," he said.

A weakness went through her.

He asked her for details of what had transpired with "la famiglia," as he put it. From the salad through the soup, they managed to ignore the heat between them while she filled him in.

A sudden lull in their conversation came when they had just begun to eat their lobster rolls. Alex took one bite and put it down. All that playfulness he had come in with had washed away. His gaze was burning with desire. He hadn't said a word, but Glory's cheeks went crimson. She put her fork down in her dish and took a few seconds to look up again. But when she did there was no turning back. She didn't move, she didn't speak. What was happening between them was thunderous.

Finally, Alex stood up. Never taking his eyes off hers, he took her hand and walked towards her bedroom. A voice spinning inside her head warned her to resist. But that voice weakened with every step she took.

They stood at the side of the bed. Still neither one spoke a word but Alex's gaze searched hers, giving her one last chance to change her mind. But the moment quickly passed, and they fell onto the bed, consumed by the thunder.

Chapter 75

Frannie had taken a liking to Sara and Tim and decided it might be a good idea to give them a crash course in food service. Glory's availability would be undependable for awhile. At least until her father is out of the hospital. She mentioned it to Glory when she stopped in that morning.

"To tell you the truth, Frannie, that would help me out. Last night it was decided that I would visit him from eleven in the morning until about two in the afternoon, when they come in. It's probably better that way. We can stay out of each other's hair."

"You mean they had a whole conversation with you? How civil of them."

Glory made a face. "I wouldn't call it a conversation. A necessary exchange of words, maybe."

Frannie blew a sigh. "Well, okay. That's a start."

Glory was glad Frannie hadn't mentioned a word about Alex. It wouldn't take much brain power for her to figure out what had happened last night. Although she was out when Glory came back from the hospital and still out when Alex had arrived, his car was there in the driveway whenever she got home and remained there until 2:00 a.m.

No, she didn't have to draw any pictures for Frannie and certainly didn't need her approval. They were each entitled to their own private lives and choice of friends. The matter of Alex was put to rest when they last discussed him. Glory had assured Frannie that he would not in any way influence their business relationship or personal friendship.

Still, she thought, I'd feel a hell of a lot better if Frannie would defrost a little. Once she had welcomed Alex into her bed last night, she could no longer tell herself that what they felt for each other was only physical. Last night wasn't about sex. It was an incredible expression of love.

***

"Wow! That's fantastic!" Sara said when Glory called to tell her the good news. "What happened to all those 'tests' we were supposed to pass first?"

"Sometimes it's necessary to waive tests. But we'll be keeping our eyes on both of you at Amore Breakfast," Glory said, her tone playful. "You and Tim made good first impressions on us. We feel confident that you'll both work out."

"Don't worry, Miss English. We won't make you sorry you recommended us. I can't wait to tell Tim. I'm going to call him as soon as I hang up."

Glory clicked off the phone and grinned. "Now that was a feel-good phone call," she said aloud. There were no worry lines in her face as she drove away from Amore Breakfast. She looked forward to seeing her father this morning. His condition had improved, according to the nurse she had spoken to earlier, and she could have him all to herself.

Only moments later, worry lines creased her forehead once again. Certainly not anytime soon, but eventually she'd have to tell her father about Alex. He won't be too happy either, she thought.

Chapter 76

Happy tears filled Glory's eyes the moment she saw her father. What a difference a day makes, she thought, and kissed his forehead.

"Morning, Glory," Dan said. "So good to open my eyes and see you." His words came out slow and labored, but his voice was much stronger than last night, his face more relaxed.

"Oh, I'm sorry. Were you sleeping?"

He lifted a hand and fanned his fingers. "On and off."

"How's it going?" His eyes darted from left to right. "Where's everybody?"

"They're coming around two. I'll be here till then."

Dan responded with one fleeting expression but it told a whole story. His lips twisted sideways and his eyes rolled upward. Glory saw tension building and tried to stop its escalation. "No, it wasn't bad, Dad, really. It works out better this way."

He gave her a disagreeable smirk, then wiped it away with a gentle smile. She could see he didn't have the strength yet to discuss his family, nor did she want him to.

"So is anything new since last night? Have you seen any doctors today?"

"Yes, Dr. Curtis, my brother-in-law. He's – "

"Your wife's brother. Yes, your children told me." Not saying how, she thought, recalling Vanessa's admonition. "What did he say?"

He shrugged. "Not much. So far, so good, is all he said, more or less."

He dismissed the subject as insignificant and moved on. "How 'bout you? Are you holding up okay? What did you do last night?"

The casual question fired up images of Alex in her bed. Her cheeks blushed. "Nothing much," she answered. "Just went home after visiting you."

"What's happening with the restaurant? You and Frannie should be closing soon, right?"

"Yes, as a matter of fact, the date's been moved up. We close Tuesday. The Duca brothers told Frannie they'll start the renovations next Friday or Saturday." Her face brightened with enthusiasm. "So all systems are go, as far as I can see. It's going to be a mad rush for us from now on, but it'll be exciting."

Dan watched how her eyes sparkled while she babbled on about renovation plans. His smile reflected the pleasure in his heart, but frightening thoughts of his mortality clouded it. More than ever now he prayed for good health so that Glory could be part of his life. He also needed time to soothe his family's angry hearts.

Somehow, he had to bring them all together.

"I'm sorry," Glory said, noticing the faraway look in his eyes. "I'm rambling on and on while you're probably still feeling lousy and want to sleep."

"No, I don't feel too bad. I was just thinking about things I have to do once I have the strength again."

"You don't have to do anything," she scolded. "You have family for your personal stuff and a crew for your business. You just rest and let them handle it."

"And what about you? Who's going to handle you?"

She gave him a proud but indignant look. "Me, of course. I make a good living and if things go our way, Amore Evenings will make it even better."

"I wasn't talking about your finances. I was talking about you. Here and here," he said, touching his heart and his forehead.

She gave him a slanted look and hoped he wasn't going to ask about Alex. "I'm not sure I know what you mean, Dad. But whatever it is can wait. I can tell by your breathing and your voice that you're talking too much." She stroked his hair and felt the warmth of a smile tugging her lips. Only days had passed since they met, yet kissing her father's forehead and stroking his face felt perfectly natural, as though she'd been doing it all her life.

Dan nodded, admitted that yes, too much talk does tire him out. "But," he said, with a warning finger raised, "don't be upset." He paused for more breath, then said only, "I'll take care of them. Please don't hate them." His voice cracked and he was suddenly silent. He closed his eyes to hide their glaze and tightened his lips.

Glory's tears were less controllable than Dan's. The pleading look in his eyes, the helplessness and the hurt they were causing him sliced right through her heart. She kissed the palms of his hands as though they were something sacred.

"I don't hate them," she managed to say, then tried to lighten up with a forced laugh. "I just don't like them very much so far – except for Amy – "

He put a finger to his lips. "Trust me, Glory. It'll be okay. I promise you. But can you do me a favor, please?"

"Of course. Anything," she said, then wiped her tears and tried for a bright smile.

"For my sake, sweetheart, try killing them with kindness."

This time her laugh was genuine. "That's a tall order, Daddy dear, but yes, I will try."

Chapter 77

This job won't be a piece of cake like Paula Grant. He had two young people to deal with now; both strong, energetic and sane. The time and the place had to be right with absolutely no opportunity for one to escape.

He never did like guns or rifles, even for hunting. But some situations don't allow you much choice. And so, he had made the trip to New York City to connect with a certain old and unfriendly friend who sold him a .38 Smith & Wesson, complete with silencer, and absolutely untraceable, the guy had assured him. He had two huge obstacles to knock down before executing this crime to perfection. The first was Alex Howard. Not only did he have to be in Maine at the time, but it had to be done within the hours of 1:00 a.m. to 4:00 a.m., when most people are asleep. More importantly, when Alex would be alone. Problem is, he thought, if he's already screwing Glory English, she could throw a monkey wrench into his plan. If Howard is in her bed, or she in his at the targeted hour, she would provide him with an airtight alibi.

Second obstacle would be the designated time frame to pull it off. How the hell would he get the two kids to be out where he wanted them at that time of night? Yes, quite a challenge this time, he mused, but a sick smile curled around his lips. A thrilling sensation rippled through his body. The challenge excited him. What a kick it would be if he could put all the pieces together, get the job done and dump the blame on Alex Howard.

Unconsciously, he picked up his darts and threw one at the board on his bedroom wall. Bullseye! The game amused him more than ever tonight. He was always a believer in omens. If he could consistently throw four consecutive bullseyes, he told himself, that would be his sign of imminent success.

Repeatedly, he aimed carefully and threw each dart, calling out names with each one. Timothy Waite, Sara Baisley, Glory English, Alex Howard. These were the principal players in his game. And there they were, all together, nice and neatly tucked within the bullseye of his dart board.

And then there was his silent partner. The ultimate prize. He threw one for her too, right on target.

Chapter 78

Maybe it was just as well that her father's discharge from the hospital fell on Tuesday of the following week, closing day for Amore Evenings. And although Glory hadn't believed it at the time, what she told him about the hospital visitation arrangement turned out to be true. It had worked out better. They didn't have to get upset at the sight of me, she thought, I didn't have to feel like the family lepor and Dad didn't have to get caught in the middle.

The skies were dark and angry this late August morning. Relentless torrential rain and wind would disappoint many vacationing families and anyone else who planned to soak in the tail end of summer. But the inclement weather did nothing to diminish the spirits of Glory English and Frannie Oliveri, co-owners of what they hoped would become Ogunquit's finest restaurant.

After the closing, they returned to Amore Breakfast, where they were pleasantly surprised. They walked in to a burst of congratulatory applause from not only the employees but the customers as well. A huge good luck banner hung from the ceiling and a mountainous tray of miniature pastries wrapped in pink cellophane stood on a table in the center of the restaurant along with bottles of sparkling cider.

Frannie was frozen in surprise at first, then filled with emotion. She burst into tears, triggering the same reaction for Glory.

"I'm stunned. This is so...so..." Frannie began, "Somebody give me a word," she said and laughed.

"Touched," somebody said. Frannie's finger went out to acknowledge that person. "Yes, touched. Glory and I want to thank all of you. We hope to make Amore Evenings a very special place that will make all of Ogunquit proud." She waved an arm to the pastry table and said, "Now help yourselves. And those of you who are still enjoying breakfast, it's on me. Enjoy!"

Glory swallowed the lump in her throat as she scanned the faces of everyone standing before them. What she saw was sincere, demonstrative enthusiasm for this dream she and Frannie had brought to life. But it was her idea to begin with, and Glory hoped with all her heart that Amore Evenings would not be a disappointment, or worse, a financial disaster.

But she smiled wide and refused to entertain such thoughts. With Frannie at the helm, they had no reason to anticipate failure.

Tim and Sara were on the job today and both appeared delighted to be part of the festivities. She stopped Tim as he was serving and said, "This was so nice. Who engineered this little celebration? Do you know?"

"Oh, it was a concerted effort," Tim answered with a grin.

"But it was his idea," Viola threw in. "His and Sara's."

Glory gave a knowing smile. "I sure know how to pick 'em, huh?"

Chapter 79

Friday night dinner with Alex could have been skipped entirely. Glory's wall of resistance had crumbled like a sand castle in a rush of water. But surprisingly, she was comfortable with their intimacy now and told him so as they lay sated in his bed.

"I'm glad we decided on Ratherbee, not my apartment. The total privacy here makes it more romantic, don't you think? When you were at my place, I cringed a little thinking of Frannie upstairs possibly hearing us."

Alex brushed a finger over her lips and smiled. "Really? I got the impression you were too preoccupied to be worrying about Frannie or anyone else."

Glory looked up at him with feigned shyness. "It flashed through my mind once or twice," she said, then rested her head in the crook of his arm. Her face grew serious, her eyes veiled in thought.

"What's going on in that pretty little head of yours? Are you thinking good thoughts of me or are you planning your next column?"

"I wish I were simply thinking of my column. That's not nearly as complicated."

"As complicated as what?"

She was sorry she had raised the subject. How could she tell him everyone frowns at the mention of his name? Sometimes it angered her, made her want to argue in his defense. Other times she wondered if what she felt for Alex was not pure and simple love, but an obsessive attraction that clouded her ability to see him for what he really is.

She took too long to answer his question so he repeated it. Her eyes locked with his. She stared into them one long moment, but saw only the love she wanted to see. "As complicated as us," she said finally.

Alex sat up to listen. He braced himself for the negatives he saw in her troubled face.

"Alex, I've been trying to fight it off, to make all kinds of excuses, but the plain truth is I'm in love with you – "

Alex beamed. "Well, there's nothing complicated about that since I – "

She stopped him with a finger to his lips. "No. This is not a simple girl-meets-boy love story." She paused. The ten percent of her brain that harbored the doubt, the fear of that other Alex Howard prompted her to search for the right words. "I know you for the kind and gentle person you really are. Truthfully it bothers me that people think of you differently. You talked to me about Elena, but you still haven't told me about Allison. I need to hear it, Alex, here and now." She got out of bed and threw on the terrycloth beach robe he had given her. "I'm going to the kitchen to make a pot of coffee so we can finish our talk."

Alex blew a sigh and followed her to the kitchen. "It's not a pretty story."

Glory nodded, silently prepared the coffee and sat opposite him, arms folded.

Alex's eyes narrowed as he began his story. "I think Allison was on a collision course from her early teens. I don't know exactly when it started…maybe when she was about fifteen. She started hanging out with a fast crowd and no matter how I tried to warn my parents, they turned a blind eye. They were good friends with a few of Allison's friends' parents and they just laughed me off. They thought it was "cute" – that's the word they used – cute of me to play the concerned big brother, but I was overreacting, they said. Meanwhile, Allison actually enjoyed watching me try to get through to them. She'd always give me a triumphant smirk.

She had them wrapped around her finger, always pouting to them like the sweet and innocent child who was constantly bullied by her brother. My parents saw only what they wanted to see. They were too busy partying to be bothered with parental responsibility."

Glory tried to look objectively at the picture Alex presented. "Well, what made you suspect Allison was on this collision course, as you put it? Is it possible she was just a little more extroverted than the average teen?"

Alex's brows shot up. He gave her a sidelong glance and laughed. "Now there's a nice polite term to describe Allison, 'extroverted.'"

Glory's serious expression never changed, so Alex raised a hand. "I'm sorry. I'm not trying to put you down or anything, but if you had known Allison then, 'extroverted' would not be your word of choice." His eyes rolled upward and he drew a breath. He didn't even like to think about what Glory insisted on hearing, much less discuss it. "Okay. But first I want to say I've never told this to anyone. You know how I feel about you, Glory, so I trust that this will never go any further – "

A ripple of fear went through Glory. She thought maybe she'd be better off not knowing. "Forget it, Alex. I can see this is painful for you. And I get the feeling it's extremely personal, so why don't we forget it and I'll never bring it up again. Okay?"

Alex gave her a long look then nodded as though he agreed, but the words were already on his tongue. "I came home unexpectedly that day…"

Glory's entire body tensed. She wanted to hear and didn't want to hear.

"I heard laughter coming from my bedroom. One of the voices was definitely male. I was already sick to my stomach, knowing what I would find. But it was worse. Much worse. He bit his lower lip and squinted as though blinded by the memory. "There was a man in our bed, as I suspected. But there were three nude bodies in that bed, not two. The third was my sweet and innocent baby sister, Allison."

Glory's hands flew over her mouth. "Oh dear, God!"

Alex swallowed hard. Bitter pain was visible on his face but he went on. "The worst part was their reaction when I walked in on them. At first Elena looked frightened, or maybe it was just shock. But when Allison burst out laughing, Elena laughed too. I have to admit I wanted to kill them all, but I was so stunned, I went numb – couldn't move, couldn't scream. The fat, hairy bastard ran like a bat out of hell before I could go after him. But I didn't give a damn about him. It was my wife and sister I wanted to kill. Two people I had loved who had reduced themselves to this and betrayed me beyond belief.

"I think I was still just staring at Elena when Allison laughed and brushed it off. 'Don't make such a big f---ing deal out of it. Maybe if you weren't such a bore your wife wouldn't have to find her own fun,' she said.

Glory left their unfilled coffee cups on the counter and sat on his lap. Gently and wordlessly she kissed his forehead. After a few silent moments, he looked up at her. "I can read your thoughts, Glory, but don't be sorry. You were right. I needed to get it out, to say it aloud. Believe it or not, I do feel better. Probably because I have you now to help me forget."

The sound of the doorbell brought them to their feet. If there ever was an inopportune time for a visitor, it was now, Glory thought. But then again, she quickly recalled the last time the bell had rung here at another inopportune time.

Together, Glory and Alex looked out from the dining room window. Then, with a defeated sigh, Alex opened the door for his uninvited guests and brought them into the kitchen.

Both Detective Sergeant Tony Gerard and Detective Patricia Carney acknowledged Glory's presence and her silent statement with a polite nod. She made no attempt this time to shield the fact that she and Alex were lovers. Maybe it could help Alex if someone reputable shows support for him, she reasoned.

Still, she raked nervous fingers through her hair knowing full well the gesture was useless. One quick glance from anyone would reveal that she had just rolled off a bed. She imagined her lips, cheeks and neck were swollen and reddened with telltale signs of their lovemaking. She brushed off the tinge of embarrassment and tilted her face upward. A little defiance, a little pride.

"We're sorry to bother you again, Mr. Howard, but we need only a few minutes more of your time."

Alex did make an effort to mask his annoyance but knew it wouldn't pass the detectives' scrutiny. "It would be nice to get an advance phone call, Sergeant, but okay. What else do you need to know?"

Glory cut in before the detective could respond. "Alex, I'll wait in the den while you speak to them," she said and made a quick exit.

In less than fifteen minutes the detectives were gone and Alex joined her in the den. He looked drained, defeated. "What happened? What did they want?" she asked.

"Apparently, they're giving more credence to Josephine Britton's statement than anything I tell them. They seem to believe her insistence that she locked Paula's bedroom door, and since it wasn't forced open…"

He didn't have to complete the sentence to know where it was going. "Oh, come on!" she said and punched the air. "They can't believe you'd unlock the door with a key! That would be so obvious. Even if you were an idiot and wanted to kill her, you would have known enough to make it look like forced entry. What did you tell them?"

Alex shrugged. "I said, assuming Josie was right and she *had* locked the door, maybe the assailant found the key. For all we know it could have been on her lap or still dangling from her fingers. Then they asked me if there were any spare keys to that room. There was one originally, but I couldn't tell them where it is. I hadn't been coming to Ratherbee on a regular basis. How can I keep tabs on small details like that?"

"Absolutely. Did they accept that?"

"More or less. They said they'd question all the aides Paula ever had. In the beginning there were several who didn't last. Then they said they also wanted to speak to Allison. Maybe she'd know something."

"They haven't questioned her?"

"Not yet. They said they haven't been able to locate her."

Chapter 80

The season was nearing a close in Ogunquit. Frannie said the next two weeks would remain busy, but after that, business would decline steadily. Amore Breakfast would be forced to close its doors until spring.

It was a depressing time of year for everyone involved in tourism here in Ogunquit, but for some it provided a welcome respite. They could travel, relax or do whatever they couldn't do during their hectic summer.

Glory and Frannie accepted that leisure would take a back seat indefinitely, but neither one cared. Both were fired up and anxious to see their dream materialize. And today the Duca Brothers and their crew would begin to make that happen.

All the tables at Amore Breakfast were still occupied, but the waiting list had finally been exhausted. Frannie couldn't leave Amore Breakfast while it was still open, but Glory could, she said, and urged her to go. Glory didn't hesitate to accept her offer. She was so thrilled about this new venture that she wished she could watch every inch of its progress. Anxiety put those familiar butterflies in her stomach. She felt like a schoolgirl on her first date. Even her appetite had vanished today. She hadn't had the patience or desire to finish eating one piece of toast.

Glory was headed for a back table where someone had signaled for a coffee refill. Sara took the pot right out of her hand. "Go," she said with a finger to the door. "You've had ants in your pants all morning. I know you want to fly out of here and down to Amore Evenings. We can handle your tables. Go."

Glory squeezed Sara's arm and smiled wide. She ripped off the checks for her two remaining tables and gave them to Sara. "Thanks. You're a doll."

"No problem. I don't blame you for wanting to run down there. I'm dying to see the place myself."

"Well, right now it's just a house. A huge house."

Sara smiled and shrugged. "Still. I'd love to see the before and after and the progress in between. Especially since Tim and I are among the first to be hired, I kind of feel an attachment to it already."

Glory patted her cheek. "That kind of enthusiastic attitude is what got you guys hired in the first place." She pulled a business card out of her bag and handed it to Sara. "Look, why don't you call me on my cell later this afternoon? Maybe I can ride you both down for a quick look."

Sara's eyes brightened. "Oh, that'll be great! Are you sure you don't mind? I know you'll be running ragged from now on. And with Mr. Madison sick – "

"Sara, if it were a problem, I wouldn't have offered. Just call me. And if things back up today, there's always tomorrow. Okay?"

"Okay," Sara responded with a grin. She was going to love watching this dream of theirs grow from the bottom up. But Glory and Frannie weren't the only ones with stars in their eyes. Sara too was already dreaming that someday she'd have a managerial position at Amore Evenings. You couldn't beat the atmosphere! The thought excited her. She fingered the card and called out to Glory just as she was heading out the door. When Glory stopped Sara held up the little New York-based card. "I already have one of these, but you're gonna have to dump them anyway."

Glory didn't answer, just smiled as she walked out. It still amazed her how little she missed her life in New York.

Chapter 81

Glory pulled into the driveway of Frannie's house, left the car running, and came out with her digital camera. No one could have been more surprised than she at her reaction to this new venture. Since the success of her *Glorious Cooking* column she should have considered it just another step up the ladder, but instead she giggled like a kid.

The Duca Brothers trucks and equipment were already parked on the old Crawford property that now officially belonged to Frannie and Glory. Carl saw her coming and walked out to meet her. Her camera was already filming to capture what it all looked like before their work had begun. He took her hands in his and kissed her on the cheek. "Hey, this is an unexpected pleasure. Let me be the first to wish you luck." He kissed her again, this time on the lips.

Glory smiled politely despite his lingering hug. "I didn't mean to interrupt, but I couldn't resist riding down now that it's ours. Frannie will be down later, after she closes up. I hope you don't mind. Will we be in your way?"

"Not at all. Just keep a safe distance from the crew. We wouldn't want anybody getting hurt. Otherwise, it'll be a pleasure for us to look up and see a pretty face for a change."

She accepted his compliment with an amiable grin, as though his remark was nothing more than harmless friendly flattery. But Glory saw something deeper in his eyes and the expression around his mouth. That cat-that-ate-the-canary look. She wasn't quite sure, but his next remark confirmed her instinct.

"Let me know when you get tired of Pretty Boy Howard," he said, brushing a finger on her chin. "Money doesn't buy everything, you know."

An angry flame shot up inside her sending a flash of heat to her neck. She was about to tell him off when better judgment made her bite her lips shut. This guy is Frannie's cousin for one, and second, he has a contractual obligation to be here every day. It would not behoove her to begin their business relationship with an argument, but eventually she'd have to put him in his place, calmly and tactfully.

Glory put on a plastic smile and let the moment pass. She excused herself and began to walk away. Her anger was probably mirrored in her face because he stopped her with a gentle touch on the arm. "Hey, I was just kidding. You know me. I like to joke around. If I offended you, I'm sorry."

She gave him a hard sidelong look, then relaxed with a sigh and a half-smile. "Okay. No harm done. I guess I'm a little sensitive about Alex Howard. I think the guy got a raw deal. People are too quick to make assumptions and condemn him without full knowledge of the facts. And that's all I care to say on the subject." She tried to keep the smile on her face but couldn't fake it anymore. "Except for your insinuation about money," she added. "I've done very well for myself. I don't need Alex Howard's money, and I have to say, Carl, that remark was a low blow."

Carl went instantly contrite. "Glory, I'm *really* sorry. I've got a big mouth and I put my foot in it sometimes. Please accept my apology. To tell you the truth, I think I was a little jealous. Maybe if we had met sooner, you'd be defending *me* to someone, not Alex. So what do you say – friends?"

He looked at her with such remorse that Glory melted. "Sure. I'm sorry too. I let my emotions get the best of me sometimes and I overreact. I like you, Carl. You're a nice guy with a great sense of humor. Yes, let's stay friends." She put out a hand and Carl eagerly shook it.

"You got it," he said with all the sincerity he could muster, then walked away to rejoin his workers.

Glory walked around the property and put her imagination to work. Several new ideas danced in her head that she'd discuss with Frannie tonight. When her thoughts shifted to her father, weariness set in. Sometime today he was being released and she couldn't be there. They had left it that either he or Amy would call her tonight, depending on how he was feeling. But he'd be recuperating at home now, with his wife and family. Where does that leave me? Glory wondered.

Chapter 82

The sun was strong and blazing in an almost clear sky this Saturday afternoon. Only soft threads of clouds streaked through the blue. It brought a bittersweet smile to Glory's lips as she thought about how it resembled her life these days. Strong and blazing was her spirit for Amore Evenings; the soft threads of clouds her problems with the Madison family and the suspicion that hovered over Alex.

She changed into shorts and a tee shirt, grabbed a blueberry yogurt and went out on the patio. She toyed with the idea of calling her father's house. *What's the worst that could happen?* she mused. *Someone might hang up on me? Big deal. With what they've put me through so far, I've practically developed an immunity.*

Glory considered it only until she finished her last spoonful of yogurt. Wiping the sweet and creamy excess from the corners of her mouth, she made her decision. If I don't get word by eight o'clock tonight, she told herself, I'm calling.

While Glory waited for Frannie to get home, she decided to put the time to good use by getting a jump on her next column. She sat at her computer and threw herself into her work. Dozens of emails had come in with questions and comments and she lost herself in the pleasantries of her responses.

Almost two hours had passed before she came up for air and only because the phone was ringing.

"Glory, it's me," Frannie said. "I'm stuck here for a while. The air conditioning died on us. By the time I waited through all those recorded messages we were sweating bullets. Finally I got through to someone. He said he'd be here within an hour."

Glory didn't want to interrupt her work, especially since she was on a roll, but she had to offer. "Oh, darn. That's too bad. And I had planned to go down to the property with you. Do you want me to wait there for the guy so you can run down and talk to your cousin?"

"No, I have to talk to the air conditioning guy. He might give me a song and dance and try to talk me into a new one."

Glory laughed. "Frannie, some things do fall apart eventually. Maybe you *do* need a new one."

"Maybe. But not until he convinces me I have absolutely no choice."

"You're some piece of work. No wonder you're so successful. No one gets past you without a fight," Glory said, but her tone reflected her admiration. "If that were me, I'd just say, 'Fine, if you can't fix it, replace it.' And whatever price he threw at me, I'd humbly pay."

It was Frannie's turn to laugh. "Exactly. And that's why you'll take charge of customer relations and good will promotion. I'll take care of the business until you get the hang of it."

"Hey, you'll get no argument from me," Glory said, playing along. "I'll be happy to bow to your expertise."

"Listen, Frannie," she said, changing the subject. "We might not connect until tomorrow, so don't worry. In case of an emergency, call me on my cell."

"You got it. Enjoy."

Glory knew that Frannie understood the message. She was seeing Alex again and would probably spend the night at Ratherbee. And yes, enjoy she would.

Chapter 83

Glory spent another hour at her computer, enjoying her work and pleased that she had accomplished so much today. But then the phone rang. She heard Sara's voice and remembered her promise.

"If you're too busy, Glory, we can make it another day."

"No, actually I'm in good shape with my column. Sometimes I can glide right through it and other times it's like pulling teeth. Today was one of my 'glide through' days.

"So where are you guys now? Where and when should I pick you up?"

"Can you hold on a minute?" Sara said, then posed Glory's question to Tim. "Tim says how about 4:30 at Amore Breakfast? We can sit on the porch and wait for you."

"Four-thirty it is. See you then."

She was polishing up the last paragraph on her column when the phone interrupted again. "It's no use," she mumbled, "When you want to get something done, you have to leave your phone at home and do your work at the library."

Her annoyance drained when she heard his voice. Alex. Glory went warm all over.

"Hi, sweetheart. What's going on? You busy?"

"I'm at the tail end of my column. I'd like to finish it before I have to run out again. Once I send this off, I'll have some breathing space."

"Where do you have to run? Anything important?"

"No, not really. Those two high school kids I told you about, Tim and Sara, they want to see the house and property. They're excited too because they'll be working there."

Alex was a little disappointed with her answer. He had hoped she had gotten an invitation to visit her father at home. Fat chance. He wished he had the right to intervene. It killed him to hear how they were treating her.

"I'm excited too," he teased. "I hope to spend a lot of time there in the future. One of these days I'd like to take the grand tour myself."

The thought hadn't occurred to Glory to invite him at this early stage, but she was pleased by his interest and she'd love sharing her plans and ideas. "Want to come along today? We can swing by and pick you up." She was about to add that they also had the choice of stopping at the site tonight before they went to dinner, but there was a good chance Frannie would be there at that time. She didn't want to shove Alex in her face that soon. It's exactly what Frannie was afraid of.

"No, I'll pass this time. The kids might feel funny having me tag along. Do they know we've been seeing each other?"

That put a grin on Glory's face. "Alex, I get the feeling that's common knowledge around Ogunquit. And that's fine with me." *Unfortunately not fine with my dad and Frannie.*

Alex loved her a little more for that. If it were possible to love her more. "Well, that brings my fan club to a total of one," he joked.

"If it's the last thing I do, Alex, I'm going to increase that fan club. And today I'll start with Tim and Sara. Listen, would you mind if I give them a look around Ratherbee? The grounds are so beautiful. I think they'd enjoy it."

"If it means I get to see you sooner than tonight, I'm all for it. Especially if it'll bring my fan club up to three."

Glory smiled and inhaled slowly, as though to fill her insides with his loving words. "Okay, Mr. Wonderful, we'll be there five-ish."

She clicked off the phone and rubbed her hands on her cheeks, feeling and basking in the warmth Alex had put there.

*****

Tim and Sara appeared thrilled with the unexpected opportunity to tour Ratherbee. Although both their homes would catch the eyes of many passersby and tourists, Ratherbee ranked among Ogunquit's oldest and finest. A moment later, though, when Glory wasn't looking, they exchanged a piercing look that needed no words. They could get a closer look at the scene of the crime.

Alex had no trouble winning their hearts. For some inexplicable reason he felt an immediate affection for the youngsters. Probably because Glory liked them at first sight and took them under her wing. Tim and Sara were full of questions and Alex was happy to answer them all with enthusiasm and pride.

"If you two want to sit and relax out here on the porch," Sara said, "Tim and I can walk the grounds on our own."

"Sure, you guys look around," Alex said gladly. He couldn't wait to steal a moment to get Glory in his arms. "We'll finish our iced tea and catch up with you later."

Tim and Sara explored the grounds and disappeared for twenty minutes. They too were looking to steal a moment in total privacy. The thick trunk of an old oak tree provided that privacy for them and they took full advantage.

Later, they rounded the property and sat on a concrete bench that overlooked a meticulously maintained flower garden bursting with color, and, of course, the magnificent ocean beyond. They held hands and talked, mostly about Glory and Alex.

"He seems so nice," Sara said. "Am I that gullible or is everybody else nuts?"

Tim didn't hesitate to answer. "No. Everybody else is nuts, in my opinion. There's no way he could have killed his sister. Did you notice how he choked up a couple of times when he talked about her?"

"Yes, and I know he could have faked it, but I can't find the slightest trace of evil in that man. For Glory's sake, I hope to God we're right."

They fell silent a few moments and watched Glory and Alex walking the oceanfront path.

Sara jolted to her feet. "Holy shit, Tim! Did you see what I just saw?"

Perplexed, Tim looked around, saw nothing but beauty and tranquility. "No. What the hell did you see?"

"Forget it. I'll tell you later. They're walking towards us."

Chapter 84

Sara dreamed up an excuse for Glory to drop them off near Amore Breakfast. She babbled on about meeting their friends for pizza.

Glory gave her a curious glance through her rearview mirror. "On our way to Ratherbee you said you had to get home because you had relatives coming for dinner."

"I did. I do," she stammered, "but my parents' dinner parties run late. There's usually a two-hour cocktail party before they actually sit down to eat."

Glory detected a sour tone to Sara's voice and another flash glance through the mirror reflected her disdain. She opted to let the subject die. "So what did you guys think of Ratherbee? Gorgeous, isn't it?"

"Breathtaking," Sara quickly replied. "We always admired it from a distance, but naturally once you get onto the property, there's so much more to see." She wished she could tell Glory that what she had seen today at Ratherbee could change someone's destiny.

"And Alex Howard seems like an okay guy. We feel bad for him," Tim said, not bothering to say why, but he wanted Glory to know he and Sara trusted her judgment and supported her decision to stick by him. Not that the support of two eighteen-year-olds should carry that much weight, but he had a strong feeling that it did to Glory.

"That's nice to hear, Tim. It means a lot to me. I guess you both know that Alex and I have something going." She forced a laugh. "I'm not quite sure yet what that something is, but it's there, that's for sure."

"I think it's a four-letter word that starts with L and everyone wants," Sara offered, but she couldn't wait to get out of the car.

***

At Perkins Cove, Sara grabbed Tim's hand and led him to the railing since all the benches were occupied.

"What the hell's going on? You look like you're about to bust a gut," he said. "What did you see that made you this jumpy?"

"I saw the same thing you saw, Tim. Only difference is I noticed something that you apparently didn't."

Tim arched a brow.

"He ducked," she said, then giggled and repeated herself, louder this time.

Tim's face creased with confusion. "Who ducked? What the hell are you talking about?"

Sara would have enjoyed dangling the good news and turning it into a guessing game a little longer, but she couldn't hold it in another moment. "Alex ducked, Tim. When we were sitting at that flower garden, we watched Glory and Alex walk the path towards the dock, remember?"

"Yes…"

"Well, think about that scene – about what you *saw*."

Tim's eyes went high and wide with the revelation. "Holy damn shit!" Now I know what you mean by 'ducked.' He had to duck under the branch when they reached that tree just before the dock."

"And the person who walked Paula that night was taller than Paula, we told Sergeant Gerard, but he never ducked at that tree. It couldn't possibly be Alex, like everyone's thinking." Sara was so excited her eyes sparkled.

"Everyone except Glory."

"I was dying to tell her, Tim, and him, but we promised Sergeant Gerard that if we remembered anything else, we'd keep it to ourselves and contact him immediately."

"You were dying to tell her? Are you kidding, Sara? Nobody knows about us and what we saw that night. It's a good thing you didn't slip and let the cat out of the bag. We're talking murder here."

"Okay, okay, don't beat up on me. I only said I was dying to tell her, not that I would."

Tim cooled. "I'm not beating up on you. I'm just excited about this piece of information. It may not help catch her killer, but it should definitely get Alex off the hook. Let's get out of here. We need to call Sergeant Gerard from somewhere private."

They left Perkins Cove and walked along Shore Road silently since they were surrounded by tourists. Both were fired up and anxious to share this news with Tony Gerard. But Sara's excitement was clouded by her conscience. She had confided in her friend Jennifer and she hoped to God that Jennifer had kept her promise not to breathe a single word.

Chapter 85

He used a disposable cell phone to call her. The sultry sound of her voice thrilled him and his maleness came to life. But it wasn't her sensuality alone that sent a rush of blood to the right places; it was the incomparable feeling of knowing that the time to move was close.

"You ready for some action?" he asked.

"Well, that depends. What did you have in mind, lover boy?"

"Anything you'd like, sugar, and more."

"And more? Now that's giving me goose bumps all over. I can't imagine what we've left out. But it's been so long since we were together, I'm getting withdrawal. When do you think it'll be safe to sneak a little visit? It's tough for a woman to be faithful when her man neglects her."

He did not see the humor in her playful banter. "That's not funny," he said through clenched teeth. "And I told you, it's safe when I say it's safe. If I left that up to you, we'd be in orange jumpsuits already."

"Okay, don't get your bowels in an uproar. I'm just teasing. Do you miss me?"

"If you were here I could show you how much I miss you, but a lot of shit's been happening. I've got it all under control, though, sugar. You just stay cool and let me work it all out."

"Hey, don't leave me in the dark like that. Tell me what's going on. What shit's been happening?"

"Nothing I can't handle. Don't worry."

"But I *am* worried now that you threw that line out at me. What shit?"

"Two kids with big eyes screwing around where they didn't belong. But that's my problem, not yours."

"Two kids? What two kids? Don't tell me they saw you! Where were they?"

He heard the panic in her voice and wanted to kick himself in the ass for opening his mouth. "They're not little kids, they're high school kids," he said as though that made his intent to kill them a lesser crime. His tone implied this was just a minor detail as he briefly explained how the teenagers were involved. "And they couldn't have seen anything that could possibly identify me, but still, if we want this to work, we have to cover all the bases. They've already been running loose too long, but I had to come up with a plan before I make a move."

"Are you saying what I think you're saying?" Her panic was rising.

"I'm saying don't you start losing it now. We came this far and we don't want to screw anything up. It's important that you do exactly as I say and just trust me, Allison."

"That's what I've been doing since you first had this get-rich-quick brainstorm. I let you talk me into Paula. You convinced me she'd never be the person she used to be and she'd never know the difference anyway if she were dead. I'm not saying I'm sorry, Carl, but high school kids! Is this absolutely necessary? You said they could never identify you."

"Yes, I did, but we need to be one hundred percent sure of that."

"But you're talking about two more lives, young lives! Just the thought makes me sick. And it's too risky, Carl."

"No, 'risky' would be eliminating your brother too. We could have the whole pie, not just half, but I'm not stupid, Allison. And I'm not doing it for pleasure. Look, we have a goal, simple as that, and in order to reach that goal, we have to remove all the obstacles."

Allison sighed with resignation. "Okay, that makes sense, I guess. I'll leave the ugly details up to you. But try to get it over with fast. I don't want to think about it. Once it's done, it's done. I can't say I won't feel a little remorse this time, but that six million dollars will help me forget. Just be careful, Carl. Very careful."

He laughed complacently. "Sugar, you're talking to the wrong person. I'm always careful. Gotta go. I'll be in touch soon."

"Carl?" She called out before he could hang up.

"What?"

"I love you."

"I love you too, sugar."

I'd *better be damn sure we reach that goal,* he thought when he hung up. His mind was sharp and shrewd, but this time he'd be dealing with three people in one sweep. And all of them had working brains and strong legs.

But I have the gun.

Chapter 86

Forty miles away in Freeport, Allison paced the thick cream-colored carpeting in her living room. Her sprawling ranch house could comfortably accommodate a family of five. But she hated it because her sister Paula had selected and paid for it, along with all its furnishings. That was the deal Paula had made to keep Allison away from Ratherbee. Living under the same roof, the two sisters were like fire and ice. One of them had to go.

But now the tables are turned, sister dear, she thought with a satisfied smile. Now you're dead and buried and I'm calling the shots. Ah, yes, revenge is sweet.

Still, revenge does not come easily, she mused, as her thoughts switched back to the present. The more she thought about Carl's phone call, the more her heart hammered away. She didn't like this "shit happening" problem. They'd already had a close call when Carl had found Paula's door locked. He had blamed her for not alerting him to that possibility. And he was right. If he hadn't spotted that key right next to the nurse's teacup, he would have had to force the door open. Alex would have come running, the nurse would have been screaming and who knows how much blood would have been shed. Maybe Carl's.

She had thought that the only thing worse than their plot to kill Paula would be to get caught, but she hadn't lost much sleep over it. But now if he gets rid of two teenagers, they'd probably have the whole damn state of Maine breathing down their backs.

Carl had delivered his brief lecture with that condescending tone Allison hated. There was so much she loved about Carl; his devil-may-care attitude, his flair for humor and even his animal instinct, In bed he was half-lover, half-predator. The danger he evoked excited her more than any lover before him. And after.

But she knew not to push him too far. She needed him as much as he needed her. Her sister Paula could have lived for heaven knows how many more years. Carl had unlocked the door to her share of Paula's vast fortune. She had to credit him for his plan and willingness to carry it out. Six million dollars could buy them plenty of good times now while they're young enough to enjoy it.

Too bad the other six million has to go to Alex. That straight-laced bastard brother of mine doesn't deserve it, she told herself, fuming at the memories. He expected me to shoot for sainthood like him. Her mood shifted quickly as she laughed at the irony. After the way Elena died, Mr. Goodytwoshoes became known as just another guy who got away with murder.

As much as Allison hated her brother, though, she was glad she had convinced Carl to alter his original plan. At the time he was flying high with the thought of seeing Ratherbee in flames with Paula and Alex trapped by tongues of fire. When she had suggested they – or at least Alex – might escape, he relented and focused on a scheme to blow up the place. A tragic accident, he'd said, totally covered by insurance.

When he filled her in on all the details, she had nixed both ideas; told him to come up with something better. And he did. He sure did. She smiled at the simple ingenuity of Carl's final plan. Smooth, easy and effective.

This turn of events wiped the smile off her face. Her brows furrowed with concern. He hadn't given her any details on how he planned to pull this off. Maybe he's so anxious to get his hands on that money that he'll screw it up.

Long hours passed while the troubling thoughts pulsated in her head. She couldn't stop thinking about those two kids. Two faceless kids who would soon be dead. *But why should I give a shit about two nosy brats? Are their lives worth giving up six million dollars?*

The choices were agonizing.

She needed the comfort of a good friend to get her through this. In her den, she walked behind her bar and pulled out a bottle of Tequila. She decided to F it all and have her own private party. "Worry and guilt are wasted emotions," she said as she downed her first glass.

Chapter 87

As they walked along Shore Road, Tim suggested that since Amore Breakfast was closed, they could easily go around the back to make their call to Sergeant Gerard.

"Sergeant Gerard is not available right now," the dispatcher said. "Is this an emergency or do you want his voice mail?"

Tim hesitated. Well, it wasn't as if Alex Howard was on death row and his message could stop the execution. "His voice mail will be okay, I guess. Does he check it often?"

"Absolutely. I'll connect you."

Tim waited for the beep and stuttered through his message. "Sergeant, this is Timothy Waite. Sara and I want to tell you something that might be important. It is important actually. Can you call us back?" He left his cell phone number, hit the off button and turned to Sara. "Are you going to get in trouble if you don't get home for another hour?"

"I don't think so. As long as I show up in time for dinner with my relatives, they won't miss me now. But I'd better call, just in case." Sara smiled when the recording came on. She could bypass all her parents' usual questions and leave her brief message that she was with her friends and would be home by 7:00.

"If he doesn't return our call in the next hour," Tim said, "I'll call again and say it's an emergency."

Sara frowned with uncertainty. "He might not like that, Tim. It's not really an emergency."

"Yeah, that's what I thought too, but on second thought, what if something else comes up to make them more suspicious of Alex? What if they arrest him? If we can stop that from happening, I'd say that's an emergency, right?"

Sara studied his face a second and laughed. "Who are you trying to convince, me or yourself?"

Tim's confident look melted away with his smile. Sara could always see through him. "Both of us, I guess. I must be getting paranoid like you. But now that we know Paula Grant's murderer couldn't possibly be Alex Howard, we'll have to keep looking over our shoulders, sort of. Sara, we have to be very careful of who we talk to and definitely can't discuss Paula Grant's death with anyone. We might slip and say something we shouldn't. Remember, we don't know if that guy got a good look at either of us before we took off..."

Sara scrunched her face doubtfully. "I don't think so. They had already passed us. He would have had to look back, and since he intended to shove Paula into the ocean seconds later, his attention was totally on her, I'm sure."

Tim disagreed. "Not if you heard an unexpected sound somewhere behind you. Particularly if you were about to kill someone, you'd sure as hell take a hard look around first."

Sara shivered. The possibility that the killer might have seen either or both of them, coupled with the guilt she suffered for stupidly opening her big mouth to Jennifer, filled her with fear. "Stop it, Tim. You're scaring me. You call me paranoid but your imagination is worse than mine."

"We're not dealing with imagination anymore, Sara. Sure as shit Paula Grant was murdered by some sicko who might have seen us. So yes, I am trying to scare you. We're going to need eyes in the back of our heads from now on."

Sara waved her hand dismissively, but his words were chilling. "Okay, Tim. I hear you, loud and clear and I'm getting sick at the thought. I liked it better when Alex Howard was the likely suspect. At least we would have known who to watch out for. But this guy now..." She shook her head, not wanting to think about what could happen. "I hope Sergeant Gerard calls us soon."

"Don't worry. One way or the other, Sara, we'll talk to him tonight."

Chapter 88

From across the narrow street, Carl Duca sat leisurely on a tree-front bench, his head behind a newspaper. He heaved a satisfied sigh and smiled triumphantly. He couldn't grab them now, but it had to be soon. And if his vibes served him correctly, he knew just where and when that would be.

He followed them just long enough to be sure he had assumed correctly. Yes, they walked across Route 1, bought a cold drink at an outdoor stand, then walked over to the trolley stop.

That was all he needed to know. Carl did an about-face and walked leisurely, like any other tourist, to where he had parked his car. An easy hideaway he had discovered years ago, close to the action but out of sight. He had taken several girls there when he was young and had never been caught. It had to work for him one last time.

Fifteen minutes later he sat in his car in the parking area of a new 110-room motel and waited for the trolley. This was the closest trolley stop to their homes and he felt confident home was their destination because of what he had overheard earlier at the Amore Evenings site. She had complained how she dreaded sitting through dinner with her relatives, but she absolutely had to be there, like it or not.

He laughed thinking about that. "Don't worry, Sara," he mumbled. "You won't have to sit through that ordeal. I'll take care of that for you."

Carl grinned when the trolley came and discharged its passengers. Sure enough, the two stupid kids were the only ones to get off. He waited just a little longer until they reached the perfect spot to grab them. They had to walk past a brick privacy wall that ran along the motel property adjacent to the pool area. Directly opposite it was undeveloped property.

He pulled his car up to them at precisely the right time. Once they passed that wall, it would be chancy. In a crowd, people don't notice much around them. Everyone is preoccupied. But here, he thought, walkers are rare. Two people getting into a car with someone would be noticed. And once those kids went missing, everyone in the whole damn town would be searching their memories hoping to become heroes.

Tim and Sara looked at him, startled by his surprise appearance, but both gave him warm hellos.

"Hey, man, what's going on? What are you doing here?" Tim asked when Carl's window slid down.

It took Sara only a split-second to realize that this wasn't a coincidence. Carl had tracked them down for some reason. The moment her eyes locked with his, she stepped away, afraid to hear whatever he had to say.

"Why are you here?" she asked. "Were you looking for us?"

"I'm sorry, kids. I have to ask you to come with me. There's been an accident. Something happened to Glory. She needs you, Sara."

Sara was horrified and confused by his message. "What the heck are you talking about, Carl? That's impossible. We just left Glory an hour ago."

"Then it happened right after you left her, I guess."

"*What* happened, Carl? Where is she? Will she be okay?" Sara was too stunned to cry, but her lips trembled. Without hesitation, she opened the back door and they both got in.

Tim was equally shocked and full of questions too. "Where are we going? To the hospital? Was it a car accident, or what? Does Frannie know?" he asked, then slapped his forehead. "Oh, damn! Her father just got out of the hospital. Does he know?"

Carl saw Tim pull his cell phone out of his pocket, ready to call whoever had to be notified. Panic filled him like fire and he cursed himself for not thinking of that before. The whole friggin' world carries cell phones. How could he have forgotten that important detail?

"No, wait, Tim," Sara said, putting her hand over his phone. "Don't call anyone until Carl tells us what happened. We're not giving him a chance to talk. C'mon, Carl, tell us. And tell us why you said she needs *me*."

Sara had unknowingly saved him with her interruption. He had to come up with something fast to stop them from using their phones until he had them completely under his control. And that wouldn't happen until his ignition was turned off and the gun was in his hand.

"Listen to me, both of you. You're right, Sara. We can't make any calls until I take you to Glory. This is not the kind of accident you guys are thinking. Glory's in big trouble. That's all I can tell you. I found her crying like a baby. When I asked her who I could call, she panicked. She only wanted you, Sara. Don't ask me why. I promised I would find you and bring you to her."

"Where did you find her?" Tim asked. He wrapped his arms around Sara, whose fears had escalated. Her whole body was shaking now. He gave her a comforting peck on the forehead and noticed that the color had drained from her face.

Carl had no idea what he was talking about. The availability of their cell phones had changed everything. He was forced to ad lib this performance. "Look Tim, Sara, I know I upset you both, but please bear with me. I'm upset too, but once we get past this damn traffic, we'll be there in minutes."

Fear for Glory ripped away Sara's fight for control. "*There! There!* Where the heck is *there*, Carl?" She didn't expect an answer, just screamed it out and buried her head against Tim's chest and cried for whatever it was she didn't know.

Tim stroked her hair and kissed the top of her head. "C'mon, Sara, try to shake it off. You don't even know why you're crying. All he said was that Glory's in trouble. If she asked for you, she has to be alive and conscious, right?" His question was meant more for Carl than Sara, but if Carl had noticed Tim gaping at him through the rear mirror, he pretended not to.

Once they were off Route 1 and on a back road, the traffic was minimal and eventually thinned out to nothing. They rode for a while in silence, each thinking separate thoughts. *Maybe she was involved in a hit and run accident,* Tim thought. *And she was the one who ran. That would explain "trouble."* He didn't like the smell of this. Carl's demeanor irked him. Why all this secrecy? He was annoyed as hell that Carl had upset Sara like this without telling them a damn thing. He tried to control his feelings, but they slipped out anyway when he spoke again.

"Carl, I wish you could fill us in on what the hell's going on. You're scaring the shit out of her."

You ain't seen nothing yet, Carl thought to himself, but he kept the smile buried inside him. "In a little while you'll know it all. I don't even know it all yet."

"But you know more than you're saying," Tim said.

"Just hang in," Carl said with the same calm but serious tone, but this time Tim caught a hint of his buried smile and jerked forward. "What the hell are you smiling at? Is this some kind of sick joke?"

Carl didn't answer, but with a quick turn of the steering wheel, he entered onto property that appeared to be a construction site. A site presently inactive or abandoned.

"Oh, God, I don't like this," Tim said and hugged Sara closer.

In a flash, Carl was out of the car, gun in hand. A proud grin crossed his face.

Realization that they were being kidnapped or worse sent shock waves through Sara. She opened her mouth to scream but instead collapsed in Tim's arms.

This is insane, Tim thought. This has to be the most realistic nightmare I've ever had. He shook his head but didn't wake up. Carl was still there, his .38 Smith & Wesson shining in the sun. Tim's eyes darted in all directions. Not a soul in sight. Not even Glory. The only remains of this once active construction project was the old weather-beaten trailer right before their eyes.

"Where's Glory?" he asked, but the two words were rife with defeat as his eyes stared at the gun with fear and disbelief.

Sara's eyes, though, were dry and staring straight at Carl, blazing with anger. "Answer him, you shit! He asked you where Glory is."

Tim threw her an are-you-crazy look, but Carl roared with laughter. "Well, you're a regular tigress, aren't you, little Miss Spitfire?" He grabbed her bag, dumped out the contents and took her cell phone. "Well, you can scream your ass off, but I'm the guy with the gun." His smile was openly sinister now and he kissed the gun that ruled him king. Then to Tim he said, "I'll take yours too, if you don't mind, kid," and pulled it out of his T-shirt pocket. "And I don't mind answering your questions. Actually, Glory is probably fine right now getting ready for her dinner date with Mr. Shithead Howard. But I'll bring her here to keep you company on your long voyage."

Sara was about to ask, "What long voyage?" but she swallowed the words, afraid to hear the answer.

Carl opened the door and yanked them out, knocking them both off their feet. Next he pulled out a bunch of wire strips from under the driver's seat of his car and threw them towards Tim. His beefy right hand gripped the gun and his eyes never left their target. "Tie her up. First her ankles, then her hands behind her back. And remember, I'm watching. If you try anything cute, she'll get the brunt of my anger first, then you. Understand?"

Tim's jaws were clenched so tight, the veins at his temples were visibly pulsating. He returned a venomous look at the man he had conversed with amiably only hours ago, but now obeyed his command. Like the bastard said, he had the gun.

A moan escaped from Tim's throat when he wrapped the wire around Sara's ankles. The terror he saw in her eyes made him want to lunge out, throw the bastard down and punch him till he begged for mercy. And long after.

But gun or no gun, Tim would never get the chance to try. A smashing blow to his head sent his body down and crumbling like a dead balloon. The last sound he heard was Sara's distant scream before everything went black.

Her scream infuriated Carl. Again he used his gun to crush Sara's cheekbone. "What the hell are you trying to do, wake up the f---in' dead?"

But no further sound came from Sara. The violent blow had stunned her into silence.

Carl tied Tim's hands and feet and dragged them both into the trailer. "Shit," he mumbled to himself when he realized he'd left the duct tape in the trunk of the car. He spotted a roll of masking tape on the desk and improvised. Not nearly as good, but who the hell would hear them anyway? And he had to get Glory.

He left Tim and Sara on opposite ends of the floor, their bodies both in fetal positions. It struck him funny to look at them. To think they'd be checking out the same way they checked in.

"There now," he said, stepping back for one last look. "At least you guys can blink at each other till I get back. Your friend Glory doesn't know it, but she's getting all dolled up for me, not Shithead."

Sara squirmed with frustration and fear. Carl smiled down on her, enjoying her desperate but hopeless moves. Her eyebrows curled in question and the whites of her eyes glared like snow in sunlight. "Why?" they silently pleaded.

Carl laughed. "You haven't got a clue, do you? You haven't figured out who the hell I really am yet." He clicked his tongue and shook his head. "I thought you were smarter than that," he said, then paused for effect. "Allison Howard and I are gonna get hitched when this is all over." He waited, arms crossed, and watched her eyes until she could connect the dots. He threw his head back, clapped his hands and laughed again when her eyes widened. "Got it now? Sure you do. You're bright but a little slow. Your biggest problem, though, is your mouth. That's what got you in trouble in the first place."

Tim's moans caught Carl's attention momentarily, but he turned back to Sara. "If you hadn't blabbed about seeing someone walking with Paula that night, you and your boyfriend wouldn't be here and neither would I. Believe it or not, I have better things to do than this."

He gave her a too-late-now shrug of his shoulders and a grin to match.

Sara's terror-filled eyes swelled with tears that streamed down her face. She shook her head violently and cried mournful sounds; sounds of words crushed in her throat.

Carl had no time to waste. He'd heard Glory mention to Sara that she needed an ice cream since dinner wouldn't be before 8:00. He had to grab her before Shithead picked her up. But this was such an incredible high, he hated to leave. This feeling of absolute power over other human beings. Like God, he had the power to choose who should live and who should die. Back when he had first dreamed up this Paula Grant thing, it was simply a job to be done; a plan to be executed strictly for the almighty dollar – millions of them. But he hadn't anticipated this unexpected pleasure.

The hell with it. Another minute or two won't matter. He decided to savor the moment. To watch the kid beg. "You bustin' to say something, sugar?" he asked. "Don't excite yourself. I'll give you your chance." He pulled a knife from his pocket and snapped it open. "Don't you move now."

Before Sara could react to this new wave of terror, he had sliced the tape on her mouth and set off a pool of crimson red.

His smile mocked contrition. "Oops, sorry, but I told you not to move."

Carl reached for a dirty roll of paper towels that had been left on the trailer floor. He grabbed a few and gently blotted Sara's oozing blood, pretending to be sorry and sympathetic. "Oh, poor baby," he said. "But don't worry, it's not deep. You have worse things to worry about than this little cut. I'll patch it up a little better." He howled with laughter as he slapped strips of masking tape haphazardly all over her face. Only her eyes were exposed and when she rolled them upward, above and beyond where eyes could see, he easily read her thoughts. "Yeah, you'd *better* pray," he said.

The bloody knife was barely an inch from Sara's terrified eyes. Fear set off spasms that rocked her body. She tried to spit away the blood that flowed back into her mouth. If he didn't kill her first with one thrust of the knife, her own blood would surely choke her to death.

But all he did was smile. He looked down at her with a look of feigned bewilderment. Like he couldn't imagine why she was making such a fuss. Then he blew a sigh and stood up. "Gotta go," he said reluctantly. "I hate to leave this fun party, but you know how it is – business before pleasure."

Tim's moans had faded to chilling silence. His body appeared lifeless. Carl was just about to take off when he decided to check him out one last time. He gazed across at Sara with that signature smile that would make anyone's skin crawl. "Don't you worry, little Sara. He's fine. Not that it matters. But we'll let him sleep. Your big hero is just as scared as you are." His hand was on the doorknob. "Now don't you cry for me. I'll be back real soon. Glory will be dying to see you." His sadistic joke amused him further and his laughter bellowed within the confines of the small trailer. But it stopped abruptly.

Sara couldn't see the door from where he had left her, but she had heard it slam, followed by the sound of his car engine. She wasted no time. A trail of blood followed as she snaked her body, inches at a time, across the floor, praying fervently to God to help them escape this madman.

Chapter 89

He had a narrow slice of time to make this workable. If he couldn't get Glory into his car unseen between now and her dinner date with Alex, he could forget about the cushion of dumping suspicion on Mr. Shithead. All he knew was that she planned a late dinner. So chances were great Alex would be home alone waiting for her call.

He would have liked better odds, but at least tonight he'd get rid of those kids. Killing them scared him less than letting them run loose. He had relived that scene over and over again in his mind trying to remember exactly when he had pulled off that damn ski mask. But it was no use. He'd never know for sure. And who's to say those nosy brats won't remember the face they saw for a second or two and wake up with bells ringing?

"And that, ladies and gentlemen, is why Timothy Waite and Sara Baisley had to die," Carl said aloud, pretending to plead his case to a jury. "Glory English, unfortunately, was in the way. That's what she gets for falling for a shit like Alex Howard." The toothpick he was chewing on slipped out when he grinned.

* * *

So far, so good. Carl drove up to Frannie's house, pleased to see his cousin wasn't home yet. He had spoken to her hours ago to casually get a sharper picture for his game plan. His smile swelled his cheeks and narrowed his eyes. "Must be the devil working with me," he mumbled with sick satisfaction. "That air conditioner couldn't have died at a more opportune time." He had a Plan B in case she was home, but since she wasn't, Step One was about to be executed.

Glory answered the doorbell with a look of surprise. If Carl were looking for his cousin, he would have rung the upstairs bell. His look was so deadpan serious that Glory reacted to it. "Carl, what are you doing here? Is something wrong?"

"I'm afraid so."

Glory stepped back and opened the screen door to let him in.

"No, Glory. I don't want to waste time. I need you to come with me. Now."

Her brows furrowed at the urgency of his tone. She had never seen this happy-go-lucky guy so serious and it scared her. "What's wrong, Carl?" she asked again. "Did something happen to Frannie? I just spoke to her a while ago."

He gave her the softest, most gentle look he could manage. The kind that always braced someone for bad news. "No, Frannie's fine, as far as I know. It's Sara. She's in big trouble. Says she needs to talk to someone she can trust. Something she can't tell her mother. I found her crying like a baby. She asked me to find you and bring you to her."

Carl looked like the face of doom. But how bad could this be if Sara is alive and well? she reasoned. "Where's Tim? Is he with her? Did she tell you what her problem is?"

"No, Tim is not with her. And yes, she talked to me a little. Tim is part of her problem, but I'll let her tell you."

Glory lifted a brow but the concern left her face. She relaxed when the obvious dawned on her. This was about life, not death. "She's pregnant?"

"Not that I know of. I wish that were the reason. But no, Sara's problem is far more serious than that."

Fear swept through Glory like a sudden storm. Carl wasn't giving her details but this was a guy who wore a perpetual smile. That smile was nowhere in sight now.

"Let's go," he said.

His gaze was so intense it frightened her. She grabbed her bag and thought of Alex. They hadn't decided on a time and place for dinner, only that it would be later than usual. She was supposed to call him when she got home but hadn't yet. Something told her their dinner date would have to be cancelled, judging by Carl's strange behavior. Her cell phone was in her bag. Once she learned the severity of Sara's problem, she'd call him.

As he drove, Carl's gaze could have burned a hole in the road. He never looked at her to offer explanation or assurance that she could eventually help Sara. The silence sent her imagination on a horrific whirlwind. Her heart raced and her mouth was dry as cotton.

She broke the silence and tried again. They were on the outskirts of town now, in unfamiliar territory. "Carl, this is scary. You haven't given me the slightest hint as to where we're going or why. Whatever it is can't be worse than anything I'm imagining. Talk to me, Carl," she pleaded.

"Be patient, pretty girl. In a few minutes we'll be there." Still his gaze never wavered, but Glory could have sworn she saw a quick smile curl at the corner of his mouth. And he had called her "pretty girl." The term was clearly incongruous to the gravity of this situation.

"We'll be where, Carl? Where the heck are you taking me? How am I connected to whatever is wrong, and how the hell did you get involved?" Glory's fear and anger raced along a parallel course.

Something was definitely wrong. The moment Carl was at her door, she'd had a strong sense of foreboding but hadn't followed her instincts. Once he had mentioned that Sara was in some kind of trouble, she hadn't hesitated to get in his car. But once she did, Carl had become a different person. Instead of focusing on what could have happened to Sara, Glory now concentrated on Carl. He had seemed so concerned when he came to her door, but those traces of concern were soon gone.

She drew a deep breath and tried again, her voice softer. "Carl, this mystery is killing me. Can't you tell me what's happening? I'll know soon enough anyway. I'd rather be prepared."

Silence.

Her heart thumped. The more she looked at him, the more her instincts kicked in. The Carl she had known was not the same man sitting beside her now.

"I'll tell you this much," he said, then took another long · pause. Once again, he made that quick turn and reached the trailer. He turned off the ignition and looked at her with a wide smile, devoid of warmth. "It's a matter of life and death. My life. Your death."

Glory's hand flew to her mouth. A scream froze in her throat. Her eyes were pools of fear.

"No, don't be afraid," he said. "Death can be a lonely ride, I know. But you won't be alone. You'll have good company."

With shaking hands, she fumbled to release the door lock, but Carl was faster. He pulled the gun out of his driver's door compartment. "Don't bother, pretty girl. You won't get very far."

Chapter 90

The phone calls started about 7:00 p.m. Alex made several futile attempts to reach Glory at her apartment and on her cell phone. He made up probably a dozen excuses for her but nothing short of a medical emergency could justify her not calling.

Maybe something happened to her father and when she got the call, she went flying out of the house. If that were the case, she'd be too distraught to think about him and their dinner date.

"I assumed she was with you or getting ready to see you," Frannie said when Alex called her at Amore Breakfast. "Her car was in the driveway when I got home. I assumed she was out with you. But I got called back here again so I don't know what happened after that. Why don't you drive by the house and see if her car is still there? If it is and you still haven't made contact, call me back and I'll use my key to her apartment. God forbid she fell in the bathroom or something. You never know."

"That thought did occur to me too. I'm in the car now on my way there. I'll be in touch as soon as I see what's what."

Their brief conversation seemed to knock down that imaginary wall between them. Their shared concern for Glory united them, if only temporarily. They both hoped they could breathe a sigh of relief later.

***

Amy considered it mighty strange that Glory was unreachable. There was no denying the love her half-sister had for their father, and Amy knew how much she wanted to visit him at home. Her mother had remained stiff-lipped and adamant about melding Glory into the family, but relented only because of her husband's fragile condition. God forbid anything happened to Dan as a result of her obstinance, she'd never forgive herself, she'd said. Dan's face had brightened like a Christmas tree when her mother caved in. Amy couldn't wait to give Glory the good news.

So now that Glory could step on the Madison welcome mat, why the hell isn't she answering her calls?

Amy saw the pain of disappointment reflected in her father's eyes when she told him. He had been sitting at the umbrellaed table on the patio, happy to be home and relaxing with the newspaper and a glass of Louise's freshly squeezed lemonade.

Dan stared into space. His face creased while he pondered Amy's message. He looked at her, pursed his lips, and said, "I don't want to push the panic button, Amy, but I don't like this. It's so unlike Glory." He paused to study her face, hoping she agreed with him.

"I know, Dad. I'm hoping she'll call me with some simple explanation, but right now I'm a little uneasy too. She loves you, Dad. She made me promise to call her as soon as we got you home."

"I'm more than uneasy. I'm worried." Dan wouldn't let his thoughts escape into spoken words, not wanting to give them credibility. His daughter had shielded herself with blind faith about Alex Howard. She's a thirty-five-year-old woman. He had allowed himself to trust her judgment. But now bizarre images crossed his mind. "Do me a big favor, Sweetheart," he said to Amy. "Call Frannie Oliveri first. See if she can tell you anything about where Glory might be. If not, try to track down Alex Howard."

Amy turned to go back in the house for the phone. Vanessa, Todd and Louise were inside and she wasn't sure she wanted to share this budding problem with them. Why invite their snide remarks? Amy was losing patience with their unyielding attitudes.

Dan broke through her ruminations as she approached the patio door. "Amy, just bring me the phone and the directory. I think I'll make those calls myself."

***

Frannie was still at Amore Breakfast when the second call came in. This time it was Sara's mother. She hadn't been able to reach her daughter on her cell phone and was concerned. "I'm sorry to bother you, Ms. Oliveri, but I thought maybe she was still working there unexpectedly?"

Frannie was silent a few seconds. Her stomach was sinking fast. First Alex called looking for Glory, now Laura Baisley was looking for her daughter.

And Sara is with Glory. She also had to make a fast decision about whether to mention Tim. She was well aware of Tim and Sara's parental problem. They were two decent kids but their parents had to be Class A jerks.

"No, I'm sorry, Mrs. Baisley, she's not here. I do know she went down Perkins Cove with my partner, Glory English, to look over the new restaurant property."

"Oh, would you mind giving me her cell number? Sara left me a message and should have been home a while ago. When I couldn't get through...well, you know how mothers are. I'm worried."

Me too, Mrs. Baisley. "I'll give you her number, but I should warn you that someone was trying to reach her earlier and she hadn't answered. I'm going to try myself."

"Maybe they're somewhere where they can't get a signal? Do you think that's possible?"

Laura Baisley's tone revealed her struggle to stay calm. She had hoped Frannie could offer something to allay her concern, but instead her fears intensified. She drew a breath and steeled herself. "Look, I'm sorry to bother you. We have family visiting and everyone is telling me I worry too much. After all, she's eighteen...they're probably right. If you hear from them, will you tell Sara to call me immediately?"

"Of course. The minute I hear."

Frannie didn't like this one bit. Where the hell are they that both cells don't work? An instant flash of relief washed through her when she realized Tim was with them and he too had a cell phone. She fumbled in her tote bag for her pocket-sized telephone book that listed her employees' numbers. And there it was: Timothy Waite. With a hopeful smile, she punched out the numbers.

"Party unavailable," the recording said.

While she was thinking of who to call next, her phone rang again. Frannie shivered when she heard the caller's first line. "Frannie, this is Dan Madison. When she didn't respond quickly enough, he added, "You know, Dan of Finestkind Tours?"

"Of course, Dan. I'm sorry. My mind was elsewhere." Her heart pounded while she waited for him to say what she already surmised.

Dan started with an embarrassed laugh. "It seems we can't find my daughter. Have you heard from her?"

Chapter 91

"What the hell is this?" Glory's shaky words spilled out of her mouth.

"I'm real sorry, pretty girl. You were never part of the plan but since you started screwing around with Alex Howard, you became a risk to me."

"What plan? How could I possibly be a risk to you? And where's Sara? Oh, dear God," she cried, afraid to ask what he'd done to her. *And why.*

"Sara's absolutely fine. She'll be happy to see you," he said. His gun made him feel ten feet tall. He poked it directly at her temple. "Not get out of the car, slowly and carefully, if you want to see your young friends."

She did as she was told. Her heart was pounding so hard, she thought she'd collapse and die on the spot. He pulled the trailer door open and kicked her inside. Glory's breath caught in her throat and the sound that followed resembled that of a trapped and wounded animal. Such was her shock that her mind was incapable of shaping words.

Sara and Tim were huddled close together, their bodies immobilized by wires at their hands and feet. A mess of blood-soaked masking tape covered most of Sara's face. The tape on Tim's mouth was partially ripped away and also covered with blood.

A gasp escaped from Glory's mouth and her eyes were glazed with fear, but she remained speechless. The sight at her feet was more than her conscious mind could accept as reality. Sara had chewed a hole in the tape large enough to expose her front teeth. The moisture from her blood had hastened that job. With her hands and feet bound, she had used her teeth to rip the tape off Tim's mouth. The blood Glory tried to wipe away with her bare hands was Sara's, not his.

"Oh, here. Be my guest," Carl said. He threw the roll of paper towels at her feet and stood leaning against the sink, arms folded and wearing that devil's-delight grin.

Glory cradled Sara in her arms, unrolled the paper towels and ripped out clean ones. While Carl hovered over them looking like this was the most fun he'd ever had, Glory wiped Sara's blood from their faces as best she could. She wanted so much to be courageous for them, but like Sara, her sobs were beyond control.

Tim, who had been temporarily blessed with oblivion, now stirred into consciousness. His face was distorted with pain, his teeth clenched.

"Hey, welcome back, hotshot," Carl said. "I wouldn't want you to miss the finale of this party."

Tim had a mouthful of bloody saliva he wanted to spit at him but didn't want to set him off. There was nothing he could do to save them, but every second they remained alive carried a sliver of hope.

Glory was their only chance. Her hands and feet were free, but that .38 still dangled from Carl's finger like a harmless toy.

"Why are you doing this?" Glory screamed. "What could these poor kids have done to put them through this hell? What do you want from them?"

"Hey, if I wanted to, I could have made them feel a lot worse. Besides, I don't plan to let them suffer too long."

"But why?" Glory cried. The whys no longer mattered. She was only trying to buy time.

"You want to know why? I'll tell you why." The sadistic smile disappeared but anger filled every crevice in his face. His eyes were fiery. He dragged a stool closer to them and spit out his poison. With maniacal passion, the gun aimed and his finger on the trigger, he began...

"They thought they were big shits, the Ducas. They wanted everyone to kiss their asses for all their do-gooder shit. Pillars of the community, they wanted to be, the bastards. I didn't ask to be their f---in' foster child. And I didn't ask them to adopt me. I hated their guts. And Mike too. Who the hell were they? All trying to control my life! Always telling me what to do and what not to do. All I needed was love and guidance, they said. Bullshit! They called it love and guidance so everyone could pat them on the back, but I called it torture!"

Glory stared at him with rapt attention while he rambled on and expunged his hatred. Not because he had grabbed her attention with his poison, but he seemed lost within himself. It was as if he had released a lifetime of suppressed violence. It poured out of him now like water rushing over a dam. He didn't need an audience and was barely aware of the captive audience he had at his feet.

Glory had no background whatsoever in mental disorders, but was certain this switch in Carl's behavior was some kind of breakdown. She flashed a look at Tim and gave Sara's shoulder a quick squeeze. Her eyes and fingers sent an urgent message to both. *Don't make a sound or a move.* His defenses were down but the knuckles of the hand that squeezed the gun were fright-white.

Chapter 92

Frannie left Amore Breakfast and prayed she wouldn't get stuck in traffic. God must have been listening because she made it home in record time. As she turned into her street, she saw Alex's car pull into the driveway. She parked right behind him, got out and waved for him to follow.

They acknowledged each other with merely a nod, but exchanged a look that mirrored their apprehension. No more than thirty seconds after Frannie rang the doorbell, she unlocked the door. Initially they were relieved not to find Glory seriously hurt and helpless, unconscious or – God forbid – dead. But their relief was short-lived.

Frannie stood rigid at the foot of the bed while her mind raced with unsettling thoughts. She turned to Alex and saw his Adam's apple protrude when he swallowed. He apparently had similar thoughts. There were three sets of clothes on the bed, all on hangers, and a matching set of pink lace bra and panties. The light in the bathroom was turned on.

"She was supposed to go out with you, wasn't she?" Her voice quivered when she spoke. "Glory was obviously deciding what to wear when something urgent intervened."

"Oh, damn," Alex murmured with a sigh. "It has to be her father – "

Frannie sliced the air to cut him off. "No. Dan Madison called me after I spoke to you. He and his daughter have been trying to reach her too. They hoped I could tell them something about where she could be."

"I'm sure she probably told you, but she was hoping they'd invite her to visit him briefly at the house. That's why we had planned to meet later."

"I'm getting seriously worried, Alex. Did you ever get a really bad feeling in your gut, a premonition?" She paused to bite her lip and wipe the tears that filled the corners of her eyes. "There's something else you don't know."

"What?" Alex asked, his gaze piercing with concern.

"Laura Baisley also called me looking for her daughter." Her voice cracked but she drew a deep breath and fought back the tears. "Her daughter and Tim Waite had both gone with Glory to look at the property."

"They did go. And then she brought them to my place. I had invited them for a brief tour of Ratherbee."

"And then what? Do you know where they were going after that?"

"I wish I did, but no. I assumed they were all going home. Actually, I didn't assume anything about where Sara and Tim were headed next. It was none of my business, nor did I care, so it never entered my mind. Glory, though, was going home, hoping for the chance to see her father. But now, since he called you, that possibility is dead."

They were standing in the kitchen now, both fighting to stay calm and think. Glory's digital camera was on the counter and Frannie picked it up with hope reflected in her eyes. "Let's look at what shots she took today. Maybe we'll find something helpful." She was already thinking they might have to tell the police what they were all wearing, if it came to that.

Alex didn't want to waste the time but agreed anyway. As he suspected, they found nothing that could possibly lead them to Glory. Frannie's hopes were equally deflated until a new thought entered her mind. "Wait a minute. What about those shots they took with my cousin Carl? They probably had talked with him a little and one of them might have casually mentioned something about later plans."

Alex nixed the idea with a frown. "That's a stretch. I doubt it. Glory wouldn't have made other plans. She wanted to be available in case that invitation to her father's house came through."

"But maybe the kids said something. It's worth a try. I'm going to call him."

When she couldn't reach Carl, Frannie tried his brother. "Hey, Mike, it's me. I was trying to reach Carl. He doesn't answer his cell. Do you by any chance know where he is?"

Mike's laugh had a sour ring to it. "I never was my brother's keeper, Frannie, but I'm sure he'd tell you otherwise."

That sounded to Frannie like a prelude to a conversation she had no head for now. Carl had carried a lifelong chip on his shoulder because he was a foster child, adopted by the Ducas when he was twelve. Growing up, he and Mike were like oil and water, but she assumed maturity had smoothed the rough spots of their sibling rivalry.

"I don't mean to cut you off, Mike, but I'm in a big hurry. We'll get into this another time soon if you need to talk."

"Fine. I'll hold you to that. But anyway, I have no idea where he is. Sorry. Is it anything I can help you with?"

"Not at the moment, Mike, but I might call you later. Thanks." She hung up before he could ask questions. This was no time for extraneous conversation. Glory and those kids had to be found.

She looked up and met Alex's gaze. His eyes told their own silent story. "You're scared too, aren't you?" she asked.

"Let's get out of here. Fast," he answered.

***

Alex drove while Frannie made calls. She tried Tim's parents. His mom hadn't heard from him but wasn't in the least concerned. Her laugh was a bit condescending when she said, "After all, he's a big boy now. I can't hold his hand."

Alex caught the gist of Tim's mother's attitude from Frannie's facial expressions and her responses. He took the phone. "Mrs. Waite, this is Alex Howard. I don't want to alarm you, but I think you should start calling Tim's friends or anyone who might know where he is. And you can start with the Baisleys because your son is with their daughter, Sara, and Glory English. We haven't been able to reach any of them and we're seriously concerned." He handed the phone back to Frannie. "She wants to know *why*. Explain it to her, Frannie, please."

Chapter 93

Anxiety wrapped around Dan Madison like the arms of an octopus. He was supposed to relax, take it easy, and eventually he'd be good as new, his doctor had said. But with each passing minute, his fears spiraled. He could do nothing more than stare at the clock and the phone. His wife and children sat with him at their patio table. Dan had no patience for their small talk. His heart and mind were elsewhere.

Amy took it upon herself to stifle them. "Look, guys, Dad's a nervous wreck because he hasn't heard from Glory. She had asked me to call as soon as he came home but we can't find her."

Vanessa, the opportunist, jumped right in. "Well, maybe she had something better to do," she said and punctuated it with an *I-told-you-so* smirk.

Dan's fist pounded the table and startled them all. "Stop it!" he yelled.

Louise remained open-mouthed and shot a dagger look at Vanessa for provoking this abnormal anger in her father. Inwardly Louise compared Dan's damaged heart to a house of cards; afraid it could easily collapse. She relaxed her gaze and fixed it on her husband. "Dan, please try not to get excited. Since when do you have a temper?" She said it with a smile but it troubled her. In all the years they'd been married, he'd never been this demonstrative with his emotions. Whenever he was angry, he was more likely to give her the silent treatment until it passed. But now, after a motorcycle accident, a heart attack, and a missing daughter he alone loved, she figured he's entitled to a small explosion.

After her mother's silent message, Vanessa approached Dan with caution. "I'm sorry, Dad. That was a dumb thing to say. I should have realized how you'd react. Give us time. After all, the emergence of an older sibling from out of the blue is a unique family problem. We have to learn how to deal with it."

Dan kept his eyes downcast for a few seconds and said nothing while he cooled. Then he patted her cheek and simply said, "I know." The affectionate gesture stabbed Vanessa with guilt. She loved her father so much she couldn't bear to share him and it was turning her into a monster. She recognized it but hadn't been able to do a damn thing to stop it.

The depth of Dan's concern was etched in the wrinkles that draped his face. Behind his back, Todd fanned his fingers discreetly to signal Vanessa that he would handle the problem. He dragged his chair closer to his father and put a hand on his shoulder. "Tell me exactly what's going on, Dad. Maybe we can help find her and put your mind at ease." He didn't want to fuel his anger by adding that Dan might be overreacting, but he didn't have to. Dan was quick to notice.

"I can see right through you, Todd, but you ought to know me better. I'm not the type to worry for no reason. You have to trust my judgment. Glory would not take off on some spur-of-the-moment pleasure trip. Not today; no way. Ask Amy, she'll tell you," he said, then shifted his gaze to his youngest child.

"Dad's right, Todd. Glory was hoping you guys would let her come here for a half-hour or so. I was supposed to call her, one way or the other."

Todd pondered the situation a moment, hoping some bright idea would register in his head. "And you say no one is answering all three cell phones?"

"That's right," Dan answered for her. "And I talked to Alex Howard and Frannie Oliveri. They had spoken to the kids' parents, their friends..." He threw his hands up and shook his head. "Nobody can reach them, has heard from them or has any idea where the hell they can be."

They were all silently digesting the facts, searching for answers when Louise said, "Has anyone contacted the police? If not, I think it's time. Todd, why don't you do it? Your father will be a wreck until they're found."

Todd picked up the phone while his family hovered over him with anxious eyes. "They might not act on this yet. They're only missing a couple of hours. They'll think we're crazy."

"Not if two teenagers are missing," Louise offered.

"All the more reason. They can be anywhere doing their thing and it might never occur to them that everyone is worried."

"Even if that were true, Todd," Dan said, "what about Glory? She's certainly more responsible."

Todd blew a sigh. He didn't want to alarm his father any more than he already was, but he couldn't ignore the facts. He cringed when his imagination flashed a few ugly pictures. "Okay," he said to his father. "What we need for immediate police action is someone who might do it as a favor. My friend Bobby has an older brother who's a detective. I'll try to reach him."

Five minutes later Todd had the cell number he needed and made the call. "Sgt. Gerard, this is Bobby's friend, Todd Madison. My family and I need a favor and hope you can help us. My sister is missing."

A smile spread across Dan's face for a second when he heard Todd refer to Glory as his sister, but it faded just as quickly while he strained to hear the conversation between his son and Sgt. Gerard.

Chapter 94

"Where are we going, Alex? I don't know where the hell to start looking." Frannie's fingers went to her mouth. Unconsciously she began nibbling on her nails, an old habit she thought she had conquered. When she realized what she was doing, she pulled her hand away and laced her fingers together in her lap.

"Neither do I," Alex said. "I thought we'd start with Perkins Cove. That's Glory's favorite spot, especially since her dad's sightseeing boat docks there. And the kids had mentioned something about hanging out there often with their friends."

"I guess that would be the logical place to start. Then we can take a fast look around The Square, although I doubt that we'll find them."

"Because of the phones, right?"

She nodded. "Because of the phones, yes. If it were just one that went unanswered, it wouldn't bother me this much, but three?"

Alex left her question to hang between them. He had no encouraging response to offer, so he said nothing.

***

At Perkins Cove, Frannie did most of the talking since she knew most of the people who owned or worked in the businesses nestled there. She started with Finestkind. "Maybe they impulsively decided to catch a ride on Dan's boat?"

Alex gave her a sidelong glance. That idea was highly unlikely and Frannie knew it. Not only did Glory have a dinner date with him, but she also wanted to avail herself should Amy's call come through. Sara too had promised to be home in time for dinner with her relatives.

They asked around anyway, hoping someone had seen them, but no one had. They moved on to check out the Amore Evenings site even though Glory's car was nowhere in sight.

Next they drove along Shore Road, turned in and around Amore Breakfast, although they couldn't imagine why. None of the three had a key. They moved on to The Square across Rt. 1. There Alex and Frannie parted again to search the busy area; she'd cover the shops on the left, he'd take the right. They met a short time later where they had parked. Frannie arrived first, trying again to reach any one of them on their cell phones. Frustration and fear made her want to fling the phone, but her eyes widened when she saw someone running towards her. As the young girl came closer, Frannie recognized her. Her name was Melanie and she worked at a popular restaurant with outdoor tables that faced Rt. 1.

"I heard you were looking for Sara Baisley and Tim Waite?" Melanie asked, slightly out of breath.

"And my partner, yes."

Alex gave Frannie's arm a hopeful squeeze. The gesture was impulsive; he'd never touch someone he barely knew under normal circumstances, but this night was far from normal.

"Well, I ran out to catch you when I heard," Melanie continued. "I saw them earlier. From a distance, though. I didn't speak to them or say hello. I was here working and you know how crazy this place is – "

Frannie pushed her along. "Where did you see them?"

"At the trolley stop," she said, pointing.

Frannie's heart pounded. "What time was that, do you remember?"

"Was anyone with them?" Alex threw in.

Melanie answered Alex first. "Oh, I'm sorry," she said ruefully. "If they were with anyone else, I never would have noticed. The area was pretty crowded." She turned to Frannie then, raised a finger and looked away thoughtfully. "The time. Wait a minute. Let me think." Her brows curled while she paused a few seconds, then her face brightened with a smile. "It had to be a little past 6:00, because that's when I started my shift. My guess would be 6:15, 6:20?" Her tone posed it as a question, as though she hoped her answer would work for them.

"Did you see them get on the trolley?" Alex asked.

"Oh, no. This place was a zoo by then, but I assume they did. Why would you stand there if you weren't waiting for the trolley?" Melanie shrugged, then said, "Anyway, I have to get back to work, but I'm sure they'll turn up. Don't worry." She left them with a cheerful smile that died as she walked away.

Frannie turned to Alex. "Now what?"

"Well, Sara and Tim live in the same neighborhood, right?"

"Yes."

"Her mother said Sara left a message that she'd be home at 7:00, so I agree with Melanie. She probably took the trolley home. And even if Tim wanted to stay and hang out with his friends, he strikes me as the kind of kid who would have taken the ride home with her."

"Most likely," Frannie said. "So why didn't either of them ever arrive home and if Glory left them, where the hell did she go?" She said it with frustrated anger but she was getting sicker by the minute.

And again, why do three phones go unanswered? Alex thought but didn't say it aloud. Frannie is a strong, independent woman, and she was beginning to fall apart, so he had to stay in control. But suddenly he wanted to vomit.

Chapter 95

Sergeant Tony Gerard was about to go off duty when Todd Madison's call came through. He rolled his eyes when he heard about the guy's thirty-five-year-old sister who was "missing" a couple of hours. While Todd apologized for bothering him, explaining about his father's recent heart attack and the need to keep him calm, Tony shaped the words he would use to bow out graciously. On his list of priorities, this would not even earn honorable mention.

But he jumped to attention when the names Sara Baisley and Timothy Waite were mentioned. More bells went off when he learned Glory English was with them. Ogunquit's new celebrity resident was also involved with Alex Howard, the murder victim's brother. She was there with him at Ratherbee the day of Paula Grant's funeral and again when they questioned him a second time. How she fit into the quagmire he didn't yet know, but intended to find out.

"Todd, back up a minute," he said. "What exactly did your father tell you? Is he well enough to speak to me?"

Todd glanced at his father who was already giving his son hand signals to let him speak to the detective. "Sure," he said and gave the phone to Dan with an admonishing wave of his finger. "Stay calm," he mouthed.

Dan provided Tony Gerard with the facts as he knew them, which added up to the basis for his apprehension. Tony maintained his professional tone, but his body felt the familiar rush of adrenaline pumping. After receiving Tim's message, he had tried several times to reach them but couldn't make contact. He had assumed the kid had inadvertently turned off his phone, but that sixth sense he developed over years in law enforcement left him uneasy.

He had listened to the voice mail message a few times and could detect no sense of danger in Tim's voice. Conversely, what he did detect sounded like enthusiasm. Tim had seemed anxious to tell him something, and Tony had the impression it was something positive. But in the case of Tim and Sara, a positive could easily turn negative. If they happened to stumble on anything that could identify Paula Grant's killer...

Alex Howard's name and face pulsated brightly in his mind like a blinking neon sign. The guy already had a questionable history before his sister was fed to the fish. Sure he had a lot to gain from his sister's death, but Alex Howard is too smart to leave such obvious tracks, he mused. Tony decided to first find out where exactly Howard was from the time of Tim's phone call to the time he met Frannie at the house. If the result of that inquiry worked in Howard's favor, he'd circle the wagons around the other sister, Allison. She was no angel either but after Paula's death, their investigation into Allison as a possible suspect had been cursory. After all, Alex Howard was conveniently at Ratherbee that weekend, with motive and opportunity.

And that's what's wrong with this case, Tony told himself. He chastised himself for letting his judgment get clouded by a heavy workload and sheer pride. If he had accepted the help initially he could have given Paula Grant's case the attention it deserved.

He called out for Pat Carney to activate his crew, then called Ogunquit P.D. to request assistance. In a few minutes, Tony Gerard's team was assembled and headed for Ogunquit.

Chapter 96

On their way to Ogunquit, Tony Gerard and Pat Carney discussed the critical situation they were faced with. Who, what, where, why, when and how. They had a few of the answers but not enough.

While Tony drove, Pat called Frannie and Alex. They arranged to meet at Amore Breakfast. Tony then assigned another detective to go up to Dan Madison's place to interview him and his family, particularly his daughter Amy, who had spoken with Glory often enough to possibly have some helpful information.

The rest of the team, with the added support of the OPD, would question Tim and Sara's parents, their friends, the trolley driver and any passengers they could locate, including everyone in the immediate area of the trolley stop where they probably got off. The Sun & Surf Inn is right there at that stop and with all the summer tourists walking, riding or lounging, someone had to see something.

But such canvassing would consume precious time. That could mean life or death for Tim, Sara and Glory if Tony's worst fears were realized.

Frannie and Alex were standing in the parking lot of Amore Breakfast when the detectives arrived. Both rushed to meet them with anxiety and fear all over their faces.

"We've got people out everywhere looking for them," Tony said before they could ask.

"Where's everywhere?" Alex asked. "What does that mean?"

Tony briefed him on all the interviews that would be conducted by the canvassing team. "Can either of you think of any other person, any casual acquaintance that Glory might contact besides you two and her father?"

Alex gave Frannie a blank look, hoping she could provide an answer, then turned to Tony. "No one that I know of, Sergeant. She hasn't been in Ogunquit long enough to meet many people, except the workers here," he said, pointing behind him to the restaurant.

"Don't waste time there, Sergeant," Frannie said. "I've already made those contacts even though I knew it was a long shot. No one had a clue as to where any of them could possibly be."

"How about the people at Ocean Cliff Lodge?" Detective Carney asked. "Isn't that where she stayed before moving to your place? Had she ever mentioned anyone she particularly liked or disliked there?"

Frannie's hand pressed against her cheek and her eyes squinted thoughtfully. "Sorry, I can't recall her ever mentioning anyone."

Tony took a deep breath and exhaled. If this turned out bad, he'd never forgive himself for not giving those kids adequate protection. "Okay, don't knock yourself out," he said to Frannie. He saw that familiar look of frustration when someone wants so much to help but can't. "We'll question the staff there if we need to." The detective's cell phone rang and he stepped aside to take the call. He listened intently for about thirty seconds, then said, "Good work, Pete. Just stay put. We're on our way."

All three looked at him with hopeful eyes. "Was that about Glory and the kids?" Frannie asked.

Alex bit his dry lips and tried to read through the detective's impassive expression.

"Possibly," Tony answered. "It could be nothing, but it could be a start. We'll check it out."

Alex stepped forward. "Can't you tell us, Sergeant? We can use a little hope to hang on to right now."

Sergeant Gerard gave him a penetrating look which Alex interpreted as reluctance to divulge what Detective Peter Granger had reported. But Tony was just taking another long hard look to be absolutely sure he had pegged him correctly. "One of my detectives found a woman – a guest at the Sun & Surf Inn – who might have seen the kids get off the bus. But don't get your hopes up. The woman is eighty-three years old with failing eyesight...you know." He shrugged and made a face that said he wasn't too optimistic but he'd certainly talk to her.

Detective Carney was apparently anxious to hear exactly what Peter had said. She was already in the car ready to head back on Route 1 to the Sun & Surf Inn.

Tony Gerard opened the passenger door of their State Police vehicle, a black 2002 Chevrolet Impala, and held it. "Call me immediately if you think of anything you might have forgotten or anyone else we can talk to."

"Absolutely, Sergeant. I'm hoping my cousin Carl calls me back. Maybe he knows something. I left a message on his cell."

Tony's interest piqued. "Why? What could he know? And what's his full name?"

"His name is Carl Duca. You've probably seen the Duca Brothers trucks around town. He and his brother Mike are partners. And he probably doesn't know anything. But he and Glory obviously talked a little this afternoon and you never know..."

"How do you know they talked?"

"Because Alex and I found Glory's digital camera in her kitchen. Someone took a picture of Carl and Glory talking together. Probably the kids."

Tony Gerard got out of the car and Pat Carney turned off the ignition.

"Where's that camera?" he asked.

Chapter 97

Frannie and Alex were back in her SUV headed home to retrieve the camera and bring it to Sergeant Gerard. They were both strangely quiet on the ride back. Frannie was lost in her troubled thoughts wondering why it had seemed so important to the detectives to check the camera. She and Alex had looked at every shot and they were all exactly what she had expected. Interior and exterior photos of the weather-beaten house, the neglected weedy grounds surrounding it, and the ocean view that had excused it all and commanded an outrageous market value. Sara, Tim and Glory were in a few, all with beaming smiles, and so were a few of the Duca Brothers' workers, busy at work.

Except for Carl. He smiled broadly for the camera, looking tall, handsome and confident with his arm wrapped snugly around Glory's waist.

A few weeks ago that might have pleased Frannie, but now it irked her. All the disturbing thoughts she'd had previously had just about washed away. In the short time she had spent with Alex tonight, she had learned all she needed to know. Like Glory, she trusted him and had no doubt that his feelings for her were honorable and his love genuine.

Her skepticism about Alex had apparently rubbed off on Carl. That hand around her waist could have been a casual gesture, but cousin or no cousin, his reputation with the ladies made her think otherwise. Was he working on winning her away from Alex? If so, was it because he had real feelings for her or because he liked the challenge?

But would he use force and take her somewhere against her will just to get in her pants? To rape her, actually? And with Tim and Sara tagging along? Ludicrous, she thought.

Crazy images started to take shape in her mind, images of the young and devilish Carl she thought was long dead. The guy he used to be before he grew up and became Ogunquit's Mr. Congeniality, so to speak. The guy who could make anyone laugh. She shook off the chilling spasms her imagination had ignited.

Alex remained silent, staring out the car window, trying to make sense of this insanity. *There has to be a reason they're all unreachable*, he thought. *Maybe they're not all together, as everyone is assuming. Maybe they all forgot to charge their cell phones this morning. Maybe Sara and Tim took off somewhere in defiance of their parents. Maybe they eloped! And maybe Glory is stuck in some obscure spot with a flat tire and a dead phone.*

Or maybe they're all dead somewhere. He swallowed his fear when they pulled into Frannie's driveway. "Want me to run in for the camera?" he asked.

She nodded and handed him the key. Seconds later he was back in the car and Frannie was temporarily through with her ruminations. "I came to a conclusion," she said, looking into her rearview mirror to back out. When she had straightened the car onto the road, she turned to Alex, whose brows were raised in anticipation. "I'm afraid to say it," she continued, "but I think this situation is a lot worse than those detectives are letting on. Don't you get the impression they're more concerned than they should be, given the facts? It's only been a couple of hours. For us it's scary, but for them....?"

Alex tossed it around and nodded. "But there are kids involved – "

"Not really. They're both over eighteen. They can do anything or be anywhere without answering to anyone."

"True. So what are you saying?"

"I'm not sure. But those detectives seemed to know Tony and Sara. Did you happen to pick that up?"

"Well, it's a small town. That's certainly possible."

Frannie waved it off. "No, that's not what I mean. It's more than that. I'd bet my bottom dollar on that. When we get there, I'm going to ask them outright what they're not telling us."

Chapter 98

If Allison had been struck by a bolt of lightning the surge could not have been more powerful. The guilt that charged through her laid heavily on the conscience she never knew she had.

"I've got to stop him! Please God, help me stop him," she cried out, pacing her living room floor and biting her knuckles. She hadn't uttered the name of God in sincere prayer probably since her childhood, yet she remembered vividly the presence of religion in her family. But somewhere between childhood and maturity she had rebelled against it. Religion had slipped away. No, not slipped away, more like avalanched into that black hole of darkness.

But Allison was not completely without faith. She believed in omens; signs sent with silent messages. An hour ago she had raised the lid of her dead mother's jewelry box and ran a finger over the little 3" x 5" photo. "Tell me what to do, Mom. I'm *lost* without you!" Sobs came with a rush and she talked to the photo as if it were Emily Howard herself. "Why did you leave me?" she screamed. "I was just a kid. I needed you. I hate you! I hate you!" She flung the photo on the floor and stomped on it as though it were the devil himself smiling up at her.

She shivered from the chill that ran through her. Her mother's presence enveloped her. That face she hadn't seen in almost thirty years was there before her with fire in her eyes. And that's when she called to God. But God didn't answer; not in words or deeds that she could hear or see.

She looked up, tears streaming down her face. "Sure. You hate me too. I don't blame you. But if you hadn't taken my mother – " Allison succumbed to the pains of guilt, rejection and remorse. She threw herself on the floor and cried it out until the well ran dry. Then she got up, blotted away her tears, tucked stray hairs behind her ears and grabbed the phone. Her heart pounded while she listened to the rings, but her determination was stronger than her fear.

***

At the trailer, Carl looked at the caller ID on his ringing phone. He had no intention of taking any calls tonight but, under the circumstances, he had to know who called. He would need to prepare a good cover story, should an explanation become necessary.

This call he took.

"What the hell are you doing? Didn't I tell you to stay put and wait for my call?"

"Carl, you can't go through with this. *Please*, I'm begging you." Sobs cracked her voice rendering it nearly incoherent. "Where are you? Did you get to those kids? Carl, please don't do this!"

He listened while she vented her hysteria. His eyes peered down on his terrified trio and the fear in their eyes thrilled him. Even Tim was conscious now and had joined the farewell party. Carl entertained the thought of pleasuring himself first with the two lovely females, but he couldn't chance it. He had to maintain total control and control would be easy to lose if he let his body's sexual demands take charge.

The .38 was still in his hand, its barrel aimed between Glory's eyes. Only Allison's frantic pleas, which all three victims could hear, broke the deafening silence. Carl clenched his teeth and struggled to stay calm so he could decide how to handle her before she blew. *Damn. I should never have told her about these kids. I should have known she'd crack eventually.*

Allison's hysterical pleas only fueled his anger. If she were there, he could have squeezed those screams silent with his bare hands.

But that would defeat the whole purpose of this execution party, he mused.

"Listen to me, sugar, and listen good. I'm a little busy now, but if you do as I say, we might be able to work something out." He kept a sharp eye on Glory whose arms and legs weren't tied yet. Not that she was going anywhere with a loaded gun in her face. He gave her a grin to remind her in case she was planning something stupid. Like moving.

"The kids are fine," he said to Allison. "I don't know where you got this maternal instinct all of a sudden," he said with a slight laugh, as though it had endeared her to him. "They're a little tied up at the moment, but I'll let you say hello." He looked down and smiled again, almost expecting them to appreciate his humor. "Here's Glory first," he said, holding the phone at her mouth and the gun under her chin.

Glory obediently uttered the one word and the phone was moved to Tim who did the same. When he brought it to Sara's mouth, her emotions overwhelmed her. "Help us!" she cried. For that disobedient act, Carl shoved the gun into her mouth while Glory and Tim looked on, horrified and helpless. He pulled the gun out and stood up, then pointed a finger at Sara and smiled his evil smile, as if to say, "That's a sample of what you'd get for another stunt like that."

Allison's cries ebbed to a mournful plea weakened to a whisper. "Carl, please don't hurt them. *Please*. We'll work this all out. We'll think of something."

"I already did, sugar. I told you to put your trust in me. Now stop worrying and get your pretty little rump here. I decided to forget the whole damn thing and let them go, but I need you with me." He watched the three pairs of eyes go wide with hope and smiled at them. "This could be pretty messy and an unnecessary risk. After all, when you come right down to it, who are they gonna tell? They'd know for sure that before they could prove me guilty, I'd gun down any one of them or their family. And even if I couldn't get to them, trust me, I'll connect with friends who will. You get my drift, guys?"

They all nodded and eagerly mumbled their acquiescence. Carl shot them a sour smirk, shaking his head. He almost felt sorry for them. The hope he had put in their hearts actually put smiles on their dumb faces.

His attention went back to Allison, whose pleas were nonstop. "Now, sugar, you just come straight here, understand?" No phone calls, no stops along the way because if I even smell betrayal, let me tell you, these three will make their exit in the worst possible way. You hear me, sugar? They're fine and they'll stay fine if you do what I say. I'll give you forty minutes to get here or all bets are off."

Allison steeled herself to stay calm. She felt as though she were trying to defuse a bomb. "Just tell me where you are, Carl, and I'll leave right now."

His sardonic smile took shape again. "At the very spot where you lost your virginity, sugar, a long, long time ago, remember?" He roared with laughter.

Chapter 99

Detectives Tony Gerard and Pat Carney pulled up at the front entrance of the new Sun & Surf Inn. Detective Pete Granger was there waiting on the front porch with the elderly witness who was seated on a white wicker rocker. Pete Granger introduced the woman to his fellow detectives as Marjorie Lauder. The silver-haired, blue-eyed lady was frail, suffering the effects of time, but her eyes were sharp and danced with eagerness to share what they had seen.

Pat leaned against the porch railing, but Tony chose the rocker next to Mrs. Lauder rather than hover over her with questions. "Now, Mrs. Lauder, take your time, but I'd like you to repeat for me what you told Detective Granger." He went on to assure her that whatever she could tell them to the best of her recollection would be helpful.

The woman nodded politely as he spoke, but was clearly anxious to tell her story. Tony realized that to Marjorie this was her fifteen minutes of fame and he hoped she didn't embellish her story with exaggerations or imaginary details.

"Oh, call me Marjorie, Detective," she began. "Everyone does."

Tony nodded and smiled.

Marjorie looked a little perplexed at first. "Now where should I begin..." She quickly unscrambled her thoughts and smiled with confidence. "Okay. I had taken a little nap, but when I woke up, I was freezing. The air conditioner made my room like a refrigerator. I hate that about summers. You dress lightly to stay cool and every time you go indoors you freeze to death!"

Out of Marjorie's line of vision, Pat shot Tony a here-we-go-again smile, knowing he would have to gently put her on fast forward.

"Yes, I know what you mean," Tony said. "So you came outside to warm up, right?"

"Yes, right. But it was too hot in the sun so I sat here on the porch. It was cool and shady."

"And then what happened?"

"Then I picked up a magazine to read, but I get sick of looking at all those half-naked people – "

"So you put the magazine down and just sat in this rocker, correct?" Tony prompted.

"No, not this one, that one," she said pointing.

Tony sat in the rocker she indicated to check visibility from that point. "And from this rocker what did you see?"

"Well, if I were down on the lawn I probably wouldn't have seen anything, but from up here on the porch you can sort of look down on that side street. See?" Again she pointed.

"Yes, you're absolutely right," Tony said, as though crediting her for a detail he never would have noticed on his own. "Go on, please, Marjorie."

"I remember seeing the trolley come to a stop – I don't know why they call them trolleys, they might look like trolleys but they ride like a bus – well, anyway, to tell you the truth, I didn't see who got off. That wall is in the way a little and besides, I wasn't paying attention. God, if I only knew how important it would be – that these kids would be missing…" She thinned her lips and shook her head ruefully.

"You couldn't have known, Marjorie. Don't start punishing yourself. Continue, please."

"Well, a minute or so later, after the trolley had taken off again, I see this car – don't ask me what kind or year; I'm no good at that – all I know is it was silver. At first I only saw the front of the car, but when it started to make a turn – like to go out on the street again, well, that's when I saw these two kids talking to the driver. You know, bending down to talk through the window. Then they got in and the car drove off." She shrugged. "I'm sorry, but where they went I couldn't tell you."

"Did you notice which way they went, left or right?"

Without hesitation, Marjorie pointed left.

"What else can you remember, Marjorie? Something you might recall about the kids, the driver, whatever. But don't guess if you're not fairly sure. No one expects you to remember details that were of no concern to you at the time. Just think back and give us your best recollection." He said it with a warm, friendly smile as though it were no big deal, but his heart was racing worrying about those kids.

Marjorie's hand, liver-spotted and bronzed by the sun, went to her cheek. She concentrated a moment, then said, "The car, like I said before, was silver. You know, grayish. Maybe...No, forget it," she said.

"Maybe what, Marjorie?"

"Well, I'm not sure now, but maybe it was a BMW. My son has one and for a second I thought it was him because it had that little blue and white emblem. At least that's what it looked like."

"You might be right, Marjorie. If so, that's a big help. Just to be sure, was it a small car, a big car, a station wagon, a van? Any memory?"

Again Marjorie gave a quick, sure-of-herself response. "No, it was a regular car. Like yours," she said, shifting her gaze to the police Impala. "The driver I didn't see, though. I couldn't even tell you if it was a man or a woman. They were sort of leaning in, from the passenger side, talking to him. Or her."

"What can you tell us about the kids? Approximate age, tall, short, that sort of thing. I know from this porch it's a bit of a distance, but roughly, anything you might remember..."

"They both had dark hair, I'm pretty sure, and I would guess they were somewhere in their teens. I *do* remember that the boy was a good head taller than the girl, like Mutt and Jeff," Marjorie said with a laugh, then quickly stifled it when she realized the young detective had probably never heard of the famous cartoon characters. "She was like that petite type, you know."

"What about their clothes? Any recollection, Marjorie?"

She wrinkled her nose. "That I can't help you with. Everyone walks around looking pretty much the same. Who pays attention?"

Tony parted his lips to speak but she stopped him. "They were both in shorts; that I'm sure of. I remember because he was wearing those ugly knee-length shorts that make all the young men look like long drips of water, and she was wearing regular shorts." A nostalgic smile curled her lips showcasing her milk-white dentures. "I know because I was admiring her legs, remembering when mine looked like hers. About fifty years ago, though." She forced a laugh and sent the fifty years behind her with a hand wave. "So that's about it, Mr. Detective." She gave Tony an apologetic grin. "Sorry, my memory for names is awful."

"Gerard. Sergeant Tony Gerard," he offered.

"Gerard. Oh, yes. I'm sorry I couldn't help you more, Sergeant."

"Don't be sorry, Marjorie. You helped us plenty."

Chapter 100

Something's happening. I feel it," Frannie told Alex. "He knew we intended to grab the camera and get right back, so why did they call to give us the rush treatment?"

Alex made no attempt to play it down. They were beyond the point of pretending. His thoughts were on the same track. "I don't know either, but we'll soon find out."

"This must be spreading like wildfire, Alex, judging by all these calls I've been ignoring. I want to know who pushed the panic button and why. Since when do the police get involved in searching for people missing only a few hours? More importantly, why is Tony Gerard heading the investigation? State Police don't get involved in small potatoes. They come in for high priority cases, like kidnapping or murder." She cringed and a shiver curled up her back. "Oh, God, I hate to even think those words."

Alex watched her as she drove. He was terrified too but with Frannie it was something more. "Talk to me, Frannie. Just as you're afraid that Sergeant Gerard is holding something back, I feel the same way about you. There's a lot written on your face that you're not saying."

She smirked and tried to make light of it. "How can you read my face when you can only see my right side?" She shook her head and smiled as though dismissing it as nonsense. But the tight worry lines quickly returned. She kept her gaze fixed on the traffic ahead, then stole a sideways glance at Alex. His eyes still held an analytical stare.

"Okay, don't make it worse than it is. I'm just anxious to hear from Carl. There's a good chance he can tell us something."

"And there's another cell phone that goes unanswered. Do you call him on his cell often? Does he usually answer or return your call right away?"

"Not often, but when I do call, he usually answers. If I leave a message he's good about getting right back to me."

Alex didn't answer right away. He was deep in thought. Nothing added up right and he didn't like Frannie's body language. "I'm hoping your cousin will call too, but I'm not banking on him leading us straight to Glory and the kids. Unless you know something I don't." He paused for her response but Frannie remained silent. "Frannie, this is no time to hold back information. I think something else is bothering you and if so, you'd better spill it out. First to me and then to Sergeant Gerard."

Frannie tried to smile but her quivering lips wouldn't let her. "I'm just worried. The more I think, the more I worry."

They were just pulling into Shore Road, headed back to Amore Breakfast where they were supposed to meet the detectives again, but they hadn't yet arrived. The words rolled off her lips unexpectedly. "I think my cousin Carl had or has an eye for Glory."

Alex ignored her unconvincing smile. He looked her straight in the eye then held her chin. "And what else should we know about Carl, Frannie?"

Frannie parked the car, turned off the ignition and looked back at him. She swallowed hard. "A long time ago, maybe ten years ago, Carl was accused of rape. The charges were dropped but we were never sure..." Her hands went to her mouth but they couldn't hold back her emotions.

Momentarily stunned, Alex watched her cry until his long dormant temper surfaced. "Damn! Damn! Damn!" he screamed.

Chapter 101

Allison drove to her destination blindly, zeroed in on what she must accomplish.

She remembered well where she had lost her virginity. It had not been an explosive culmination of love. Drugs and alcohol had brought Allison to that secluded spot decades ago. It had begun at a summer party with wild fun, raucous laughter and freedom for all. But not the kind of freedom that sends flags flying. It was more like a free-for-all where anything goes.

The "anything" that night, under the stars and nestled among the trees, was gang rape. Only three, but a gang nevertheless.

And Carl Duca was number one. With all the casual sex she had allowed in subsequent years, why did she still shiver with repulsion at that memory? And why did she later allow Carl to twist what happened into an irresponsible act caused by their over-indulgence?

His remorse seemed so believable at the time. Even his friends had apologized profusely. They too blamed it all on the drugs and alcohol.

And she bought it. She was so young and stupid.

"Now I'm forty-two and still stupid," she mumbled, then slapped the steering wheel and yelled out. "What friggin' jackass falls in love with her rapist? And how did I allow him to talk me into killing *my own sister*?"

Tears streamed her face and she was shaking uncontrollably. "Oh, dear God, I must have been out of my mind. How can I possibly expect You to forgive me for that?"

By stopping him before he kills again that other voice in her head replied.

She pulled in a deep breath and wiped away her tears with the back of her hand. "Yes, by stopping him. If it isn't too late when I get there."

Sobered by her resolve to make peace with God, she allowed her mind to roll back the years. She lost herself in memories now fraught with guilt. But nothing she had ever done, whether for her own wicked pleasure or as an act of defiance, could ever be equated with the cold-blooded, premeditated murder of her own feeble-minded sister. No, that even topped having a strange man sandwiched between you and your brother's wife.

An inexplicable tranquility enveloped Allison as she cut off the highway and headed for "Put Out Point," as it had been labeled generations ago. If she had her way, "Put Out Point" would take on new meaning tonight.

Chapter 102

The Baisley family's dinner was long forgotten but everyone remained to offer support until Sara was found.

At Dan Madison's house, his family pleaded with him to relax and wait. Tony Gerard had promised to call the moment he had something to report. But their pleas only upset Dan more. How could they expect him to relax when his daughter was missing?

He picked up the phone again to call the Baisleys first, then the Waites. He had never met either of the couples but this crisis prompted his call.

But the Waites were not at home. They had set aside the ugliness that had soured their relationship with the Baisleys and, with contrite and humble hearts, presented themselves at the Baisleys' door. No words were exchanged at first, only emotional embraces were shared between the two couples who had once been friends.

"We programmed our phone to forward calls here," Douglas Waite said. "I hope you don't mind. We were starting to get crazy and thought we should see this through together."

Jonathan Baisley ushered them in. "Of course we don't mind," he said and led them into the living room where the Baisleys' extended family had gathered. Everyone was grim-faced and silent.

Both the Baisleys' phones rang almost simultaneously. Marcia picked up one and Jonathan answered the cell.

"It's Sergeant Gerard," Jonathan announced.

"And I have Dan Madison here," Marcia said to her husband, then to Dan she said, "Mr. Madison, please hold on. Sergeant Gerard is on my husband's cell."

"They'll be here in a few minutes," Jonathan said. "They haven't found them yet, but have some important information to share."

The vague message only frustrated Marcia. "Well, didn't he say whether the information was good or bad?"

Jonathan sat down on the edge of a club chair, steepled his hands together against his face, and gazed downward. "No, he didn't say. And I was afraid to ask."

Marcia told Dan what was happening and promised someone would call him back.

Exactly seven minutes later, Tony Gerard, Pat Carney and Sara's friend, Jennifer, were at the door. The moment Jennifer saw the anxious, distraught faces of the Baisleys and the Waites, she burst into tears. At Tony Gerard's request, Jonathan led Jennifer and the Waites to the den where they could talk privately.

"First I should let you know something I couldn't divulge before," Tony said, "and I'll explain why. Sara and Tim had come to me the week after Paula Grant drowned to tell me that she might have been murdered." He paused for their shocked reaction to subside, then continued with the facts that Sara and Tim had confided. "Under the circumstances, because it was information pertinent to a possible murder investigation, confidentiality was essential."

"But we're their parents!" Douglas Waite said, shocked and angered.

"Yes, but Sara and Tim are both over eighteen. We therefore had no legal obligation to have their parents present while we took their statements."

Now Jonathan Baisley had anger in his eyes. "I don't give a damn what the law books say. If they witnessed a murder, they were in danger, and you denied us the right to protect them!"

Tony's hands went palms up. "Hold it. Let me go on. First of all, they did not *witness* a murder. All they saw was someone leading Paula Grant to the water. They were almost certain they were not seen – "

"*Almost* isn't good enough," Jonathan bellowed.

Jennifer's sobs surfaced again.

"Jennifer, why are you here?" Jonathan asked, his voice softened. "What do you have to tell us?"

"Do you want me to tell them?" Tony asked gently.

"No. This might be my fault. I have to tell them." She sucked in a breath and repeated what Sara had told her in confidence, making her swear never to tell a living soul. "But that same night, I broke my promise," she sobbed. "I ended up calling three of my friends and God only knows who else they told." She covered her face with her hands, too ashamed to face the parents.

Everyone was stunned into silence; their emotions gripped by fear.

Marcia Baisley was first to speak. "Someone should call Dan Madison. I can't handle that now." Her voice cracked and she too burst into tears. Her husband wrapped his arms around her. It took Evelyn Waite a little longer, but she succumbed as well and buried her head in her husband's chest.

Pat Carney sat with Jennifer and tried to calm her.

Tony Gerard stepped out of the picture to use his phone. He summoned all the help he could get and blanketed the area in and around Ogunquit with teams of detectives and criminal investigators. He had a feeling that Marjorie Lauder's description of the car would lead them straight to Carl Duca. And as soon as they picked up Glory's camera, Duca's smiling face would be spread everywhere.

Everyone had to move fast before he killed them all. If he hadn't killed them already. Tony took one moment more to call Dan Madison and hoped the information he provided didn't trigger another heart attack.

Chapter 103

"What the hell do you think you're doing?" Carl screamed at Glory. "You want my gun? I'll give you a gun!" He grabbed his crotch and sneered at her, then slammed the .38 against the back of her head. Glory let out an agonizing cry and fell over Sara. Her blood spurted out and spilled over Sara's face and chest while Sara coughed and gagged in her futile attempt to spit it away. Her sobs were convulsive now.

Tim couldn't bear to look at her but he did, and the sight tore away at his heart. Her face and hair were covered with blood and her body quaked violently. As she turned her head slightly their eyes met and a mournful cry escaped from Tim's mouth. The whites of Sara's eyes stood out against her bloodied face, their gaze fixed and crazed, like a person gone mad.

A moment ago Glory was their last hope, but now Tim couldn't even tell if she was dead or alive.

Carl peered down at Tim with a broad, sadistic grin. "See? It's no use. These dames all want equality with us, but look at them. One goes bonkers and the other wouldn't last two seconds in combat." He shook his head as though disappointed by their early defeat, then a new idea brightened his face. "How about you, hotshot? You in the mood for a little fun? I'll give you some slack to allow for your headache." The whole scene struck him so funny that as he rocked with laughter, the gun almost slipped from his hand.

"So what do you say, hotshot? I'm trying to be sociable here while we wait for more company. I think it would behoove you – is that how you say it, 'be-H-O-O-V-E?'" He made a wide-eyed mimicking gesture. "See? I'm not so dumb. I picked up a few Sunday words on my own." He played with the loaded toy in his hand, twirling it with one finger. "Anyway, as I was saying, hotshot, it would *behoove* you to entertain me while we wait for our company. Just one more person to join our party. Another woman, but she's mine, so don't get any ideas," he said, shaking a fist in his face, then laughed again at the absurdity of his suggestion.

His laughter faded and his expression switched to mocked sympathy as he looked down at Glory and Sara. He sighed and shook his head, his lips twisted. "But I don't see much fun here. One's looney-tunes and the other looks dead as a doorknob."

Tim hadn't said a word but Carl hadn't noticed. Judging by his evil grin, he was obviously enjoying his thoughts. He peered down at Glory's limp body like The Big Bad Wolf. "So, what do you say, Tim? Wanna have some fun before you check out?"

Tim held his breath, repulsed by what the bastard might do to entertain himself or, worse yet, command him to do. His eyes went to Glory now, hoping this maniac wouldn't violate her dead body.

But Glory's eyelids lifted slightly and for a second Tim saw her blue but vacant eyes.

"Well, do ya?" Carl yelled down at Tim and stomped on his leg to demand an answer.

But Tim never got the chance to answer. A gunshot blast came from the trailer door.

Chapter 104

It had taken only seconds to identify the make and color of Carl Duca's two vehicles, and sure enough, one of them was a 2001 silver BMW.

"I'm glad you guys are here already because we couldn't hang around to wait. We would have called you. Looks like we got a break."

Tony was about to fill them in about what Marjorie Lauder had seen, but Frannie saved him the trouble. Tears welled in her eyes and her lips quivered for control. "Sergeant, I'm afraid to say this – God, I hope I'm wrong – " She threw her gaze upward, not wanting to look Tony in the eye. "But there's a small chance..." She couldn't get the words out and looked to Alex for help.

"What she's trying to tell you, Sergeant, is that her cousin Carl Duca could be the guy we need to find."

"It's okay, Frannie. Don't bother," Tony said softly. "I was about to tell you the same thing. I'm sorry, but we have a credible witness. No positive ID but it looks like all roads lead to Carl Duca."

Frannie sniffed and wiped away her tears. Never in her lifetime had she ever lost control and cried among people. But then never had she been in a situation that compared to this. "This can't be, Sergeant. He's been so good. For *years* he's been good. I've been so proud of how he turned himself around. I just can't believe he'd do something as insane as this – whatever the heck *this* is anyway." She threw her hands out in surrender.

"We did a background check on him, Frannie. We know all about his run-ins with the law. And we know about the alleged rape."

"That's just the point, Sergeant. It was only *alleged.* No one could prove it was Carl."

Tony was understanding and sympathetic to her reaction. She probably knew as well as he did that the sixteen-year-old he attacked had made a positive ID immediately after the assault but, like most victims, she lacked the courage to see it to the end. The charges were dropped before they could *smell* a courtroom.

And another degenerate had walked away, grinning ear-to-ear.

"Frannie, believe me, I hope for your sake that he comes out clean. But I have to warn you, we're not optimistic." He glanced at his watch. "I'm sorry, but we've got to get out of here. I'll take that camera now, please. We'll want to circulate that photo of him, especially since it was taken today."

Frannie's denial weakened and died. Acceptance drained her and settled on her face, aging her ten years. She handed him the camera and asked, "If Carl is involved, have you learned where he might have taken them?"

"And why?" Alex asked.

"The why is clear," Tony answered ruefully. "The kids had witnessed what most likely was Paula Grant's murder."

Frannie's mouth opened and her eyes widened, but disbelief left her momentarily dumbfounded. When she found her voice, she said, "Are you telling us that you suspect my cousin Carl of *murder?* What possible motive could he have to murder Paula Grant?"

"We're working on that," was all Tony could answer.

For Frannie's sake, Alex steeled himself to remain calm but rage and fear burned inside him. "What can we do to help, Sarge? Anything at all?" he asked.

"Well, one of my detectives is directing a search party. As word spreads, people are volunteering like crazy. Why don't you guys jump in on that?"

"How do we reach him, Sergeant?" Frannie asked, wanting to feel useful.

Tony provided the information and got into the police car. Pat Carney's hands were on the wheel, ready to take off.

"What's next, Sarge?" Alex asked. "Can you tell us where you're going?"

"We're going hunting for that shiny silver car that Marjorie Lauder saw."

Frannie had an instant flashback of the day her cousin Carl came to proudly show off his new BMW. Then she thought about how she had hoped to steer Glory's affection from Alex to Carl. A dry lump lodged in her throat.

Chapter 105

The entire Madison family sat with Dan on the patio, all as worried as he, but all faked optimism with their far-reaching theories.

"I know I had a heart attack and I know you're all trying to keep me calm because of it," Dan said, "but this waiting and not knowing what the hell's going on is killing me anyway. What is it you guys are not telling me?" He pointed an admonishing finger at them. "And don't tell me 'nothing' because I can see trouble all over your faces."

Louise couldn't face him. Surely if their eyes met for one split-second, she'd break down and cry. She glanced over to her son Todd, silently asking him to handle it however he thought best.

"Don't get excited, Dad," Todd began. "You're absolutely right. This is one of those damned if you do, damned if you don't situations." He blew a sigh and paced to avoid his father's perceptive eyes. "I called Tony Gerard a few minutes ago when I went inside the house. He was reluctant to give me details, but then said information had already leaked out through various sources – "

"Get to the point, Todd," Dan said. He leaned forward on the patio table, clenched his hands into fists and braced himself.

"It seems they spoke to an elderly woman, a guest at the Sun & Surf Inn, who saw the two kids talking to someone inside the car. She didn't see the driver but remembered the car was silver and might have been a BMW, like her son's, she said."

"And?"

"And the kids got into the car willingly," he said. "They apparently knew him."

"Do they know it was a him? She hadn't seen the driver yet, you said."

"It seems, Dad, that they're not only pretty sure it was a him, but they think they know who. A few other factors all point to one guy." He paused, not wanting to go on as he watched the tension build on his father's face. But now that he had begun, he had no choice.

"C'mon, Todd. Don't stop there," Dan urged. "What guy?"

"Well, they're not sure, but Glory and the kids were last seen this afternoon with Carl Duca."

Dan's brows furrowed with confusion and disbelief. "Carl Duca? You mean of Duca Brothers Construction?"

"Yep," Todd answered with an angry grimace. "The same guy who put the new deck on this house last year who just happens to own a silver BMW."

Still perplexed, Dan said, "And so do a million other people," he said and paused to digest the facts. "Carl Duca just doesn't make sense. I've spoken to him several times. He seems like such an okay guy. Besides, how do they know he wasn't innocently giving them a lift somewhere?"

"They don't. But nobody can find him either."

Todd could see by his father's bewildered expression that he apparently had never heard anything about Carl Duca's troubled past. He probably had only met and talked to Duca when he came to give an estimate for the deck.

On the basis of that assumption, Todd opted not to tell Dan that the kids had probably witnessed Paula Grant's murder. And who else but a desperate killer, intent on saving his own ass, would abduct and kill any possible witnesses?

No, no way am I telling him that, Todd decided.

Chapter 106

Allison's three bullets all met their target. Two in the stomach and one through the heart. Carl's crazed eyes blazed with fury and fear as his body slumped down, his blood pooling over his three victims. He made one final attempt to fire his gun back at her, but his hands went limp. He collapsed with a thunderous sound. Allison watched him gasp for his last breath and die with his eyes wide open.

The horrific scene triggered hysterical cries of terror from his victims, but the realization that someone had saved their lives turned those cries to relief.

Allison stood over them, staring down with an eerie calm. "The police are on the way," she said, then turned to Glory. "Please tell my brother that I'm sorry. For my whole life, I'm sorry." Her words spilled out with a rush of tears. Before Glory could utter a word, Allison fired the gun one last time. Her brains exploded and splattered like strings of a wet mop. They settled on the open mouth and eyes of Carl Duca, the man she thought she had loved.

Sirens could be heard in the distance but no one had the strength to react.

***

Throngs of curious tourists and locals followed the screeching sounds and flashing lights of police and emergency vehicles all racing towards Put Out Point. No one knew what had happened, but everyone knew it had to be some kind of tragedy or horrible accident.

A wide area surrounding the trailer had already been cordoned off with yellow crime scene tape. As the crowds gathered in frightened apprehension, word spread rapidly from those who had already heard about the three missing people to those who were shocked to hear it for the first time. Detectives had been questioning people everywhere and, as always, bad news had traveled faster than lightning.

Everyone waited to hear what the police had discovered inside or outside that trailer.

The Baisleys and the Waites were insane with grief, not knowing if their children were dead or alive.

Dan's three children hugged each other in silence. Remorse filled Todd and Vanessa's hearts for the emotional pain they had caused their half-sister. Each of them held one of Amy's hands in theirs which silently pleaded for her forgiveness as well. Both had lashed out at her for "betraying" them by befriending Glory. Vanessa cringed at the memories of their cruel and selfish treatment.

An hour ago, when word had come to them at the house that the three victims were being held at Put Out Point, Dan had insisted that his children take him with them. He had become so enraged by fear for his daughter that they almost gave in. But Louise cried mournfully, begging him to wait at home with her. She was so terribly afraid of how this trauma would affect his healing heart. Surely they'd be notified immediately after the police stormed the area, she pleaded. "She's our children's half-sister and I have to accept her as part of our family. And I will, Dan. I promise you. You were right. She was conceived long before we met. I had no right to be hostile or jealous. Can you ever forgive me?"

Dan melted when he took a long look at her pleading eyes. His heart swelled with love and pathos for Louise as she sobbed, kissed the back of his hand and held it to her cheek. He took a long slow breath and stroked her hair. "I'll stay, sweetheart. Please stop crying. Those tears will break my heart for sure." He smiled down at her and the smile she returned reminded Dan of how much he had to live for.

***

Frannie and Alex abandoned their car at the foot of the hill, as everyone else had done. Together they climbed upward. Unparalleled tension ripped through them.

Without warning Alex lost control. All the pent-up emotions surfaced and he cried openly, unashamed. He realized now more than ever the depth of his love for Glory and he prayed that they'd find her and the kids alive and unharmed.

But he had a bad feeling that was too much to expect. It had to be Carl Duca who killed Paula. Once the news was out that Sara and Tim had seen Paula being led to her death, who else but her killer would abduct them?

But no one knew why Carl wanted Paula dead.

***

After what seemed like an eternity, Alex saw Tony Gerard walking toward him. Slowly.

He grimaced and squeezed Frannie's hand. Instinct told him to back away. He didn't want to hear that Carl Duca had viciously massacred Glory, Sara and Tim.

But Alex was totally unprepared for the message Tony Gerard was about to deliver. He pulled them both aside while a hundred eyes watched from a distance.

"First let me say that Glory and the kids are all fine…well, not fine, really, but they'll be fine, I'm sure." Tony was referring to their physical injuries only. He wouldn't dare suggest the emotional impact. Nor would he or could he disclose the horrific scene they found inside that trailer.

Tony watched the tension drain from their faces. Relief formed a smile on Alex's lips, but it would be wiped away with his next breath.

"Alex, I'm very sorry to inform you, but there were two fatalities in there. One was your sister, Allison."

For seconds Alex's mouth opened but no sound came out. His eyes went wide with shock. Then his agonizing screams pealed through the quiet stillness.

This is the only part of police work we all dread, Tony thought to himself. *No matter how many years you pile up behind you, it never gets easier.*

He decided to let Alex's first wave of shock settle before telling him the rest. But Alex looked at him with shocked disbelief. "Allison! Why Allison?" he cried.

Tony continued softly but there was no way he or anyone else could stop the pain. "Your sister called 911 only moments before she arrived at the scene." He paused to look at Frannie because he was about to give her bad news as well. "She was hysterical but told the dispatcher that she and Carl Duca had come up with a plan to get rid of your sister Paula. She had lost her mind anyway, Duca told her, and why shouldn't they enjoy Allison's half of Paula's fortune? She let her six million dollar share overshadow her guilt, she said, but when he told her about the two teenage kids he'd have to eliminate, she couldn't let him do it. She cracked and set out to kill him first."

Frannie's hands flew to her mouth. "Oh, my God, my God, no!" she cried.

"But he got her first, didn't he?" Alex said, his voice laced with rage.

"No, Alex, she got him good with a bullet through the heart. Then she left a message for you with Glory." Tony had trouble suppressing his own emotions. This horror was a first for him. And he had never seen a man cry like Alex cried for his sister. Both his sisters, probably. "She said, 'Tell my brother I'm sorry. For my whole life I'm sorry.'" He still had to tell him that Allison had put the gun to her head and blew her brains out. Instead he said, "She took her own life, Alex. She just couldn't live with the guilt, I'm sure."

Frannie and Alex embraced, sobbing on each other's shoulder. Before tonight they were merely acquaintances, not even friends. Now they would forever be bonded by tragedy.

Tony stepped aside to leave them alone with their grief.

Epilogue

Nine months had passed since that tragic night in Ogunquit. For the first few months, Glory and Frannie were completely dispirited. But too much was at stake and too many new employees were depending on the success of Amore Evenings. Glory had the added responsibility of her column. Fortunately she had always produced enough to stay ahead of schedule, but the well was running dry and she absolutely had to write. And once she did, she was surprised to see the old feeling returning. That rush of adrenaline. *Glorious Cooking* was indeed gloriously therapeutic.

Their grand opening, originally scheduled for Thanksgiving week, had been unavoidably postponed until after the holidays. Mike Duca was in bad shape for a long time after his brother's death and his job commitments had fallen way beyond schedule.

The holiday season passed without the usual festivities for those who mourned their losses, but for others like the Baisley and Waite families, Dan and Louise Madison and their children, which now included Glory, there was quiet celebration. It was a time to reflect and give thanks for the precious lives that were nearly lost.

Amore Evenings opened its doors on a bitter cold night in mid-February. The locals stayed huddled in front of their fireplaces or curled up on a sofa to watch TV. Tourism was practically nil during January and February anyway, but this particular February the freezing temperatures were down to a record low. And so were the diners.

But opening in the dead of winter had certain advantages. Everyone had time to work out the kinks so that when the in-season crush came, they'd all be ready.

Like Glory and Frannie, Sara and Tim had also been through months of therapy. Their night in hell could never be erased completely, but hopefully time would dull the memory like a bad dream. They were both young with bright futures to look forward to. As they had planned, they were both in local colleges and home on weekends. That arrangement enabled them to have a steady diet of rigorous on-the-job training at Amore Evenings and they loved every minute. Working together was a convenient pleasure and they adored their employers. Glory and Frannie had become like adoptive mothers to them and often served as on-the-spot counselors.

On a personal level, Sara and Tim's love grew stronger than ever. "Nothing like nearly dying together to strengthen a relationship," Tim had teased.

"At least something good came out of our suffering," Sara said. "Now that our parents are friends again, I don't have to climb out the window to meet you!"

After Amore Evening's "deep-freeze" opening, Glory had convinced her reluctant father to enjoy the rest of the winter in Florida with Louise. After what his daughter had been through, he had wanted to be there for her. But Glory assured him that she'd be well-covered. She had siblings now; two sisters and a brother to spend time with and get to know. She had Frannie, her dear friend and business partner. And then she had Alex, her *very special friend*. He came to Maine every weekend now and he'd soon be back in Ogunquit as a permanent resident.

After the tragedy, Alex's grief weighed heavily with guilt. *If only I hadn't slept through Paula's abduction that night....If only I had tried to make peace with Allison years ago before her rebellion tied her to the likes of Carl Duca.* But with the passage of time Alex was learning not to dwell on the *if onlys*. Glory needed his love and support. Frannie too needed his friendship and, on a business level, they both welcomed his temporary assistance.

Although Alex had been doing quite well financially with his drug stores, he was now the sole heir to Paula's twelve million dollar estate. But Paula's fortune was stained with the blood of his sisters. It had claimed the lives of three people and nearly three more. He couldn't fathom how he could derive pleasure from any of that money.

Then when an idea dawned on him, he smiled. Yes, he would find the right property and build a full-care facility for Alzheimer's patients. He imagined a beautiful place with a wraparound porch and lots of rockers, all painted in cheerful colors. There would be acres of lush green grounds, shade trees and an abundance of flowers and shrubs. It would be designed to include other amenities the patients' families might enjoy, thereby encouraging visitation.

On the Sunday of Memorial Day Weekend, Glory and Frannie held an open house cocktail party to launch Amore Evening's first summer season. Among their special guests were Dan, Louise and their family, Frannie's parents, Mike Duca and his wife, the Baisleys and the Waites. Sara and Tim were also present but had little time to spare. They were both on the job, enthusiastically doing their share to ensure Amore Evening's success.

Everyone was so grateful that God had spared their lives; that all three of Carl Duca's victims had survived his maniacal attack. They all shared the same feelings, but no one expressed them verbally, at least not in Frannie's presence. Perhaps in some way her pain was deeper. She still struggled to accept that the cousin she had loved was a violent man and a vicious killer. But Frannie was strong. She resolved to get past it, to accept Carl's shocking behavior as an obsessive mental disorder over which he had no control.

Carl's death brought Frannie and Mike Duca closer than they had ever been. It was as if they had each lost a piece of themselves and the shameful weight of having a murderer in the family was a burden easier to bear if shared. Her friends all came through for her too. It had taken them months but eventually she agreed to join them once again, as long as they switched to Tuesdays, when Amore Evenings was closed. Their perseverance had paid off because once she did, Frannie realized that she had been denying herself the best medicine of all. Laughter.

Alex chose this happy occasion to announce his plans. As he spoke Glory's eyes welled with tears but this time they were happy tears. "That'll be such a beautiful tribute to Paula, Alex. I'm all choked up just thinking how she must be smiling down at you."

Dan hugged the man who might someday be his son-in-law. "You're a special person, Alex. I'm glad you and my daughter are friends." He silently admonished himself for prejudging Alex on the basis of idle gossip. But he was confident Alex and Glory would rise above it.

"I think you know, Dan, that Glory and I are more than friends," Alex said with a glance that waited for approval.

"I'm glad about that too, Alex. Glory's told me many times how much you've done for her and Frannie – and the kids too. You've helped them heal. That means a lot to me, especially knowing you were grieving yourself."

Todd interrupted their conversation. "C'mon, Dad. Let's get a few family photos before the guests start pouring in." He took his father's arm and led him to Glory. "First just the two of you alone, then we'll take all of us." He snapped the photo, then handed the camera to Alex. Dan, Louise and their three children joined hands and opened their semi-circle to make room for Glory. The camera captured the sincerity and pride in their smiles.

Champagne glasses were handed out and Alex lifted his for the toast. "To Amore Evenings and all the love, hard work and dedication that made it possible."

Everyone fell silent thinking back to those two horrible nights. Frannie brought them back to the present. "Not to mention a bundle of money!" she said and everyone welcomed the laughter.

"Can I make a toast of my own?" Glory asked. "I don't want to get us all mushy again, but I want to say thanks for all the good things that happened to me since I set foot in Ogunquit. Sure, I fell in love with the area but I probably would have gone back home eventually. Then I met Frannie and although I didn't know it at the time, our friendship would open a whole new life for me here. Then along came Alex and now I had two special friends." She paused to blink back tears but they fell anyway. Glory forced a smile but her mouth quivered with emotion. She darted a look at Alex and Frannie. "Sorry, guys," she said, "but as much as you both mean to me..." She couldn't finish. Her father's arms were open wide and she ran to accept his embrace.